STARTER FOR TEN

Starter For Ten

DAVID NICHOLLS

FLAME
Hodder & Stoughton

First published in Great Britain in 2003 by Hodder and Stoughton
A division of Hodder Headline

A Flame Book

1

A CIP catalogue record for this title is available from the British Library

ISBN 978-1-4447-0563-8

Typeset in Sabon by Palimpsest Book Production Limited,
Polmont, Stirlingshire

Printed and bound by
Clays Ltd, St Ives plc

Hodder and Stoughton
A division of Hodder Headline
338 Euston Road
London NW1 3BH

To Ann and Alan Nicholls.
And Hannah, of course.

ACKNOWLEDGEMENTS

Thanks are due to the following people for their input, support and jokes: everyone at Hodder for their enthusiasm, in particular Mari Evans for her superb editing; Jonny Geller and all at Curtis Brown. A particular debt of thanks is also owed to Hannah MacDonald for her invaluable advice and to Roanna Benn, for her early enthusiasm. Also Douglas Kean, Michael McCoy, Josh Varney, Nicola Doherty, Emma Longhurst, Justin Salinger, Tamsin Pike, Christine Langan, Camilla Campbell, Nicholas Wilson-Jones, Olivia Trench, Susie Phillips, Crispian Balmer, Sophie Carter, Eve Claxton, Matthew Warchus and Nell Denton for wearing *that* dress. For dramatic purposes, certain deliberate alterations have been made to the *University Challenge* rules and filming procedure – apologies to any purists.

I am indebted to innumerable reference books, but in particular the *Encyclopaedia Britannica* and Peter Gwyn's *University Challenge: The First 40 Years*, both of which no home should be without. I would also like to offer sincere thanks to Bamber Gascoigne, Kate Bush, Jeremy Paxman and the 2002 champions, Somerville College, Oxford, for their unwitting inspiration.

Most of all, I would like to thank Hannah Weaver, who is on every page whether she's aware of it or not.

Round One

She knew this type very well – the vague aspirations, the mental disorder, the familiarity with the outside of books . . .

E.M. Forster, *Howards End*

1

QUESTION: Stepson to Robert Dudley and one-time favourite of Elizabeth I, which nobleman led a poorly planned and unsuccessful revolt against the Queen, and was subsequently executed in 1601?

ANSWER: Essex.

All young people worry about things, it's a natural and inevitable part of growing up, and at the age of sixteen my greatest anxiety in life was that I'd never again achieve anything as good, or pure, or noble, or true, as my O-level results.

I didn't make a big deal about them at the time of course; I didn't frame the certificates or anything weird like that, and I won't go into the actual grades here, because then it just gets competitive, but I definitely liked having them; Qualifications. Sixteen years old, and the first time I'd ever felt qualified for anything.

Of course, all that was a long, long time ago. I'm eighteen now, and I like to think I'm a lot wiser and cooler about these things. So my A-levels are, comparatively, no big deal. Besides, the notion that you can somehow quantify intelligence by some ridiculous, antiquated system of written examinations is obviously specious. Having said that, they were Langley Street Comprehensive School's best A-level results of 1985, the best for fifteen years in fact, three As and a B, that's 19 points – there, I've said it now – but I really, honestly don't believe that's particularly relevant, I just mention them in passing. And anyway, compared to other qualities, like physical courage, or popularity, or good looks, or clear skin, or an active sex-life, just knowing a whole load of *stuff* isn't actually that important.

But like my dad used to say, the crucial thing about an education is the opportunity that it brings, the doors it opens, because otherwise knowledge, in and of itself, is a blind alley, especially from where I'm sitting, here, on a late September Wednesday afternoon, in a factory that makes toasters.

I've spent the holiday working in the despatch department of Ashworth Electricals, which means I'm responsible for putting the toasters in their boxes before they're sent out to the retailers. Of course, there are only so many ways you can put a toaster in a box, so it's been a pretty dull couple of months over all, but on the plus side it's £1.85 an hour, which isn't bad, and as much toast as you can eat. As it's my last day here, I've been keeping an eye open for the surreptitious passing-round of the goodbye card and the collection for the leaving present, and waiting to find out which pub we're going to for farewell drinks, but it's 6.15 now, so I think it's probably safe to assume that everyone's just gone home.

Just as well though, because I had other plans anyway, so I get my stuff, grab a handful of biros and a roll of sellotape from the stationery cupboard and head off to the pier, where I'm meeting Spencer and Tone.

At 2,360 yards, or 2.158 kilometres, Southend pier is officially the longest pier in the world. This is probably a little bit *too* long, to be honest, especially when you're carrying a lot of lager. We've got twelve large cans of Skol, sweet-and-sour pork balls, special-fried-rice and a portion of chips with curry sauce – flavours from around the world – but by the time we reach the end of the pier, the lagers are warm and the takeaway's cold. As this is a special celebration Tone's also had to lug his ghetto-blaster, which is the size of a small wardrobe and, it's fair to say, will probably never blast a ghetto, unless you count Shoeburyness. At the moment it's playing Tone's home-made compilation *The Best Of The Zep* as we settle down on a bench at the end and watch as the sun sets majestically over the petrol refinery.

'You're not going to turn into a wanker, are you?' says Tone, opening a can of lager.

'What d'you mean?'

'He means you're not going to get all *studenty* on us,' says Spencer.

'Well, I am a student. I mean, I will be, so . . .'

'No, but I mean you're not going to get all twatty and up-your-own-arse and come home at Christmas in a gown, talking Latin and saying "one does" and "one thinks" and all that . . .'

'Yeah, Tone, that's *exactly* what I'm going to do.'

'Well don't. Because you're enough of a twat already without becoming even more of a twat.'

I get called 'twat' a lot by Tone, either 'twat' or 'gaylord', but the trick is to make a sort of linguistic adjustment, and try to think of it as a term of affection, in the same way as some couples say 'dear' or 'darling'. Tone's just started a job in the warehouse in Currys, and is starting to develop a nice little sideline in knocked-off portable hi-fis, like the one we're listening to now. It's his Led Zeppelin tape too; Tone likes to call himself 'a Metallist', which sounds more vocational than 'rocker' or 'heavy-metal fan'. He dresses like a Metallist too; lots of light blue denim, and long, flicked-back lustrous blond hair, like an effeminate Viking. Tone's hair is actually the *only* effeminate thing about him. This is, after all, a man steeped in brutal violence. The mark of a successful evening out with Tone is that you get home without having had your head flushed down a toilet.

It's 'Stairway to Heaven' now.

'Do we have to listen to this fucking hippie bollocks, Tone?' says Spencer.

'This is The Zep, Spence.'

'I know it's The Zep, Tone, that's why I want you to turn the fucking thing off.'

'But The Zep rule.'

'Why? Because you say they rule?'

'No, because they were a massively influential and important band.'

'They're singing about *pixies*, Tony. It's embarrassing . . .'

'Not pixies . . .'

'Elves then,' I say.

'It's not just pixies and elves, it's *Tolkien,* it's literature . . .' Tone loves that stuff; books with maps in the front, and cover-illustrations of big, scary women in chain-mail underwear, holding broad-swords, the kind of woman that, in an ideal world, he'd marry. Which, in Southend, is actually a lot more feasible than you'd think.

'What's the difference between a pixie and an elf anyway?' asks Spencer.

'Dunno. Ask Jackson, he's the cunt with the qualifications.'

'I dunno, Tone,' I say.

The guitar solo has kicked in and Spencer's wincing now. 'Does it ever end or does it just go on and on and on and on . . .'

'It's seven minutes, thirty-two seconds of pure genius.'

'Pure torture,' I say. 'Why's it always your choice, anyway?'

'Because it's my ghetto-blaster . . .'

'Which you *nicked*. Technically, it still belongs to Currys.'

'Yeah, but I buy the batteries . . .'

'No, you *nick* the batteries . . .'

'Not these, I bought these.'

'So how much were the batteries then?'

'One pound ninety-eight.'

'So if I give you sixty-six pence, can we have something decent on?'

'What, like Kate Bush? Alright then, Jackson, let's put some *Kate Bush* on then, all have a really good time listening to *Kate Bush*, all have a *really, really good dance* and a *singalong* to *Kate Bush . . .*' And while Tone and I are bickering, Spencer leans over to the ghetto-blaster, nonchalantly ejects *The Best Of The Zep*, and skims it far out to sea.

Tone shouts 'Oi!' and throws his can of lager after him as they both run off down the pier. It's best not to get too involved in the fights. Tone tends to get a little bit out of control, possessed by the spirit of Odin or something, and if I get involved it will inevitably end with Spencer sitting on my arms while Tone farts in my face, so I just sit very still, drink my lager, and watch Tone trying to hoist Spencer's legs over the pier railings.

Even though it's September, there's the beginning of a damp chill in the evening air, a sense of summer coming to an end, and I'm glad I wore my army-surplus greatcoat. I've always hated summer; the way the sun shines on the TV screen in the afternoons, and the relentless pressure to wear T-shirts and shorts. I hate T-shirt and shorts. If I were to stand outside a chemist in T-shirt and shorts, I guarantee some old dear would try and put a coin in the top of my head.

No, what I'm really looking forward to is the autumn, to kicking through leaves on the way to a lecture, talking excitedly about the Metaphysical Poets with a girl called Emily, or Katherine, or François, or something, with black opaque woolly tights and a Louise Brooks bob, then going back to her tiny attic room and making love in front of her electric bar fire. Afterwards we'll read T.S.Eliot aloud and drink fine vintage port out of tiny little glasses while listening to Miles Davis. That's what I imagine it's going to be like, anyway. The University Experience. I like the word *experience*. It makes it sound like a ride at Alton Towers.

The fight's over, and Tone is burning off his excess aggression by throwing sweet-and-sour pork-balls at the seagulls. Spencer walks back, tucking his shirt in, sits down next to me and opens another can of lager. Spencer really has a way with a can of lager; watching him, you could almost imagine he's drinking from a martini glass.

Spencer's the person I'll miss the most. He isn't going to university, even though he's easily the cleverest person I've ever met, as well as the best-looking, and the hardest, and the coolest. I wouldn't tell him any of that of course, because it would sound a bit creepy, but there's no need as he clearly knows it, anyway. He could have gone to university if he'd really wanted to, but he fouled up his exams; not deliberately as such, but everyone could see him doing it. He was sat at the desk next to me for the English Set-text Paper, and you could tell by the movements of his pen that he wasn't writing, he was *drawing*. For his Shakespeare question he drew *The Merry Wives of Windsor*, and for Poetry he did a picture entitled 'Wilfred Owen Experiences the Horror of the Trenches at First Hand'. I kept trying to catch his eye, so I could give him a friendly 'hey, come on mate' kind of look, but he just kept his head down, drawing away, and then after an hour he got up, and walked out, winking at me on the way; not a cocky wink, a slightly tearful, red-eyed wink, like a plucky tommy on his way to the firing squad.

After that, he just stopped coming in for exams. In private, the phrase 'nervous breakdown' was mentioned a couple of times, but Spencer's far too cool to have a nervous breakdown. Or if he did, he'd make the nervous breakdown seem cool. The way I see it, that whole Jack Kerouac, tortured existential thing is fine up to a point, but not if it's going to interfere with your grades.

'So what are you going to do, Spence?'

He narrows his eyes, looks at me. 'What d'you mean, "*do*"?'

'You know. Job-wise.'

'I've got a job.' Spencer's signing on, but also working cash-in-hand at the all-night petrol station on the A127.

'I know you've got a job. But in the future . . .'

Spencer looks out across the estuary, and I start to regret raising the subject.

'Your problem, Brian my friend, is that you underestimate the appeal of life in an all-night petrol station. I get to eat as much confectionery as I want. Road atlases to read. Interesting fumes to inhale. Free wine glasses . . .' He takes a long swig of lager, and looks for a way to change the subject. Reaching into his Harrington, he pulls out a cassette tape with a hand-written inlay card: 'I made this for you. So you can play it in front of your new university friends, trick them into thinking you've got taste.'

I take the tape, which has 'Bri's College Compilation' written down the spine in careful 3-D capitals. Spencer's a brilliant artist.

'This is fantastic Spencer, thanks mate . . .'

'Alright, Jackson, it's only a sixty-nine pee tape from the market, no need to cry about it.' He says that, but we're both aware that a ninety-minute compilation tape represents a good three hours of work, more if you're going to design an inlay card. 'Put it on will you? Before the muppet comes back.'

I put the tape in, press play, and it's Curtis Mayfield singing 'Move On Up'. Spencer was a mod, but has moved on to vintage soul; Al Green, Gil Scott-Heron, that kind of thing. Spencer's so cool he even likes *jazz*. Not just Sade and The Style Council either; proper jazz, the irritating, boring stuff. We sit and listen for a while. Tone's now trying to wheedle money out of the telescopes with the flick-knife he bought on a school trip to Calais, and Spencer and I watch like the indulgent parents of a child with acute behavioural problems.

'So are you coming back at weekends?' asks Spencer.

'I don't know. I expect so. Not every weekend.'

'Make sure you do though, won't you? Otherwise I'll just be stuck here on my own with Conan The Barbarian . . .' and Spencer nods towards Tone, who's now taking running jumps and drop-kicking the telescope.

'Shouldn't we make a toast or something?' I say.

Spencer curls his lip 'A *toast*? What for?'

'You know – to the future or something?'

Spencer sighs, and taps his can against mine. 'To the future. Here's hoping your skin clears up.'

'Piss off, Spencer,' I say.

'Piss off, Brian,' he says, but laughing.

By the time we're on to the last cans of lager, we're pretty drunk, so we lie on our backs, not saying anything, just listening to the sea and Otis Redding singing 'Try A Little Tenderness', and on this clear late summer night, looking up at the stars, with my best mates either side of me, it feels as if real life is beginning at last, and that absolutely everything is possible.

I want to be able to listen to recordings of piano sonatas and know who's playing. I want to go to classical concerts and know when you're meant to clap. I want to be able to 'get' modern jazz without it all sounding like this terrible mistake, and I want to know who the Velvet Underground are exactly. I want to be fully engaged in the World of Ideas, I want to understand complex economics, and what people see in Bob Dylan. I want to possess radical but humane and well-informed political ideals, and I want to hold passionate but reasoned debates round wooden kitchen tables, saying things like 'define your terms!' and 'your premise is patently specious!' and then suddenly to discover that the sun's come up and we've been talking all night. I want to use words like 'eponymous' and 'solipsistic' and 'utilitarian' with confidence. I want to learn to appreciate fine wines, and exotic liqueurs, and fine single malts, and learn how to drink them without turning into a complete div, and to eat strange and exotic foods, plovers' eggs and lobster thermidor, things that sound barely edible, or that I can't pronounce. I want to make love to beautiful, sophisticated, intimidating women, during daylight or with the light on even, and sober, and without fear, and I want to be able to speak many languages fluently, and maybe even a dead language or two, and to carry a small leather-bound notebook in which I jot incisive thoughts and observations, and the occasional line of verse. Most of all I want to read books; books thick as a brick, leather-bound books with incredibly thin paper and those purple ribbons to mark where you left off; cheap, dusty, second-hand books of collected verse, incredibly expensive, imported books of incomprehensible essays from foreign universities.

At some point, I'd like to have an original idea. And I'd like to be fancied, or maybe loved even, but I'll wait and see. And as for a job, I'm not sure exactly what I want yet, but something that I don't despise, and that doesn't make me ill, and that means I don't have to worry about money all the time. And all of these are the things that a university education's going to give me.

We finish off the lager, then things get out of hand. Tone throws my shoes into the sea, and I have to walk home in my socks.

2

QUESTION: Loosely derived from a Hans Christian Andersen story, in which 1948 Powell and Pressburger film does Moira Shearer dance to her death in front of a steam locomotive?

ANSWER: *The Red Shoes*.

Sixteen Archer Road, like all the other houses on Archer Road, is a maisonette, the diminutive form of the French noun (feminine) *maison*, literally meaning 'little house'. I live here with my mum, and if you want to see a really uncomfortable living arrangement, then you can't really beat an eighteen-year-old man and a forty-one-year-old widow in a maisonette. This morning's a case in point. I'm lying under the duvet at 8.30, listening to 'The Breakfast Show' and watching the model aeroplanes dangling from the ceiling. I should have taken them down, I know, but at some point, a couple of years ago, they went from being endearingly boyish to amusingly kitsch, so I left them up there.

Mum comes in, then knocks.

'Morning, sleepyhead. Big day today!'

'Don't you ever knock, Mum?'

'I do knock!'

'No, you come in, and *then* you knock. That's not knocking . . .'

'So? You're not *doing* anything are you?' She leers.

'No, but . . .'

'Don't say you've got a girl in there with you,' and she tugs at the corner of the duvet. 'Come on, sweetheart, don't be embarrassed, let's talk about it. Come out, come out, whoever you are . . .'

I yank the duvet back over my head. 'I'll be down in a minute . . .'

'It smells in here, actually *smells*, did you know that?'

'Can't hear you, Mum . . .'

'Smells like boys. What do boys actually *do* to make a smell like that?'

'Just as well I'm leaving then, isn't it?'

'What time's your train?'

'Twelve-fifteen.'

'So why are you still in bed then? Here; a going-away present for you . . .' and she throws a carrier bag onto the duvet cover. I open it; inside is a see-through plastic tube, the kind you get tennis balls in, but here containing three tightly balled-up pairs of men's cotton slips in red, white and black, the colours of the Nazi flag.

'Mum, you shouldn't have . . .'

'Oh, it's only little.'

'No, I mean I wish you hadn't.'

'Don't be clever, young man. Just get up. You've got packing to do. And open a window please.'

After she's gone, I shake the pants out of the plastic tube onto the duvet, relishing the potent solemnity of the occasion. For, truly, these are The Last Pants My Mother Will Ever Buy Me. The white ones are okay, and I can see the black ones having a certain durability, but *red*? Are they meant to seem a bit *racy* or something? To me, red pants are pants that say 'stop' and 'danger'.

But in a bold spirit of adventure, I get out of bed and pull on the red pants. What if they're like *The Red Shoes*, and I can never take them off? I hope not, because when I check the effect in the wardrobe mirror it looks as if I've been shot in the groin. I pull on yesterday's trousers anyway, and with woolly teeth and sweet-and-sour breath, and still a little woozy from last night's Skol, I head downstairs for breakfast. Then I'll just have a bath, then pack, then go. I can't believe I'm actually leaving. I can't believe that I'm *allowed*.

But of course the big challenge today is to pack, leave the house and get on the train without Mum saying the words, 'Your dad would have been proud of you.'

A Tuesday night in July, still bright outside, and the curtains are half-drawn so we can see the telly properly. I'm in my pyjamas and dressing gown after a bath, smelling slightly of Dettol, concentrating hard on the Airfix 1/72 scale Lancaster Bomber on a tea-tray in front of me. Dad's just got in from work, he's drinking a can of bitter, and the smoke from his cigarette hangs in the evening sunlight.

'Your starter for ten; Which British sovereign was the last to see active military combat?'

'George V,' says Dad.

'George III,' says Wheeler, Jesus College, Cambridge.

'Correct. Your bonus round begins with a question on geology.'

'Know anything about geology, Bri?'

'A bit,' I say, boldly.

'Crystalline or glassy in appearance, which of the three main classes of rock is formed by the cooling and solidification of molten earth matter . . . ?'

I know this, I'm sure I know this. 'Volcanic!' I say.

'Igneous,' says Armstrong, Jesus, Cambridge.

'Correct.'

'Nearly,' says Dad.

'Igneous rocks which contain large conspicuous crystals called phenocrysts are said to be what in texture?'

Have a stab. 'Granular,' I say.

Johnson, Jesus, Cambridge says 'Porphyritic?'

'Correct.'

'Almost,' says Dad.

'Porphyria's Lover, *in which the protagonist strangles his beloved with a braid of her hair . . .' – hang on,* I do *know this one – 'is a narrative poem by which Victorian poet?'* Robert *Browning. We did it in English last week. It's Browning, I know it is.*

'Robert Browning!' I say, trying hard not to shout.

'Robert Browning?' says Armstrong, Jesus, Cambridge.

'Correct!' and there's applause for Armstrong, Jesus, Cambridge from the studio audience, but we both know that the applause is really for me.

'Bloody hell, Bri, how d'you know that?' says Dad.

'I just know it,' I say. I want to look around and see his face, to see if he's smiling – he doesn't smile much, not after work anyway – but I don't want to look smug, so I just stay still and watch his sunlit reflection in the telly screen. He draws on his fag, then lays his cigarette hand lightly on the top of my head, like a cardinal, smooths my hair down with his long, yellow-tipped fingers, and says;

'You'll be on there one day if you're not careful,' and I smile to myself and feel clever and smart and right about something for a change.

Of course, then I get cocky, and try answering every question, and get every question wrong, but it doesn't matter because for once I got something right, and I know one day I'll get it right again.

I think it's fair to say that I've never been a slave to the fickle vagaries of fashion. It's not that I'm *anti*-fashion, it's just that of all the major youth movements I've lived through so far, none have really fitted. At the end of the day, the harsh reality is that if you're a fan of Kate Bush, Charles Dickens, Scrabble, David Attenborough and *University Challenge*, then there's not much out there for you in terms of a youth movement.

That's not to say I haven't tried. For a while I used to lie awake and worry that I might be a Goth, but I think that was just a phase. Besides, being a male Goth basically means dressing up as an aristocratic vampire, and if there's one thing that I'm never going to convince as, it's an aristocratic vampire. I just don't have the cheek-bones. Also, being a Goth means that you have to listen to the music, which is unspeakable.

So that was pretty much my only brush with youth culture. I suppose you could say that my own personal sense of style might best be described as informal yet classic. I favour the pleated cotton slack over denim, but dark denim over light. Overcoats should be heavy, long, and with the collar worn up, scarves should be lightly tasselled, black or burgundy, and are essential from early September through to late May. Shoes must be thin-soled and not too pointy, and (very important, this) only black or brown shoes to be worn with jeans.

But I'm also not afraid to experiment, especially now I'm getting my chance to reinvent myself. So with Mum and Dad's old suitcase lying open on the bed, I go through some of the new purchases that I've been saving for this special day. First up is my new donkey jacket, an incredibly dense, black heavy thing that's a bit like wearing a donkey. I'm pretty pleased with it, and the implied mix of artiness and rough-handed labour – 'enough of this Shelley, I'm off to tarmac something'.

Then there's the five granddad shirts, assorted shades of white and blue, which I got for £1.99 each on a day-trip up to Carnaby Street with Tone and Spencer. Spencer hates these, but I think they're great, especially combined with the black waistcoat, which I got second-hand for three quid from Help the Aged. I've had to hide the waistcoat from Mum, not because she's got anything against The Aged as such, but because she thinks second-hand is common and one step away from picking up food off the floor. What I'm aiming for with this waistcoat/granddad shirt/round spectacles combination is the look of a shell-shocked young army officer with a stammer and a notebook full of poetry who's been sent back from the brutalities of The Front, but is fulfilling his patriotic duty by working on a farm in a remote Gloucestershire village, where he's treated with gruff suspicion by the locals, but secretly loved from afar by the vicar's beautiful, bookish, suffragette daughter, who's into pacifism, vegetarianism and bisexuality. This really is a great waistcoat. And besides, it's not *second-hand*, it's *vintage*.

Then there's Dad's brown corduroy jacket. I lay it flat on the bed and fold the arms carefully across the chest. There's a slight tea-stain on the front from a couple of years ago, when I made the mistake of wearing it to a school disco. I know that could be seen as a bit morbid, but I thought it might be a nice gesture, a sort of tribute. I probably should have asked Mum first though, because when she saw me standing in front of the mirror dressed in Dad's jacket, she screamed and threw a mug of tea at me. When she finally realised it was just me she burst into tears and lay on the bed weeping for half an hour, which I have to tell you is a *real* boost just before a party. And when she'd calmed down, and I actually got to the disco, I had the following conversation with the love-of-my-life that week, Janet Parks.

ME: Slow dance, Janet?
JANET PARKS: Nice jacket, Bri.
ME: Thanks!
JANET PARKS: Where d'you get it?
ME: It's my dad's!
JANET PARKS: But isn't your dad . . . *dead*?
ME: Yep!
JANET PARKS: So you're wearing your dead dad's jacket?
ME: That is correct. So, about that dance?

. . . and at this point Janet put her hand in front of her mouth, and drifted off and started pointing and whispering in the corner with Michelle Thomas and Sam Dobson, then went and got off with Spencer Lewis. Not that I bear a grudge about it or anything. Besides, at university, none of this history will matter. No one will know any of this, except me. At university, it will just be a nice corduroy jacket. I fold it up and put it in the case.

Mum comes in, then knocks, and I close the case quickly. She looks teary enough as it is, without Dad's jacket starting her off again. She has, after all, taken the morning off work especially so that she can cry.

'Nearly done then?'

'Nearly.'

'D'you want to take a chip pan with you?'

'No, I'll be fine without, Mum.'

'But what are you going to eat?'

'I do eat things other than chips, you know!'

'No, you don't.'

'Well, maybe I'll start. Anyway, there's always oven-chips.' I look around to see that she's almost smiling.

'You'd better get going, hadn't you?' The train's not for ages yet, but Mum thinks catching a train is a bit like international air travel, and that you should check in four hours before departure. Not that we've been on a plane or anything, but still, it's a wonder that she hasn't made me go and get jabs.

'I'll go in half an hour,' I say, and there's a silence. Mum says something but can't quite get the words out, which means it's probably along the lines of Dad being proud or something, but she decides to save it for later, and turns and goes. I sit on the suitcase to close it, and then lie on my bed and look round my room for the last time – the kind of moment where, if I smoked, I'd smoke.

I can't believe it's actually happening. This is independent adulthood, this is what it feels like. Shouldn't there be some sort of ritual? In certain remote African tribes there'd be some incredible four-day rites of passage ceremony involving tattooing and potent hallucinogenic drugs extracted from tree-frogs, and village elders smearing my body with monkey blood, but here, rites of passage is all about three new pairs of pants and stuffing your duvet in a bin-liner.

When I get downstairs I find that Mum's made a package for me, two large crisp-boxes containing most of the house's contents. Sure enough the chip pan's in there, craftily hidden under a full dinner service, the toaster that I nicked from Ashworth Electricals, a kettle, a copy of *Marvellous Meals with Mince*, and a bread bin complete with six floured baps and a loaf of Mighty White. There's even a cheese-grater, and she knows I don't eat cheese. 'I can't really carry all this stuff Mum,' I say, and so the symbolic and touching final moments of my life in my childhood home are spent bickering with Mum about whether or not I'm going to need an egg whisk – yes, there will be a grill to make toast, yes, I do need the record player *and* the speakers – and when negotiations are finally over we've narrowed it down to a suitcase, a rucksack with my stereo and books in, two bin-liners full of duvet and pillows and, on Mum's insistence, a vast number of tea towels.

Finally it's time. I'm very insistent that Mum doesn't walk me to the train station because it somehow feels more potent and symbolic this way. I stand on the doorstep while she goes to get her purse, and solemnly presses a ten-quid note, folded very small, into my hand, like a ruby.

'Mum . . .'

'Go on, take it.'

'I'll be all right, really . . .'

'Go on. You take care of yourself . . .'

'I will . . .'

'Try and eat a piece of fresh fruit every now and then . . .'

'I'll try . . .'

'And . . .' here it comes. She gulps and says '. . . you do know Dad would have been proud of you, don't you?' and

I kiss her quickly on her dry, pursed lips, and run, in short bursts, as best as I can, to the train station.

On the train journey I put my headphones on and listen to my own specially prepared compilation tape of absolute, all-time favourite Kate Bush tracks. It's a pretty good collection, but we don't have a proper hi-fi at home, so you can hear Mum shouting upstairs to tell me the chops are ready halfway through 'The Man With The Child In His Eyes'.

I solemnly open my crisp new edition of Spenser's *The Faerie Queene,* which we're doing in the first term. I like to think I'm a pretty good reader, and open-minded and everything, but this just seems like nonsense to me, so I put down *The Faerie Queene* after the first eighteen lines, and instead concentrate on Kate Bush, and the English countryside speeding by, and on looking brooding and complex and interesting. I've got a big window, four seats and a table to myself, a can of Coke and a Twix, and the only thing that could make life any better for me now would be if an attractive woman came and sat opposite me, and said something like . . .

'Excuse me, but I can't help noticing you're reading *The Faerie Queene.* You're not by any chance on your way to read English at university are you?'

'Yes, yes I am!' I'd say.

'That's wonderful! Do you mind if I join you? My name's Emily, by the way. Tell me, are you familiar with the work of Kate Bush . . . ?'

And my conversation is so sophisticated and urbane and witty, and there's such tangible sexual electricity arcing between us, that by the time we pull into the station, Emily is leaning over the table, and coyly biting her plump bottom lip, and saying, 'Look, Brian, I barely know you, and I've never said this to a man before, but maybe we could go to . . . a hotel or something? It's just I don't think I can fight it any longer' and I acquiesce with a weary smile, as if to say 'why must this happen every time I get on a train' and take her hand and lead her to the nearest hotel . . .

Hang on a minute though. For a start, what am I going to do with all my luggage? I can hardly turn up at the hotel with two black bin-liners, can I? And then there's the cost. My money from the summer job's already gone on accommodation, my grant cheque doesn't arrive till next week, and though I've never actually stayed in a hotel before, I know it's not going to be cheap – forty, fifty quid maybe – and let's face it, the whole thing's going to last, what, ten minutes if I'm lucky, fifteen tops, and I don't want to be approaching the moment of ecstatic sexual crisis, and simultaneously worrying about value for money. I suppose Emily *might* suggest we go halvesies on the room, but I'll have to refuse or she'll think I'm cheap. And even if she does insist and I agree, she'll still have to hand over cash, and whether we do that before or after we've made love, it's bound to take some of the melancholy, bittersweet longing out of the encounter. Will she think I'm weird if I stay on afterwards, to make the most of the hotel facilities? 'Darling Emily, our love-making was both beautiful and strangely poignant. Now can you help me get the towels in my rucksack?' Also, is it a good idea to leap straight into bed with someone I'm going to be studying with? What if the sexual tension between us gets in the way of our academic work? In fact, maybe it's not such a good idea after all. Maybe I should wait till I know Emily a bit better before we get into a physical relationship.

And by the time the train pulls into the station, I find myself actually relieved that Emily's only a figment of my imagination.

I drag my bin bags and suitcase out of the station, which is on a hill overlooking the city. It's only the second time I've been here since my interview, and okay, it's not Oxford or Cambridge, but it's the next best thing. The important thing is it's got *spires*. The dreaming kind.

3

QUESTION: Which popular novel by Frances Hodgson Burnett, written in 1886 and dramatised many times since, inspired a fashion among young boys for long curly hair and velvet suits with lace collars?
ANSWER: *Little Lord Fauntleroy.*

This is what I put in the 'Hobbies and Interests' section of my application to the University Accommodation Office: Reading, Cinema, Music, Theatre, Swimming, Badminton, Socialising!

It's not a very revealing list, obviously. It's not even entirely true. 'Reading' is true, but everyone puts reading. Likewise 'Cinema' and 'Music'. 'Theatre' is a lie, I *hate* the theatre. Actually I've done plays, I've just never really seen much theatre, except for a touring educational show about road safety which, whilst performed with élan, brio and panache, didn't really do it for me aesthetically. But you have to pretend you like theatre – it's the law. 'Swimming' isn't strictly true either. I *can* swim, but only in the same way that any drowning animal can swim. I just thought I ought to put in something a bit sporty. Likewise 'Badminton'. When I say I'm interested in badminton what I really mean is that if someone held a gun to my head and forced me, on pain of death, to play one sport, and they were refusing to accept Scrabble as a sport, then that sport would be badminton. I mean, how hard can it be? 'Socialising!' is a euphemism too. 'Lonely and Sexually Frustrated' would be more accurate, but also more weird. Incidentally, the exclamation mark at the end of 'Socialising!' is meant to convey an irreverent, insouciant, devil-may-care outlook on life.

So admittedly I didn't give the people in the Accommodation Office a lot to go on, but that's still no explanation as to why they've put me in this house with Josh and Marcus.

Richmond House itself is in a red-brick terrace on the top of a very steep hill above the city, conveniently sited several miles from the nearest bus stop so that by the time I finally get there I've sweated right through my donkey jacket. The front door's already open, and the hall is crammed with boxes and racing bikes and two oars, a cricket bat and pads, ski-ing equipment, oxygen tanks and a wet-suit. It looks like a raid on a sports shop. I dump my suitcase just inside the door and, with a growing sense of trepidation, clamber over the pile of sporting goods to find my new flatmates.

The kitchen is strip-lit and institutional and smells of bleach and yeast. By the sink, two boys, one huge and blond, the other dark, squat, with a spotty rodent-face, are filling an empty plastic dustbin with water via a rubber shower attachment. 'She Sells Sanctuary' by The Cult is playing very loudly from the ghetto-blaster, and I'm stood in the doorway for some time, saying 'Hi!' and 'Hello there!', before the blond one finally looks up and sees me with my black bin-liners.

'Hullo! It's the dustbin man!'

He turns the music down a notch, bounds over like a friendly Labrador, and shakes my hand vigorously, and I realise it's the first time I've shaken hands with someone my own age.

'You must be Brian,' he says. 'I'm Josh and this is Marcus!'

Marcus is small and carbuncular, with all his features bunched up in the centre of his face, behind aviator frames that singularly fail to make him look capable of flying a plane. He looks me up and down with his ratty face, sniffs, and turns his attention back to the plastic dustbin. But Josh chatters on, not waiting for answers, in a voice that's straight out of a Pathe newsreel. 'How did you get here? Public transport? Where are your folks? Are you feeling all right? You're absolutely sodden with sweat.'

Josh is wearing burgundy pixie boots, a beige velvet waistcoat – that's a *velvet* waistcoat – a puffy purple shirt, and black jeans so tight that you can actually make out the whereabouts of each individual testicle. He has Tone's haircut, the Effeminate Viking, the badge of the confirmed Metallist, but here complemented by a tentative downy moustache; a sort of foppish, cavalier look that makes it almost look as if he's mislaid his rapier.

'What's in the bin?' I ask.

'Home-brew. We thought the sooner we get the fermentation going, the better. Obviously you can join in if you want to, we'll just split the cost three ways . . .'

'Right . . .'

'It's a tenner now, for the yeast and hop concentrate and tubes and barrel and everything, but in three weeks' time you'll be enjoying traditional Yorkshire Bitter for six pence a pint!'

'Bargain!'

'Marcus and I are quite the moonshiners, ran an illicit still in the dorms, made quite a tidy profit actually. Though we did accidentally blind a couple of day-boys!'

'You were at school together?'

'Absolutely. Joined at the hip, aren't we, Marcus?' Marcus snuffles. 'Where did you go to school?'

'Oh, you wouldn't have heard of it . . .'

'Try me.'

'Langley Street?'

Nothing.

'Langley Street Comprehensive?'

Nothing.

'Southend?' I offer. 'Essex?'

'Nope! You're absolutely right, never heard of it! Want me to show you to your quarters?'

I follow Josh upstairs, with Marcus slouching behind, along

a battleship-grey hallway decorated with instructions about what to do in case of a fire. We pass their new rooms, full of boxes and suitcases but still clearly spacious, and at the end of the corridor, Josh flings open the door to what at first glance looks like a prison cell.

'Da-da! Hope you don't mind, but we allocated for the rooms before you got here.'

'Oh. Right . . .'

'Tossed for them. We wanted to start unpacking, get settled, you see.'

'Of course! Right!' I sense I've been taken for a ride here, and resolve never again to trust a man in a velvet waistcoat. The trick now is to assert myself without being noticeably assertive.

'Quite *small*, isn't it?' I say.

'Well they're *all* small, Brian. And we did toss, fair and square.'

'How do you toss between three people?'

Silence. Josh frowns, his mouth working silently.

'We can always toss again if you don't *trust* us,' snuffles Marcus indignantly.

'No, it's not that, it's just . . .'

'Well, we'll leave you to get settled then. Glad to have you on board!' and they run back to their home-brew, whispering.

My digs look as if they've been dug. The room has the appeal and ambience of a murder scene; a single mattress on a metal frame, a matching plywood wardrobe and desk, and two small wood-effect Formica shelves. The carpets are mud-brown and seem to have been woven from compacted pubic hair. A dirty window above the desk looks out on to the dustbins below, whilst a framed sign warns that using Blu-Tack on the walls is punishable by death. Still, I wanted a garret, and I got a garret. Better get on with it, I suppose.

The first thing I do is set up the stereo, and put on *Never for Ever*, Kate Bush's triumphant third album. The rest of the records are stacked next to the turntable, and there's a bit of an internal debate as to which album should go face-out into the room; I experiment with The Beatles' *Revolver*, Joni Mitchell's *Blue*, Diana Ross and the Supremes, and Ella Fitzgerald before settling on my brand-new recording of Bach's *Brandenburg Concertos* on the Music For Pleasure label, a snip at £2.49.

Next I unpack my books, and experiment with different ways of arranging them on the Formica shelves; alphabetically by author, alphabetically by author but sub-divided by subject; genre; nationality; size; and finally, and most effectively, by colour – black Penguin classics at one end, fading through to white Picadors at the other, with two inches of green Viragos, which I haven't got round to reading yet but definitely will, in the middle of the spectrum. This takes some time, obviously, and by the time I've finished it's dark, so I set up the anglepoise on the desk.

Next I decide to turn my bed into a futon. I've been wanting to do this for some time actually, but Mum just laughed at me when I tried it at home, so I'm going to give it a go here. I manhandle the mattress, mysteriously stained and damp enough to grow cress, on to the floor without letting it come into contact with my face, then with some difficulty I up-end the metal bed frame. It weighs a ton, but I eventually get it stowed safely away behind the wardrobe. Obviously this means I lose a couple of feet of valuable floor space, but the finished effect is worth it – a kind of minimal, contemplative, oriental atmosphere that's only marginally undermined by the bold navy, red and white stripes on the British Home Stores duvet cover.

In keeping with the Zen-like minimalism of the futon, I want to limit decoration to a montage of postcards of favourite paintings and photographs, a kind of pictorial manifesto of heroes and the things I love, on the wall above my pillow. I lie on my futon, and get out the Blu-Tack; Henry Wallis's *The Death of Chatterton*, Millais' *Ophelia Drowning*, Da Vinci's *Madonna and Child*, Van Gogh's *Starry, Starry Night*, an

Edward Hopper; Marilyn Monroe in a tutu looking mournfully into the camera; James Dean in a long overcoat in New York; Dustin Hoffman in *Marathon Man*; Woody Allen; a photograph of Mum and Dad asleep in deckchairs at Butlins, Charles Dickens, Karl Marx, Che Guevara, Laurence Olivier as Hamlet, Samuel Beckett, Anton Chekhov, me as Jesus in the sixth-form production of *Godspell*, Jack Kerouac, Burton and Taylor in *Who's Afraid of Virginia Woolf?* and a photograph of Spencer, Tone and me on a school trip to Dover Castle. Spencer is posing slightly, head tilted down and to the side, looking cool and bored and clever. Tone, as usual, is flicking the 'V's.

Finally, just by my pillow, I put up a picture of Dad, looking whippet-thin and vaguely menacing, like Pinky in *Brighton Rock*, but on Southend sea front, with a bottle of beer and a cigarette smouldering in the long fingers of one hand. He's got a black quiff, high, sharp cheek-bones, a long thin nose, and a sharp, slim-collared three-button suit, and though he's half-smiling at the camera, he still looks pretty intimidating. It was taken around 1962, four years before I was born, so he must have been the same age as I am now. I love this photograph, but I still have a nagging feeling that if my nineteen-year-old dad had met the nineteen-year-old me on Southend pier on a Saturday night, there's a pretty good chance he'd have tried to beat me up.

There's a knock on the door, and instinctively I hide the Blu-Tack behind my back. I assume it's Josh, asking me to fag for him or something, but instead in walks a huge blonde woman with Viking hair and a milky blonde moustache.

'How are you getting on? Alright?' says Josh in drag.

'Fine, fine.'

'Why's your mattress on the floor?'

'Oh, I thought I'd try it as a futon for a while.'

'A futon? Really?' says Josh, pursing his lipstick-ed mouth as if it's the most exotic thing he's ever heard in his life, which is pretty rich, coming from a man in drag. 'Marcus, come and have a look at Jackson's futon!' and Marcus, in a curly black nylon wig, hockey skirt and laddered stockings, sticks his nose into the room, snuffles, then disappears.

'Anyway, we're off now – are you coming along or what?'

'Sorry, coming . . . ?'

'Tarts and Vicars Party, Kenwood Manor. Should be a laugh.'

'Right, well, maybe. It's just I thought I might stay in and read . . .'

'Oh, don't be so wet . . .'

'But I don't have anything to wear . . .'

'You've got a dark shirt, haven't you?'

'Uh-huh.'

'Well, there you go then. Stick a bit of white cardboard under the collar and away you go. See you in five minutes. Oh, and don't forget that tenner for the home-brew, yeah? *Love* what you've done to the room, by the way . . .'

4

QUESTION: The interaction energy of two protons relates to the separation between them. What are the forces between the protons when the separation between them is respectively a) small and b) intermediate?

ANSWER: Repulsive and attractive.

As a man of sophistication and experience, I know the value of 'lining your stomach' before an evening out, so for supper I buy a bag of chips and a battered sausage, and eat them on the way to the party. It starts to rain quite steadily, but I eat as many chips as I can before they get too cold and wet. Marcus and Josh stride self-confidently on ahead in their high heels, seemingly indifferent to the mirthless glances of passers-by. I suppose that posh-boys-in-drag must be one of the inevitable miseries of living in a university town. For soon it will be rag-week, the leaves will turn to bronze, the swallows will fly south, and the shopping arcade will be full of male medics dressed as sexy nurses.

On the way, Josh bombards me with questions.

'What are you studying, Brian?'

'English.'

'Poems eh? I'm Politics and Economics, Marcus is Law. Play any sports, Brian?'

'Only Scrabble,' I quip.

'Scrabble's not a sport,' sniffles Marcus.

'You haven't seen the way I play it!' I say, quick as a flash.

But he doesn't seem to find this funny, because he just scowls and says, 'Doesn't matter how you play it, it's still not a sport.'

'No, I know, I was just . . .'

'Are you soccer, cricket or rugby?' says Josh.

'Well, none of them really . . .'

'Not a sportsman, then?'

'Not at all.' I can't help feeling that I'm being assessed for admission into some un-named private club, and failing.

'How's your squash? I need a partner.'

'Not squash. Badminton occasionally.'

'Badminton's a *girls'* game,' says Marcus, adjusting the straps on his slingbacks.

'Take a year out?' asks Josh.

'No . . .'

'Go anywhere nice this summer?'

'No . . .'

'What do your parents do?'

'Well, Mum works on the tills in Woolworths. Dad sold double-glazing, but he's dead now.' Josh squeezes me on the arm and says, 'I'm *so* sorry,' though it's unclear whether he means Dad's death or Mum's job.

'How about yours?'

'Oh, Dad's Foreign Office, Mum's Department of Transport.' Oh my God, he's a Tory. Or at least I assume Josh is Tory if his parents are Tory, it does tend to run in families. As for Marcus I wouldn't be surprised to discover that he's in the Hitler Youth.

Finally we arrive at Kenwood Manor. I'd avoided the halls of residence as I'd been advised on the university open-day that they were dull and institutional and packed full of Christians. The reality is somewhere between a lunatic asylum and a minor public school – long echoing corridors, parquet floors, the smell of damp underwear drying on a luke-warm radiator, and the sense that somewhere, something terrible is happening in a toilet.

The distant thud of Dexys Midnight Runners beckons us along a corridor to a large, wood-panelled room, with high windows and sparsely populated with students – about seven parts Tart to three parts Vicar, and with a roughly fifty-fifty split between female and male Tarts. It's not a pretty sight. Burly men and quite a few women, in artfully torn tights with sports socks stuffed in their bras, leaning against the walls like, well, Tarts, whilst patrician Edwardian vice-chancellors peer down from their portraits in despair.

'By the way, Bri, I don't suppose you've got that tenner . . . ?' says Josh, frowning '. . . for the home-brew?'

I can't really afford it of course, and it's the tenner that Mum pressed into my hand, but in the spirit of new friendship I hand over the money, and Josh and Marcus skip off like dogs on a beach, leaving me to make some more of these friendships that will last me a lifetime. I decide that, generally speaking, at this early stage of the evening it's best to go for a vicar, rather than a tart.

On the way to the makeshift bar, a trestle table selling Red Stripe for a very reasonable 50p a can, I put on my talk-to-me-please face, a simple-minded close-mouthed grin accompanied by tentative nods and hopeful glances. Standing waiting to be served is a lanky hippie with a matching village-idiot grin to mine and, remarkably, an even worse complexion. He glances around the room, and in a high Brummie accent says, 'Absolutely *looooony*, isn't it!'

'Insane!' I say, and we both roll our eyes as if to say 'Tch, kids today!' His name's Chris, and it soon transpires that he's studying English too; 'Synchronicity!' exclaims Chris, and then proceeds to tell me the whole of his A-level syllabus, and the precise contents of his UCCA form, and the plot of every book he's ever read in his whole life, before embarking on a description of his summer spent travelling round India, in *real time*, and I pass the days and nights that follow by nodding, and drinking three cans of Red Stripe, and wondering whether his skin really is worse than mine, when all of a sudden I realise that he's saying . . .

'. . . and d'you know what? I never used toilet paper once in all that time.'

'Really?'

'Nope. And I don't think I'll ever use it again either. It's much fresher this way, and much more environmentally friendly.'

'So what do you . . . ?'

'Oh, just my hand, and a bucket of water. This hand!' and he thrusts it under my nose. 'Trust me, it's *loads* more hygienic.'

'But I thought you said you kept getting dysentery?'

'Well, yes, but that's different. *Everyone* gets dysentery.'

I decide not to pursue the point, and say, 'Great! Well, well done you . . .' and we're off again, travelling on bare wooden benches by rickety bus from Hyderabad to Bangalore until, somewhere in the Erramala Hills, the Red Stripe does its work and I realise with joy that my bladder's full and that I'm really sorry but I have to go to the toilet – 'Don't go away, I'll be right back, stay *right* where you are' – and as I'm leaving he grabs me by the shoulder, holds his left hand up in front of my face and says, evangelically, 'And don't forget! No need for toilet paper!' I smile and head off briskly.

When I come back I realise with relief that he *has* gone away, so I go and sit on the edge of the wooden stage, next to a small, neat woman dressed neither as tart nor vicar, but as a member of the KGB Youth Wing – a heavy black coat, black tights, a short denim shirt, and a black soviet-style cap, pushed back behind an oily black quiff. I give her a 'mind-if-I-sit-here?' smile and she gives me a 'yes-go-away' smile, a tight little spasm, and there's a glimpse of tiny, sharp white teeth, all the same size, behind an incongruous smear of crimson lipstick. I should probably just go, of course, but the lager's made me fearless and over-friendly, and so I sit next to her, anyway. Even over the gurgling bass-line of 'Two Tribes', you can still hear the muscles in her face tightening.

After a while, I turn and glance at her. She's smoking a rollie in nervous little puffs, and staring doggedly out at the dance-floor. I have two choices, speak or leave. Maybe I'll try speaking. 'The ironic thing is, I actually *am* a vicar!'

No response.

'I haven't seen this many prostitutes since my sixteenth birthday!'

No response. Maybe she didn't hear me. I offer her a swig of my can of Red Stripe.

'You're too kind. I'll pass though, thanks very much,' and she picks up the can by her side, and waggles it at me. Her voice precisely fits her face, hard and sharp; Scottish, Glaswegian I think.

'So! What did you come as?' I say brightly, nodding at her clothes.

'I came as a normal person,' she says, unsmilingly.

'You could at least have made an effort! Just put on a dog-collar or something!'

'Maybe. Except I'm Jewish.' She takes a swig from her own can. 'Funnily enough, fancy-dress has never really taken off amongst the Jewish Community.'

'You know, I sometimes wish I was Jewish,' I say. As a conversational gambit, I realise that this is pretty bold, and I'm not entirely sure why I say it; partly because I think it's important to be up-front about issues of race, gender and identity, and also because by this stage I'm pretty pissed.

She narrows her eyes, and looks at me for a moment, a spaghetti-western look, sucking on her rollie, deciding whether to take offence or not, then says quietly: 'Is that right?'

'I'm sorry, I'm not being racist, I just mean that a lot of my heroes are Jewish, so . . .'

'Well, I'm glad that my people meet with your approval. Who are these heroes, then?'

'Oh, you know, Einstein, Freud, Marx . . .'

'Karl or Groucho?'

'Both. Arthur Miller, Lenny Bruce, Woody Allen, Dustin Hoffman, Philip Roth . . .'

'Jesus, of course . . .'

'. . . Stanley Kubrick, Freud, J.D.Salinger . . .'

'Of course, strictly speaking Salinger's not Jewish.'

'Oh, he is.'

'Trust me, he's not.'

'Are you sure?'

'We know – we have a special sense.'

'But it's a Jewish name.'

'His father was Jewish, his mother was Catholic, so technically he's not. Jewishness passes through the female line.'

'I didn't know that.'

'Well there you go, the beginnings of your university education,' and she goes back to glowering at the dance-floor, now crammed with Tarts hobbling along to the music. It's a pretty grim sight, like a newly discovered circle of hell, and the girl watches with knowing contempt, as if waiting for the bomb she's planted to go off. 'Christ, will you take a look at this little lot,' she drawls wearily, as 'Two Tribes' segues into 'Relax'. 'Frankie Says "Ab-so-lute-ly Noooo Fucking Idea . . ."' Deciding that world-weary cynicism is definitely the way to go here, I make sure that I chuckle audibly at this, and she turns to me, half-smiling. 'You know the greatest achievement of the English boarding-school? Generations of floppy-haired boys who know the correct way to adjust a suspender belt. What's amazing is how many of you lot arrive at university with your women's clothing already packed.'

You lot?

'Actually, I went to a comprehensive school,' I say.

'Well, bully for you. You know, you're the sixth person to

tell me that tonight. Is it some kind of weird left-wing chat-up line I wonder? What am I meant to be more impressed by? Our state school system? Or your heroic academic achievements?'

If I know anything, I know when I've been beaten, so I pick up my three-quarters-full can and wave it in the air like it's empty; 'I'm just going to the bar, can I get you something, um . . . ?'

'Rebecca.'

'. . . Rebecca?'

'I'm fine.'

'Right. Well. See you around. I'm Brian, by the way.'

'Goodbye, Brian.'

'Bye, Rebecca.'

I'm about to go over to the bar, but notice Chris the hippie lying in wait, up to his elbow in a big bag of crisps, and so head out of the hall and decide to go for a walk.

I wander down the wood-panelled corridor, where the last batch of new students are saying goodbye to their parents to a soundtrack of Bob Marley's 'Legend'. One girl sobs in her sobbing mother's arms whilst her impatient dad stands stiffly by, a little roll of banknotes clutched in his hand. A lanky, embarrassed black-clad Goth with a prominent dental brace is almost physically pushing his parents out of the room, so that he can get on with the serious business of letting people know the dark and complex creature that lies behind all that metal and plastic. Other new arrivals are introducing themselves to their next-door neighbours, delivering little potted biographies: subject, place-of-birth, exam grades, favourite band, most traumatic childhood experience. It's a sort of polite, middle-class version of that scene in war movies, where the raw young recruits arrive in the barracks and show each other photos of the girl back home.

I stop at the Student Union notice-board, sip my lager and idly scan the posters – a drum-kit for sale, calls to boycott Barclays, an out-of-date meeting of the Revolutionary

Communist Party in support of the miners, auditions for *The Pirates Of Penzance* – I note that Self-Inflicted and Meet Your Feet are playing at the Frog and Frigate next Tuesday.

And that's when I see it.

On the notice-board, a bright red photo-copied A4 poster reads:

> **Your Starter for Ten!**
>
> Know your Sophocles from your Socrates?
> Your Ursa Minor from your Lee Majors?
> Your *carpe diem* from your *habeas corpus*?
>
> Think you've got what it takes to take on the big boys?
>
> Why not come along to the *University Challenge* auditions?
>
> Qualification by brief (and fun!) written exam.
> Friday lunchtime, 1.00 p.m. prompt,
> Student Union, Meeting Room 6.
>
> Commitment required. No slackers or chancers.
> *Only the finest minds need apply.*

Here it is then. This is the one. The Challenge.

5

QUESTION: Which black American entertainer, the self-proclaimed 'hardest-working man in show-business' and a pioneer of funk music, is commonly known as 'the Godfather of Soul'?

ANSWER: James Brown.

The thing that used to strike me most was their hair; great, improbable waves of brittle hair like parched wheat; swooping curtains of silky fringe; Sunday tea-time costume-drama mutton-chop sideburns. Dad could be reduced to a white-faced rage by anything other than a short-back-and-sides on Top of the Pops *but if you made it on to* University Challenge *then you'd earned the right to any damned hair-do you wanted. It was almost as if they couldn't help it, as if the crazy hair was just an outlet for all that incredible, uncontrollable excess mental energy. Like a mad scientist, you couldn't be that clever and still expect to have manageable hair, or decent eyesight, or the ability to wash and dress yourself.*

And the clothes; the arcane, olde-English tradition of scarlet gowns combined with the self-consciously wacky piano-keyboard-ties, the endless home-knitted scarves, the Afghan jerkins. Of course, when you're a kid watching telly, everyone seems old, and retrospectively I suppose they must have been young, technically, in earth years, but if they really were twenty, then they were twenty going on sixty-two. Certainly there was nothing in the faces that suggested youth, or vigour, or good health. Instead they were tired, pasty, care-worn, as if struggling with the weight of all that information – the half-life of Tritium, the origins of the term 'éminence grise', *the first twenty perfect numbers, the rhyme scheme of a Petrarchan sonnet – had taken a terrible physical toll.*

Of course, Dad and I rarely got any of the answers right, but that wasn't really the point. This wasn't trivia *– it wasn't about feeling smug and complacent about all the things you* knew, *it was about feeling humbled by the whole, vast universe of things about which you had absolutely* no idea; *the point was to watch in awe, because it really did seem to me and Dad as if these strange creatures knew everything. Ask any question: what's the weight of the sun? Why are we here? Is the universe infinite? What's the secret of true happiness? – and even if they didn't know the answer immediately, they could at least confer, muttering to each other in low, lisping voices, and come up with something that, if not quite correct, still sounded like a fairly good guess.*

And it didn't matter that the contestants were clearly social misfits, or a little grubby or spotty, or ageing virgins, or in some cases just frankly strange, the point was that somewhere was a place where people actually knew *all these things, and loved knowing them, and cared about that knowledge passionately, and thought it was important and worthwhile, and that one day, Dad said, if I worked really, really hard, I might actually get there too . . .*

'Fancy your chances?' she says.

I turn around and I swear she is so beautiful that I nearly drop my can of lager.

'Fancy your chances?'

I don't think I've ever stood this close to anything this beautiful. There's beauty in books of course, or in a painting maybe, or a view, like on that geography field-trip to the Isle of Purbeck, but up until now I don't think I've ever experienced *true* beauty, not in a real live, warm, soft human being, something that you might be able to touch, in theory anyway. She's so perfect that I actually flinch when I see her. The muscles in my chest tighten up and I have to remind myself to breathe. It sounds like outrageous hyperbole, I know, but she really does look like a young, blonde Kate Bush.

'Fancy your chances?' she says.

'Hmhm?' I riposte, sharp as a tack.

'Think you're up to it?' she says, nodding at the poster.

Quick, say something witty.

'Ffnagh' quip I, and she smiles at me sympathetically, like a kindly young nurse smiling at the Elephant Man.

'See you there tomorrow, then?' she says, and walks away. She's in fancy dress, but very cannily, with great wit and aplomb and taste, she's gone for the *far* superior French Tart option – a tight black-and-white striped top, wide, black elasticated ballet-dancer's belt, black pencil skirt, fishnet tights. Or are they stockings? Stockings or tights, stockings or tights, stockings or tights . . .

I follow her back along the corridor, a decent, non-threatening distance behind, and watch her walk her metronomic walk, like Monroe coming out of the steam in *Some Like It Hot*, stockings or tights, stockings or tights, and as she passes each bedroom door someone will pop their head out and say hi, and hello, and how are you and you look great; but she can only have been here eight hours, a day at most, so how come she seems to know *everyone*?

Then she enters the party, walks through a crowd of gaping vicars and across to a little cluster of girls stood by the edge of the dance-floor, the kind of hard, pretty, trendy girls who always sniff each other out and flock together. The DJ is playing 'Tainted Love' now, and the atmosphere in the room seems to have got darker, more sexually predatory and decadent, and if it's not quite Weimar Republic Berlin, then it's at least an East Sussex Sixth-form-college production of *Cabaret*. I stand in the shadows and observe. I'm going to have to have my wits about me, if I'm going to do this properly, and I'm also going to need more lager. I go and buy can number six. Or is it seven? Not sure. Doesn't matter.

I hurry back, in case she's gone, but she's still there at the edge of the dance-floor with her gang of four, laughing and joking as if she's known them for a lifetime rather than for a whole afternoon. I arrange my face into something like a look of wry, amused boredom and make a couple of sorties, walking close by her with a nonchalant air, in the hope that she'll catch my eye, grab me by the elbow and say, 'Tell me *everything* about yourself, you fascinating creature.' She doesn't, so I decide to walk by her again. I do this maybe fourteen or fifteen times, but she doesn't notice me, so I decide to take a more direct approach. I go and stand behind her.

I'm stood behind her for the whole of the extended twelve-inch version of 'Blue Monday' by New Order. Eventually, one of her new friends, a triangular-faced, thin-lipped girl with cat's eyes and a bleached-blonde crop, catches my eye and instinctively puts her hand on her handbag as if she thinks I'm there with the intention of stealing someone's purse. So I grin reassuringly, and her eyes start to flick madly round the group, and maybe she emits a high-pitched warning signal or something, because finally the group turns and looks at me, and all of a sudden the blonde Kate Bush is right there, her beautiful face just inches away from mine. I've got my wits about me this time so, pithily, I say: 'Hullo!'

This intrigues her less than I'd hoped, because she just says 'Hi' then starts to turn her back on me.

'We met? Just now? In the corridor?' I gabble.

Her face is blank. Despite the volume of liquid I've drunk, my mouth feels thick and gluey, as if the saliva has been thickened with cornflour, but I lick my lips and say, 'You asked me if I fancied my chances? On *University Challenge*?'

'Oh, yes,' she says, and turns again, but her friends have

scattered, sensing the electricity between us, and we are alone at last, as fate has decreed.

'The ironic thing is I actually *am* a vicar!' I say.

'Sorry?' She leans in closer, and I take the opportunity to put my hand to her ear, and let it brush against her lovely head.

'I actually am a vicar!' I shout.

'Are you?'

'What?'

'A vicar?'

'No, I'm not a vicar.'

'I thought you said you were a vicar?'

'No, I'm not . . .'

'What did you say, then?'

'Well, yes, I mean, I did, yes, say, I was a vicar, yes, but I was, I was joking!'

'Oh. Sorry, I don't underst . . .'

'I'm Brian by the way!' *Don't panic . . .*

'Hello Brian . . .' and she starts to look around for her friends. *Keep going, keep going . . .*

'Why? Do I look like a vicar?!' I say.

'I don't know. A little bit, I suppose . . .'

'Oh! Right! Well, *thanks*! Thanks *a lot*!' I'm trying mock-indignation now, arms folded high across my chest, trying to make her laugh, to get some witty, light-hearted banter going. 'A vicar eh! Well, thank you *very much*! In that case, you look like a . . . like a real . . . a real *tart*!'

'I'm *sorry*?'

She can't have heard me properly, because she's not laughing, so I raise my voice.

'A TART! You look like a prostitute! A high-class prostitute, mind you . . .'

She smiles at me, one of those very small, subtle smiles that resemble contempt, and says, 'Will you excuse me, Gary, I'm *desperate* for the loo . . .'

'Okay! See you round!' but she's already gone, leaving

me with a vague feeling that things might have gone better. Perhaps she's taken offence, even though I was obviously putting on a funny voice. But how does she know it's a funny voice, if she's not accustomed to my usual voice? Maybe now she just thinks that I've got a funny voice? And who the hell is Gary? I stand and watch her head off to the toilets, except she only goes as far as the dance-floor, where she stops, and whispers in another girl's ear, and they both laugh. So she doesn't need the toilet after all. The toilet was just a ruse.

Then she starts to dance. They're playing 'Love Cats' by The Cure, and in a witty and incisive interpretation of the song's lyric, she's dancing a little bit like a cat, bored and aloof and supple, with one arm occasionally flung up above her head like a, well, like a cat's tail! She is the most amazing dancer in the world! Now she's got her hands under her chin like two little paws, and she *is* the eponymous Love Cat, and she is so wonderfully, wonderfully, wonderfully, wonderfully pretty, and an idea hits me, a plan so beautiful in its simplicity and yet so ingenious and infallible, that I'm amazed I haven't thought of it before.

Dance! I will woo her through the medium of contemporary dance.

The record changes, and it's 'Sex Machine' by James Brown, which is fine by me, because I *do* feel like getting up and being a sex machine now you come to mention it. I carefully place the can of Red Stripe on the floor, where it is immediately kicked over, but I don't mind, and it doesn't matter. I won't be needing it where I'm going. I start to do some warm-up moves at the edge of the dance-floor, a little gingerly at first, but I'm glad I wore my brogues instead of my Green Flash, as the flat soles slide gratifyingly on the parquet floor, giving me a kind of funky, loose-limbed feel. Then warily at first, like I'm back at the ice-rink, clinging to the walls, I carefully make my way on to the dance-floor itself, and get up get on up over to her.

She's dancing in her little group of five again, tight as a fist, one of those impregnable defence formations that the Roman infantry used to repel the barbarians. The cat-eyed girl sees me first, and emits her high-pitched warning signal, and Blonde Kate Bush breaks formation, turns and sees me and looks me in the eye and I take my cue, let the music enter me, and dance like I have never danced before.

I'm dancing as if my life depended on it, biting my lower lip seductively, both as an erotic signifier and an aid to concentration, and looking her straight in the eye, daring, just *daring* her to look away. Which she does. So I slide on round, back into her eye line, and I let rip. I'm dancing as if I was wearing the Red Shoes, and then I think maybe I was right, maybe it's because of those pants, the pants Mum gave me, the Red Pants, but whatever it is, I'm dancing like James Brown, I've got funk and soul and a brand-new bag, I'm the hardest-working man in show-business, I'm a machine made specifically for the purpose of sex, sliding and spinning through 360, 720 degrees and once actually through 810 degrees, which leaves me facing the wrong way, and momentarily disorientated, but it's okay because James Brown is saying 'take it to the bridge' so I do, I take it to the bridge, wherever that is, and on the way to the bridge my hand goes to my neck and rips away the white cardboard dog-collar in a gesture of righteous contempt for organised religion, and I hurl the cardboard dog-collar onto the floor, into the middle of a group of people who've formed a circle around me now, and are clapping and laughing and pointing in awe and admiration, as I spin and duck and touch the floor, my cardigan flying free behind me. My glasses have steamed up a bit, so I can't see Kate Bush's face amongst them, just a glimpse of that chippy, dark-haired Jewish girl, Rebecca whatsername, but it's too late to stop dancing now, because James Brown is asking me to shake my moneymaker, shake my moneymaker, and I have to think for a minute because I'm not sure what my moneymaker is specifically. My head?

No, my ass, of course, so I shake it as best I can, anointing the crowd around me with sweat, like a wet dog, and then all of a sudden there's a jab of horns and the song is over and I.

Am.

Spent.

I look for her face among the cheering crowd, but she's definitely gone. Not to worry. The important thing is to have made an impression. Our paths will cross again, tomorrow, one p.m., at The Challenge auditions.

The ironic, tongue-in-cheek slowies are beginning now, 'Careless Whisper', but everyone's either too cool or too drunk to dance, so I decide it's time for bed. On the way out along the corridor, I go into the toilets and wipe the syrupy sweat off my spectacles with the corner of my cardy so that I can get a better look at myself in the mirror above the urinals. My shirt is stuck to my skin with sweat and undone to my belly-button, and my hair is matted to my forehead, and all the blood has rushed to my head, specifically to my acne, but I still think that on the whole I look pretty good. The room's spinning now, so I rest my forehead on the mirror in front of me to make it stay still while I pee, and from one of the cubicles comes the smell of marijuana smoke, and two low voices, giggling. Then there's the sound of the toilet flushing, and two tarts come out, one female and wet-faced, adjusting her hockey skirt, the other a broad-shouldered rugby-player tart. Both have lipstick smeared over their faces. They look at me challengingly, daring me to say something disapproving, but I'm full of elation, and passion and love for the sheer, joyous recklessness of youth, so I smile woozily back at them.

'The ironic thing is I actually *am* a vicar!' I say.

'Oh, *do* fuck off,' he says.

6

QUESTION: Book IX of Wordsworth's *The Prelude* contains the exhortation: 'Bliss was it in that dawn to be alive . . .'?

ANSWER: But to be young was very heaven.

As new dawns go, this one is depressingly like the old dawn.

It's not even dawn, it's 10.26. I thought I'd wake up on my first day here full of health and wisdom and academic vigour, but instead I just get the usual; shame, self-loathing and nausea, and a vague feeling that waking-up needn't always be like this.

I'm also pretty indignant because someone has clearly come into my room while I was sleeping, lined my mouth with felt and then stamped on my head. I'm finding movement difficult, so I lie for a moment and count how many consecutive nights I've gone to bed drunk, and come up with the approximate figure of 103. And it would have been more if it weren't for that last bout of tonsillitis. I contemplate the idea that maybe I'm an alcoholic. I get this occasionally, the need to define myself as a something-or-other, and at various times in my life have wondered if I'm a Goth, a homosexual, a Jew, a Catholic or a manic-depressive, whether I am adopted, or have a hole in my heart, or possess the ability to move objects with the power of my mind, and have always, mostly regretfully, come to the conclusion that I'm none of the above. The fact is I'm actually not *anything*. I'm not even an 'orphan', not in the strict sense, but 'alcoholic' seems the most plausible yet. What other name is there for someone who goes to bed drunk every night? Still, maybe alcoholism wouldn't be the worst thing in the world; at least half the people in the postcards on the wall by my head are alcoholics. The trick is, I suppose, to be an alcoholic without letting it affect your behaviour or your academic work.

Or maybe I've just read too many novels. In novels, alcoholics are always attractive and funny and charming and complex, like Sebastian Flyte or Abe North in *Tender is the Night*, and they're drinking because of a deep, unquenchable sadness of the soul, or the terrible legacy of the First World War, whereas I just get drunk because I'm thirsty, and I like the taste of lager, and because I'm too much of a div to know when to stop. After all, it's not as if I can blame it on the Falklands.

And I certainly smell like an alcoholic. After less than twenty-four hours, the new room has started to smell. It's Mum's 'boy' smell – warm and salty, a bit like the back of a wrist-watch. Where does it come from? Do I just carry it around with me? Sitting up in bed, I find my shirt from last night on the floor nearby, still soaked with sweat. Even my cardigan's damp. A little momentary flash of suppressed memory comes back to me . . . something about . . . dancing? I lie back down, and pull the duvet up over my head.

In the end, it's the futon that forces me up. In the night it seems to have compacted, and I can feel the hard, cold floor against my spine, so that now it's like lying on a large moist towel, one that's been left in a plastic bag for a week. I sit on the edge of it, knees up under my chin, and search through my pockets for my wallet. It's there, but worryingly only contains a fiver plus 18p in change. That's got to last me till next Monday, three days' time. How much lager did I actually drink last night? And, oh God, there it is again, the suppressed memory, bubbling to the surface like a fart in a bath. Dancing. I remember dancing, in the centre of a group of people. But that can't be right, because usually I dance like St Vitus, and these people were smiling and clapping and cheering.

And then it comes to me, with a terrible clarity, the realisation that *the applause was ironic.*

The Student Union building is an ostentatiously ugly rain-streaked concrete hulk, marooned in the middle of terraces of neat Georgian house like a bad tooth. This morning they're pouring in and out the swing doors, singly and in tight little groups with their day-old best friends, because it's the last day of Freshers Week, and there are no lectures till Monday. Instead today is our opportunity to join Socs.

I join FrenchSoc, FilmSoc, LitSoc, PoetrySoc, and the writing staff of all three student magazines; the literary-minded *Scribbler*, the irreverent, salacious *Tattle*, and the earnest, campaigning, left-wing *By Lines*. I sign up for Darkroom Soc ('Join us and see what develops!') even though I don't have a camera, and then contemplate joining the FeministSoc, but whilst queuing at their trestle table I get glared at confrontationally by a Gertrude Stein look-alike and start to wonder if maybe joining FeministSoc might be trying just a bit too hard. I made this mistake once before, on a school trip to the Victoria and Albert Museum, when I followed a sign marked 'Women', thinking it was an exhibition on the changing role of women in society, and actually ended up standing in the ladies' toilets. In the end I decide to give FeministSoc a miss, because while I firmly support the women's liberation movement, I'm not entirely confident that I'm not just joining as a way to meet girls.

I hurry past the fresh-faced, pastel-coloured sweaters of BadmintonSoc, just in case someone calls my bluff, then wave to Josh who's surrounded by pals in the queue for BeefyToffSoc, or whatever it is, something to do with ski-ing and drinking and harassing women and extreme right-wing views.

I also decide not to join TheatreSoc. Like FeministSoc, it's a pretty good way of spending time with girls, but the down-side is that it's usually just a ruse to trick you into putting on a play. This term TheatreSoc will be producing

Charley's Aunt, Sophocles' *Antigone* and *Equus*, and I just know I'd get cast either as a member of the Greek chorus, all shouting simultaneously through papier-mâché masks in ruined bed-sheets, or one of those poor saps in *Equus* who spends the whole evening in a leotard wearing a horse's head made out of coat hangers. Well, TheatreSoc, thanks but no thanks. Besides, I'll have you know that in my last year at school I played Jesus in *Godspell*, and once you've been whipped and crucified in front of the whole school, there isn't really anywhere to go performance-wise. Tone and Spencer laughed all the way through of course, and shouted 'More! More!' during the forty lashes, but everyone else said it was a very affecting performance.

When I think I've had enough Socs, I wander the room looking for the mystery girl from last night, though God knows what I'll do if I see her. Certainly not dance. I do two circuits of the sports hall, but there's no sign of her, so I head upstairs to the room where The Challenge heats are taking place, just to make sure I've got the right room and the right time. Sure enough, the poster's on the door; *Your Starter For Ten. Only the finest minds need apply*. 'Fancy your chances?' she'd said last night. 'Maybe see you there?' she'd said. Was she serious? And if so, where is she? I am an hour early though, so I decide to go back to the sports hall, to have another look round.

Walking back downstairs, I pass the dark-haired Jewish girl from last night on the stairwell; Jessica, was it? She's standing with a bunch of skinny, pale men in Harringtons and tight black jeans, handing out leaflets for the Socialist Workers Party and all looking fuckingangryactually, so in a spirit of solidarity, I approach and say, 'Greetings, comrade!'

'Morning twinkle-toes,' she drawls, glancing at my clenched fist, unamused, and quite right too, because it's not funny. She goes back to handing out the leaflets. 'I think DanceSoc's through there somewhere.'

'Oh God, was it really awful?'

'Let's just say I was all for putting a pencil between your teeth, stop you biting your tongue off.'

I laugh self-deprecatingly, and shake my head, in an I'm-mad-me kind of way, but she doesn't smile so I say, 'You know, life's taught me two things; Number *One* is don't dance when you're drunk!!!' . . . silence . . . 'Actually, I wondered if I could take a leaflet?'

She looks at me quizzically, intrigued by my hidden depths.

'You're sure I wouldn't just be wasting paper?'

'Absolutely not.'

'So are you already a member of any political parties?'

'Oh, you know. CND!'

'That's not a political party.'

'So you don't think defence policy is a political issue?' I say, enjoying how it sounds.

'Politics is economics, pure and simple. Single-issue groups, pressure groups like CND or Greenpeace, have an important and valid role to play, but saying that whales are big and nice, or a nuclear holocaust is nasty, is not a political stance, it's a truism. Besides, in a true socialist state the military would be disenfranchised automatically . . .'

'Like it is in Russia?' I say.

A-ha!

'Russia isn't truly socialist.'

Oh . . .

'Or Cuba?' I say.

Touché!

'Yes, if you like. Like in Cuba.'

Um . . .

'Oh, so I suppose Cuba doesn't have an army then?' I say. *Nice recovery.*

'Not really, none to speak of, not in terms of Gross National Product. Six per cent of tax is spent on defence in Cuba, compared to forty per cent in the USA.' She must be making this stuff up. Not even Castro knows this stuff. 'If it wasn't under constant threat from the USA it wouldn't even need to spend the six per cent. Or do you lie awake at night and worry about being invaded by Cuba?'

It seems a bit too school-playground to accuse her of making stuff up, so I just say, 'So do I get a leaflet or what?' and grudgingly she hands me one.

'If it's too outspoken for you, the Labour Party's over there. Or you could just go the whole hog and join the Tories.'

She says it like a slap, and it takes me a moment to take it in, and then while I'm thinking of what to say, she turns her back on me, just turns around and carries on handing out leaflets. I want to put my hand on her shoulder, spin her round and say '*Don't* turn your back on me, you prissy, bigoted, self-righteous little cow, because my dad's job actually killed him, more or less, so don't lecture me about Cuba, because I've got a better sense of fucking social injustice in my little finger than you and your whole gang of bourgeois, art-school boyfriends have got in your whole complacent, smug self-satisfied bodies.' And I almost say it, I really do, but in the end what I choose to say is, 'Of course you do realise that if you shortened your name, you could just become SocSoc!'

She turns to me, quite slowly, narrows her eyes and says 'Look. If you're really committed and passionate about opposing what Thatcher's doing to the country, then you should come along. If on the other hand you're just interested in making a whole load of sixth-form jokes and banal comments, then I think we can probably manage without you, thanks very much.'

She's right, of course. Why do I always sound facetious and unconvincing when I talk about politics? I don't *feel* ironic about it. I think about trying to convey this to her, just by having a proper intelligent adult conversation, but a skirmish has broken out between one of the skinny boys in black denim and someone from Class War, so I think better of it, and move on.

7

QUESTION: Devised by the German psychologist William Stern, what controversial measurement was originally defined as the ratio of a person's mental age to his physical age, multiplied by 100?

ANSWER: IQ.

I walk back upstairs to Meeting Room 6, where a tall, fair man is setting out tables and chairs in exam formation, thirty or so, with an air of bureaucratic officiousness. He's clearly a lot older than me, twenty-one or twenty-two or something, tall and fit in an official burgundy university sweatshirt, tanned and blandly handsome with very neat, short reddish-blond hair, the kind of hair that looks as if it's been moulded from a single piece of plastic. I watch him for a while through the glass door. He looks like an astronaut, if Britain had astronauts, or a non-threatening Action Man. What's troubling about him is that I seem to remember him from somewhere . . .

He catches sight of me, so politely I stick my head around the door and say, 'Excuse me, is this the room for the University Chal . . . ?'

'Fingers on the buzzers, your first starter question – can you read the sign?'

'Yes.'

'What does it say?'

'Meeting Room 6, one o'clock.'

'What time is it now?'

'Twelve forty-five.'

'So I presume that answers your question?'

'I suppose so.'

So I sit down outside the door and limber up by running through some lists in my head; the Kings and Queens of England, the Periodic Table, the American Presidents, the Laws of Thermodynamics, the planets of the solar system, just in case; basic exam technique. I check that I've got a pencil and pen, a tissue, a box of Tic-Tacs, and wait for the other contestants to turn up. After ten minutes I'm still the only one here, so I sit and peer at the guy sitting at his teacher's desk, as he solemnly sorts out and staples question papers. I assume he must be something pretty high up in the *University Challenge* selection committee, and is giddy on the sheer intoxicating power of it all, but I must keep on his good side, so at 12.58 precisely, and no earlier, I get up and enter the room.

'Okay now?'

'Fine. You can come in. How many others out there with you?' he says, without looking up.

'Um – none?'

'Really?' He looks past me, because I clearly can't be trusted. 'Oh bugger! It's nineteen eighty-three all over again.' He tuts and sighs, and perches on the edge of the desk, and picks up a clipboard, then looks me up and down appraisingly, and glances at my face, before settling on a point twelve inches to the side of my face, which he seems to prefer. He sighs mournfully again. 'Oh well, I'm Patrick. What's your name?'

'Brian Jackson.'

'Year?'

'First year! Just arrived yesterday!'

Tut and sigh. 'Specialist subject?'

'You mean what am I reading?'

'If you like.'

'English Literature.'

'Christ, another one! Well, at least you're not completely wasting three years of your life.'

'I'm sorry, I . . .'

'Whatever happened to all the mathematicians, that's what I want to know. All the bio-chemists? All the mechanical engineers? No wonder the economy's going to the dogs; everyone knows what a metaphor is, no one can build a power station.'

I laugh, then check to see if he's joking, but he isn't. 'I have science A-levels!' I say, defensively.

'Really? What in?'

'Physics and Chemistry.'

'Well there you go then! A Renaissance Man! What's Newton's Third Law of Motion?'

Oh, my friend, you're going to have to try a lot harder than that . . .

'Reaction is equal and opposite to action,' I say.

Patrick's reaction is pretty equal and opposite too; a brief, begrudging raising of the eyebrows, before he goes back to his notepad.

'School?'

'Pardon?'

'I said "school"? Big building, made of bricks, teachers in it . . .'

'I understood the question, I just wondered why you wanted to know?'

'Alright then, Trotsky, you've made your point. You've got a pen? Good. Here's your paper, and I'll be with you in a minute.' I take a seat near the back of the room as two more people arrive behind me. 'Ah, the cavalry!' says Patrick.

The first potential team-mate, a Chinese girl, causes a bit of a stir, because she seems to have a panda bear clinging to her back. Closer scrutiny reveals this not to be a real-life panda, but an ingeniously designed rucksack! It shows a quirky sense of humour I suppose, but doesn't bode well for her chances on a serious, advanced general knowledge quiz. Anyway, from her conversation with Patrick I hear that she's called Lucy Chang, that she's a second year, reading Medicine, and so may possibly have an edge on me with some of those science questions. Her English seems pretty fluent, though she speaks incredibly quietly, with a slight American accent. What do the rules say about foreign nationals?

The next contestant is a big, loud-voiced Mancunian, dressed in olive-green army surplus, big heavy boots and with a little blue RAF knapsack at his hip with, somewhat inconsistently, a CND sign magic-markered onto it. Patrick interviews him with a kind of begrudging civility, NCO to corporal, and it transpires that he's a third-year Politics student from Rochdale called Colin Pagett. He glances round the room, nods, and then we wait in silence and fiddle with our pens, all sitting as far away from each other as the laws of geometry will allow, waiting ten, fifteen minutes, until it's absolutely clear that no one else is going to turn up. Where is she? She said she'd be here. What if something's happened to her?

Finally Patrick the Astronaut sighs, stands up behind his desk and says, 'Right, well let's begin shall we? My name's Patrick Watts from Ashton-Under-Lyme, reading Economics, and I'm the captain of this year's *University Challenge* team' . . . hang on, who says? . . . 'Regular viewers of the show may recognise me from last year's tournament.'

That's it, that's where I know him from. I remember watching the episode extra carefully because I'd been filling out my UCCA form, and I'd wanted to know what the standard was like. I remember thinking then that they were a pretty poor team, and this Patrick obviously still carries the emotional scars with him, because he looks at the floor, shame-faced, at the mention of it. 'Obviously, it wasn't a flawless performance' – they were knocked out in the first round if I remember rightly, against soft opponents too – 'but we're very hopeful about our chances this year, especially with so much ... promising ... raw material.'

The three of us look around the room, at each other, and at the rows of empty desks.

'Right! Well, without further ado, let's get cracking on the test. It's in written form, forty questions, and covers a diverse range of subjects, similar to those we'll be facing on the programme. Last year we were particularly weak in the science area' – he glances at me – 'and I want to make sure we're not too arts-orientated this time ...'

'And it's a four-person team, yeah?' the Mancunian pipes up.

'That is correct.'

'Well if that's the case, then surely ... we *are* the team.'

'Well, yes, but we need to make sure we're up to an appropriate standard.'

But Colin's not letting go. 'Why?'

'Well, because if we're not ... we'll lose again.'

'And?'

'Well, if we lose again ... if we lose again ...' and Patrick's mouth is working wordlessly now, opening and closing like a dying mackerel. It's the same face he had on national television last year, trying and failing to answer a perfectly simple question on the East African lakes: the same haunted look, with every single member of the audience knowing the answer, willing it to him; Lake Tanganyika, Tanganyika, you idiot.

Then he's distracted by a noise at the door – a cluster of grinning female faces briefly pressed against the glass, a muffled burst of laughter, a scuffle, and she's shoved into the room by unseen hands, and just stands there, giggling, trying to regain her composure, looking round the room at the four of us.

I swear, for a moment I think everyone's going to stand up.

'Whoops! Sorry, everyone!'

She's slurring a bit, and seems a little unsteady on her feet. She's not thinking of taking an exam pissed, is she?

'I'm sorry, am I too late?'

Patrick runs his hands over his astronaut's hair, licks his lips, and says, 'Not at all. Glad to have you on board . . . um . . . ?'

'Alice. Alice Harbinson.'

Alice. Alice. Of course, she's an Alice. What else could she be?

'Okay, Alice. Please – take a seat . . .' And she looks around, smiles at me, and comes over and sits at the desk directly behind mine.

The first few questions are pretty easy; basic geometry and some stuff about the Plantagenets, just there to soften us up really, but it's hard to concentrate because Alice is making this snuffling noise over my shoulder. I turn and glance at her, and sure enough she's hunched forwards over her exam paper red-faced, shaking with suppressed laughter. I go back to the test paper.

Question 4. What was ancient Istanbul known as, *before* it was called Constantinople?

Easy. Byzantium.

Question 5. Helium, neon, argon and xenon make up four of the so-called 'noble gases'. What are the other two?

No idea. Krypton and hydrogen maybe? Krypton and hydrogen.

Question 6. What is the precise composition of the aroma emanating from Alice Harbinson, and why is it so delightful?

Something expensive, flowery but light. Is it perhaps Chanel No 5? Mixed with a tiny hint of Pears soap, and Silk Cut, and lager . . .

That's enough now. Concentrate.

Question 6. Where is Mrs Thatcher's parliamentary seat?

Easy. I know this one, but there's the noise again. I turn, and look and catch her eye this time, and she pulls a face, mouths 'sorry . . .' and seals her lips with a little imaginary zip. I smile laconically down one side of my face, as if to say, hey, phew, don't mind me, I'm not taking this seriously either, then go back to the test. Must concentrate. I pop a Tic-Tac into my mouth, and press my fingers against my forehead. Concentrate, concentrate.

Question 7. The colour of Alice Harbinson's lips might best be described as . . . ?

Not sure, can't see. Something from that Shakespearean sonnet. Damask'd hue or coral or something like that? Maybe I'll have another look. No. Don't. Don't look. Just concentrate. Head down.

8, 9 and 10 are fine, but then there's a long stretch of ridiculously hard maths and physics questions, and I start to flounder a little, skip two or three that I just don't understand but have a stab at the one about mitochondrion.

'Pssst . . .'

Question 15. The energy liberated by the oxidization of the products of cytoplasmic metabolism is converted into adenosine triphosphate . . .

'Psssssssst . . .'

She's leaning forward over her desk, eyes wide, trying to pass me something in her clenched fist. I check that Patrick's not looking, and then reach behind me, and feel her press the little scrap of paper into my cupped hand. Patrick looks up, and I quickly turn the motion into a stretch, arms up over my head, and when the coast is clear, I unwrap the note. It says, *'Your strange, unnatural beauty intrigues me. How soon till I can feel your lips against mine . . . ?'*

Or, more accurately, *'Hey swot! Help me! Am very STOOPID and also PISSED. Please save me from COMPLETE humiliation. What are the answers to 6, 11, 18 and 22? And 4 is Byzantium, right? Cheers mate, in anticipation, da thicko behind you xxx. p.s. Split on me to the teacher, and I'll have you afterwards.'*

She's asking me to share my general knowledge with her, and if that's not a come-on, then I don't know what is. Of course cheating in an exam is a terrible thing, and if it was anyone else I wouldn't get involved, but these are exceptional circumstances so I quickly check the questions, then turn the piece of paper over and write: *'No. 6 is Finchley, 11 is Ruskin's Stones of Venice maybe, 18 is Schrodiger's Cat maybe, and 22 I don't know either; Diaghilev? And yes, 4 is Byzantium.'*

I read and re-read this several times. It's pretty dry, as love letters go, and I want to say something more tantalising and provocative, without actually just writing 'you're lovely', so I think for a minute, take a deep breath, then put: *'By the way, you owe me! Coffee afterwards? Best wishes, the Swot!'* . . . then before I can change my mind, I spin around in my seat and place it on her desk.

Question 23. Whales of the sub-order Mysteciti have a specialised feeding structure called . . . ?

Baleen.

Question 24. Which French verse form, utilised by Corneille and Racine, consists of a line of twelve syllables, with major stresses on the sixth and last syllable?

The Alexandrine.

Question 25. Increased heart rate, cold sweat and a feeling of elation are usually a symptom of which emotional condition?

Come on, head down, concentrate, this is The Challenge, remember?

Question 25. How many vertices has a dodecahedron?

Well, dodec- is twelve, so that's twelve plane faces, which means 12 times four if you separated it all out, which is 48, but then you have to minus the number of shared corners which would be, what, 24? Why 24? Because each vertex is the junction of three plane faces? Threes into 48 are 16.

16 vertices? Isn't there a formula for this? What if I were to draw it?

And I'm trying to draw a deconstructed dodecahedron when the little ball of paper is lobbed over my head and skitters across my desk. I catch it before it rolls off the edge, open it and read '*Okay. But you have to promise* not to dance.'

I smile to myself, and play it cool by not turning round, because after all, that's what I am, a pretty cool guy, and I go back to deconstructing my dodecahedron.

8

QUESTION: If incandescence is light emitted by a hot material, what is the term for light emitted from a relatively cool material?

ANSWER: Luminescence.

'I expect you didn't recognise me without my dog-collar on!'

'What? Oh, no. I didn't to begin with,' she says.

'So – Alice!'

'That's right.'

'As in Wonderland?'

'Uh-huh,' she says, glancing longingly towards the exit.

We're sat at a little marble table in Le Paris Match, a café that's straining very hard to be French; all 'authentic' wooden chairs and Ricard ashtrays and reproduction Toulouse-Lautrec posters, and 'croque monsieur' on the menu instead of 'ham-and-cheese toastie'. It's full of students in black polo-necks and 501s leaning forward in intense conversations over their pommes frites, and jabbing the air with their fags, wishing they were Gitanes rather than Silk Cut. I've never been to France, but is it really like this?

'And is that who you're named after, Alice in Wonderland?'

'So I'm told.' Pause. 'How about you, why did they call you Gary?'

I think for a moment, and actually try to come up with an interesting and amusing anecdote as to why I'm called Gary, before deciding that it's probably easier to come clean.

'Actually, my name's Brian.'

'Of course. Sorry, I meant Brian.'

'Not sure. I don't think there are any Brians in literature. Or Garys, come to that. Except isn't there a Gary in *The Brothers Karamazov*? Gary, Keith and . . .'

'. . . and Brian! Brian Karamazov!' she says and laughs, and I laugh too.

Today's turning out to be quite a big day for me actually, because not only am I sat here with Alice Harbinson, laughing at my own name, but I'm also enjoying my very first ever cappuccino. Do they drink cappuccinos in France? Anyway, it's okay; a bit like the milky coffees they do in the caff on Southend pier for 35p, except instead of little, bitter globules of undissolved instant coffee on the top, this has a grey musky scum of cinnamon. My fault; I overdid it a little, thinking it was chocolate powder, so it smells a bit like a hot, milky armpit. But then I expect that cappuccinos are a little bit like sex in that I'll probably enjoy it much more the second time. Though at 85p a throw, I'm not sure if there'll be a second time. Again, a little bit like sex.

There it is again. Sex and Money. Stop thinking about sex and money. Especially money, it's awful, you're here with this amazing woman, and all you can think about is the price of a cup of coffee. And sex.

'I'm starving,' she says. 'Shall we have some lunch? Some french fries or something?'

'Absolutely!' I say, and look at the menu. £1.25 for a lousy bowl of chips? '. . . though I'm actually not that hungry, but you get some.'

So she waves to the waiter, a whippet-thin guy with a Morrissey quiff, a student by the looks of it, and he comes over and talks over my head, greeting her with a big, friendly 'Hiya!'

'Hello, how are you today?' she says.

'Oh, fine. Except I'd rather not be here. Double shift!'

'Oh, God. Poor you!' she says, rubbing his arm in sympathy.

'How are you, anyway?' he says.

'Very good, thank you.'

'You're looking lovely today, if I may say so.'

'Aw, gee,' says Alice, and puts her hands over her face.

Zut alors.

'So what can I get you?' he says, finally remembering what he's here for.

'Could we just get a bowl of pommes frites, d'you think?'

'*Absolument!*' says the garcon, and more or less sprints off to the kitchen to commence the preparation of the precious, gold-plated chips.

'How do you know him?' I ask when he's gone.

'Who? The waiter? I don't know him.'

'Oh.'

And there's a silence. I sip my coffee, and rub the cinnamon dust out of my nostrils with the back of my hand.

'So! I wasn't sure if you'd recognise me without my dog-collar!'

'You said that already.'

'Did I? I do that sometimes, get muddled up about what I've said or haven't said, or I find myself saying things aloud that I'd only meant to say in my head, if you know what I mean . . .'

'I know *exactly* what you mean,' she says, grabbing my forearm. 'I'm *always* getting muddled up, or just blurting things out . . .' It's sweet, what she's doing here; trying to establish common ground between us, though I don't believe her for a second. 'I swear, half the time, I don't know what I'm doing . . .'

'Me too. Like the dancing last night . . .'

'Ah, yes . . .' she says, pursing her lips '. . . the dancing . . .'

'. . . yes, sorry about that. I was a little bit pissed, truth be told.'

'Oh, you were fine. You're a good dancer!'

'Hardly!' I say. 'You know, I'm just surprised no one tried to put a pencil between my teeth!'

She looks at me puzzled. 'Why?'

'Well . . . to stop me biting my tongue off?' Still nothing. 'You know, like an . . . epileptic!'

But she doesn't say anything, just sips her coffee again. Oh, my God – maybe I've offended her. Maybe she knows an epileptic. Maybe there's epilepsy in her family! Maybe *she's* an epileptic . . .

'Aren't you hot in that donkey jacket?' she asks, and the garçon returns with the exquisite chips, about six of them, arranged artfully in a large egg-cup, then loiters around, grinning, pleased with himself, trying to strike up another conversation, so I keep talking.

'You know, if life's taught me two things so far, the first is don't dance when you're drunk.'

'And the second?'

'Don't try and put milk through a Soda Stream.'

She laughs, and recognising defeat, the garçon retreats. Keep going, keep it up . . .

'. . . I don't know what I was expecting, I just thought I'd get this amazing fizzy, milky drink, but there's a name for fizzy milk . . .' (pause, sip) '. . . it's called yoghurt!'

Sometimes I could make myself throw up, really I could.

So we talk some more and she eats her chips, dipping them into a Pyrex contact-lens of ketchup, and it's a bit like an afternoon spent in that café in T.S. Eliot's *The Love Song of J. Alfred Prufrock*, but with pricier food. *'Do I dare to eat a peach? Not at these prices, no . . .'* I find out more about her. She's an only child, like me – something to do with her mum's tubes she thinks, but isn't sure. She doesn't mind being an only child, it just means she has always been a bit bookish, and she went to boarding-school, which is politically not very *right-on*, she knows, but she loved it anyway, and was Head Girl. She's very close to her dad, who makes arts documentaries for the

BBC and lets her do work-experience there in the holidays, and she's met Melvyn Bragg on many, many occasions, and apparently he's really, really funny in real life, and actually quite sexy. She loves her mum too, of course, but they argue a lot, probably because they're so similar, and her mum works part-time for TreeTops, a charity that builds tree-houses for deprived kids.

'Wouldn't they be better-off living with their parents?' I say.

'What?'

'Well, you know, kids living on their own up in the trees – that's *got* to be dangerous, hasn't it?'

'No, no, they don't *live* in the tree-houses, it's just a summer holiday activity thing.'

'Oh, right. I see . . .'

'Most of these kids from underprivileged homes have only got one parent, and they've never had a family holiday in their whole lives!' Oh my God, she's talking about *me*! 'It's fantastic really. If you're not doing anything next summer you should come along.' I nod enthusiastically, though I'm not entirely sure whether she's suggesting I help out, or actually offering me a holiday.

Then Alice tells me about her summer break, some of which was spent up in the tree-tops with the deprived, and no doubt anxious, kids. The rest was divided between their houses in London, Suffolk and the Dordogne, then performing with her school drama group at the Edinburgh Festival.

'What did you do?'

'Bertolt Brecht's *Good Woman of Schezuan*.' Of course, it's clear what she's done here, isn't it? It's a classic opportunity to use the word 'eponymous'.

'And who played the eponymous . . . ?'

'Oh, I did,' she says. Yes, yes, of course you did.

'And were you?' I ask.

'What?'

'Good?'

'Oh, not really. Though *The Scotsman* seemed to think so. Do you know the play at all?'

'Very well,' I lie. 'Actually we did Brecht's *Caucasian Chalk Circle* at our college last term' – pause, sip cappuccino – 'I played the chalk.'

God, I think I *am* going to throw up.

But she laughs, and starts talking about the demands of playing Brecht's eponymous Good Woman, and I take the opportunity to get my first proper look at her sober, and without perspiration on my spectacles, and she really is beautiful. Definitely the first truly beautiful woman I've ever seen, other than in Renaissance art or on the telly. At school people used to say Liza Chambers was beautiful, when what they really meant was 'horny', but Alice is the real thing; creamy skin that seems to be entirely without pores, and is lit from within by some organic under-skin luminescence. Or do I mean 'phosphorescence'? Or 'fluorescence'? What's the difference? Look it up later. Anyway, she's either wearing no make-up, or, more likely, make-up that's artfully contrived to seem as if it's not there, except around the eyes possibly, because surely no one has eyelashes like that in real life, do they? And then there are the eyes; brown's not really the word, it's too dull and dun, and I can't think of a better one, but they're bright and healthy, and so wide that you can see the whole of the iris, which is speckled with green. Her mouth is full and strawberry-coloured, like Tess Derbyfield, but a happy, well-balanced, fulfilled Tess who's found out that, thank God, she actually is a D'Urberville after all. Best of all there's a tiny raised white scar on her lower lip, which I imagine she probably got in some harrowing childhood blackberrying incident. Her hair is honey-coloured and slightly curly, and pulled back from her forehead, in a style that I imagine is called 'a Pre-Raphaelite'. She looks – what's that word in T.S. Eliot? Quattrocento. Or is it Yeats? And does it mean fourteenth century or fifteenth century? I'll look that up too when I get back. Note to self; look up 'Quattrocento', 'Damask', 'Dun', 'Luminescence', 'Phosphorescence', and 'Fluorescence'.

And now she's talking about the party last night, how awful it was, and about the terrible men she met, lots of awful, naff, no-neck rugger-buggers. She leans forward from her chair when she talks, long legs coiled around the chair-legs beneath her, and touches my forearm to emphasise a point, and looks me in the eye as if daring me to look away, and she also has this trick of tugging on her tiny silver-stud earrings while she talks, which is indicative of a subconscious attraction towards me, or a mildly infected piercing. For my own part, I'm trying out some new facial expressions and postures too, one of which involves leaning forward and resting my hand on my chin with my fingers splayed over my mouth, occasionally rubbing my chin sagely. This serves several purposes; 1) it looks as if I'm lost in deep thought, 2) it's sensual – the fingers on the lips, a classic sexual signifier – and 3) it also covers up the worst of the spots, the raised red clusters round the corners of my mouth that make it look as if I've been dribbling soup.

She orders another cappuccino. Will I have to pay for that too I wonder? Doesn't matter. The Stephane Grappelli/Django Reinhardt cassette is on a permanent loop in the background, buzzing away like a bluebottle against a window, and I'm pretty happy to just sit and listen. If she does have a failing, and it's obviously only a tiny one, it's that she doesn't seem particularly curious about other people, or me anyway. She doesn't know where I'm from, she doesn't ask about Mum, or my Dad, she doesn't know my surname, I'm not entirely convinced that she still doesn't think I'm called Gary. In fact, since we've been here she's asked me only two questions – 'Aren't you hot in that donkey jacket?' and 'You do know that's *cinnamon*, don't you?'

Suddenly, as if she's read my mind, she says, 'I'm sorry, I seem to be doing all the talking. You don't mind do you?'

'Not at all.'

And I don't really mind, I just like being here with her, and having other people see me with her. She's talking about this amazing Bulgarian Circus Troupe that she saw at the Edinburgh Festival, which means it's a good time to drift off and work out the bill. Three cappuccinos at 85p, that's £2.55, plus the chips, sorry, pommes frites, £1.25, which incidentally works out at about 18p per pomme frite, so that's, 25 plus 55, that's 80, £3.80, plus a tip for laughing boy over there, 30, no, say 40p, so that's £4.20, and I've got £5.18 in my pocket, so that means 98 pence to last me until I can pick up my grant cheque on Monday. God, she's beautiful though. What if she offers to go halvsies? Should I accept? I want her to know that I firmly believe in gender equality, but I don't want her to think I'm poor or, even worse, mean. But even if we do go halvsies, I'll still be down to three quid, and I'll have to ask Josh for Mum's ten pounds back till Monday, and that will mean I'll probably have to fag for him till the Christmas hols, white his cricket pads and toast his crumpets or something. Hang on a second, she's asking me a question.

'D'you want another cappuccino?'

NO!

'No, better not,' I say. 'In fact, we'd better get back – have a look at the results. I'll get the bill . . .' and I look around for the waiter.

'Here, let me give you some money,' she says, pretending to reach for her purse.

'No, really, my treat . . .'

'Are you sure?'

'Absolutely, absolutely,' I say, and count £4.20 out on to the marble table, and feel pretty ritzy.

Outside Le Paris Match, I realise it's getting dark; we've been talking for hours, and I had no idea. For a while, I even forgot about The Challenge. But I've remembered now, and it's all I can do not to break into a run. Alice is a stroller though, so we stroll back to the Student Union in the autumn evening light, and she says, 'So who put you up to it, then?'

'What? The Challenge?'

'Is that what you call it? The Challenge?'

'Doesn't everyone? Oh, I just thought it would be a laugh,' I lie, nonchalantly. 'Also, there's only me and Mum at home, so there weren't enough of us for *Ask The Family* . . .' I thought she might pick up on this, but instead she just says, 'The girls in my corridor put me up to it, for a dare. And after a couple of pints in the bar at lunch it suddenly seemed like a good idea. And I want to be an actress, or something in TV, a presenter or something, so I thought it might be good experience in front of the camera, but I'm not so sure now. It's not an obvious springboard into the Hollywood firmament is it? *University Challenge*. I just hope I get knocked out now, to be honest, so I can forget about the whole silly business.' Tread softly, Alice Harbinson, for you tread upon my dreams.

'Have you ever thought of acting as a career?' she asks.

'Who, me? God no, I'm terrible . . .' then, just as an experiment I say, 'and besides, I don't think I'm good-looking enough to be an actor.'

'Oh, that's not true! There are lots of actors who aren't good-looking . . .'

Which serves me right, I suppose.

As we approach the notice-board outside Meeting Room 6, it feels like getting my O-level results all over again; the quiet confidence, mixed with just the appropriate amount of anxiety, the awareness of how important it is to be in control of your face, not to look too pleased with yourself, too cocky. Just smile, nod knowingly, and walk away.

Approaching the notice-board, I can see Lucy Chang's panda peering over her shoulder at the test results, and there's something about the angle of Lucy's head that tells me it's not good news for her. She turns and walks away, and gives a sweet little disappointed smile. Looks like Lucy won't be joining us at Granada studios then, which is a shame, because she seemed nice. I smile my commiseration at her as she hurries away, and head over to the notice-board.

I look at the notice.

I blink, and look again.

UNIVERSITY CHALLENGE AUDITIONS

The results of the 1985 University Challenge selection heats are as follows;

Lucy Chang – 89%
Colin Pagett – 72%
Alice Harbinson – 53%
Brian Jackson – 51% *

So this year's team is as follows; Patrick Watts, Lucy, Alice and Colin. Our first rehearsal is next Tuesday. Many congratulations to everyone who took part!

Patrick Watts.

* (In case of <u>absolute emergency</u> or <u>extreme, life-threatening</u> ill-health, Brian Jackson is our first reserve.)

'Oh God! I don't believe it, I'm on the team!' squeals Alice, jumping up and down and squeezing my arm.

'Hey, well done you!' I find a smile from somewhere, and nail it to my face.

'Hey, you realise if you hadn't given me those answers, you'd be on the team instead!' she squeals. Well, yes Alice, I do realise that, actually.

'What shall we do now? Shall we go to the bar and get

completely pissed?' she asks. But I've run out of money, and I suddenly don't feel like it any more.

I haven't made the team, I've got 98p in my pocket, and I'm hopelessly in love.

Not hopelessly. Uselessly.

Round Two

'He calls the knaves, Jacks, this boy,' said Estella, with disdain, before our first game was out.

Charles Dickens, *Great Expectations*

9

QUESTION: George, Anne, Julian, Timmy and Dick are better known as . . . ?
ANSWER: The Famous Five.

There are three things that I always expected to happen at university – one was to lose my virginity, two was to be asked to become a spy, three was that I'd be on *University Challenge*. The first of these, virginity, went out the window two weeks before I left Southend, thanks to a drunken and begrudging fumble up against a wheely-bin, round the back of Littlewoods, courtesy of Karen Armstrong. There's not a great deal to be said about the experience really; the earth didn't move, but the wheely-bin did. Afterwards, there was some debate as to whether we'd actually 'done it properly', which gives you some idea of the awesome skill and artful dexterity of my love-making technique. Walking home on that memorable summer night, as we enjoyed the post-coital dregs of a bottle of warm Merrydown, Karen kept saying over and over again, 'don't tell anyone, don't tell anyone, don't tell anyone', as if we'd just done something really, truly awful. Which in a way I suppose we had.

As for being asked to spy for Her Majesty's Government, well, even leaving aside my ideological reservations, I'm pretty sure that languages are important to a career in spying, and I do only have O-level French. It's a Grade A, but still, in terms of actual espionage this pretty much limits me to infiltrating, say, a French primary school, or maybe, at a push, a boulangerie.

Red Cobra, it's Dark Swallow here; I have details of the bus timetable . . .

Which just leaves The Challenge, and now I've managed to cock that up too. It's the first meeting tonight, and it's taken all my powers of persuasion to even get invited. Patrick refused to return my calls, and when I did finally catch up with him he said it wasn't really necessary for the reserve to come along, as he was pretty sure that no one was going to get run over. But I kept on and on until he caved, because if I don't come along, then I don't get to see Alice, not unless I start hanging around outside her halls of residence.

And don't think I haven't thought about it either. In the six days since we met, I haven't seen her once. And I've been looking. Whenever I visit the library, I find myself doing a circuit of all the desks, or loitering suspiciously in the Drama section. When I go to the bar with Marcus and Josh, and am being half-heartedly introduced to some new James or Hugo or Jeremy, I'm watching the door over their shoulder in case she comes in. Just walking between lectures, I'm constantly on the look-out, but there's been no sign of her at all, which suggests that she's having a very different university experience to me. Or maybe she's seeing someone else? Maybe she's already fallen in love with some handsome, cheek-boned bastard, a Nicaraguan poet in exile or a sculptor or something, and she's spent the last week in bed, drinking fine wines and reading poetry aloud. Don't think about it. Just ring the doorbell again.

I wonder if Patrick has deliberately given me the wrong address, and am about to head off when I hear him trot down the stairs.

'Hi!' I say, smiling brightly as he opens the door.

'Hello, Brian,' he groans, addressing that point to the right of my head which he seems to prefer, and I follow him up the communal staircase to his flat.

'So is everyone coming tonight?' I ask, innocently.

'I think so.'

'You've spoken to them all?'

'Uh-huh.'

'So you've spoken to Alice?'

He stops on the stairs, turns and looks back. 'Why?'

'Just curious.'

'Don't worry. Alice is coming.' He's wearing his official university sweatshirt again, which puzzles me a little. I mean I'd sort of understand it more, if it said Yale or Harvard or something, because then it would be a fashion choice. But why advertise the fact that you're at a university to all the other people who are at the university with you? Does he worry that people will actually think he's just *pretending*?

We enter the flat, which is small and plain, and reminiscent of an Eastern-bloc show-home. It smells of warm mince and onions.

'I've bought some wine!' I say.

'I don't drink,' he says.

'Oh. Right.'

'I suppose you'll want a corkscrew. I think I've got one somewhere. D'you want tea, or do you want to start straight on in with your alcohol?'

'Oh, booze please!'

'Right, well if you just go through there, I'll be with you in a minute. You don't *smoke* do you?'

'No.'

'Because it's strictly no-smoking . . .'

'Okay, but I don't smoke . . .'

'Right, well, it's just through there. Don't touch anything!' Because he's a third year, and because he's obviously got parents with money, Patrick seems to have got his life in some kind of semi-adult order: proper, non-institutional furniture, which he probably *owns*, a television, a video, a living room which doesn't have a bed or a gas-cooker or a shower in it. In fact he's barely a student at all; everything in its place and a place for everything, like the living quarters of a monk, or a particularly fastidious serial-killer. While he's searching for the corkscrew, I look around the living room. On the wall above his desk is the flat's only decoration; a poster of a beach, with a set of footprints disappearing into the sunset, and that inspirational poem about how Jesus is beside you always. Though it would be fair to point out that if Jesus had been beside him in the TV studio last year, then he might have got more than 65 points.

There's a ring on the doorbell, and I hear Patrick lollop downstairs, so I take the opportunity to examine his shelves; economic textbooks mainly, neatly alphabeticised, a Good News Bible. Another shelf of videos – *Monty Python and the Holy Grail* and *The Blues Brothers* – reveals the lighter side of Patrick Watts.

But beside them are a series of about twenty identical VHS cassettes; a shelf of home-recorded videos with immaculately hand-typed white labels placed precisely along the spines. I step up to get a closer look and let out an involuntary gasp. The labels read:

03/03/1984 – Newcastle versus Sussex

10/03/1984 – Durham versus Leicester

17/03/1984 – King's, Cambridge versus Dundee

23/03/1984 – Sidney Sussex versus Exeter

30/03/1984 – UMIST versus Liverpool

06/04/1984 – Birmingham versus UCL

. . . and so it goes on, Keele versus Sussex, Manchester versus Sheffield, Open versus Edinburgh. On top of the cassettes is a picture in a frame, lying face down. I'm feeling fairly Marion Crane now, but I pick it up and look at it, and yes, it is indeed a photograph of Patrick shaking hands with Bamber Gascoigne and I realise with a sudden spasm of horror that this is Patrick's shrine, and that I have *stumbled blindly into the lair of a madman . . .*

'Looking for something, Brian?'

I spin around, and look for a weapon. Patrick is stood in the doorway, with Lucy Chang peeking over his shoulder, and Lucy Chang's panda rucksack peeking over her shoulder.

'Just admiring your photo!'

'Fine, but could you put it back exactly where it came from?'

'Yes, yes of course . . .'

'Lucy – tea?'

'Yes, yes thank you.'

He shoots me a hands-off look, and heads back to the kitchen. Lucy sits on the hard-backed chair at Patrick's desk, but right on the edge, so as not to squash her panda. We sit in silence, and smile at each other, and for no apparent reason, she lets out a nervous little tinkling laugh. She's very small and neat, wearing a very clean and neatly ironed white shirt with the top button done up. Not that this is at all important, but she's quite attractive too, even with the disconcertingly low hairline that seems to be creeping down her forehead to meet up with her eyebrows, like a wig that's slipped forward.

I try and think of things to say. I contemplate telling her that according to the *Guinness Book of Records*, Chang is officially the commonest surname in the world, but I assume she already knows that, so instead say, 'Hey, well done on that amazing score! Eighty-nine points!'

'Oh, thank you. And well done to you, well done for . . .'

'. . . losing?'

'Well . . . yes, I suppose so!' and she laughs again, high and brittle. 'Well done for losing!'

Out of politeness, I laugh too, and say, 'Still, never mind. Fail again, fail better!'

'Samuel Beckett, right?'

'That's right,' I say, taken aback. 'What are you studying, again?'

'Oh, second year Medicine,' she says, and I think, my God, she's a genius. I watch in frank awe as she struggles out of her novelty rucksack.

'I like the panda,' I say.

'Oh – thank you!'

'Peeking over your shoulder! Or should I say *Beijing* over your shoulder!'

She looks at me uncomprehendingly, so by way of clarification, I say, 'Did you bring it with you from home?'

'Pardon me?'

'Did you bring it from *home*?'

She looks puzzled. 'You mean my halls of residence?'

I have the sensation of falling. 'No, your, you know . . . your *original* home.'

'Oh, you mean China! Because it's a *panda*, right? Well actually, I'm from Minneapolis, so no.'

'Yes, but *originally* you're from . . . ?'

'Minneapolis . . .'

'But your *parents*, they're from . . .'

'Minneapolis . . .'

'But *their* parents are from . . .'

'Minneapolis . . .'

'Of course. Minneapolis,' and she smiles at me with perfect, sincere kindness, despite the fact that I'm clearly ignorant, racist scum. 'Where Prince comes from!' I add, funkily.

'Exactly! Where Prince comes from,' she says. 'Though I've never met the guy.'

'Oh,' I say. I try again. 'Have you seen *Purple Rain*?'

'No,' she replies. 'Have. You. Seen. *Purple Rain*?'

'Yes. Twice,' I reply.

'Did you enjoy it?' she asks.

'Not really,' I reply.

'And yet you saw it twice!'

'I know,' I say, and add humorously, in a pretty good American accent, 'Go figure!'

And then, thank God, the door opens and it's Big Colin Pagett, carrying four bottles of Newcy Brown and a cardboard bucket of Kentucky Fried Chicken. Patrick shows him in like a head butler showing in the chimney-sweep, and in the awkward silence that follows, I take time to ruminate on the complex art of conversation. Ideally, of course, I'd like to wake up in the morning and be handed a transcript of everything I'm about to say during the day, so that I could go through it and rewrite my dialogue, cutting the fatuous remarks and the crass, idiotic jokes. But clearly that's not practical, and the other option, of never speaking again, isn't going to work either.

So maybe it's better to think of conversation as being a bit like crossing the road; before I open my mouth I should take a few moments to look both ways, and carefully consider what I'm about to say. And if this means that my conversation gets a little slow and stilted, like a transatlantic phone call, if it means I spend just a little extra time standing on the metaphorical conversational kerb, looking left and right, then so be it, because it's clear that I just can't keep stumbling blindly out into traffic. I can't keep getting run over like this.

Thankfully there's no need for conversation right now because while we wait for Alice to arrive, Patrick pops on one of his precious video cassettes – last year's grand final, and we sit and watch the Dundee team win again, while Patrick mumbles the answers and Colin eats his bucket of chicken, and for fifteen minutes, those are the only sounds: Colin sucking on a chicken thigh, Patrick muttering insanely from the arm of the sofa.

'. . . Kafka . . . nitrogen . . . nineteen fifty-six . . . the duodenum . . . trick question, none of them . . . C.P.E. Bach . . .'

And every now and again, I'll chip in with an answer, or Colin will, through a mouthful of brown meat – Ravel, Dante's *Inferno*, Rosa Luxembourg, Veni Vidi Vici – but clearly Patrick's marking his territory, showing who's boss, because his voice gradually gets louder . . .

'. . . THE MOODY BLUES . . . GOYA . . . TYPHOID. MARY . . . THEY'RE ALL PRIME NUMBERS . . .'

. . . and whilst I love the show as much as anyone, I can't help thinking that this is maybe taking things a little too far . . .

'. . . RHINE, RHONE, DANUBE . . . MITOCHONDRIA . . . FOUCAULT'S PENDULUM . . .'

. . . has he learnt them by rote? Are we meant to think he's never seen it before, or are we meant to think that he just knows all this stuff anyway? And what does Lucy Chang make of all this? I glance to my side, and she's staring at the floor with her eyes closed, and I think maybe she's upset, or embarrassed, understandably, but then I notice a slight shudder across her shoulders and I realise that *she's trying not to laugh* . . .

'. . . ODE TO A GRECIAN URN . . . BO DIDDLEY . . . THE ST BARTHOLOMEW'S DAY MASSACRE . . . THE BERLIN AIRLIFT . . .'

. . . and just as it seems she might burst, the doorbell goes downstairs, and Patrick heads off, leaving the three of us staring straight ahead at the telly. In the end, it's Colin who speaks first, in a low, conspiratorial voice.

'Is it just me, or is this fella completely round the fuckin' twist?'

With Alice's appearance the atmosphere lightens considerably. She arrives breathless and bundled up in scarf and coat and suede mittens, and looks round the room, smiling and greeting everyone. 'Hi, Bri!' she says warmly, and gives me a provocative little wink. Patrick buzzes around her, the sap, running his hands over his beige plastic hair, offering up his seat, and pouring her a glass of the Bulgarian Cabernet Sauvignon that *I* brought along at great personal expense as if it was his own. When Alice asks, 'D'you mind if I smoke?' he says 'Of course!' as if it's suddenly a terrific idea, why hadn't he thought of it himself, then he looks round for something to use as an ashtray, and finds a little desk-tidy containing paper clips, which he empties onto the desk with wild, punky abandon.

Alice squeezes in next to me on the sofa, her hip pressed up tight against mine, Patrick clears his throat, and addresses the team.

'So, here we are then! "The Fantastic Four!" And I really think that we've got something special this year . . .'

Hang on a second – Fantastic *Four*?

'Just to explain how things work then . . .'

I count the people in the room; one, two, three . . .

'. . . the first stage is that we need to qualify for the actual televised competition . . .'

Why not say 'Famous Five'? It wouldn't have hurt him to say 'Famous Five'.

'This is in two weeks' time, and it's informal, but pretty tough so, we're going to need our wits about us if we're to actually make it on air. So up until then, I suggest the four of us meet up here this time every week, and just run through some questions that I'll prepare in advance, and maybe watch a tape or two, just to keep our hands in . . .'

Hang on a second – why can't I come? I have to come, if I don't come then I don't get to see Alice. I put my hand up to ask a question, but Patrick's putting a tape in the video, and can't see me, so I clear my throat and say, 'Um, Patrick . . . ?'

'Brian?'

'So I don't need to come then?'

'I don't think so, no . . .'

'At all . . . ?'

'No . . .'

'You don't think it's a good idea then . . . ?'

'Well, we'll only need you in an emergency. I just think it's best if the four of us get used to each other as a team, seeing as, you know, we *are* the team.'

'So you don't need me?'

'No.'

'Not even to come along and, you know, observe . . . ?'

'Not really, Brian, no . . .' and he presses play on the video. 'Right, this is Leeds versus Birkbeck in the quarter finals from two years ago. A really good match . . .' and he sits back on the sofa, with Alice squeezed in between us, her hip pressed up tight next to mine, while I try to come up with a plan to murder Patrick Watts.

10

QUESTION: What is the meaning of the Latin motto that accompanies the roaring lion at the beginning of Metro-Goldwyn-Mayer films?
ANSWER: *Ars Gratia Artis* – Art for Art's Sake.

'Well, personally speaking, I have to say that I just absolutely *hate* it. I mean, the idea that this is some great lyrical *love* poem is rubbish. It's just this horny guy's poem, just this sexually frustrated, little twerp trying to get into his mistress's knickers by banging on about "Time's Winged Chariot", and not taking no for an answer. There's nothing lyrical or romantic, and certainly nothing *erotic* about this poem at all, not if you're a woman anyway,' drawls Alice's friend, Erin, the cat-eyed woman with the bleach-blonde crop. 'In fact, if a guy sent this poem to me or read it to me or something, I'd call the police. No wonder his mistress is coy. The poet's a complete misogynist.'

'You think Andrew Marvell's a misogynist?' says Professor Morrison, slouching back in his armchair, the long fingers of his hands linked across his belly.

'Basically, yes. Certainly in this poem, anyway.'

'So the voice of the poet and the voice in the poem are one and the same?'

'Why shouldn't they be? There's nothing to suggest any kind of distancing device . . .'

'What d'you think, Brian?'

To be honest, I'm actually thinking about Alice, so I pause

for a second and play for time by rubbing my ears, as if my critical faculties were somehow located in the lobes and I just need to warm them up. It's only my third tutorial, and I got caught out last time by pretending to have read *Mansfield Park* when in fact I'd only seen half of the first episode on telly, so this had better be good. From my arsenal, I select the phrase 'historical context'.

'I think it's more complicated than that, especially if you place the poem in its historical context . . .' and Erin smacks her lips and sighs, as she tends to whenever I open my mouth in tutorials. Erin clearly hates my guts, though I don't know why, because I'm always smiling at her. Unless of course that is the reason. Anyway. Concentrate. 'For a start there's clearly a strong element of humour here. The use of rhetoric is self-conscious, and in that sense it's a bit like Shakespeare's sonnet 130, "My mistress' eyes are nothing like the sun" . . . (nice one) . . . except here the poet's rhetoric renders him foolish – the desperation, the extremities to which he goes to persuade his lover to succumb make him an essentially *comic* figure. It's the comedy of sexual frustration and romantic humiliation. It's actually the eponymous "coy mistress", the object of his unrequited passion, who has all the power here . . .'

'Well that's a load of reactionary, chauvinistic crap,' snaps Erin, who's been wriggling in her chair throughout, making the vinyl squeak with indignation. 'The coy mistress has no *power*, and no *personality* either, she's just a cipher, a blank, defined solely by her beauty and her unwillingness to have it off with the poet. And the tone clearly isn't comic, or lyrical, it's hectoring, manipulative and oppressive.'

Then Chris the Hippie with the dirty hand starts talking, and I decide to let Erin use him as her scratching post for a while instead. Professor Morrison gives me a little fatherly smile, letting me know that he agreed with me all along. I like Professor Morrison. I'm scared of him too, which is probably the right combination for an academic. He looks a bit like

David Attenborough, which has also got to be a good thing in an academic, and wears a lot of corduroy, and knitted ties, and is stick thin, apart from a compact little pot-belly that looks like a cushion strapped on underneath his dirty shirt. And he listens intently when you're talking, head slightly cocked, pressing his long fingers together into a church-and-steeple in front of his mouth, exactly like Intellectuals do on the telly.

While Erin flays Chris alive, and Professor Morrison looks on, I drift off for a bit and look out of the window at the garden outside, and go back to thinking about Alice again.

Walking back along the High Street after the tutorial, I see Rebecca whats-her-name and a couple of the fuckingangry-actuallys that she's always hanging around with. They're thrusting leaflets into the hands of indifferent shoppers and for a moment I contemplate crossing the road. I'm a bit wary of her to be honest, especially after our last conversation, but I've made a promise to myself to make as many new friends as possible at university, even if they give every indication of not actually liking me very much.

'Hiya,' I say.

'It's the Dancing Queen! How you doing?' she says, and hands me a leaflet, urging me to boycott Barclays.

'Actually my grant money's with one of the other caring, humanitarian, multinational banking organisations!' I say, with an incisive, wry, satirical glint in my eye, but she's not really looking and has gone back to handing out leaflets and shouting 'Fight apartheid! Support the boycott. Don't buy South African goods! Say no to apartheid! . . .' I start to feel a bit boycotted too, so start to walk away when she says, in a marginally softer voice, 'So, how ya' settling in, then?'

'Oh, alright. I'm sharing my house with a right pair of bloody Ruperts. But apart from that it's not too bad . . .' I had thrown in the hint of class-war for her benefit really, but I don't think she gets it, because she looks at me, confused.

'They're both called Rupert?'

'No, they're called Marcus and Josh.'

'So who are the Ruperts?'

'They are, they're, you know – Ruperts,' but the remark is starting to lose some of its cutting edge, and I wonder if I should offer to hand out leaflets instead. After all, it is a cause I'm passionate about, and I have a strict policy of not eating South African fruit that's almost as strict as my policy of not eating fruit. But now Rebecca's folding up the remaining leaflets and handing them to her colleagues.

'Right, that's me done for today. See you later, Toby, see you Rupert . . .' and suddenly I find myself walking down the street side by side with her, without quite knowing whose idea it was. 'So, where're we off to now, then?' she asks, hands stuffed deep into the pockets of her black vinyl coat.

'Actually, I'm just on my way to the City Art Gallery.'

'The *Art Gallery*?' she asks, intrigued.

'Yeah, I thought I'd, you know, check it out?'

She wrinkles her nose, says, 'Okay. Let's "check it out"!' and I follow her down the street.

Ah, the timeless old check-out-the-art-gallery ruse. I've been waiting to try this for some time actually, because it's not really possible in Southend, but this is a proper art gallery; hushed library atmosphere, marble benches, security guards dozing on uncomfortable chairs. My plan, ideally, was to bring Alice here on a date, but it's good to have a dry run with someone else first, so that I can work out my spontaneous reactions in advance.

I don't mind admitting that my response to the visual arts can be pretty superficial; for instance, I often have to resort to pointing out that someone in the painting looks like so-and-so off the telly. Also, there's a certain amount of art gallery etiquette that I need to get the hang of – how long to stand in front of each of the paintings, what noises to make, that kind of thing – but Rebecca and I soon settle into a nice, comfortable rhythm; not so fast as to seem shallow, not so slow as to be deathly bored.

We're checking out the Eighteenth Century room, standing in front of a not particularly remarkable painting by someone I've never heard of, a Gainsborough-esque Lord and Lady stood under a tree.

'Amazing perspective,' I say, but drawing her attention to the way objects get smaller as they get further away seems a little basic, so instead I decide to take a more Marxist, socio-political approach.

'Look at their faces! They certainly seem pleased with their lot!'

'If you say so,' says Rebecca, uninspired.

'Not an art-lover then?'

''Course I am. I just don't think that because something's been put in a big, bloody gilt frame, I should be obliged to stand around in front of it for hours, rubbing my chin. I mean, look at this stuff . . .' Hands still plunged in coat pockets, she gestures dismissively round the room, with the bat's wings of her coat '. . . portraits of the idle rich surveying their ill-gotten gains, chocolate-box portrayals of back-breaking rural toil, paintings of spotlessly clean pigs. I mean, look at this monstrosity' – she gestures towards a creamily pink, plump nude reclined on a chaise-longue – 'soft-porn for the slave-trading set. Where's her pubic hair for crying out loud! Have you ever in your life seen a naked woman who looked like *that*?' I contemplate telling her that I've actually never seen a naked woman, but I don't want to blow my artistic credentials, so I stay quiet. 'I mean, who's it actually *for*?'

'So you don't think art has any intrinsic value?'

'No, I just don't think it has intrinsic value because someone somewhere decides to call it "art". Like this stuff – it's the kind of crap you see on the walls of provincial Conservative Clubs . . .'

'So I suppose, come the revolution, you'd burn this all down . . .'

'Och, that's a really endearing little habit you've got there, reducing people to a stereotype . . .' I follow her through to a room full of still-lifes, and decide to steer the conversation away from politics. 'What's the plural of "still-life"? Is it "still-*lives*" or "still-life*s*"?' This strikes me as a pretty sophisticated Radio 4 kind of thing to say, but she's not biting.

'So what are your politics, then?' she says.

'Well, I suppose I'm a sort of left-wing liberal-humanist.'

'Nothing at all in other words . . .'

'Well, I wouldn't say th . . .'

'And what are you studying again?'

'Eng. Lit.'

'What's *Inglet*?'

'English Literature.'

'Is that what they're calling it these days? And what attracted you to *Inglet,* apart from the fact that it's obviously just one big, fat, juicy *skive*.'

I choose to ignore the last comment, and go straight into my number. 'Well, I wasn't sure what to do really. I had a fairly broad base of qualifications at O and A-level, and I thought about history, or art, or maybe one of the sciences. But the thing about Literature is, well, basically it encapsulates all the disciplines – it's history, philosophy, politics, sexual politics, sociology, psychology, linguistics, science. Literature is mankind's organised response to the world around him, or her, so in a way it's only natural that this response should contain a whole . . .' – take a little run-up – '. . . *panoply* of intellectual concepts, ideas, issues . . .'

Etcetera, etcetera, etcetera. If I'm completely honest, this isn't the first time I've said any of this. In fact I used this little number in all of my university interviews, and whilst it's not exactly 'We shall fight them on the beaches . . .' it usually goes down a storm with academics, especially if accompanied, as here, with lots of hair tousling and emphatic gestures. I bring the speech to its shattering climax '. . . so as the eponymous Hamlet says to Polonius in Act Two Scene Two, it's all ultimately about "words, words, words", and what we call "literature" is in fact just the vehicle for what might more accurately be described as the Study of . . . Everything.'

Rebecca contemplates this, nods sagely. 'Well, *that*'s certainly the biggest pile of bogus horse-shit I've heard for some time,' she says, and starts walking off.

'You think so?' I say, trotting after her.

'I mean, why not just say you want to sit round on your arse and read for three years? At least it would be honest. Literature doesn't teach you about "*everything*", and even if it did, it'd only be in the most useless, superficial, impractical way. I mean, anyone who thinks that they can learn anything practical about politics or psychology or science by flicking through *Under Milk Wood* is talking out their arse. Can you imagine someone saying to you, 'Well, Mr-whatever-your-name-is, I'm about to remove your spleen, and, okay, I haven't actually studied medicine as such, but don't worry, because I very much enjoyed *The Pickwick Papers* . . . ?'

'Well, medicine's a special case.'

'And politics isn't? Or history? Or law? Why not? Because they're *easier*? Less deserving of rigorous analysis?'

'So you don't think novels and poetry and plays contribute to the quality and richness of life?'

'I didn't say that, did I? I'm sure they do, but so does the three-minute pop song, and no one feels the need to study *that* for three years.'

I'm sure Alexander Pope said something pertinent that would help me out here, but I can't remember what, and I contemplate using the word 'utilitarianism', but am not sure how. So instead I say, 'Just because something isn't *practical*, it doesn't mean it isn't *useful*.'

Rebecca wrinkles her nose at this, and I realise I'm on pretty sticky ground here, semantically speaking, so I decide to take a different tack, and go on the offensive.

'So what are *you* studying then, that's so *useful*?' I say.

'Law. Second Year.'

'Law! . . . right, well, I suppose law is pretty useful.'

'Well, let's hope so.'

Law makes sense. If I was in a court of law I definitely wouldn't want to argue with Rebecca Epstein. She'd slap you around the face with her Glasgow accent, she'd bark things at you like 'define your terms!' and 'your argument is specious!' In fact I don't want to argue with her now, so I just stop talking and we walk silently through the City Museum, with its glass cases of fossils and Roman coins and antique farming implements. I suppose this is my first taste of the lively intellectual cut-and-thrust of academic life. There are those arguments in tutorials with Erin of course, but they're like Chinese burns; it's just a matter of how much you can take. With Rebecca, it feels like I've been stabbed in the eye. Still, it is only my third week, I'm sure I'll get better at it, and I know deep down that I am capable of coming up with an eloquent and incisive reply, even if it won't be for another three to four days. In the meantime I decide to see if I can change the subject.

'So what d'you want to do afterwards then?' I say.

'Dunno. We could go for a drink if you fancy it . . .'

'No, I mean, after uni, when you qualify . . .'

'When I qualify? Dunno. Something that actually makes a difference to people's lives. Not sure if I want to do that whole barrister thing, but I'm interested in immigration law. The Citizens' Advice Bureau do good work. Maybe I'll move over into politics or journalism or something, help shift those Tory bastards. How 'bout you?'

'Oh, maybe teaching or academia. Maybe writing in some way or other.'

'What do you write?'

'Oh, nothing yet.' I decide to try something out, and add, 'Just a little poetry.'

'Well there you go. You're a poet and I wasn't aware of it.' She looks at her watch. 'Right, I'd better be getting back.'

'Where d'you live?'

'Kenwood Manor, where that lousy party was.'

'Ah, the same as my friend Alice?'

'Beautiful-blonde-Alice?'

'Is she beautiful? I hadn't noticed.' I'm testing out a kind of wry, post-feminist humour here, but Rebecca just tuts and scowls and asks, 'So how d'you know her, then?'

'Oh, we're on the *University Challenge* team together . . .' I say, shrugging casually. Rebecca's cackle bounces off the museum's stone walls.

'You're joking!'

'What's funny about that?'

'Nothing, nothing at all. I'm so sorry, I had no idea I was talking to a TV personality, that's all. So what are you trying to prove then?'

'What d'you mean?'

'Well, going on something like that, must mean you've got something to prove.'

'I haven't got anything to prove! It's just a bit of fun. And anyway, we haven't qualified for the TV tournament yet. We've got the selection heats next week.'

'Tournament, eh? Makes it sound quite macho. Like you've got to wear protective clothing or something. What position d'you play? Centre-forward? Goal defence . . . ?'

'Actually, I'm the first reserve.'

'Ah, so you're not technically *on* the team then.'

'No. No, I suppose not.'

'Well, if you want me to break anyone's buzzer finger for you, just give me the word . . .' We're standing on the steps of the gallery now, and it's started to turn dark since we've been inside. 'Nice talking to you . . . I'm sorry, I've forgotten your name again.'

'Brian. Brian Jackson. Shall I walk you home?'

'I know the way, I live there, remember? See you around then, Jackson,' and she heads down the steps, then stops and turns. 'And Jackson? Of course you should study whatever subject you want. The written appreciation and understanding of literature, or any kind of artistic endeavour, is absolutely central to a decent society. Why d'you think books are the first things that the fascists burn? You should learn to stick up for yourself more,' and she turns, and trots down the steps and off into the evening.

11

QUESTION: What word, German in origin, describes pleasure obtained from the misfortunes of others?
ANSWER: Schadenfreude.

Today I finally got my first lucky break. Big Colin Pagett has contracted hepatitis.

I find out in the middle of a lecture on Coleridge and Wordsworth's *Lyrical Ballads*. Dr Oliver's been talking for some time now, and I've been trying to concentrate, really I have, but to my mind a Lyrical Ballad is something like Kate Bush singing 'The Man With The Child In His Eyes', and that's my central problem with The Romantics; they're just not *romantic* enough. You imagine it's going to be a lot of love poetry that you can plagiarise in Valentine's cards, but generally speaking it's all about lakes and urns and leech-collectors.

From what I can glean from Dr Oliver, the primary concerns of the Romantic Mind were 1) Nature 2) Man's relationship with Nature 3) Truth and 4) Beauty, whereas I tend to respond best to poetry that explores the themes a) God, you're really nice b) I fancy you, *please* go out with me c) going out with you is really, *really* great and d) *why* won't you go out with me any more? It's the sensitive and profound handling of these themes that makes the poetry of Shakespeare and Donne the most affecting and lyrical in the English canon. I'm contemplating entitling my next illuminating essay 'Towards a Definition of "Romance", a comparative study of the "lyrical" in Coleridge and Donne' or something, when, appropriately enough, I see Alice Harbinson's face appear at the door to the lecture hall.

Everyone looks up, as well they might, but she seems to be jabbing her finger at me, and mouthing something. I point at myself and she nods urgently, then ducks down and scribbles something on an A4 pad and presses it up to the glass.

'Brian, I Need You – *Urgently*,' it says.

For sex, I wonder? Presumably not, but still, I clearly have no option but to go, so as discreetly as I can I pick up my books and files, crouch down and head towards the door. Dr Oliver, in fact the whole lecture hall, look across at me.

'Sorry – doctor's appointment,' I say, and place my hand on my chest, as if to emphasise that I could drop dead at any moment. Dr Oliver doesn't seem to mind much either way, and goes back to the Lyrical Ballads, and I sneak out to find Alice in the corridor, red-faced, sweaty, breathless and lovely.

'Sorry, sorry, sorry, sorry, sorry . . .' she gasps.

'That's fine really, what's up?'

'We need you! For the qualifying round this afternoon.'

'Really? But Patrick told me not to bother . . .'

'Colin can't make it – he's got hepatitis.'

'You're joking!' Of course, I don't punch the air or anything, because I quite like Colin and I am genuinely concerned for him, really I am, so I look anxious and say, 'Is he okay?'

'Absolutely. It's not the serious one, it's Hepatitis A or something. He's bright yellow apparently, but he's going to be fine, completely fine. But it means you're on the team! Now!' and we do a little excited victory shuffle, nothing indecent or anything, then run over to the Student Union.

There are moments when mankind's achievements seem to stretch our very conception of what is humanly possible – the sculptures of Bernini or Michelangelo for instance, Shakespeare's tragedies or Beethoven's string quartets. And this afternoon in the empty student bar, for some reason that defies rational explanation – fate, or luck, the unseen hand of God, or a state of grace – I seem to know just about *everything*.

'If Adenine is paired with Thymine, then Cytosine is paired with . . . ?'

Know it. 'Guanine.'

'What is the full name of the organisation that awards Oscars?'

Know it. 'Academy of Motion Pictures Arts and Sciences.'

'Correct. Reed, bush, swamp and chiff-chaff are all varieties of the family Sylviidae and are better known as . . . ?'

Know it. 'Warblers?'

'Correct. Which Canadian folk-singer's real name is Roberta Joan Anderson?'

Know it. 'Joni Mitchell.'

'Correct.'

The *University Challenge* people have sent down a researcher called Julian, who's a nice softly spoken young man, mid-twenties, in a v-neck jumper and tie; Bamber Gascoigne's stunt-double basically. It's a straightforward quiz format – forty questions in fifteen minutes, no starters, conferring allowed – to see if we're up to appearing on the televised championship. And we are. Oh, we so obviously are. In fact, I don't mind saying we're on fire.

'Which twelfth century figure, Queen Consort of both France and England, was the inspiration for many of the poems of Bernard de Ventadour, the troubadour poet?'

'Eleanor of Aquitaine,' I say.

'Hold on, hold on – can we go through the *captain* please?' hisses Patrick, indignantly. 'Now, Brian, how do you know that?'

I actually know it because Katharine Hepburn plays her in that dodgy film that's always on Sunday afternoon telly, but I don't tell him that, I just nod sagely and say, wide-eyed, 'I just . . . know,' as if the sheer, awesome world-conquering power of my general knowledge is an enigma, even to me. Sceptically, Patrick looks to Lucy Chang for confirmation, but she just shrugs, so he says 'Eleanor of Aquitaine?'

'Correct', says Julian.

I feel a hand squeeze my arm, and glance to my right, where Alice is sat smiling at me, eyes wide open in frank awe. That's my ninth correct answer *in a row*, and I feel like Jesse Owens must have felt at the 1936 Berlin Olympics. The others aren't getting a look-in, not even Lucy Chang, and all of a sudden it seems as if Colin Pagett's hepatitis is the best thing that could have possibly happened, for everyone except Colin Pagett that is, because it really does seem as if I know everything about everything.

'Which parallel of latitude was chosen at the 1945 Potsdam conference as the approximate demarcation of North and South Korea?'

I don't know this one actually, but it's okay, because we've got Lucy.

'The Thirty-eighth Parallel?'

'Correct.'

And so it goes on – Andalucia – correct, 1254 – correct, calcium carbonate – correct, Ford Madox Ford – correct. Of course, if any of this was actually happening on telly, it would have a nation transfixed, fork-full of pie frozen halfway between plate and mouth in breathless awe. But it's not, it's just happening in an empty student bar that reeks of fags and lager, at three in the afternoon on a damp November Tuesday, and no one's watching, not even the cleaners, one of whom has started to hoover the bar carpets.

'Um, is there any chance we could . . . ?' mumbles Julian.

Patrick leaps to his feet and shrieks indignantly. 'Excuse me! WE'RE TRYING TO DO A QUIZ AND IT'S AGAINST THE CLOCK!'

'It's got to be done some time!' says the cleaner, still hoovering.

'*THIS* MAN . . .' declaims Patrick, pointing his finger at Julian, like an Old Testament prophet '. . . HAS BEEN SENT FROM THE MANCHESTER OFFICES OF *UNIVERSITY CHALLENGE*!' and for some reason, this seems to clinch it, because the cleaner turns the Hoover off, mumbles and returns to emptying the ashtrays.

Back to the quiz. I wonder if perhaps the spell's been broken, and if we can retain our championship form, but I needn't have worried because the next question is about the Anglo-Saxon ship burial uncovered in Suffolk in 1939, which provided valuable insights into ancient burial rituals.

Know it.

'Sutton Hoo,' I say.

'Correct.'

'The Rorschach test,' I say.

'Correct.'

'Epithelium . . .' Lucy says.

'Correct.'

'Uganda?' Patrick says.

'No, I think it's Zaire . . .' I say, and Patrick scowls at me like Caligula for daring to question his authority, then turns back to Julian and says, firmly 'Uganda.'

'Incorrect. It's actually Zaire,' says Julian, giving me a little consolatory smile. I think I see a little involuntary twitch in the corner of Patrick's eye, but I'm way too mature to gloat about it, because after all, Patrick, it's not about petty individual point-scoring, it's all about team-work, you fat-head . . .

'The house sparrow,' I say.

'Correct.'

'a is congruent to b modulo m?' whispers Lucy.

'Correct.'

'The Corn Laws,' shouts Patrick.

'Correct.'

'*The Woodlanders* by Thomas Hardy,' I suggest.

'Correct.'

'Buster Keaton?' offers Alice.

'No, I think it's Harold Lloyd,' I say, kind but firm.

'Okay, Harold Lloyd?' says Alice.

'Correct. Which aeronautical engineer died in 1937, several years before his most famous design came to dominate the skies during the Battle of . . . ?'

'R.J. Mitchell,' I say.

'*What?*' says Patrick.

'R.J. Mitchell, designer of the Spitfire.' I remember the name from the blurb on the box of the classic 1/12th scale Airfix kit, and I know I'm right, it's R. J. Mitchell, definitely, I'm sure of it. But Patrick's looking at me now, and frowning as if he's willing me, aching for me to be wrong. 'It's R.J. Mitchell – trust me.'

'R.J. Mitchell?' he says reluctantly.

'Correct,' says Julian, who can't help but smile now. Patrick looks at me with eyes narrowed, but Lucy leans around him and gives me the thumbs-up sign, and Alice, well, Alice slides her hand behind me and places it at the small of my back, just where my granddad shirt has come untucked from my jeans.

'Okay, your final question; isolated in seventeen thirty-five by Swedish chemist Georg Brandt, which ferromagnetic metal of Group VIII of the periodic table is used in the production of heat-resistant and magnetic alloys?' In all fairness, my periodic table is a little rusty, and I haven't got a clue with this one, but it's okay because again, Lucy Chang knows.

'Cobalt,' she says.

'Correct.' It's over, and we slump forwards and pat each other on the back, and Alice gives me a hug and I realise from the damp patch on my back that I'm sweating like a racehorse.

But Julian is clearing his throat and saying, 'Well, your final score was thirty-nine out of a possible forty, a really superb score, so I'm very pleased to tell you that you're definitely through to this year's *University Challenge* competition!'

And the crowd, if there had been one, would have gone wild.

Outside the Student Union building we all shake hands with nice young Julian, wish him well on his trip back to Manchester, see you again on 15 February, best regards to Bamber, ha-ha, then we all stand around in the late afternoon sunlight, not sure what to do next.

'So – how about a celebratory pint then!' I say, keen to prolong the glory.

'What? At four in the afternoon?' says Patrick, indignantly, as if I'd just invited everyone back to mine for heroin and an orgy.

'Can't, sorry, test tomorrow,' says Lucy.

'I'd better not, either,' says Alice, and there's a little hiatus while we all wonder if she's going to come up with an excuse.

She doesn't bother, so I say, 'Okay, well I'm heading your way too, I'll walk with you.' We head off, and I try to come up with a plausible explanation for why I'm walking in completely the wrong direction.

'Hey, well done you!' she says, as we walk through the park that leads to her halls of residence. 'You were *amazing*.'

'Oh, well, thanks. You too.'

'Oh, rubbish. I'm dead weight on that team. I only qualified in the first place because you gave me the answers.'

'Well, that's not true,' I say, even though it is.

'So how did you know all that stuff?'

'Mis-spent youth!' I say, but she doesn't get it, so I say, 'I suppose I just have a capacity for remembering useless knowledge, that's all.'

'D'you think there's such a thing? As *useless* knowledge?'

'Well. Sometimes I wish that I hadn't learnt how to crochet,' I say, and Alice laughs. Obviously she thinks I'm joking, which is maybe for the best. 'And lyrics to pop songs, I sometimes think that I could do without knowing so many pop lyrics . . .'

'"*Give me spots on my apples but give me the birds and the bees . . .*"?'

Know it.

'"Big Yellow Taxi" by Joni Mitchell,' I say.

'"*From Ibiza to the Norfolk Broads . . .*"'

Know it.

'"Life on Mars", Bowie,' I say.

'Okay, here we go, something new. "*She's got cheek-bones like geometry and eyes like sin/and she's sexually enlightened by* Cosmopolitan . . ."'

Of course, I know the answer to this, but I do an engaging little pantomime of not-knowing, then say, '"Perfect Skin", Lloyd Cole and the Commotions?'

'God, you're gooooood,' she says and then, bizarrely, takes my arm, and we walk on through the park as the sun goes down.

'Okay, my turn. Do your worst . . .'

So I think for a moment, and take a deep breath and say,

'"*I saw two shooting stars last night/I wished on them but they were only satellites/It's wrong to wish on space hardware/I wish, I wish, I wish you'd care.*"'

And I seem to have gotten away with it, in the sense that she doesn't projectile puke on me right there and then. And, yes, I know I should be ashamed of myself, and I am, really I am. She seems to take it fairly innocently though, and thinks for a moment then says 'Billy Bragg – "A New England".'

'Spot on,' I say.

'It's beautiful, isn't it?'

'I think so,' and we walk on through the tree-lined avenue, and the sodium lights blink on as we pass them, like the illuminated dance-floor in the *Billie-Jean* video. It occurs to me that what we most resemble at this moment is the black-and-white photograph on the cover of a TV-advertised exclusive 4-disc

Ronco compilation album entitled *The Greatest Love Songs Ever*. Ahead of us is a large pile of newly fallen leaves, all russet and ochre and gold, and I steer her towards it, saying 'Hey, let's kick through some leaves!'

'Better not. There's usually dog-shit in there,' she says.

And I have to admit, she's probably got a point.

Shortly afterwards we get back to Kenwood Manor. She's held on to my arm all the way, which has to count for something, so feeling emboldened I say, 'Hey, what are you doing next Tuesday?'

Only a highly experienced eye like my own would spot the fleeting moment of panic that passes over Alice Harbinson's features, but it's there all right, if only for a moment, before she pulls a quizzical look, and taps her chin with her finger. 'Next Tues . . . day? Let me think . . .' she says. Quick, Alice, think of an excuse, quickly girl, come on, come on, come on, . . .

'It's just it's my nineteenth birthday, you see. The big One-Nine! . . .' and I pause just long enough for her to stroll blindly into my trap.

'And you're having a party! Well I'd *love* to come . . .'

'Actually, not a party, I don't really know enough people for a party. But I thought maybe we could just go out for . . . dinner or something?'

'Just me and you?' She smiles. Is the word 'rictal' or 'rictusly'?

'Just me and you . . .'

'Okay,' she says, as if it were two words. 'O. Kay. Why not? Yes! That'll be great! That'll be fun!' she says.

And it will be great. Great and Fun. I'm determined that it will be both Great and Fun.

12

QUESTION: Lanugo, vellus and terminal are all terms used to describe the different developmental stages of which part of the human body?
ANSWER: Hair.

Today is a special day, because not only is it my nineteenth birthday, the last year of my teens, the beginning of a new and excitingly adult, mature phase in the life of Brian Jackson, but it's also the day of my romantic dinner for two with Alice Harbinson, and as a special birthday gift to myself, Alice, and the world, I've decided to completely change my image.

This has been due for some time, frankly. A lot of great artists, like David Bowie or Kate Bush stay on the cutting-edge by constantly changing their attitude and appearance, but I think it's fair to say that I've been caught in a bit of a style-rut lately. I'm not going to do anything extreme, I'm not going to start wearing knitted leotards, or get into heroin or become bisexual or anything, but I am going to get my hair cut. No, not just cut. *Styled*.

Hair has always been a bit of a bone of contention to be honest. Like using gel or washing your face or wearing slip-ons, having your hair cut was always considered a bit effeminate at Langley Street Comprehensive. This means that up until today I've been lumbered with this sort of nameless, formless thing that just flops lankly over my eyes, curling unhygienically over my collar and sticking out over the ears so that in silhouette my head looks a bit like a large bell or, as Tone would have it, the end of a knob.

But all that's going to finish today, because I've been eyeing up Cutz, a *unisex salon* – not a barber's – that I like the look of. It's modern without being avant-garde, and quite masculine, and clean, with copies of *The Face* and *id* to read, rather than a dog-eared, hairy pile of *Razzle* and *Mayfair*. I've spoken to a nice man called Sean, with a flat-top and an earring and a boys-y demeanour, who says he's going to do-me at ten.

It is, of course, massively expensive, but I've got the fiver Mum sent me in the post this morning (tucked in a card with footballers on the front – 'don't spend it all at once!'), and a fiver from Nana Jackson to go towards the romantic dinner for two tonight, so I'm feeling pretty uptown and ritzy as I stroll nonchalantly into Cutz, the first customer of the day. I approach the small group of staff, all hanging round the reception desk, drinking coffee and smoking Silk Cut.

'Appointment for ten o'clock? With Sean? Name of Jackson?'

They all look up, at my clothes and my hair, then look back down in a 'don't-get-involved' way, except for the receptionist, who strolls over and checks the appointment book. I can't see Sean, though. Where's my new friend Sean?

'Sean's not in today,' she says.

'Oh, right . . . ?'

'Nicky can do-you though. He's the apprentice. Is that alright?'

I follow her gaze to the corner where a skinny boy is half-heartedly sweeping up last night's trimmings. Is that Nicky? He looks about six.

'An *apprentice*?' I whisper.

'He's the same as Sean, he's just a bit cheaper,' says the receptionist, chirpily, but even she knows it's a gamble.

You know in westerns, when the gang go to a brothel, and the main cowboy has to pick the prostitute that he likes the most, and there's always a sexy one with a beauty spot, the one that's clearly much more attractive than the other prostitutes, who are all fat or skinny or old, or have a wooden leg, or a mole on their lip, or a glass eye, and of course the cowboy always picks the sexy one? Well, I can't help worrying about the other prostitutes' feelings. I know that prostitution is wrong, but there's a kind of resigned, disappointed shrug that the rejected prostitutes give as they head back to their chaise-longue or whatever, that shows that while they'd rather not have loveless sex for money with a strange cowboy, *it still would have been nice to be asked*. And that's the look Nicky the Apprentice gives me. I can't reject Nicky, because Nicky is the prostitute with the wooden leg.

'I'm sure Nicky will be great!' I say chirpily, and Nicky shrugs, puts down his broom, picks up his scissors, and gets ready to do-me.

They make me up an individual proper coffee in a sort of jug with a plunger, and we have what I think is called 'a consultation'. This is a tricky one for me, because I don't really have the vocabulary. I thought about bringing along a photograph as a sort of visual aid, but if I turn up with a picture of David Bowie or Sting or Harrison Ford, they're just going to laugh in my face.

'What d'you want then? The usual?'

'I don't know. What's the usual?'

'Short-back-and-sides.'

No, that can't be right – sounds too old-fashioned. 'Actually I was thinking more of sort of keeping some of the length on the top, with a loose parting on the left, and sort of combed back, and short over the ears, and at the back.'

'Shaved at the back?'

'Just a little.'

'Like in *Brideshead Revisited*?'

'No!' I laugh, meaning yes.

'Well, like what then?'

Be cool. 'Ummmm.'

'. . . because what you've just described there is a short-back-and-sides.'

'Is it? Okay then, a short-back-and-sides.'

'Want it washed?' he asks, lifting a lock distastefully between finger and thumb, like someone picking up a dirty tissue.

Will that be more expensive? 'No, no, no, I think it's fine, thanks.'

'You a student?'

'Yes!'

'Thought so.'

And so it begins. Young Nicky's actually pretty deft with the scissors, considering that the last pair he used were plastic and round-ended, and pretty soon he's hacking away with something like enthusiasm, as 'Purple Rain' plays loudly over the stereo. Meanwhile I sit and read *The Face* and pretend I understand it, and that I'm not worried about my hair, oh no, not at all, even though Nicky's the apprentice. The apprentice what? Apprentice plumber? Apprentice electrician? Apprentice lathe operator? I'm staring at an article about skate-boarding without really taking it in, so instead just look at the models in the fashion shoots, who are all skinny and androgynous and topless and languidly post-coital, and all sneer up at me, as if sneering at what Nicky's doing to my hair, and the electric razor's out now, and he's shearing the back of my head. Apprentice shepherd? I look up from *The Face*, look at the mirror, and it looks . . . quite good actually, clean and fresh, structured yet natural. I look alright. In fact, I think this might actually be the one for me, the perfect haircut, the haircut I've been waiting for all my life. Nicky, I am *so* sorry for ever doubting you . . .

But still he keeps cutting. Like when you do a great painting at junior school, and the teacher says 'stop now, or you'll spoil it' – Nicky's spoiling it! He's carving out great shaved strips over my ears, he's shaving so high up the back that the long hair on top looks like a toupee. Apprentice lawn-keeper?

Apprentice butcher? I want to reach over and yank the power cable out of the wall, but I can't, I just look dumbly back at *The Face*, something about break-dancing in Basingstoke shopping centres, and wait for the buzzing to stop.

Finally he stops. 'Gel or wax?' he asks.

God, gel or wax? I don't know. Is 'bag' an option? I've never had wax, so I say wax, and he opens a little shoe-polish container, rubs what looks like lard on his hands, and drags his fingers through what remains of my hair.

It's clear that I'm a long, long way from Brideshead here. I look like Winston Smith. I look like a shaved rabbit. I look skinny and wide-eyed and consumptive and a bit mad. Nicky gets a mirror and shows me the back of my head, where the electric razor has uncovered a Martian landscape of scars and boils that I didn't even know existed until now, one of which is bleeding slightly.

'What d'you think?' Nicky says.

'It's perfect!' I say.

Now that I've ruined my hair, it's time to pick a restaurant for our romantic dinner for two. Once again, no one teaches you how to choose a restaurant, and I've never been to a proper restaurant with just one other person before, just cafés and curries and Chinese with Spencer and Tone mainly, where more often than not, the traditional end to a meal is not a cognac and a fine cigar, but Tone shouting 'Runner!' So I'm working on instinct rather than experience, but sticking to a few basic rules of thumb.

First of all, no curries, just in case things get amorous. Also, there's nothing particularly attractive about sitting there with the object of your devotion, wafting your hand in front of your mouth going 'Bloody hell, that's *hot*!' Secondly, try to avoid restaurants that are located within large department stores or supermarkets. I once treated Janet Parks to a slap-up sit-down lunch in Basildon British Home Stores, and I don't think it went down that well actually. Carrying your own food back to your table on a tray, generally speaking, is to be avoided; remember, waitresses are *not* a luxury. Thirdly, don't be *too* flash. Impulsively, I told Alice that I'd take her to Bradley's Bistro, which is pretty swanky, but I went to look at the menu and it's way out of my league, so we're going to have to go somewhere which combines fine cuisine with value-for-money. Even with Nana Jackson's fiver taken into account, I've still only got £12.00 for dinner for two, to include wine, two courses and a dessert with two spoons.

Walking around town, looking in restaurant windows, I keep catching sight of my new haircut, my face looking haunted and afraid. That hair wax is a rip-off too. They make you think it's going to give you control, but all it's done here is make the fringe cling lankly to my forehead, like an oil-slicked seagull. Maybe it'll look better by candle-light. As long as it doesn't combust.

I browse the restaurants in the chintzier village-y part of town, and finally make my decision – a traditional Italian trattoria called Luigi's Pizza Plaza. It does burgers and ribs too, and deep-fried whitebait, and has red-check tablecloths, and candles in wine bottles under great red vesuviuses of congealed wax, and complimentary breadsticks and gigantic pepper mills on every table, so I book the table for two, eight-thirty, name of Jackson, from a red-faced man with dirty fingernails who may or may not be the eponymous Luigi, then head back to my digs.

13

QUESTION: A durable blue twill taking its name from 'serge de Nimes'; the exuded sap of the tree 'hevea brasiliensis'; and woven filaments from the genus Bombyx. Name the three materials.

ANSWER: Denim, rubber and silk.

I'm meant to be doing an essay on 'Nature Imagery in John Donne's Holy Sonnets', but I've been looking for a week now and still can't actually find any.

My pencil-notes in the margin don't help much either; I've written things like 'the Annunciation!' and 'irony?' and 'cf. Freud' and 'here he turns the tables!', and I can't remember why, so instead I pick up Jacques Derrida's *Of Grammatology*. It occurs to me that there are six ages of book-reading. The first is picture books, then 2) books with more illustrations than words, then 3) books with more words than illustrations, then 4) books with no illustrations, just a map maybe, or a family tree, but lots of dialogue, then 5) books with long paragraphs and hardly any dialogue, then 6) books with no dialogue, no narrative, just great long paragraphs and footnotes and bibliographies and appendixes and very, very small writing. Jacques Derrida's *Of Grammatology* is very much a book of the sixth kind, and, intellectually speaking, I'm still stuck somewhere between ages four and five. I read the first sentence, flick through in a fruitless search for a map or photo or illustration then fall asleep.

When I wake up, I suddenly realise it's 4.30, and I've

only got three hours to get ready for dinner. I head to the bathroom, but Josh has been using the bath to soak a load of dirty denim in detergent. I have to scoop the clothes out of the cold, blue stew, and pile them in the sink before I can run the bath, and it's not until I get in that I realise that I haven't got rid of all the washing powder, and that I am, to all intents and purposes, giving myself a 70-degree non-biological cotton/polyester wash. So the bath isn't quite the relaxing experience I'd hoped for, especially as I have to rinse myself off with cold water through the shower attachment to try and prevent the worst of the chemical burns. Looking in the mirror, I notice that I've turned slightly blue.

I transfer the wet denim back in the bath, then in a spirit of righteous vengeance, I nip down the corridor to Josh's bedroom door, and when I'm sure he's not there, I nip in and steal his Apri facial scrub, which basically is grains of ground-up peach-stone in soap that you rub your face with. I do so, and get a pretty satisfying lather going, but when it comes to washing it off, the results aren't good. It looks like I've been through a plate-glass window. Either that or someone's rubbed my face very hard with ground-up peach-stone. There's a lesson to be learnt here, I suppose, and it's this; acne doesn't rub off.

Tight-faced now, and scared to smile in case my face starts to bleed, I go back to my room, where my futon is up against the wall, drying out, put my dirty clothes away, and carefully choose what books to leave lying around just in case Alice comes back '*for "coffee"*' or more likely, for coffee. I go for *The Communist Manifesto*, *Tender is the Night*, *The Lyrical Ballads*, *The Female Eunuch*, some e.e.cummings and the *Songs and Sonnets* of John Donne, just in case things get steamy and I need some lyric poetry to hand. I'm in two minds about *The Female Eunuch*, because even though I'd like her to think that my sexual politics are progressive and radical the illustration on the front cover, of a disembodied naked female torso, has always seemed a bit sexy to me, so much so that I used to have to hide it from Mum.

Then I put on some brand-new black briefs, my best black slacks, a new second-hand dinner-jacket, bought from the vintage clothes shop, 'Olden Times', my best white shirt, a bow tie, and my new black braces. I arrange the dead seagull on my head, then splash my face with Dad's vintage white porcelain bottle of Old Spice, which makes me smell a bit old and spicy, and stings like hell. Then I check my wallet for the condom that I always carry with me in case of a miracle. This particular condom is number two in a proposed trilogy, the first of which met its poignant fate in the wheelie-bin at the back of Littlewoods. This one has been in my wallet for so long that it's stuck to the lining, and the foil wrapper has started to tarnish round the outline of the condom, like some grotesque brass rubbing. Still, I like to carry it with me, in the same way as some people like to carry a St Christopher's medal, despite the fact that I have about as much chance of using the thing tonight as I have of carrying the infant Jesus across a river.

On the way to Kenwood Manor I have to stop every hundred yards or so, because the metal clips on my braces refuse to gain a purchase on the waistband of my black slacks, and keep pinging off and snapping against my nipples.

I'm re-attaching them for about the twentieth time when a voice behind me says, 'Someone stolen your teddy-bear, Sebastian?'

'Hello, Rebecca, how are you?'

'I'm alright, the question is are *you* alright?'

'What d'you mean?'

'Well, what's happened to your hair?'

'Don't you like it?'

'Makes you look like Heinrich Himmler. And why the fancy dress?'

'Well, you know what they say – clothes maketh the man . . .'

'. . . look uncomfortable?'

'I'm taking someone out to dinner, if you must know.'

'Wooooooo!'

'It's just a platonic thing.'

'And who's the lucky lady? Not bloody Alice Harbinson I hope . . .' I look innocently up at the sky. 'Och, I don't believe it. You *boys*, you're sooooo predictable. Honestly, if you want to play with dolls, why don't you just go out and buy a doll?'

'What?'

'Nothing. Hey, you'd better get a move on Jackson, or you'll miss the boat.'

'What d'you mean by that?'

'I just mean that she's clearly a very popular young lady, that's all. We're on the same corridor, and every night there's this long queue of drooling rugger-buggers snaking out of her door, all clutching bottles of warm Lambrusco . . .'

'Really?'

'Uh-huh. And she's got this habit of strolling down the corridor to the communal bathroom in her little black knickers and bra. Though for whose benefit *that* display's for, I really couldn't say . . .'

I bat the image out of my mind. 'You sound as if you don't like her.'

'Och, I barely know her – not cool enough for that crowd, am I? Besides, I don't think she's what you'd call a *girl*'s girl, if you know what I mean. Personally speaking, I don't see the appeal of the kind of girl who still draws a smiley face in the middle of her letter 'O's but, hey, that's just me. So, where you taking the lovely Alice?'

'Oh, just a place in town. Luigi's?'

'KFC all booked up was it?'

'You think Luigi's is a bad idea?'

'Not at all. You're clearly a gentleman of taste and sophistication! And I hear the half-pounder with cheese, chilli and onion rings is *to die for*. Maybe you can take me there one day too, Jackson.'

And she walks on ahead, leaving me trying to think of something clever to say. 'Rebecca,' I call after her. She turns, grinning. 'Why do you always call me Jackson?'

'D'you mind?'

'Not really. It's just a bit *Grange Hill*, that's all.'

'Och, I'm sorry. It's meant with affection. Would you prefer "Brian"? Or the more perky and informal "Bri"? Or "Herr Himmler" perhaps . . . ?'

'Brian, I think.'

'Okay then, Brian it is. Have fun, Brian. Keep your wits about you, Brian. Play it cool, Brian' . . . and she disappears down the corridor . . . 'see you around, Brian.'

I hurry to Alice's room, half expecting to see this great long queue of boys, but when I get there the door's closed. I can hear voices from inside – I don't exactly press my ear to the wood, because that wouldn't be right, but I do stand close enough to hear.

'Where's he taking you for dinner?' says a voice, female, thank God.

'Bradley's, I think,' says Alice.

'Bradley's – very posh.'

'Is he rich then?'

'Don't know. Wouldn't have thought so,' says Alice.

'Well, just make sure you're back by eleven, young lady, or we'll send the police out looking for you . . .' I knock, because I don't want to hear any more, and there's some whispering and giggling, and then she opens the door.

She's wearing a low-cut charcoal-grey satin evening dress with a puff-ball skirt, and her hair's piled high on her head, so that along with the high heels, she seems about two feet taller than usual. She's wearing more make-up than usual too, lipstick for the first time, the line of that tiny raised scar still visible on her lower lip. Most remarkable of all, though is the low-cut ball gown. She must have some kind of strapless bra arrangement under there, because her shoulders are bare, as if the top half of her body were being squeezed gently out of the dress, and there's a fantastic curve of bare skin, of bare Alice, rolling, over-flowing the top of the satin bodice. In a nineteenth century novel, you'd say that she had a 'magnificent bosom'. In fact, you'd say it now too. She has a magnificent bosom. You're staring. Don't stare, Brian.

'Hello, Alice.'

'Hello, Brian.'

Behind her, Erin the Cat, and another one of her gang, are smirking at me. Close your mouth, Brian.

'You look very nice, Bri,' says Erin, without meaning it.

'Thank you! So, shall we go then?'

'Absolutely.'

And she takes my arm and we go.

14

QUESTION: Consisting of a straight chain of carbon atoms, with hydrogen atoms along its length, and a carboxyl growth at one end, Oleic acid is the most widely distributed example of which lipid component?

ANSWER: Fatty acids.

Politically, of course, I don't really approve of the concept of physical beauty. The idea that someone, man or woman, should receive any kind of extra attention or affection or popularity or respect or adulation, simply because of a quirk of genetics and some arbitrary, male-media-defined subjective notion of 'beauty' seems to me inherently wrong and unacceptable.

Having said that, Alice is clearly just . . . beautiful. In the candle-light she looks like a De la Tour. Or do I mean Vermeer? Or Watteau? She knows she's being looked at as she opens the menu, and she must know that she looks lovely, but what must that be like? To be *looked at*, rather than just glanced at, and to give pleasure, entirely passively, just by being looked at. Though looking at her now, it occurs to me that it's not even *pleasure* as such, just more of an ache, a low, dull, heavy throb in your belly, that you wish you could get rid of but can't, because it's too much temptation, to sit and look, to sit and gaze and take her in.

Ever since I met her, I've noticed people gazing at Alice in this way. I've watched Patrick do it, smoothing back his hair, with his fat, stupid astronaut's tongue lolling out, and I watch

Luigi the waiter do it as he peels her burgundy shawl off her bare shoulders and shows us to the table, then heads through the swing doors to spread the word, so that both the chef and the washer-upper come out of the kitchen on some feeble pretext, just to look at her. What must that be like? To be admired before you've even said a word, to be desired two or three hundred times a day by people who have absolutely no idea what you're like?

When Mum's watching telly, she'll often appraise a woman, a film star or something, and say 'she's beautiful . . .' then, damningly, in her best Old Testament voice '. . . *and she knows it*'. Whether or not 'beautiful and knows it' is better or worse than 'ugly and knows it' I'm not sure, and I suppose great physical beauty must be some kind of burden, but as burdens go it surely has to be one of the lighter ones.

Over the top of the menu, I steal a glance at the rectangle of peachy, candle-lit cleavage that I'm trying not to look at because I don't want her to feel she's being objectified.

'Nice, isn't it?' she says.

I assume that she means the restaurant and say, 'Is it? I hope so.' I'm having to whisper, because we're the only people here, and I don't want to offend Luigi, who's busy over by the plastic-ivy-covered bar, smearing the wine glasses with grease, and leering. It seems that reserving a table might not have been as essential as I thought. 'I tried to get us into Bradley's but they were fully booked,' I lie.

'Not to worry. This is great!'

'There's pizza and pasta, and over the page there's burgers . . .'

'Oh, so there is . . .' she says, unpeeling the plastic-sealed pages which come in an A4 binder.

'Or spare ribs if you prefer . . . ?'

'Ooooo-kay.'

'And you have to have a starter too, the works, all on me!'

'Well, we'll see about that . . .'

And we go back to the menu.

Oh, God.

Silence.

Better say something.

'Hmmmm. Breadsticks!'

I take a breadstick, peel the paper off, unwrap a pat of butter, and wipe it along the breadstick. 'You know what I always wonder about spare ribs? Who decides they're *spare*! Not the pig, surely! It's not like the pig's saying, "Well, I'm going to need *these* ribs, but *those* are *spare*, take them! Take my ribs! Eat! Eat my ribs!"' She gives me a Children-in-Need kind of smile, glances at my hand, and I look down and realise that for some reason I'm waving a knife around.

Stay calm.

Stop jabbering.

Put – the knife – down.

But the truth is I'm starting to lose faith in Luigi's as a venue for a romantic seduction. The floors, I realise, are linoleum, curling up at the skirting boards, and not particularly clean, and the chequered tablecloths are actually vinyl, for ease of wipeability. Also, even though Luigi's seated us in a romantic corner at the back, we're pretty near the toilets, which is convenient I suppose, but means there's a slightly tangy back-note of lemon Harpic to the evening. I'm anxious that Alice might feel uncomfortable here. She's certainly starting to look uncomfortable; her puff-ball evening dress has ballooned up around her, as if she's being consumed by her gown.

'Shall we order?' I ask.

'It all looks delicious, I have to say,' she says, but I'm not so sure. We concentrate on the menu, which is sticky to the touch, imperfectly typed, phonetically spelt – Chilly Concarny, is that right? – and divided up into 'For Openers!', 'The Main Event!!' and 'Oh Go On Then . . . !!!'. To be honest, it actually does all look delicious to me; with an emphasis on deep-frying and charred meats, and hardly any vegetables. Even the cheese comes deep-fried, and the portions here are obviously big, because they tell you on the menu how much all the meat weighs. But I can't help worrying that Alice is used to lighter fare, tofu and salads and things that have been *steamed*, and I think she may well be one of those quality-over-quantity types. I'm starting to perspire. And itch too, from the detergent in the bath. I look down and notice that the cuffs of my white shirt have a denim-blue tide-mark.

The theme from the Cornetto adverts plays on a loop in the background, and after some silent deliberation, we're ready. I look around for Luigi, but can tell he's approaching behind me by the sucking noise his footsteps make on the linoleum. Alice goes for the stuffed mushrooms and a margarita pizza with a side salad, while I opt for the whitebait and the barbecued half-chicken with chips and complementary relish tray. 'Hope it's not the back half!' I say, and Alice smiles, ever so subtly, and insists I choose the wine. There's stuff by the carafe, but even I know that wine shouldn't be *that* cheap, so I decide to go for something bottled and sparkling. The champagne's way too expensive so I settle on the Lambrusco. Didn't Rebecca say something about her liking it? I don't know much about wine, but I know white goes with chicken and fish, so I order the white Lambrusco Bianco.

After the waiter's gone I say, 'Oh God, Faux-Pas City!'

'Why?'

'Well, I asked for *white* Lambrusco Bianco and of course "bianco" actually means white! Tautology or *what*!' As amusing anecdotes go, I realise that this wouldn't really hold its own on the Parkinson show, but it serves to break the ice, and she smiles and we start to talk. Or rather she does, and I nod and listen, pick sticks of red wax off the candle, melt the ends, stick them back on at odd angles, and watch her. She's talking, as she often does, about school days at Linden Lodge, one of those massively expensive socialist private schools out in the country, and I have to say it sounds like a pretty cushy number to me, and not like boarding-school at all, more like a sort of seven-year slumber-party. As far as I can tell from the way Alice describes it, a typical academic day at Linden Lodge goes like this:

8.30/9.30	Smoke joint. Bake bread.
9.30/10.30	Have sex with son/daughter of Famous Person.
10.30/11.30	Build barn.
11.30/12.30	Read T.S. Eliot aloud, listen to Crosby, Stills and Nash, play cello.
12.30/1.30	Experiment with drugs, have sex.
1.30/3.30	Double skinny-dipping. Swim with dolphins.
3.30/4.30	Dry-stone-walling. Sex (optional).
4.30/5.30	Acoustic guitar lesson.
5.30/6.30	Have sex, then sketch sleeping naked partner in charcoal.
6.30/04.00	Compulsory Bob Dylan.
04.00	Lights out, but only if you want to.

Obviously, from a political point of view I don't approve of a school like this, even if it sounds frankly fantastic. What with all the dope-smoking and sex and endless singing of Simon and Garfunkel songs, you'd think they'd never actually get any studying done, but they must be doing something right, because Alice is here after all, and though I haven't asked about her A-level grades yet, not on a first date, she is doing a degree, even if it's only in Drama. Maybe if you listen to enough Radio 4 from an early age, you just get educated subliminally.

My whitebait arrive, about thirty of the little silver things washed up on a leaf of iceberg lettuce, looking up at me and saying 'we *died* for you, you bastard, at least do something amusing!' So I put one in my mouth with the tail sticking out and pretend to be a cat. This goes down only moderately well. She returns to her garlic mushrooms.

'How are they?'

'Nice! Very garlicky. No snogging for me tonight!'

And there it is, the subtle warning, like a klaxon in the ear, in case I was getting any fancy ideas. I'm not surprised really, it's pretty much what I expected, and I take comfort from the fact that it's an ambiguous warning, albeit only very, very slightly ambiguous – it's not *you*, Brian, it's the *mushrooms* – the implication being that if she'd ordered a different appetiser, the deep-fried Camembert for instance, then we'd have already made love by now.

'So did you have many boyfriends there?' I ask casually, nibbling on a fish.

'Oh, just one or two,' and she proceeds to tell me all about them.

From the point of view of sexual politics, I think it's really important not to have double standards about men and women's sexual history. Of course, there's absolutely no reason why Alice Harbinson shouldn't have had an active romantic and sexual past, but still, I think it's fair to say that 'just one or two' is a little misleading. By the time the main courses arrive, the names have started to blur, but there's definitely someone called Rufus, who's dad's a famous film director, and who had to move to LA because their love for each other was just too dark and intense, whatever *that* means. And Alexis, the Greek fisherman who she met on holiday, and who kept turning up at their London house asking for her hand in marriage, until they had to phone the police and get him deported. And Joseph, a really beautiful jazz musician who she had to finish with because he kept trying to get her to take heroin with him. And Tony, a potter friend of her father's who made stunning ceramics in this beautiful crofter's cottage in the Highlands of Scotland, and was great in bed for a sixty-two-year-old, but then wouldn't stop phoning in the middle of the night and eventually tried to commit suicide in his own kiln, but is okay now.

And Saul, a really gorgeous and wealthy American model who was amazing-looking with a (whisper it) 'really massive penis', but you can't have a relationship based on sex, even if it's mind-blowing sex. And then, saddest of all, there was Mr Shillabeer, her English teacher, who turned her on to T.S.Eliot and apparently once made a girl orgasm just by reading *The Four Quartets* aloud, and who fell in love with Alice while they were doing *The Crucible*, but became a bit obsessive. 'In the end he had a nervous breakdown and had to leave. He's gone back to live with his parents now. In Wolverhampton. It's quite sad, really, because he was a cool English teacher.'

By the time she's finished, I've stripped half-a-chicken in barbecue sauce down to its carcass, and the remains lie on my plate looking like, well, one of Alice's ex-lovers. Nearly all of her relationships have ended in madness, obsession and devastation, and suddenly my wheely-bin adventure with Karen Armstrong round the back of Littlewoods seems to have lost some of its tragic grandeur.

'It's strange isn't it – how many of them end badly?' I say.

'I know! Weird isn't it? Tony, Dad's ceramic friend, the guy in the kiln, once told me that when it came to love I was like The Four Horsemen of the Apocalypse!'

'But do you ever end up getting, you know . . . hurt?'

'Of course I do, Brian. That's why I'm not going to have any relationships at all at university. I'm going to concentrate on my work,' and then she adds, unaccountably, in an American accent, 'I'm going to get me to a nunnery!'

And there it is again, the klaxon. Casually, she goes back to peeling the melted Cheddar off the top of her margarita, and wrapping it round her index finger. 'Anyway, sorry – me, me, me. What do your mum and dad do, again? I've forgotten . . .' she says, sucking on her finger.

'Mum works in Woolworths, and Dad's dead.'

She puts her napkin to her mouth, swallows.

'You didn't tell me that . . .'

'Didn't I?'

'No, I'm sure you didn't.' She reaches across, puts her hand on my arm. 'Brian, I am so sorry.'

'Oh, it's alright, it was six, no, seven years ago now, when I was twelve.'

'What happened?'

'Heart attack.'

'Oh God, how old was he?'

'Forty-one.'

'That must have been awful.'

'Oh, well, you know.'

And she's leaning forward now, eyes wide and she's holding my hand and squeezing it, and with the other hand she takes the wax encrusted bottle, and puts it to one side so that she can see me properly.

'Do you mind talking about it?'

'No, not at all,' I say, and I start talking.

15

QUESTION: Lee J. Cobb, Frederick March and Dustin Hoffman have all played the unfortunate Willy Loman in which Arthur Miller play of 1949?
ANSWER: *Death of a Salesman*.

'Dad was a double-glazing salesman, which is a funny job really, because it's one of those jobs that people think it's okay to laugh at, like traffic warden or tax inspector or sewage worker. I suppose it's because, at the end of the day, no one loves double-glazing. Dad certainly didn't, not after ten years of it, anyway. He was in the army before that, where he'd met Mum and had me. He'd done his National Service, one of the last people to do it, and sort of liked it, and hadn't known what else to do, so he stayed on. I do remember worrying, whenever there was a war somewhere on the news, tension with Russia, or when Northern Ireland was flaring up or something, worrying that he'd be called up, stuck into uniform, given a gun. But I don't think he was that kind of soldier really, I think he was more on the clerical side. Anyway, when they had me Mum put her foot down and said he had to leave the army because she was fed up with moving round all the time, and she hated West Germany, where I was born, so he came back to Southend, and he got the double-glazing thing and that was it really.'

'Did he enjoy it?'

'God, no. I mean, he must have at first, I suppose, but I think he really grew to despise it. It's long hours, you see, because you have to catch people when they're in, which means early mornings, evenings and nighttime, so it was usually dark when he got home, even in summer. And I think there was a bit of door-to-door involved; "Excuse me madam, but are you aware of the huge difference double-glazing could make to your heating bill," that kind of thing. And I know it was paid mainly on commission, which meant that there was this constant worry about money. Whatever job I end up doing, I never, ever want to be paid on commission. I know it's meant to be an incentive, but it's just an incentive to fuck up your life, it's working with a gun to your head. It's really evil, I think. Anyway. Sorry. Boring.

'Anyway, he hated it. He never told me he did of course, because why would you, to a little kid, but he must have because he was angry whenever he got home from work; not shouting or punching or anything, but just this silent, clenched, white-knuckled, red-faced rage at the tiniest thing, like toys left out or wasted food. You want your memories of your parents to be about picnics or being carried round on their shoulders, or pooh sticks, or something, but no one's childhood is perfect and all I mainly remember is him arguing in the kitchen with Mum about money or work or whatever, his face all red, clenching and unclenching his fists.'

'That's terrible.'

'Is it? Well, I'm probably exaggerating a little bit. Mostly I remember watching telly with him, if I was allowed to stay up until he got home. Sitting on the floor between his legs. Quiz shows. He loved quiz shows, and nature documentaries, David Attenborough, educational stuff, he was always going on about how important an education was, I suppose because he thought that was the key to a good life, to not being miserable, to a job you didn't despise.'

'So, how did he, you know . . . ?'

'Well, I'm not sure exactly. I don't like to ask Mum about it, because it sets her off, but apparently he was out at work, in some strangers' house, trying to convince them of the benefits of double-glazing or whatever, and he just . . . fell over. Right there, in their living room. I'd got back from school and was watching telly while Mum was cooking tea, and there was a knock at the front door, and some talking in the hall, I went out to see what had happened, and there were two policewomen and Mum was curled up in a ball on the carpet. To begin with I thought maybe Dad had been arrested or something, but this policewoman said he'd been taken poorly, and then they rushed Mum off to the hospital while I stayed with the next-door neighbours, and he died shortly after she got there. Oh, look. No more wine. D'you want some more? Another bottle? I stayed over at the neighbours, and they told me the next morning. Another bottle of Lambrusco please, no, we've not decided about desserts yet, can we have five minutes?

'Anyway. Looking back, I'm not surprised, even though he was only forty-one, because he was just like this . . . knot, all the time. And he did drink, I mean a lot, pub at lunchtime and after work, you could always smell the beer on him. And he smoked about sixty a day. I used to buy him fags as a *Christmas present* for fuck's sake. I don't think I've got a single memory of him where he isn't puffing away on a fag. There's even a photo of him and Mum with me in the maternity ward, and he's got a fag lit up. In a hospital, with the ashtray and a bottle of beer balanced on top of my cot. The silly sod.'

'And how did you react?'

'To him dying? Um. Not sure. Weirdly, I think. I mean I cried and everything, but they wanted to keep me off school, which worried me because I didn't like missing lessons, so that should give you some idea of the kind of swotty, cold little freak I was. I was more upset by Mum to be honest, because Mum really loved Dad, and she was only, what, thirty-three at the time, and he was the only man she'd ever slept with, before or since, as far as I know, and she did take it really, really badly. Oh, she was okay as long as there were people around, and of course for the first two weeks the house was absolutely crammed – assorted vicars, and mates of Dad's, and neighbours, and my gran, and aunts and uncles – so there wasn't time for Mum to get too upset really, because she was always busy making sandwiches and pots of tea, and making up camp-beds for these strange cousins from Ireland, who we'd never seen before or since. But then after a couple of weeks they all started to drift off and it was just me and Mum. And that was the worst time, when things had calmed down and people left us alone. Quite a weird combination, a teenage boy and his mum. I mean, you're very aware that there's someone . . . missing.

'And I suppose, looking back, I could have been better with Mum, sat with her and stuff. But I used to hate sitting in that living room every night, watching her watch *Dallas* or whatever and then suddenly bursting into tears. When you're that age, that kind of thing, grief, well it's . . . just embarrassing. What are you meant to do? Put your arms around her? Say something? What are you supposed to say, a twelve-year-old boy? So in a strange, terrible way I started to resent it. I used to avoid her. I'd just go from school to the public library and from the library to my room to do my homework; there was never enough homework as far as I was concerned. God, what a creep.'

'How were they at school?'

'Oh, it was alright. Compassion doesn't come very easily to twelve-year-old boys, not at my school anyway, and why should it really? Some of them tried, but you could tell they were putting it on. Also – and this is really shameful – at the time it wasn't so much about the person who'd actually, you know, *died*, my dad, just dropping dead at the age of forty-one, or how it was for Mum even, I just thought how it was going to be for *me*. What's that word? Solipsism or solecism or something? Solecism.

'I suppose it got me noticed though, in a terrible way;

this awful, maudlin kudos, the dead-dad-boy, you know, lots of girls who've never talked to you before, coming up and offering you a finger of their Kit-Kat and rubbing your back. And there was a bit of bullying of course, and a couple of kids took the piss, calling me Barnardo-boy, that kind of thing, which isn't even witty, because it's not like I didn't have Mum. But I had one mate, Spencer, who decided to look after me for some reason, and that helped. People were scared of Spencer. Quite right too, because he's a hard bastard, Spencer . . .'

'Do you have a picture of him?'

'Spencer? Oh, Dad. No, not in my wallet. Why, d'you think I should?'

'Not at all.'

'Back at home I do. If you come back to mine. Not tonight necessarily, but, you know, whenever . . .'

'And you think about him?'

'Oh, yeah, of course. All the time. But it's hard because we never really knew each other. Not as two adults anyway.'

'I'm sure he'd have loved you.'

'D'you think so?'

'Of course. Don't you?'

'Not sure. I think he'd have thought I was a bit weird, to be honest.'

'He'd have been proud.'

'Why?'

'Lots of reasons. University. Star of the quiz team, going on telly and everything . . .'

'Maybe. The only thing I do still think, and I don't know why, because it's not rational, and it's not even technically their fault, but I'd love to meet the people who employed him, the people who made all the money from making him work like that, because I think they're cunts. Sorry – bad word. I don't really know their names or where they are now, probably in some big fuck-off villa in the Algarve or something, and I don't know what I'd say to them even if I met them, because they weren't doing anything *wrong*, they were just running a business, just making a profit, and Dad could always have left if he hated it so much, got on his bike and looked for something else, and he would have probably, you know, gone early at some point anyway, even if he was a florist or a primary school teacher or something, it's not like it was criminal negligence, or a mining accident or a fishing boat or something, he was just a salesman, but it's not right for anyone to hate their job that much, and I think the people who made him work like that, well, I do think they're cunts and I hate them, every day, whoever they are, for taking . . . anyway. Anyway, will you excuse me a minute? I've just got to go to the loo.'

16

QUESTION: The lachrymal duct and gland are primarily responsible for the production and distribution of what?
ANSWER: Tears.

In the end I suppose it was a blessing that we were sat so near the toilets.

I've been in here some time now. Too long probably. I don't want her to think I've got diarrhoea or anything, but I don't want her to see me crying either. As a seduction technique, uncontrollable sobbing is definitely overrated. Now she thinks I'm one of those boys who cries. She's probably next door right now, shaking her head, paying the bill and hurrying back to halls to tell Erin all about it; 'God, you wouldn't believe the evening I've had. He's only one of those boys-who-cry . . .'

There's a knock on the cubicle door, and I assume it's Luigi, checking to see if I've done a runner through the fire exit, but there's a voice . . .

'Brian, are you okay?'

'Oh, hiya Alice!'

'Are you alright in there?'

'Oh, I'm fine, I'm fine.'

'D'you want to unlock the door, sweetheart?'

Oh, God, she wants to come in the toilet cubicle with me.

'Unlock the door, darling . . .'

'Actually, I'm fine, I'll be with you in a minute.' Hang on – '*sweetheart*'?

'O-kay. Come back to me soon though, won't you?'

'Two minutes,' I shout, and, as she's going out the door, 'go ahead and order dessert if you want to!'

And she goes. I wait a moment, then leave the cubicle and look in the mirror. It's not so bad I suppose – the eyes are a bit red, but my nose isn't running any more, so I adjust my bow-tie, mould the fringe back in place, re-attach the braces, and walk back in, head slightly bowed so Luigi won't see me. When I approach the table, Alice stands up, and amazingly puts her arm round me and hugs me really tightly, her cheek pressed tight against mine. I don't know what to do, so I put my arms around her too, leaning forward slightly to allow for the volume of the puff-ball skirt, one hand on the grey satin, and one on her back, her beautiful back, just where the flesh swells out over the top of the satin, and she whispers in my ear – 'you are *such* a lovely man' – and I think I'm going to cry again, not because I am such a lovely man, but because I'm such a disgusting, fucking stupid, fucking twat, so I squeeze my eyes tight shut and we stay like that for a little while. When I open my eyes again I see Luigi watching, and then winking slyly at me, and giving me the thumbs-up. I don't really know how to react to this so I give him the thumbs-up back, and immediately feel despicable, because I don't quite understand what I'm giving the thumbs-up to.

Eventually of course, my braces ping off and Alice breaks the embrace, and smiles at me with the corners of her mouth turned down, the kind of rueful smile mums give to tearful kids in TV commercials. I'm starting to get pretty uncomfortable now, so I say, 'Sorry about that. I usually don't start crying until *much* later in the evening.'

'Shall we go?'

But I don't want to go yet. 'You don't want dessert? Or coffee or anything?'

'No, I'm alright.'

'They've got profiteroles? Death by chocolate . . . ?'

'No, really, I'm *stuffed*,' and from somewhere in the folds of the puff-ball dress she produces the world's smallest handbag, and goes to open it.

'Hey, I'm paying!' I say.

And so I pay the bill, which is actually pretty reasonable in the end, thanks to me having a complete mental breakdown instead of dessert, and we head out.

On the way back to her digs, we change the subject, and talk about books, how we both hate D. H. Lawrence and which Thomas Hardy we prefer; I'm *Jude The Obscure*, she's *Far From The Madding Crowd*. It's a mild late November evening, and the streets are damp despite the fact that there's been no rain. She suggests we take the scenic route back, and so we stomp up the hill that overlooks the city, breathing a little heavily, because of the exertion and the conversation, which never falters. The sound of the cars on the city streets gets fainter and the only noise apart from our voices is the wind in the trees and the whoosh of her satin ball-gown. Halfway up the hill she slips her arm through mine, and gives it a little squeeze, and rests her head on my shoulder. The last person to take me by the arm like that was my mum, on the way home after seeing my Jesus in *Godspell*. She had just watched me being crucified of course, which is bound to have an emotional effect on a mother, but I remember even then that it made me feel a little strange, partly proud, partly deeply embarrassed, like I was her proper-little-soldier or something. Alice taking my arm feels no less self-conscious, as if it's something she picked up from a TV costume drama, but it's nice too, and I feel warmer and a good two inches taller.

At the top of the hill we sit on a bench, and she nestles her hip against mine so that we sit snugly in the corner, and even though I can feel the damp soaking through my slacks, and know they'll be streaked with algae, I don't mind. In fact I wouldn't mind if we stayed here forever, looking at the city beneath us, and the lights of the motorway winding off into the countryside.

'I've just realised, I haven't wished you happy birthday yet.'

'Oh, that's okay . . .'

'Happy birthday though . . .'

'Oh thank you, same to you.'

'Except it's not my birthday.' She says.

'No, of course not. Sorry.'

'And I haven't got you a present, either . . .'

'That's okay. Tonight was a present.'

We stop talking, and I contemplate pointing out some of the constellations, like they do in films. I've learnt them off by heart for just such an occasion, but it's too cloudy, so instead I wonder if it's dark enough for me to kiss her, or if she's drunk enough to let me.

'Brian, what are you doing at Christmas?'

'Um, don't know . . .'

'D'you want to come and stay?'

'Where?'

'With me.'

'In London?'

'No, we've got a little cottage in Suffolk. You can meet Rose and Michael.'

'Who are Rose and Michael?'

'My parents!'

'Right! Well I'd love to, but I don't want to leave Mum alone . . .'

'Of course not, but you could come after Christmas, the day after Boxing Day or something. And my parents pretty much keep themselves to themselves, so it would just be me and you most of the time' – *she thinks I need persuading* – 'we can just hang out and walk and read and talk and stuff . . .'

'Okay,' I say.

'Fantastic! It's a deal then. I'm cold now. Let's go home.'

It's gone midnight when we get back to her halls of residence, but there are still a few people padding to and fro along the parquet corridors, the swots and the insomniacs and the stoners. They all say 'hello Alice' and then glance at me sceptically, but I don't really mind. I'm too busy thinking about how we say goodbye, the mechanics of it. At her door, she says, 'I'd better go straight to bed, I've got a nine-fifteen lecture.'

'Right. On . . . ?'

'"Stanislavski and Brecht, the Great Divide, question mark".'

'Right, because they're not actually that different in many ways, though people tend to think that their philosophies are mutually exclu . . .'

'Actually, Brian, I really ought to go to bed.'

'Okay. Well, thanks for agreeing to come out with me.'

'Brian – I didn't *agree* to. I *wanted* to,' and she leans forward very quickly and kisses me just near my ear. It's pretty quick, like a cobra strike, and my reflexes aren't really up to it, so I just have time to make that smacking noise with my mouth too loud in her ear, and then the door's closed and she's gone.

And once again, I'm walking up the gravel driveway, on my way home. So it was okay in the end. I think it was okay. I've been invited to a cottage, and I think she finds me 'interesting' now, even if 'interesting' wasn't really what I was going for. I'm a little uncomfortable about the reasons why, but still . . .

'Oi, Jackson!'

I look around.

'Sorry, I mean *Brian*. Brian, up here . . .' It's Rebecca, leaning out of the first-floor window, ready for bed in a long black T-shirt.

'So, how'd it go, lover-boy?'

'Oh, you know. Alright.'

'So is love in the air?'

'Not "love". "Like".'

'"Like" is in the air. I thought so. I sensed it. Like is in the air. Well done, Brian. And you hang in there, pal.'

On the way home I go to the all-night garage and treat myself to a Picnic and a can of Lilt with the money I saved by bursting into tears. When I get home to Richmond House it's nearly two o'clock. There are three handwritten notes pinned to my door . . .

7.30 Brian – your Mum rang.

10.45 Spencer rang. Says he's 'bored out of his skull'. He's at the petrol station all night. Call him.

Brian, can you please not use my Apri without asking?

17

QUESTION: What precisely does Dorothy Gale have to do to return to Kansas?

ANSWER: Click her heels three times, whilst thinking 'There's No Place Like Home'.

Mum's still out at Woolworths when I let myself in, so I make a mug of tea, flop on the sofa, pick up a pen and methodically mark up my Christmas television viewing in the bumper edition of the *Radio Times*. I feel completely exhausted, which unfortunately owes more to Josh and Marcus' home-brew than any academic fervour. The last few weeks of term have passed by in a blur of sparsely populated parties in strangers' houses, or drinking games in the kitchen with Josh and Marcus' pals; big, burly sporty boys, and hearty, perma-tanned girls from the lacrosse team, all with their shirt collars turned up, all doing French, all from the home counties, and all with the same flicked-back blonde hair. I've made up a pretty good joke about this kind of girl, i.e. that they're all from Surrey-with-a-fringe-on-top, but unfortunately have no one to tell it to.

Anyway, whatever else they teach them at those private schools, they certainly know how to drink. I feel poisoned and grey and malnourished, and glad to get home, lie on the sofa, watch telly. There's nothing good on this afternoon, just some Western, so my eyes wander up to the school photo of me on top of the telly, taken just before Dad died. Is there anything more grizzly and joyless than an old school photo? They say the camera adds five pounds, but here it seems to have been added exclusively to my acne. I look positively mediaeval, like a plague victim, all gums and boils, and I wonder what Mum gets out of it, having me grimacing out at her while she's trying to watch the telly.

The photo depresses me so much that I have to turn the telly off, and go out to the kitchen to boil the kettle and make more tea. While it boils, I look out at the backyard, a shadowy patch the size of a double-bed that Mum had paved over when Dad died, to save bother. I make the tea, and take my bag upstairs to my bedroom. Mum's turned the radiator off, to save on heating, and it's icy cold, so I get into bed fully clothed and stare at the ceiling. The bed feels smaller for some reason, like a child's bed, in fact the whole room does. God knows why, it's not as if I've got any bigger, but already, after only three months it's started to feel like someone else's room. All that's left here is the kid's stuff – the piles of comics, the fossils on the window-sill, the Brodie's notes, the model aeroplanes hanging from the ceiling covered in a fur of dust, the old school-shirts hanging in the wardrobe. I start to feel a bit sad for some reason, so I think about Alice for a while, and then I fall asleep.

I haven't spoken to her properly for ages. The Challenge team meetings broke up two weeks ago, and since then she seems to have been swallowed into her own little clique, a tight, noisy gang of cool and beautiful boys and girls that I've seen in the student bar, or driving round town, seven or eight of them stuffed giggling into her smoke-filled bright yellow 2CV, passing a bottle of red wine between them and listening to Jimi Hendrix, then all going back to someone's Georgian flat to share interesting drugs and have sex with each other. In fact the nearest I've got to Alice was in the student bar a couple of nights ago. I approached and said 'hiya', and they'd all said 'hiya' back, bright and smiley, but unfortunately there weren't enough chairs at the table for me to actually sit down with them. Also, Alice was having to crick her neck uncomfortably to turn and talk to me, and there's only so long you can stand at the edge of a group like that before you start to feel as if you should be clearing the empties off the table. Of course I have nothing but contempt for cool, self-satisfied, privileged cliques like that, but unfortunately not quite enough contempt to not want to be part of it.

But we did manage to talk long enough for Alice to confirm the cottage trip was definitely on. I don't have to bring anything except lots of books and a jumper. In fact she laughed at me when I asked if I had to bring a towel. 'We've *lots* of towels,' she said, and I thought, yes, of course you have. 'Can't wait,' she said. 'Can't wait either,' I said, but I really meant it, because I know that at college I'm never really going to be able to take up much of her time, there are too many distractions, too many lanky boys with bone structure and money and their own flats. But when we're finally away, just me and her, then that'll be my chance, my big opportunity to prove to her the absolute inevitability of us being together.

It's Christmas morning, and the first thing I do when I get up is eat a big bowl of Frosties and turn the telly on. It's about ten o'clock, and *The Wizard of Oz* has already started, so I put it on in the background while Mum and I open each other's presents. Dad's there too, in a way, like Jacob Marley's ghost, dressed like he was in an old Polaroid I have of him, looking weary and sardonic in a burgundy dressing gown, black hair slicked back, wearing new slippers and smoking the packet of fags that I bought and wrapped up for him as a present.

This year Mum's bought me some new vests and the *Collected Works of e.e.cummings* that I specifically asked for, and which she had to order specially. I check the price on the fly-leaf and feel a twinge of guilt at how expensive it was, a day's wages at least, but I thank her and kiss her on the cheek, and give her my presents in return – a little wicker basket of smellies from the Body Shop, and a second-hand Everyman edition of *Bleak House.*

'What's this then?'

'It's my favourite Dickens. It's brilliant.'

'"Bleak House"? Sounds like *this* house.'

And that just about sets the tone for the day, really. Dickensian.

We're joined for Christmas dinner by Uncle Des. Uncle Des's wife left him for a bloke from her work a couple of years ago now, so Mum invites him round for Christmas dinner every year because he doesn't have much family of his own. Even though he's not my real uncle, just the bloke from three-doors-down, he thinks he's somehow got the right to ruffle my hair and talk to me as if I was twelve years old.

'How ya' doing then, brainbox?' he says, in his children's entertainer voice.

'Fine thank you, Uncle Des.'

'Bloody hell, don't they teach you how to use a comb at university!' he says, ruffling away. 'Look at the state of you!' – ruffle, ruffle, ruffle – and it occurs to me that this is all pretty rich coming from a forty-five-year-old man with a tight blond perm and a moustache that looks as if it's been cut out from a carpet sample, but I keep quiet because Mum doesn't like me back-chatting to Uncle Des. So I squirm bashfully and count myself lucky that at least this year he isn't pulling fifty-pence pieces out from behind my ear.

Mum pops her head round the door and says, 'Sprouts are on!' A waft of warm chlorophyllic air confirms her warning, and I feel a little wave of nausea, because I can still taste the Frosties caught between my back teeth. Then she heads back to the kitchen and Uncle Des and I sit and watch *The Wizard of Oz* with the sound turned down low.

'Bloody hell, not this rubbish again!' says Uncle Des. 'Every Christmas, the bloody-Wizard-of-bloody-Oz.'

'You'd think they'd find something else to put on, wouldn't you?!' I say. Then Uncle Des asks about college.

'So what do you actually *do* all day, then?' It's a fair question I suppose, and one I've asked myself a couple of times.

'Lots of things – go to lectures, read, write essays – that kind of thing.'

'And that's all? Bloody hell – all right for some . . . !'

Change the subject. 'How about you, Uncle Des, how's your work?'

'Oh, bit quiet, Bri, bit quiet at the moment . . .' Uncle Des is in the building trade – conservatories, porches and patios – or at least he was until the divorce and the recession. Now the van sits idly in front of his house, and Des spends most of the time dismantling the engine, and then reassembling it again, not quite correctly, then dismantling it again. 'People don't seem to want extensions, not in a recession. It's a luxury really, porches and conservatories . . .' and he smooths his moustache down with his finger and thumb, and stares mournfully at *The Wizard of Oz*, those vaguely disturbing monkeys with the wings growing out of their backs, and I feel bad for asking him about work when I know it isn't going well. After a moment or two of staring blankly at the flying monkeys, he pulls himself out of it, with a visible physical effort, sitting up as straight as the settee will allow, and clapping his hands together. 'Right, how about a drink, then? It's Christmas after all. What's your poison, Bri?' then, conspiratorially '. . . apart from Brussels sprouts!'

I glance at the clock on the mantelpiece – it's 11.55. 'I'll have a lager please, Des,' and he bustles off into the kitchen, almost as if he lives here.

Over dinner, which we eat in the kitchen with Radio 2 playing, I decide to break the big news.

'By the way – I've got an announcement to make . . .'

Mum stops chewing. 'What?'

'Something that happened at university last term . . .'

'Oh, God, Brian . . .' says Mum, hand in front of her mouth.

'Don't worry, it's nothing bad . . .'

She glances at Uncle Des, then says nervously, 'Go on . . .'

'Well, I'm going to be on *University Challenge*!'

'What, that thing on telly?' says Uncle Des.

'Yep! I'm on the team!'

And Mum starts to laugh and laugh, and looks at Des, who's laughing too. 'Congratulations, Bri,' he says, and he puts his fork down to free up his hair-ruffling hand. 'That's brilliant news, really brilliant . . .'

'God, and what a *relief*,' says Mum, and takes a big swig of wine, and puts her hand on her chest to calm her heart.

'Why, what did you think I was going to say?'

'Well, to be honest sweetheart, I thought you were about to tell me that you were a homosexual!' she says, and starts to laugh again, and looks at Uncle Des, who starts to laugh again too, laughing so hard that I'm afraid that he's going to choke on his sprouts.

In the afternoon, after our attempt on the turkey, Uncle Des pours himself a large scotch and lights up a slim-line panatella, and Mum lights up a Rothman's, and we peer through the caramel fug at *Top of The Pops*. Uncle Des makes a growling noise every time the camera finds a scantily clad backing singer, and Mum laughs indulgently and slaps him on the wrist. She's methodically working her way through a large box of traditional chocolate liqueurs, biting the caps off the little chocolate bottles and trickling the various different spirits into her mouth, like a particularly dainty wino. This is a bizarre new development in Mum's boozing, and I'm not sure what to make of it, but keen not to be left behind, I continue work on my four-pack of lager. Because I'm a young hep-cat, and up with the current popular music scene, I help out in identifying the more obscure faces in the *Do They Know It's Christmas?* video, then we watch the Queen's Speech, then Uncle Des goes off to see his old mum up the road, but promises to be back at six o'clock for some leftovers and our traditional, infinitely long game of Monopoly, which Uncle Des will inevitably win, but only by nominating himself as banker and embezzling.

Then before it gets too dark Mum and I put our coats on, and head out. Mum takes my arm as we walk the mile or so to the cemetery to lay flowers on Dad's grave. The cold damp air makes her a little bit more pissed, and I have to lean down to hear what she's saying. She smells of sage and onion and Tia Maria.

As usual I stand with Mum for a while and say how the gravestone's still looking nice, then I go and stand a little way off and wait while Mum talks to Dad. I'm always a little uncomfortable waiting around without a book to read, so instead I try to identify the birds, but it's just rooks and magpies (of the family *corvidae*), starlings (*sturmus vulgaris*) and sparrows (*passer domesticus*) and I wonder why cemeteries always attract such miserable, morbid bloody birds, and after about ten minutes Mum finishes what she's got to say, touches the gravestone lightly, and walks away, head down, and takes my arm, not saying anything until she can control her breathing a little bit, and can speak normally again. It's dark now, but a couple of the local kids from the estate are riding the new BMXs that they got for Christmas in between the graves, slamming on their brakes and performing long, low sliding skids that send up waves of gravel. Mum, still with wet eyes and a little bit drunk from all the chocolate liqueurs, gets upset about this, and starts shouting at them – 'you shouldn't do that, not in a cemetery, show some respect' – and one of them flicks the V's and cycles past laughing and shouting back – 'fuck off, mind your own business, you silly cow'. I can feel Mum starting to cry again and I suddenly have this overwhelming desire to run after him, and grab hold of the hood of his parka and yank him off the back of his new bike, put my knee in his back and rub his stupid, leering face hard into the gravel, and see how long it takes for him to stop laughing. And then just as suddenly I wish that I was a long, long way away from here, lying still with someone, in a warm bed, falling asleep.

18

QUESTION: What is the name of the class of organic compounds with the general formula R-OH, where R represents an alkyl group made up of carbon and hydrogen, and OH represents one or more Hydroxyl groups?

ANSWER: Alcohol.

The Black Prince is a pub that caters specifically for the under-age drinker. At school we used to call it The Crèche, the rationale of the landlord being that anyone crafty enough to hide their school tie in their pocket was old enough to drink. On a Friday afternoon it looked like the set of *Grange Hill*, and you could barely move for satchels.

Outside of term-time, it's harder to imagine a more desolate place to meet for a drink. Brown, scabrous and dank, it's a little like sitting in someone's kidney, but at some point in the last five years it became traditional to meet here every Boxing Day night, and traditions are sacred. So here we are, me and Tone and Spencer, sat in a vinyl booth the colour of a blood clot, the first time we've met up since September. I'd been a little anxious about meeting up again, but Spencer seems genuinely pleased to see me. Tone does too, in his own special way, which basically involves rubbing his knuckles hard on the top of my head.

'What the *fuck* is going on with your hair?'

'What d'you mean?'

'Bit *bouffant*, isn't it?' Tone grabs my head by the ears, sniffs it like a melon. 'Are you wearing *mousse*?'

'No, I'm not wearing any *mousse*.' I am, in fact, wearing a little mousse.

'What's it called then, a haircut like that?'

'It's called a Brideshead,' says Spencer.

'It's called a short-back-and-sides. What do they call yours then, Tone?'

'It doesn't have a name, it just *is*. So what you drinking these days – port and lemon? Medium sherry? Sweet white wine? . . .' It's started, and I haven't even taken my donkey jacket off yet.

'A pint of lager please, Tone.'

'*Special* lager?'

'Go on then. Special lager.'

'Special lager' is lager-with-a-gin-top. Part of the landlord's educational remit here is to nurture experimentation and innovation, and he won't bat an eyelid, no matter what repulsive combination you order. Besides, lager-with-a-gin-top is actually pretty grown-up by Black Prince standards. Anything that doesn't taste of coconut or mint or aniseed counts as refined here.

This is the longest I've gone without seeing Spencer since we were both twelve years old, and I'm very anxious that there shouldn't be any awkward silences. But here it is. Silence. Spencer tries to fill it by flicking his beer mat up in the air and catching it, while I reach for the matchbox, in case there's something to read on the back of it.

'So. I thought you said you'd be down at weekends?' he says finally.

'Well, I was going to, but it got a bit busy.'

'Busy. Right.'

'Good Christmas?' I ask.

'The usual. Same as last year's, same as next year's. You?'

'Oh, you know. The same.' Tone is back with the three special lagers. 'So . . . what's new?' I ask.

'What's "*new*"?' says Spencer.

'At work, I mean . . .'

'What work?' he asks, with a wink. As far as I know, Spencer's still signing on and doing cash-in-hand night-shifts.

'At the petrol station . . . ?'

'Well, we've got a very interesting free-set-of-wine-glasses promotion on at the moment, that's causing quite a stir, and the price of four-star went up the other day, that was pretty thrilling, too. So all in all, I haven't been this excited since I had that all-chocolate Kit-Kat. Oh, and last week a bunch of students drove off without paying . . .'

'I hope you chased after them,' slurs Tone.

'Well, no, Tony, I didn't, on account of them being in a car and me being on foot. Besides, I only get one pound eighty an hour. They'd have to pay me a lot more than that before I break into a run.'

'How do you know they were students?' I ask, taking the bait.

'Well, they were very badly dressed for one thing. Long scarves, little round glasses, bad haircuts . . .' He smiles conspiratorially at Tone, then back at me. 'How's your eyesight, Bri?' This is a running gag between Tone and Spencer, who believe that I lied to my optician just to get spectacles.

'Fine, thank you, Spence,' and I decide to go and get some crisps.

On the way to the bar, I think for a moment about heading for the door and walking out. I love Spence and Tone, Spencer especially, and I think it's mutual, though God knows we'd never actually use the L-word, not sober, anyway. But for my eighteenth birthday Spencer and Tone tied me naked to the end of Southend pier and force-fed me laxatives, so it's a love that expresses itself in unconventional ways.

When I come back they've started talking about Tone's sex life, so I know I'm going to be in the clear for the next hour or so. Barmaids, hairdressers, teachers, school friends' sisters, or mothers even, no one seems immune to Tone's Nordic charms. The list is endless, and the detail is explicit, and after a while I start to feel I need a bath, but he's obviously got something going for him, Tone, something other than sensitivity or tenderness or consideration. It's far easier to imagine that, after making love, he rubs his knuckles very hard on his lover's head. I wonder, but don't ask, if Tone's practising safe sex, but suspect that he thinks safe sex is for wimps, in the same way that safety-belts and crash-helmets are for wimps. If Tone was thrown from a plane, he'd still think parachutes were for wimps.

'How about you then, Brian, any action?'

'Not really.' This sounds a bit feeble, so I add, nonchalantly, 'There is this girl, Alice, and she's invited me to stay with her tomorrow, at her cottage, so . . .'

'Her *cottage*?' says Spencer. 'What is she? A milkmaid?'

'You know, a house, in the country, her parents' . . .'

'So you're shagging her then?' asks Tone.

'It's platonic.'

'What's platonic mean then?' asks Spencer, even though he knows.

'It means she won't let him shag her,' says Tone.

'I'm not "shagging" her because I don't want to "shag" her, not yet anyway. If I wanted to, then I would.'

'Though recent evidence would suggest that not to be the case,' says Spencer.

Tone seems to find this incredibly funny, so I decide to retreat again, and go and get some more gin-and-lagers; I stumble slightly as I leave the booth, so I know they're beginning to do their work. Keenly aware of how pocket money doesn't stretch very far these days. The Black Prince is also incredibly cheap, and it's possible for three young men to get incoherent, aggressive, sentimental and violent, and still have change from a tenner.

When I sit back down, Spencer asks me, 'So what do you actually *do* all day then?'

'Talk. Read. Go to lectures. Argue.'

'It's not proper work though, is it?'

'Not work. *Experience*.'

'Yeah, well, I'm very happy in the University of Life, thank you very much,' says Tone.

'I applied for the University of Life. Didn't get the grades,' says Spencer.

'Not the first time you've said that, is it?' I say.

'Obviously not. So what about politics?' The question feels like being poked with a stick.

'What about it?'

'Been on any good demonstrations lately?'

'One or two.'

'What for?' asks Tone.

The sensible thing would be to change the subject, but I don't see why I should compromise my political views just for the sake of an easy life, so I tell them.

'Apartheid . . .'

'For or against?' asks Spencer.

'. . . the NHS, Gay Rights . . .'

Tone perks up at this. 'What *bastard*'s been trying to take away your rights?'

'Not *my* rights. There's a move by the Tory council to try and prevent schools from portraying homosexuality in a positive light; it's legislated homophobia . . .'

'Is that what they do, then?' asks Spencer.

'Who?'

'Schools. Because I don't remember anyone teaching it at our school.'

'Well, no, they didn't, but . . .'

'So why's it such a big deal, then?'

'Yeah, I mean *you* turned out gay without being taught it,' says Tone.

'Yeah, well, that's true, Tone, that's a very good point . . .'

'Well, I think it's a scandal,' says Spencer, with mock

indignation. 'I think it *must* be taught. Tuesday afternoons. Double Gayness . . .'

'Sorry, miss, I forgot my *hom*-work . . .'

'*Gay*-levels! . . .'

We all try and think of another joke and can't, so instead Spencer says, 'Well, I think it's great that you're making a stand about something important, I really do. Something that affects us all. It's like when you joined CND. Have we had a nuclear holocaust since? Nope.'

Tone lurches to his feet. 'So. Same again then?'

'No gin in it this time, please Tone,' I say, knowing that he'll put gin in it.

After he's gone, Spencer and I sit and fold up the empty crisp packets, into little triangles, knowing this is not quite over yet. The gin has made me bad-tempered, and sulky; what's the point of coming out with your mates if all they're going to do is take the piss? Eventually I say, 'So what would you protest against then, Spence?'

'Don't know. Your haircut?'

'Seriously.'

'Believe me, it is serious . . .'

'But really, there must be something you'd actually make a stand about.'

'Don't know. Lots of things. Maybe not gay rights, though . . .'

'It's not just gay rights, it's other stuff, things that affect you too, things like cut-backs in the welfare state, cuts in dole, unemployment . . .'

'Well, thanks for that, Brian mate, I'm glad you're making a stand on my behalf, and I look forward to receiving the extra cash.'

There's nothing I can say to that. I try something more conciliatory, in a mate-y tone. 'Hey, you should come up and visit me next year!'

'Sort of like a Careers Day?'

'No, just, you know, for a laugh . . .' and this is the point where I should change the subject to sex or films or TV or something. Instead I say, 'Why aren't you re-taking your A-levels anyway?'

'Ummmm, because I don't want to . . . ?'

'But it's such a waste . . .'

'Waste? Fuck off it's a *waste*! Reading poetry and wanking into your sock for three years, *that*'s a waste.'

'But you wouldn't have to do Literature, you could do something else, something vocational . . .'

'Can we change the subject, Brian?'

'Alright . . .'

'. . . because I get enough fucking careers advice at the DHSS, and I don't necessarily want it down the pub on fucking Boxing Day . . .'

'Alright then. Let's change the subject.' As an olive branch, I suggest, 'Quiz machine?'

'Absolutely. Quiz machine.'

The Black Prince has invested in one of those new computerised quiz machines, and we take our fresh pints over to it, balance them on top.

'Who plays Cagney in TV's *Cagney and* . . . ?'

'C – Sharon Gless,' I say.

Correct.

'The Battle of Trafalgar was in . . . ?'

'B – Eighteen-oh-five,' I say.

'The nickname of Norwich City FC is . . . ?'

'A – The Canaries,' says Tone.

Correct.

Maybe this would be a good time to mention The Challenge . . .

'What did Davros create?'

'A – The Daleks,' I say.

Correct.

'Whose original surname was Schicklegruber?'

'B – Hitler,' I say.

Correct.

I could just drop it into conversation, casually; 'By the way guys, did I tell you? I'm going to be on University Challenge!'

'Which American holds the record for most Olympic . . . ?'

'D – Mark Spitz,' says Tone.

Correct.

'You know, University Challenge, *on the telly . . . ?' Maybe they wouldn't take the piss. Maybe they'd think it was a bit of fun – well done Bri – we are old mates after all . . .*

'One more question, we win two quid!'

'Alright, concentrate . . .'

I'm definitely going to tell them about The Challenge . . .

'*Star Wars* was nominated for how many Oscars?'

'B – Four,' I say.

'D – None,' says Tone.

'I'm pretty sure it's four,' I say.

'No way. It's a trick question. It didn't get any . . .'

'Not *win*, nominated . . .'

'It wasn't nominated either, trust me Spence . . .'

'It was four, Spence, I swear it, B – four . . .'

And we're both looking at Spencer now, pleadingly, 'choose me, please, me not him, I'm right, I swear, choose me, there's two quid at stake here' and, yes, he chooses me, he trusts me, he presses B.

Incorrect. The correct answer's D – Ten.

'You see!' shouts Tone.

'You were wrong, too!' I shout back.

'You twat,' says Tone.

'*You're* the twat,' I say.

'You're both twats!' says Spencer.

'You're the twat, you twat,' says Tone.

'No, mate, it's you that's the twat,' says Spencer and I decide that maybe I won't tell them about The Challenge after all.

The fourth pint of gin and lager makes us sentimental and nostalgic about things that happened six months ago, and we sit and fondly reminisce about people we didn't really like and fun we didn't really have, and was Mrs Clarke the PE teacher really a lesbian, and exactly how fat was Barry Pringle, and then, finally, finally, they call last orders.

Outside The Black Prince, it's started raining. Spencer suggests maybe going to Manhattan's nite-club, but we're not *that* drunk. Tone nicked a new video recorder for Christmas, and wants to watch *Friday The 13th* for the eighty-ninth time, but I'm too depressed and drunk, and decide to head home, in the opposite direction.

'You around for New Year?' asks Tone.

'Don't think so. I think I'm staying with Alice.'

'All right mate, well see you around,' and he smacks me on the back and stumbles off.

But Spencer comes over and hugs me, his breath smelling of lager with a gin-top, and whispers wetly in my ear, 'Listen, Brian mate, you really are my mate, my best mate, and it's great that you're out there, meeting all these different people, and having all these experiences, and new ideas, and staying in *cottages* and everything, but just promise me something, will you?' He leans in really close. 'Promise me you're not turning into a complete cunt.'

19

QUESTION: If a burn that affects only the epidermis is defined as first degree, what is the term for a burn that reaches the subcutaneous tissue?

ANSWER: A third-degree burn.

No matter how predictable, banal and listless the rest of my life might be, you can guarantee that there'll always be something interesting going on with my skin.

When you're a kid, skin is just this uniform pink covering: hairless, poreless, odourless, efficient. Then one day you see that microscope cross-section in the O-level biology text-books – the follicles, the sebaceous glands, the subcutaneous fat, and you realise there are so many things that can go wrong. And they have gone wrong. From the age of thirteen onwards it's been an on-going medicated soap opera of blemishes and scars and in-growing hairs, spreading from region to region, taking on different forms, from discreetly corked pores behind the ears to lit-from-inside boils on the tip of the nose, the geometric centre of my face. In retaliation, I've experimented with camouflage techniques, but all the skin-tone creams that I've tried are a sort of albino-pink and tend to actually draw attention to the spots as effectively as a circle drawn with a magic-marker.

I didn't really mind this in my adolescence. Well, I *minded* of course, but I accepted it as part of growing up; something unpleasant but inevitable. But I'm *nineteen* now, an adult by most definitions, and I'm starting to feel persecuted. This morning, standing in my dressing gown under the glare of the 100 watt bulb, things are looking particularly bad. I feel as if I'm leaking gin and lager and peanut oil from my T-zone, and there's something new, a hard pad of matter under the skin, about the size of a peanut, that moves around when I touch it. I decide to call out the big guns. The Astringents. On the back of one of them is written '*Warning – may bleach fabrics*' and there's a momentary anxiety that something that can burn a hole in a sofa might not be a good thing to apply to your face, but I do it anyway. Then I apply a final wash of Dettol, just for luck. After I've finished the bathroom smells like a hospital, but my face at least feels taut and scrubbed, as if I've been through a car-wash strapped to the bonnet of the car.

There's a knock on the door and Mum enters, carrying my best vintage white linen granddad shirt, freshly ironed, and a foil parcel.

'It's some gammon and turkey, for your friend.'

'I think food's laid on, Mum. Besides they're all vegetarians.'

'It's *white* meat . . .'

'I don't think it's the colour that's the issue, Mum . . .'

'But what are you going to eat?'

'I'll eat what they eat!'

'What, *vegetables*?'

'Yes!'

'You haven't eaten a vegetable for fifteen years! It's a wonder you don't have rickets.'

'Rickets is Vitamin D2, Mum, scurvy is Vitamin C, lack of fresh fruit.'

'So do you want to take some fresh fruit with you then?'

'No, really, Mum, I'll be fine, I don't need fruit or meat.'

'You might as well take it, for the train journey. It'll only go off if you leave it.' For my mother, the *true* meaning of Christmas has always been Cold Meats so I give in, and take the foil parcel from her. It weighs about the same as a human head. She follows me into my bedroom, to check that I'm definitely putting it into my suitcase, like a sort of motherly customs official, and I count myself lucky she's not making me pack the sprouts.

She's sat on my bed now, and starts neatly folding my granddad shirt.

'I don't know why you wear these horrible old things . . .'

'Because I like them maybe? . . .'

'Talk about lamb dressed as mutton . . .'

'I don't criticise what *you* wear . . .'

'Boxer shorts! How long have you been wearing boxers?'

'Ever since I started buying my own underwear . . .'

'Y-fronts out of fashion are they?'

'I have absolutely no idea, Mum . . .'

'I thought you preferred those cotton brief things . . .'

'I mix. It depends . . .'

'Depends on what?'

'Mum . . . !'

'So how long are you staying with your girlfriend for?'

'Don't know. Three days, maybe four. And she's not my girlfriend.'

'So are you coming back?'

'No, I think I'm going straight back to college, Mum.' I don't know why, but I've taken to calling it 'college', maybe because 'university' still sounds snooty to me.

'So you're not here for New Year?'

'I doubt it.'

'You're with her?'

'I think so.' I hope so.

'Oh. That's a shame . . .' She's using her martyr voice. The trick here is not to catch her eye. I concentrate on my packing. 'And are you back here afterwards?'

'I can't really. I've got work to do.'

'You could work here . . .'

'I can't really . . .'

'I won't disturb you . . .'

'I need special books, Mum . . .'

'So you *definitely* won't be here for New Year?'

'Don't think so Mum, no.' From behind me comes an exhalation so mournful that I fully expect to turn around and find her lying dead on the bedroom floor. Irritated now, I say, 'You'll be out getting smashed with Uncle Des anyway, it's not like we'll see each other . . .'

'I know, it's just it's the first time you won't be here, that's all. I just don't like rattling round in the house all by myself . . .'

'Well it was bound to happen one day, Mum.' But we're both thinking the same thing. It shouldn't have happened, not like this, not just yet. There's a silence, and then I say, 'I'm going to get dressed now, Mum, so if you wouldn't mind . . . ?'

She sighs, gets up off the bed.

'It's nothing I haven't seen before.'

Recently too. New Year's Eve 1984/85, I came home so drunk that I managed to vomit in my own bed. I have a mercifully vague memory of my mother helping me into the bath at dawn, and rinsing off the Pernod and lager and half-digested chicken-and-chips with the shower attachment. That was just twelve months ago. She has never mentioned it since and I like to believe that maybe it didn't really happen, but I'm pretty sure it did.

Sometimes I think there aren't enough psychiatrists *in the world . . .*

Mum's cheered up a bit by the time I kiss her goodbye on the doorstep, though she's still trying to thrust groceries on me. I reject a loaf of Mighty White, a litre of Dry Blackthorn, a pack of mince pies, a 250ml pot of UHT single cream, a 5lb bag of spuds, a packet of Jaffa Cakes, a bottle of peppermint flavour Iced Magic, and a two-litre bottle of sunflower oil, and every no-thank-you is a knife between my mother's shoulder blades. Damage done, I head off, dragging my suitcase along the road, and not looking back in case she's started crying. On the way to the train station I stop to get a fiver out of the cashpoint, then stop off at the newsagents to buy some wine for the Harbinsons. I want to get something nice, so in the end blow three quid on the one that comes in its own carafe.

20

QUESTION: What socio-economic term originally described the artisan occupants of walled towns in eleventh century France, occupying a position between the peasants and the landlords?

ANSWER: The Bourgeoisie.

On the train from Southend I look out the window at the wet, empty streets, the handful of shops open in a half-hearted take-it-or-leave-it way. The four days in between Boxing Day and New Year's Eve are surely the longest and nastiest in the year – a sort of bloated, bastard Sunday. August Bank Holiday's the worst though. I fully expect to die at about two-thirty in the afternoon on an August Bank Holiday. Dead of terminal ennui.

I change at Shenfield, where lunch is a can of Lucozade, a packet of Hula Hoops and a Twix bought from the windswept newsagents, and then there's just time to check how my face is healing in the station toilets' mirror before I'm back on the train.

Leaving the suburbs and heading into Suffolk the rain turns to snow. Snow like this rarely seems to reach Southend. The combination of street lights and estuary air and massed central heating tends to turn it into a sort of cold, damp dandruff, but here, through fields as the sun sets, it looks fantastically thick and clean. I read the first page of Ezra Pound's *Cantos* five times without understanding a word, then give up and look at the landscape. Soulfully. Ten minutes from the station I pull on my overcoat and scarf and check the reflection in the train window. Collar up or collar down? I'm aiming for a sort of Graham-Greene, *Third-Man* look, but getting an Ultravox video.

Five minutes away, and I'm practising what I'm going to say when I see Alice again. I haven't been this nervous since Jesus in *Godspell* when I had to take my top off to be crucified. I can't even seem to *smile* properly; a lop-sided grin with my mouth closed makes me look like a stroke victim, but when I open my mouth my teeth are a jumbled cream-and-black, like a bag of Scrabble tiles. A lifetime of fresh fruit and vegetables means that Alice Harbinson has perfect teeth. I imagine her dentist looking into her mouth and just weeping at the sheer, pure, snowy splendour of it all.

As the train pulls into the station, Alice is waiting at the far end of the platform, huddled up against the snow in an expensive-looking long black overcoat that almost touches the ground, her head wrapped in a grey woollen scarf, and I wonder where she's put her balalaika. If she doesn't quite break into a run when she sees me, she at least walks a little faster, and as her face comes into focus I can see she's grinning, and then laughing, her skin whiter, her lips redder and there's something softer and warmer about her away from college, as if she's off duty, and she throws her arms around me, and says she's *missed* me, and she's *so* excited I'm there, and we're going to have *so* much fun, and for a moment this feels like perfect happiness, here on a country train station in the snow with Alice. Until I see, over her shoulder, this dark, handsome, moody man who I assume must be Alice's dad. Heathcliff in a wax-jacket.

If I'd had a forelock I'd have tugged it, but instead I offer him my hand. Recently I've been experimenting with shaking hands, because it's what I imagine grown men are meant to do, but Mr Harbinson just looks at me as if I've done something incredibly un-cool and eighteenth century, like curtseying or something. Eventually he takes the hand, squeezes it just hard enough to show that he could fracture my skull if he chose to, then turns and walks away.

As I drag my bags to the green Land-Rover in the station car park, Alice walks on ahead with her arms looped around her dad's neck, like he's her boyfriend or something. If I put my arm around my mum's neck like that she'd call social services, but Mr Harbinson seems to take it in his stride, puts his arm round Alice's waist and pulls her towards him. I trot up alongside.

'Brian's our secret weapon on the team. He's the boy-genius I've been telling you about,' says Alice.

'Well, I'm not sure if *genius* is the right word,' I say.

'No, I'm *certain* it's not,' says Mr Harbinson.

Driving through the country lanes. I sit in the back amidst the muddy wellingtons and walking boots and sodden Ordnance Survey maps, as Alice keeps up a monologue about all the parties she's been to and the old friends she's seen, and I scrutinise every word, just to check for the presence of Romantic Interlopers, a hot young actor maybe, or some lightly muscled sculptor called Max or Jack or Serge. But the coast seems clear, so far anyway. Maybe she's censoring herself in front of her father. I doubt it though. I think Alice is one of those strange people who behaves exactly the same way in front of her parents as she does in front of her friends.

Mr Harbinson listens and drives in silence, quietly emanating a subtle buzz of hostility. He's absolutely massive, and I try to imagine why someone who makes art documentaries for BBC2 should have the physique of a brickie. And hairy, the kind of man who shaves his cheeks twice a day, but obviously terrifyingly intelligent. It's almost as if he was raised by wolves, but wolves who knew the value of a decent college education. He also seems impossibly young, good-looking and cool to be a dad, as if having a family is something he slipped in between Hendrix concerts and LSD trips.

Eventually we arrive at Blackbird Cottage. Except 'cottage' isn't really the word. It's huge and beautiful, the kind of house that 'rambles', a series of converted barns and farmhouses, almost a whole village, knocked together to accommodate the country residence of the Harbinson family; all the luxury of a stately home, without any of the politically inconvenient aristocratic connotations. In the snow, it's like an animated Christmas card. There's even smoke coming out of the chimney, and it's all very rural and nineteenth century, except for the sports car, Alice's 2CV, and a tarpaulin-covered swimming-pool where the cowshed used to be. In fact any notion of practical, agricultural labour has long since been swept away, and even the dogs seem middle class; two Labradors who come bounding up as if to say '*so* pleased to meet you, tell us *all* about yourself'. I wouldn't be surprised to find out they have Grade Four Piano.

'Meet Mingus and Coltrane!' says Alice.

'Hello Mingus and Coltrane.' There's a slight lapse in dog etiquette when they start snuffling at the cold meats in my suitcase as we cross the farmyard. I hoist the bag up into my arms.

'What d'you think?'

'It's lovely. Bigger than I expected.'

'Mum and Dad bought it for about five guineas or something, back in the sixties. Come in and meet Rose,' and it takes me a second to realise Rose is her mum.

There's that old chauvinistic cliché about women turning into their mothers when you marry them, but in the case of Alice's mother, I wouldn't mind. Not that I'm going to marry Alice or anything, but Mrs Harbinson is *beautiful*. When we come into the kitchen, a vaulted barn of copper and oak, she's stood at the sink listening to *The Archers*, and for a second I think Julie Christie's scrubbing the carrots; she's small, with soft wrinkles round blue eyes, and a soft blonde perm. I march forward across the bare flagstones, arm extended like a tin soldier, determined to persevere with the handshake thing.

'So this is the Brian I've heard so much about,' she says, and smiles, and waggles the tip of my finger with her muddy hands, and smiles at me, and I have a momentary flashback to a teacher I had a crush on when I was nine years old.

'Very pleased to meet you, Mrs Harbinson.' I *sound* like a nine-year-old.

'Oh, please don't call me Mrs Harbinson, it makes me feel so old. Call me Rose.'

As she bends forward to kiss me on the cheek I have a reflex action to lick my lips, so the peck on her cheek is a bit too moist, and there's this exaggerated smacking noise that seems to bounce off the flagstones. I can actually see my saliva glistening just below her eye. She discreetly wipes it away with the back of her hand before it can evaporate, and pretends to be adjusting her perm. Then Mr Harbinson looms between us, and kisses the other cheek, the dry one, proprietorially.

'And what shall I call you, Mr Harbinson?' I ask, cheerily.

'Call me Mr Harbinson.'

'*Michael!* Don't be mean,' says Rose.

'. . . or *Sir*. You can call me Sir . . .'

'Just ignore him,' says Alice.

'I bought you some wine,' I say, tugging the bottle out of my bag and handing it to him. Mr Harbinson looks at it as if I've just handed him a carafe of my own piss.

'Oh, thank you *so* much, Brian! You can come again!' says Rose. Mr Harbinson doesn't look so sure.

'Come on, I'll show you your room,' says Alice, taking me by the arm, and I follow her up the stairs, leaving Mr and Mrs Harbinson whispering behind me.

In the maisonette on Archer Road there's a point about halfway up the stairs where, if you crane your neck ever so slightly, you can actually see into every room in the house.

Blackbird Cottage is not like this at all. It's massive. My room, Alice's old room, is at the very top of the house, under ancient oak beams, in the East Wing or something. One wall is taken up completely with enlarged childhood photos of Alice; in a flowery pinafore-dress baking scones; picking blackberries in a pair of dungarees; playing Olivia in a school production of *Twelfth Night,* and, I guess, *The Good Woman of Schezuan* with a drawn-on moustache, and dressed in a black bin-liner as a rather unconvincing 'punk-rocker' for a fancy-dress party, V's flicked demurely at the camera. There's a polaroid of her parents in their twenties, proud owners of one of the very first bean-bags, looking like members of Fleetwood Mac, in matching embroidered waistcoats and smoking what may or may not be cigarettes. Shelves of children's books indicate that Alice was obviously something pretty big in the Puffin Club; Tove Jansson, Ingrid Lindgren, Eric Kastner, Herge, Goscinny, Uderzo, Saint-Exupery – world literature for tots – and, somewhat incongruously, a broken-backed paperback edition of *Lace*. An A-level art montage of Madonnas from the Uffizi and a cut-out Snoopy comic-strip. Framed certificates proclaim that Alice Harbinson can swim 1,000 metres, play the oboe up to grade 6 and the piano up to grade 8, simultaneously for all I know. My bedroom is The National Museum of Alice Harbinson. I don't know how she expects me to get any sleep.

'D'you think you'll be alright here?' she says.

'Oh, I think I can manage.' She watches me scanning over the photographs, with no pretence of embarrassment or false modesty. Here is a record of my life – good, isn't it? At four, she was all you could wish for in a four-year-old, at fourteen she was just fine, thank you very much.

'No use looking for my diary, I've hidden it. And if you get cold, which you will do, there's a blanket in the wardrobe. Here, let me help you unpack. So what d'you want to do tonight?'

'Oh, I don't know, just hang out. *Some Like It Hot*'s on telly.'

'Sorry, no telly here.'

'Really?'

'Dad doesn't approve of TV.'

'But he's a TV producer!'

'We've got a telly in London, but he thinks it's wrong in the country. What's that look for?'

'Oh, I was just thinking – three houses, one telly. With most people it's the other way round.'

'No need to get all *Socialist Worker*, Brian, no one's listening. Boxer shorts, eh?' She's holding my underpants. A mild erotic frisson fills the air between us, and I'm profoundly grateful to Mum for ironing them. 'I had you down as a tanga-briefs man.' I'm trying to work out if this is a good or bad thing, when Alice squeals, 'Oh my God! What's *this* . . . ?'

She's found the foil parcel of assorted meats in my bag. I try to snatch it off her.

'Oh, that's just my mum's packing . . .'

'Let me see . . .'

'It's nothing, really.'

'Contraband!' She tugs the parcel open. 'Meat? You've smuggled in your own supply of meat!'

'Mum's worried I won't get enough protein.'

'Give us a bit then – I'm gasping.' She takes a piece of pallid boiled bacon, and flops onto the bed. 'Hmmmm. Bit dry.'

'That's Mum's special recipe. She cooks it overnight, slices it, leaves it on a radiator, then finishes it off with a hairdryer.'

'Well don't let Rose catch you with it. She'll be mortified. Blackbird Cottage is a strictly meat-free zone.'

'So what do Mingus and Coltrane eat?'

'Same as us. Vegetables, muesli, rice, pasta . . .' They feed their dogs *pasta*. 'What have you got there?'

'Your Christmas present.' I hold out the gift-wrapped LP. 'It's a tennis racket.'

She glances at the postcard, a provocatively romantic Chagall sellotaped to the album. I'd laboured long and hard over the message, and gone through several drafts, before coming up with the eloquent and emotive; '*To Alice, my newest, bestest (sp.?!?) friend, all my love always Brian*'. I'm particularly pleased with the way the wryly humorous '*(sp.?!?)*' comments on the '*bestest friend/love*' element without necessarily undermining the sincerity of the emotion, but in the end she doesn't even bother to read it before she starts tearing off the wrapping paper.

'Joni Mitchell! *Blue*!'

'Oh no, you've got it, haven't you?'

'Only about *six* copies. You were spot on though. I *love* Joni. I actually lost my virginity listening to Joni Mitchell.'

'Not "Big Yellow Taxi", I hope.'

'*Court and Spark* actually . . .' I might have guessed. 'How about you?'

'My virginity? Can't remember. It was either Chopin's *Funeral March* or *Geoff Love and His Orchestra Play Big War Themes*. "The Dambusters' March", I think. Followed by an eerie silence.'

She laughs and hands it back. 'Sorry. Have you still got the receipt?'

'I think so. Is there something specific I should swap it for?'

'Surprise me. No Kate Bush though, please. I'll let you finish unpacking.'

'When's tea?'

'Dinner's in half an hour.' On the way out she hugs me once again. 'I am *so* glad you're here. We are going to have so much fun, I *promise* you.'

After she's gone, I put the newly ironed granddad shirts on wooden hangers, enjoying the feeling of residency and permanence. If I play my cards right, I could actually still be here on New Year's Day. Even the 2nd, or 3rd maybe . . .

Opening the wardrobe, I half expect to find Narnia.

In the end, protein turns out to be the least of my worries. Dinner is nut-roast. I'd heard about nut-roast, and sort of always thought it was a joke, but here it is, a pile of luke-warm, gritty cake with vegetarian cheese melted on top, my first experience of nuts as something other than a bar snack. It sits on my plate like a worm-cast. I wonder what the dogs are having?

'How's your nut-roast, Brian?'

'Delicious, thank you, Rose.' From somewhere I've picked up the notion that it's polite to use the other person's name a lot – 'yes Rose, no Rose, lovely Rose' – but I think it's making me sound a bit Uriah Heep-y. Best follow it up with a little humour. 'It's my first experience of nuts as something other than a bar snack!'

'Shut your stupid, ugly face and keep your filthy, plebby hands off my beautiful daughter, you unctuous little prick,' says Mr Harbinson. Well, he doesn't *say* it, but he *looks* it.

Rose just fingers her perm, and smiles, and asks, 'Okay with those courgettes?'

'Absolutely!' In actual fact I've never eaten a courgette in my life, but just to underline my enthusiasm I pop a forkful of the damp, watery discs into my mouth, and grin idiotically. Like all green vegetables, it tastes of what it is, boiled cellulose, but so keen am I to please Rose that it's all I can do to stop myself rubbing my belly and saying 'hmmmm . . .' I wash the pond-weed taste away with some wine. There's no sign of my carafe, and I assume that it's been taken outside and shot. Or maybe the dogs are having it with their pasta, and some garlic-bread. This wine, though, is so syrupy and warm that it feels as if I should be sipping it from a plastic 5ml spoon.

'Your first time in Suffolk, Brian?'

'I've been once before. On a mountaineering holiday!'

'Really? But isn't it terribly flat?' says Rose.

'I was misinformed!'

Mr Harbinson exhales loudly through his nose.

'I don't understand. Who told you . . . ?' says Rose.

'Brian's *joking*, Mum,' says Alice.

'Oh, I see, of course!'

It's clear that I should stop trying to be funny, but have yet to work out what the alternative is. Sensing the need for assistance, Alice turns to me, puts her hand on my arm; 'If you wanted to see something really funny, Brian, you should have been here yesterday.'

'Why, what happened yesterday?'

Rose is blushing. 'Oh Alice, darling, can we keep it to ourselves please?'

'She can tell him,' growls Mr Harbinson.

'But it's *so* embarrassing! . . .'

'Tell me!' I say, joining in the fun.

'But I feel *so* foolish,' says Rose.

'Well . . .' says Alice '. . . we had some friends round, like we always do on Boxing Day, and we were playing charades, and it was my turn, and I was trying to do *Last Year At Marienbad* for Mummy, and she was getting *so* frantic and over-excited, and shouting *so* hard, that her *cap* popped out and landed right in our next-door neighbour's glass of wine!'

And everyone's laughing, even Mr Harbinson, and the atmosphere is *so* fun and adult and amusing and irreverent that I say, 'You mean you weren't wearing any underwear?!?'

Everyone is silent.

'I'm sorry?' asks Rose.

'Your cap. When it popped out. How did it get . . . past your . . . underpants?'

Mr Harbinson puts down his knife and fork, swallows his mouthful, turns to me and says, very slowly, 'Actually, Brian, I think Alice was referring to her mother's *dental* cap.'

Shortly afterwards, we all go up to bed.

I'm in the bathroom, splashing my face with cold water, when Alice knocks on the door.

'Hold on two seconds' I say, though I'm not sure why; I'm fully dressed, and there's not much I can do about my appearance in two seconds, short of wrapping a towel round my head.

I open the door, Alice steps in, closes it carefully behind her and says, very slowly and seriously, 'D'you mind if I say something – something personal?'

'Sure, go ahead!' I make a mental calculation, and decide that there's a one-in-three chance that she's going to ask me to make love to her tonight.

'Well . . . it's a real mistake to scrub your face hard with a flannel like that. You'll only bleed and spread the infection . . .'

'Oh . . .'

'And you'll scar too.'

'O-kay . . .'

'Now, do you boil-wash your flannels?'

'Well, no . . .'

'Because the flannel's probably part of the problem . . .'

'Right, okay . . .'

'I wouldn't use a flannel at all, if I were you, flannels are absolutely *crawling*, just water and a basic, non-perfumed soap . . .' How can I get out of this conversation? '. . . and not necessarily a harsh medicated soap, because they're generally far too astringent . . .' It isn't even a conversation, it's me waiting for her to stop talking. '. . . And you shouldn't use astringent creams either, they're effective in the short run, but in the long run they just make the sebaceous glands more active . . .' By now I'm eyeing the bathroom window, wondering whether or not to throw myself out of it. Alice must notice this, because she says 'I'm sorry. Do you mind me saying all this?'

'Not at all. You're very knowledgeable though. If "skin-care" comes up on *University Challenge*, we'll be laughing!'

'Oh, I've upset you, haven't I?'

'No, I just don't think there's much I can do about it, that's all. I think it must be the onset of puberty! All the hormones. Any day now I'll start taking an interest in girls!' Alice smiles indulgently, then goes to give me a sisterly kiss goodnight, her eyes momentarily scanning my face, trying to find somewhere safe to land.

Shivering in bed later, lying on my back and waiting for my face to dry so I don't get blood on the pillow, I carefully evaluate my strategy for tomorrow and, after much consideration, decide that my strategy is to be less of a twat. This will not come easily, but it's absolutely vital that she gets to see the Real Me. The problem is, I'm starting to suspect this notion that there's this wise, smart, funny, kind, brave Real Me running around somewhere out there is a bit of a fallacy. Like the Yeti; if no one ever actually sees him properly, why should anyone believe that he actually exists?

21

QUESTION: A legal writ that demands the appearance of a party in front of a court or judge, the Latin term 'habeas corpus' might be translated as . . . ?
ANSWER: You should have the body.

When I wake up the next morning I'm so cold that for a moment I think Mr Harbinson must have moved me outside in the night. Why is it that the posher people are, the colder their house? And it's not just the cold, it's the dirt too; the dog hair, the dusty books, the muddy boots, the fridges that reek of sour milk and putrescent cheese and decaying kitchen-garden vegetables. I swear the Harbinsons' fridge has a top-soil. They probably have to mow it in the summer. But maybe that's the definition of true, authentic upper-middle-class status, the ability to be cold and filthy with complete self-confidence. That, and the little washbasins in every bedroom. I splash my face with the icy water, put the copy of *Lace* back on the bookshelf, and head downstairs.

Radio 4 is broadcasting loudly from hidden speakers, and Alice is lying on the sofa, under a blanket of Blue Peter Dogs, reading.

'Morning!' I say.

'Hiya' she mutters, engrossed in her book.

I squeeze in next to a dog.

'What ya' readin'?' I say in an amusing voice. She shows me the cover. '*One Hundred Years of Solitude* – sounds like my sex-life!'

'Sleep well?' she says, when she finally realises that I'm not going to go away.

'Amazingly, thank you.'

'Cold?'

'Oh, only a little.'

'That's because you're used to central heating. It's very bad for you, central heating, numbs the senses . . .'

And as if to underline her point, Mr Harbinson strolls nonchalantly across the living room. He is naked.

'Morning!' he says, nakedly.

'Morning!' Even with my eyes staring fixedly at the top of the fireplace, it's clear that he's either a very hairy man, or is wearing a black, mohair jump-suit.

'Tea in the pot, Alice?' he says, nudely.

'Help yourself.'

And he bends down beside her, *bends down from the waist*, and pours himself a cup, then strides upstairs, *taking the steps three at a time*. When it's finally safe to look, I ask, 'So. Is that. Fairly. Normal. Then?'

'What?'

'The naked-dad thing.'

'Absolutely.'

'Oh.'

'Not *shocked* are you?' She says, eyes narrowed.

'Well, you know . . .'

'You must have seen your dad naked.'

'Well, not since he died, no.'

'No, of course, I'm sorry, I forgot, but *before* he died, you must have seen him naked.'

'Well, maybe. But it's not how I choose to remember him.'

'And what about your mum?'

'God, no! So do *you* go naked in front of your dad then?'

'Only when we're having sex,' says Alice, then clicks her tongue and rolls her eyes. 'Of course I do, we all do. We *are* family after all. God, you're really *freaked out*, aren't you?

Honestly, Brian, for someone who's meant to be *right-on*, you're really incredibly *square*.' For a moment I catch a glimpse of her as Head Girl, malicious and superior. And did she really just call me *square*? 'Well don't worry, Brian, I keep my clothes *on* when there are guests around.'

'Oh, please, don't compromise, not for my sake . . .' Alice knows I'm pushing my luck, and smiles wryly. 'What I mean is, I think I could handle it.'

'Hmm. Now I wonder if that's strictly true?' Alice licks the tip of her finger, and turns the page of her book.

Breakfast is toast made from home-baked bread that has the colour, weight, texture and taste of a heavy-loam soil. Radio 4 is broadcasting in the kitchen too. In fact as far as I can tell it's on in every room and is apparently impossible to turn off, like the telescreens in *1984*. We chew and listen to the radio, and chew, Alice reading her book throughout. I feel miserable already. Partly it's because I'm the first person to be called 'square' since 1971, but mainly I'm depressed by the mention of Dad. How could she 'forget'? And I despise the way I find myself talking about him in front of other people. I'm sure Dad would have been over the moon to know that this was his fate all along; to be used by his son as raw material for a bunch of shitty, glib one-liners, or self-pitying drunken monologues. The hunt for the Real Me is going badly, and I've not even brushed my teeth yet.

And then we go for a long walk in the snow. You couldn't call the East Anglian countryside spectacular; it's striking, I suppose, in a post-nuclear sort of way, and the view tends to stay pretty much the same no matter how far you walk, which sort of defeats the object really, but at least it's consistent. It's also refreshing to be somewhere that you can't hear Radio 4. Alice takes me by the arm, and I almost forget about the snow ruining my new suede desert boots.

Since I've been at university, I've noticed that people want to talk about the same five major topics: 1) 'My A-level

Results' 2) 'My Nervous Breakdown/Eating Disorder' 3) 'My Full Grant' 4) 'Why I'm Actually *Relieved* I Didn't Get Into Oxbridge' 5) 'My Favourite Books', and this last option is the one we alight on.

'Top of the pops for me used to be *The Diary of Anne Frank*. When I was a teenager, I used to really want to be Anne Frank. Not the ending obviously, just the idea of living very simply in an attic, reading books, keeping my diary, falling in love with the pale, sensitive Jewish boy in the attic next door. That probably sounds a little bit perverse, doesn't it?'

'A little bit.'

'I think it's just a phase all us girls go through at a certain age, like cutting yourself, and throwing up, and lesbianism.'

'You tried lesbianism?' I ask casually, in near falsetto.

'Well, you more or less *had* to at boarding-school. It was compulsory; lesbianism, French and netball.'

'So what did you . . . do?'

'Wouldn't you like to know.' Well, clearly, yes. 'Nothing much really. I just dipped my toe in.'

'Well, maybe that was where you were going wrong!' She gives a tired smile. 'Sorry. So – what happened?'

'It just didn't really do it for me, I suppose. I've always liked sex with men too much. I'd miss the penetration.' We walk on a little further. 'How about you?'

'Me? Oh, I miss the penetration too.'

'I'm trying to be serious, Brian,' she says, punching me on the arm with her mitten. 'So have you?'

'Have I what?'

'Well, I'm assuming you've had sex with men.'

'No!'

'Really?'

'Absolutely not. What makes you say that?'

'I just assumed you would have.'

'You think I'm effeminate?' I ask. The falsetto's back.

'No, not *effeminate*. And besides, effeminacy is not a signifier of homosexuality . . .'

'Well, no, of course not.'

'. . . and it's not a *bad* thing anyway.'

'No, of course it isn't. It's just you sound like one of my mates from school, that's all.'

'Well, methinks the lady doth protest too much.'

Change the subject. I'm keen to bring the conversation back to lesbianism, but then dimly remember that she'd said something earlier about cutting herself. I probably should have picked up on that.

'What about the . . . self-harm?'

'What self-harm?'

'You said you used to cut yourself?'

'Oh, only now and again. A cry-for-help, I think they call it. Or more accurately a cry-for-attention. I got a bit depressed at school, a bit lonely, that's all.'

'I'm amazed,' I say.

'Really? Why should that surprise you?'

'It's just I suppose I can't imagine you having anything to be depressed about.'

'You really have to get over this notion that I'm silver-plated, Brian, some sort of Perfect Being. It's really not the case at all.'

But that afternoon she's pretty perfect.

When we're nearly home from the walk we have a frisky little snowball fight on the front lawn, which differs from all the previous snowball fights I've ever had in that no one is packing dog shit or broken glass into the centre of their snowballs. It's not even a snowball *fight* as such, just a mildly aphrodisiacal tussle, the kind of self-conscious fooling around that feels as if it's being filmed, ideally with a black and white cine-camera. Then we go in and sit on the sofa by the fire to dry out, and she plays her favourite records, lots of Rickie Lee

Jones and Led Zeppelin and Donovan and Bob Dylan – even though she was sixteen in 1982, there's definitely something very 1971 about Alice. I watch as she jumps around the room to 'Crosstown Traffic' by Jimi Hendrix, then when she's out of breath and tired of changing records every three minutes she puts a crackly old Ella Fitzgerald LP on, and we lie on the sofa and read our books, and steal glances at each other every now and then, like that bit between Michael York and Liza Minnelli in *Cabaret*, and talk only when we feel like it. And, miraculously, for nearly a whole afternoon I manage not to say anything fatuous or pretentious or priggish or unfunny or self-pitying, I don't break or spill anything, I don't slag anyone off, I don't whine or moan or flick my hair back or pick at my face while I'm talking. In fact, I'm just about the best person I'm capable of being, and if that person's not quite *love*able, at least he's fairly *like*able. And then at about four o'clock Alice lolls over and lies with her head in my lap and falls asleep, and for the time being at least, it does seem true, she is absolutely and entirely perfect. We're listening to *Blue*, side 2, track 5 now, and Joni's singing '*The last time I saw Richard was Detroit in '68/ and he told me all romantics meet the same fate/Cynical and drunk and boring someone in some dark café* . . .' and when the record finishes, and the room is silent except for the sound of the log fire, I just sit very, very still and watch her sleeping. Her lips are slightly parted and I can feel her warm breath on my thigh, and I find myself staring at the tiny raised scar on her lower lip, white against the red, and have this overwhelming desire to run my thumb across it, but don't want to wake her, so instead I just look at her, look and look and look. In the end I have to wake her up though, because I'm worried that the weight and warmth of her head on my lap will get me over-stimulated, if you know what I mean, and let's face facts, no one likes to be woken up that way. Not with *that* in their ear.

And then, would you believe, it gets even better. Her parents are out for the evening, eating more vegetables at someone's converted mill in Southwold, so it's just me and Alice alone in the house. As we stand drinking large beakers of gin and tonics in the kitchen, I'm ashamed to say that I entertain myself by fantasising that we live here together. We turn out all the lights in the house and play Scrabble by candle-light, peering hard at the letters, and I win, by quite a long way as a matter of fact, but with modesty and good grace. 'Foxed' and 'amazed' on triple letter scores, incidentally.

Supper is brown-rice-stir-fry, which looks and tastes a little like we've stir-fried the dust-pan sweepings, but is just about edible if you add enough soy sauce. Besides, by the time we get around to eating it, we're fantastically drunk, and talking over each other and laughing and dancing around the living room to old Nina Simone songs, then seeing how far we can slide along the varnished wooden floors in our socks. Then when we're lying in a crumpled, giggling heap, Alice very suddenly takes me by the hands, smiles mischievously and says, 'D'you want to go upstairs?'

My heart pops up into my mouth.

'Well, that depends. What's upstairs?' I say, foxed and amazed.

'Come with me and find out,' and she scrambles up the stairs on all fours, shouting behind her, 'Your bedroom, two minutes – bring the wine!'

Concentrate. Just concentrate.

I go to the kitchen sink, move the soaking wok to one side, run the cold tap, and splash my face, partly to sober up, partly to check I'm not dreaming, then holding the wine bottle and the half-filled glasses precariously with the tips of my fingers, I follow her upstairs.

Alice isn't in my room yet, so I go to the sink and very quickly brush my teeth, listening out for her footstep so that she doesn't catch me at it and think I'm taking things for granted. Then when I hear her coming along the corridor,

I rinse and spit, and turn off the overhead light and arrange myself nonchalantly on the bed and wait.

'Da – daaaaa!'

She's standing in the doorway, arms out-flung like an Oscar winner, but I can't tell what I'm meant to be looking at. Her breasts maybe? Hoping against hope, I wonder if maybe she's put on special underwear, and then I spot the Rizlas in one hand and the tiny cling-film pouch in the other.

'What is it?'

'Skunk, man. Wick-ed skunk. We can't do it downstairs – Michael's like a sniffer-dog. That Bohemian Dad thing only stretches *so* far.' She grabs a copy of Richard Scarry's *It's a Busy, Busy World* from the bookshelf and starts rolling the joint on it.

'What about your mum?'

'Oh, Mum actually gets it for me, from this creepy guy in the village. What can I say! Housewife's ruin. Still, she's got to fill her days somehow, I suppose. It's amazing stuff. Amaaaaazing!' God help me, she's putting on a West Indian accent, Jamaica-cum-Aldeburgh, and for the first time ever I find myself really embarrassed by her. 'Really strong gan-ja, mon, reeeeeally nice weeeeed . . .' *Please, stop that Alice, please?* Now she's lit it, and is inhaling deeply, and holding the smoke in her lungs while her eyes roll back in her head, then she pouts and blows the smoke out towards the paper lampshade, and I wonder if marijuana is an aphrodisiac.

Alice looks at me with one lazy eye, and offers me the joint, as if it were a challenge. Which it is.

'Your turn, Bri.'

'Actually, I don't think I can, Alice.'

'Why not? Why don't you want to get high, Bri?'

This strikes her as very, very funny, and while she bangs her head against the headboard I say, 'No, I'd love to, it's just I never learnt to smoke, not even tobacco, I'm useless, I can't take it back, not without coughing my lungs up anyway.' Actually, smoking was one of the things I hoped to do at university, like reading *Don Quixote*, growing a beard and learning to play the alto sax, but I just haven't got round to it.

'You're a strange one, aren't you, Brian Jackson?' she says, suddenly very serious. 'How can you not smoke! Smoking's pretty much the thing I do best. Or *second* best anyway . . .' she says, winking the other lazy eye. Marijuana *must* be an aphrodisiac. 'Okay, we'll try something a little more provocative. But first, some music!' And she stumbles over to the clunky, flat-deck, childhood tape-recorder, which has 'Alice's' written on it in Tippex, then digs around in her old desk drawer for a tape, jams it in and presses play. It is, I believe, Brian Cant, singing 'A Froggy Went A Courtin'.'

'Wow – Proustian Rush!' she says. 'This song *is* my childhood. I fucking *love* and *adore* this song! Don't you? Right, come here, young man, sit up straight . . .' We kneel up on the bed, facing each other, and she brings her face up to within a couple of inches from mine.

'Okay, put your hands here . . .' and she takes my wrists, and pushes them behind my back '. . . and purse your lips, like this.' Her mouth is just inches away, I can smell the sweetness of the soy sauce and ginger on her breath. Then she takes her hand and pinches my cheeks together into an exaggerated pout.

'Froggy went a courtin', he did ride, uh-hum . . .'

'Now, what you are about to receive, Mr Brian Jackson, is called a *blow-back*, and no, it's not what you think it is, so nooo sauciness please. I'm going to blow the smoke into your mouth, and you are to inhale deeply and hold the smoke in your lungs and you *will not cough, d'you understand? I forbid it!* Instead you will hold your breath for as long as physically possible, and only then will you exhale. Is that clear?'

'Perfectly clear.'

'Okay then. Here we go!'

She places the joint between her lips, and inhales deeply,

then smiles, raises her eyebrows as if to say 'ready?', and I nod, yes, I'm ready. She brings her lips right up to mine so that they are centimetres, millimetres away, surely not even that, surely they're touching, and then she blows, and I suck in my breath, which is only natural really, given the circumstances, and I want the moment to go on forever.

'Froggy went a courtin', he did ride
A sword and pistol by his side
A Froggy went a courtin' he did ride, uh-hum . . .'

Finally, when my lungs are about to burst, I exhale and she flops back and asks, 'What d'you think?'

Once I've worked out how to operate my mouth, I say, 'Okay!'

'Feel anything?'

'Not massively.'

'Want to go again?'

Oh, God, yes, Alice, do I? More than anything in the world . . .

'Yeah, yeah, all right . . .'

'Are you sure? It's very strong.'

'Really, Alice, trust me. I can handle it.'

When I regain consciousness, Alice has gone, and I'm under the duvet, and Froggy's still going a-courtin'. The tape's on auto-reverse. I've no idea how long I've been under, so I jab at the stop button and look for my travel alarm clock. 1.30 a.m. I'm suddenly desperately thirsty, but thank goodness there's still half a bottle of refreshing red wine by my bed, so I sit up and drain most of the bottle. I check to see if Alice took my trousers off before she put me to bed, find that she didn't, but am too stoned to know whether to be pleased or disappointed.

Besides, I'm too busy thinking about food. I have never been hungrier in my life. Even courgettes seem appealing. Then thank God, I remember I am the possessor of Cold Meats, bless you Mum. I dig the foil parcel out of my suitcase, tear a ribbon of fat off a piece of boiled bacon, and stuff the lean into my mouth. It's good, but something's missing. Bread. Need sandwich. Must have bread.

Walking is less easy than I remembered, and getting downstairs seems almost impossible. I don't want to turn any lights on, but it really is pitch black here, so bracing myself against the walls on either side I take fairy steps along the hallway and down the stairs into the kitchen. Time stretches, and the journey seems to take maybe several days, but I get there eventually and begin the physically demanding task of chiselling myself two slices of home-made wholemeal bread. The resulting sandwich is the size, weight and texture of a household brick, but I don't care any more, because it contains Cold Meats. I settle down at the table and pour myself some milk first, to try and make the bread less gritty, but the milk has curdled and separated, and I'm about to cross to the sink to spit it out, when the landing light clicks on and I hear a creak at the top of the stairs.

Maybe it's Alice! Maybe we can carry on from where we left off. But it isn't. It's Mrs Harbinson. Rose. Naked Rose. I swallow the curdled milk.

Of course, I should just say something straight away, just a sexless, casual 'Hullo Rose!' but the dope and the wine have made me fuzzy and muddled, and I don't want a naked woman screaming at me at two in the morning, so I just sit there, very quietly, and hope she'll go. She opens the door of the fridge, and then she bends over, and the white fridge-light and the bending-over make her look *really* naked. Closer scrutiny reveals she's actually wearing a pair of thick grey socks, which gives her nudity a sort of wholesome, muesli-quality, like a line drawing from *The Joy Of Sex*, and in my drug-fuddled state I find myself wondering if there is such a word as *pubicy*. What is she looking for? And why is it taking so long? I imagine that she 'looks-good-for-her-age' too, but then I've never actually seen a whole woman naked, not in real life and all at once, only odd bits and pieces, and even then none of them were older than nineteen, so I'm not really an authority on the subject. Still, I suppose the situation isn't without a sort of hackneyed eroticism, albeit one that's tempered slightly by the parcel of body-temperature gammon nestling on my lap. Suddenly anxious that maybe she'll smell the meat, I try to fold the foil over silently, and the resultant crackling seems to reverberate round the kitchen like an electrical storm.

'Oh my God! Brian!'

'Hello Mrs Harbinson!' I say brightly. I expect her to cover her nakedness with her arms, but she doesn't seem that bothered really, and just reaches nonchalantly for a National Trust tea-towel, which she wraps around her waist and holds at her hip like a sarong. I can see the word 'Sissinghurst' running down her thigh.

'Oh dear, I do hope I haven't shocked you,' she says.

'Oh, not really . . .'

'But then I'm sure that you've seen hundreds of naked women before.'

'You'd be surprised, Mrs Harbinson.'

'I've told you before, call me Rose. Mrs Harbinson makes me feel so *old*!'

There's a momentary silence, and I search for something to say that will rid the situation of any embarrassment or discomfort, and come up with the *perfect* solution.

In an American accent I say, 'Are you trying to seduce me, Mrs Harbinson?!'

What did I just say? . . .

'I beg your pardon?'

Don't say it again . . .

'Are you trying to seduce me?' I say.

Quick, explain, explain . . .

'You know – like Mrs Robinson?' I explain.

Rose stares at me blankly. 'Who's Mrs Robinson?'

'It's a quote. From *The Graduate* . . .'

'Well I can tell you now, Brian, I have no intention of seducing *you* . . .'

'I know, I know, and I don't *want* to be seduced by you . . .'

'Right, well, just as well then . . .'

'That's not to say that I don't find you *attractive* . . .'

'I *beg* your pardon?'

'What the *fuck* is going on down here?' says a voice, and another figure is loping down the stairs, the muscular legs and barrel chest – the muscular, *naked* legs and barrel chest of Mr Harbinson. He seems to be clutching a rolled umbrella between his legs but closer examination reveals it to be a penis. Now I *really* don't know where to look. Not looking at Rose's genitals seems to bring my eye-line directly down to Mr Harbinson's genitals, and suddenly it's hard to find anywhere in the kitchen that's genital-free, so finally I pick a point on the ceiling just above the Aga, and concentrate, concentrate, concentrate.

'Nothing's *going on*, Michael. I just came down for a drink and Brian was here, that's all . . .' Why is she sounding so guilty? Is she *trying* to get me killed?

'So what were you talking about?'

Oh, good Christ, he heard me. I'm already dead.

'Nothing! Brian just made me jump, that's all . . .'

Mr Harbinson and his penis look unconvinced, and I realise that he's not actually *covering* his penis with his hand, but *holding* it, and for a moment I have an irrational fear that he's going to hit me with it.

'Well keep it down, will you? And Rose, come to bed!' and he thumps back upstairs, holding his rolled umbrella. Clearly deeply embarrassed, Rose takes a floral, vinyl apron from a hook by the Aga, and puts it on grumpily, whilst I brush the meaty evidence from the table into the foil pack, and stuff it into the cutlery drawer.

Finally she comes over to the table, and hisses, 'I think it's best if neither of us ever mention this again, don't you, Brian?'

'Okay, but I do just want to say that I really was just quoting . . .'

'Let's forget about it, shall we? Pretend it never happened . . .' She's peering at my face. 'Brian, are you feeling all right?'

'Absolutely!'

'You look a bit grey.'

'Oh, this is my normal colour, Rose!'

She looks at the glass in front of me.

'Is that the milk?'

'Uh-huh.'

'So you had it all along?'

''Fraid so, Rose.'

'I've been looking for that, Brian.'

'Sorry' – she reaches for the glass – 'I wouldn't drink it though, if I were you!'

'Why on earth not?'

'It's off, it's curdled, really, it's disgusting . . .'

And she takes the glass of curdled milk, sniffs it, sips it, and looks me with utter disdain and says, 'It's *soya milk*, Brian.'

From somewhere in Blackbird Cottage comes the sound of hysterical laughter, an awful, mad cackle, the laughter of some pitiable, depraved child, and it takes a little while to realise that the laughter's coming from me.

When I wake up the next morning, there's the usual three-second delay between knowing that I should feel deeply ashamed, and remembering the reason why. I groan, actually, physically groan aloud, as if someone had just jumped on my chest. I look at the alarm clock. It's 11.30 and I feel like I'm coming out of a coma.

I lay there for a while, trying to work out the best way to

deal with this. The *best* way to deal with it would be to kill myself, but the second best way is going to involve a great deal of grovelling and pleading and self-mockery, so I start to get dressed, to get it over with, when there's a knock at the door.

It's Alice, looking sombre, as well she might. Does she know that her naked mother thinks I attempted to seduce her?

'Hello, sleeping beauty . . .' she whispers.

'Alice, I am so, so sorry about last night . . .'

'Oh, God, that's all right, it's nothing, forget about it . . .' She obviously doesn't know. 'Look, Brian, something's come up, I've got to go to Bournemouth . . .' She's sat at the edge of the bed, and it looks like she's going to cry.

'Why, what's happened?'

'It's Granny Harbinson, she fell downstairs late last night, and she's in hospital, with a fractured hip, and we've got to go and see her . . .'

'Oh, God, Alice . . .'

'Mum and Dad have already gone, but I've got to follow on, so I don't think New Year's going to work out, I'm afraid.'

'Oh, that's okay. I'll find out the times of the . . .'

'Already done it. There's a train to London in forty-five minutes, I'll give you a lift to the station. Is that okay?'

And so I start to pack, cramming books and clothes in my bag like it's an emergency evacuation, and in ten minutes we're in the Land-Rover, with Alice driving. She looks tiny behind the wheel, like a Sindy doll driving an Action Man jeep. The snow has turned to a dirty grey slush in the night, and we seem to be driving much too fast, which all just contributes to the general air of tension and anxiety.

'I have a terrible headache today!' I offer.

'Me too,' she replies.

Two hundred yards of country lane go by.

'I ran into your mum and dad in the kitchen last night,' I say, nonchalantly.

'Oh, really!'

Another two hundred yards.

'Did they say anything about it?'

'Not really. No. Why should they?'

'No reason.' I'm safe it seems. Obviously I'm not *glad* Granny Harbinson fell down the stairs, but at least she's created a diversion.

We arrive at the station with fifteen minutes to spare, and she helps me carry my bag on to the empty platform.

'I'm *so* sorry you can't stay for New Year.'

'Oh, that's all right. Send my love to Granny Harbinson.' What for? I've never even met the woman for Christ's sake. 'And I'm really sorry about overdosing on you last night.'

'Really, that's fine. Look, d'you mind if I don't wait for you to get the train? It's just I should get going . . .' And we embrace, but don't kiss, and then she's gone.

I get home at about teatime, and let myself in. Mum's dressed in her track-suit and is lying on the sofa in the lounge watching *Blockbusters* on full volume, with an ashtray balanced on her belly, a bucket of Quality Street and a bottle of Tia Maria on the coffee table in front of her. As I come into the room she sits up and stuffs the bottle under a cushion, then realises she's left the sherry glass of Tia Maria out, and tries to conceal it by wrapping both hands around it, like it's a tiny mug of cocoa or something.

'You're back early!'

'Yes, Mum, I know . . .'

'I'll take a P, Bob . . .'

'What's up, then?'

'Alice's nan fractured her hip.'

'How did that happen?'

'I pushed her downstairs.'

'No, really.'

'I've no idea, Mum.'

'Which P is the main chemical ingredient in the manufacture of matches?'

'Poor thing. Is she going to be all right?'

'How should I know? I'm not the doctor-in-charge, am I? Phosphorous.'

'Correct.'

'What?' says Mum.

'The telly!' I snap.

'I'll take an H please, Bob . . .'

'Something wrong, Bri?'

'No, nothing's wrong!'

'Which H gave his name to the . . . ?'

'Did you fall out with your girlfri . . . ?'

'She is *not* my girlfriend!'

'All right, no need to shout!'

'Bit early for cocktails, isn't it, Mother?'

And then I turn and run upstairs, feeling seedy and mean. And where did that nasty, peevish 'Mother' come from? I've never called her 'Mother'. I go to my room, slam the door, lie on my bed and put on my headphones to listen to my cassette copy of *Lionheart*, Kate Bush's staggeringly beautiful second album, 'Symphony in Blue', side A, track one. But almost immediately I realise something's missing.

The Cold Meats.

I left the parcel of cold meat in the kitchen drawer last night. I don't have the Harbinsons' Bournemouth number, so I decide to phone the cottage and leave a message for when Alice gets back. After four rings the answering-machine clicks on, and I'm just working out what to say, when someone unexpectedly picks up.

'Hello . . . ?'

'Oh. Hello, is that . . . is that *Rose*?'

'Who is this?'

'It's Brian, Alice's friend?'

'Oh, hello, Brian. Hold on, will you.'

There's a rustling noise, as she puts her hand over the receiver, and some vague mumbling, and then Alice comes on.

'Hello, Brian?'

'Hi! You're still there!'

'Yes, yes, we're here.'

'Only I thought you'd be in Bournemouth . . .'

'We were, but . . . then it turned out Granny was feeling much better, so we drove back. We've just got in, actually.'

'Right. So she's okay then?'

'She's absolutely fine!'

'No fractured hip?'

'No, just bad bruising, and, um, shock.'

'Good. I'm glad to hear it. Well, not glad that she's in *shock*, obviously, I mean I'm glad it's not life-threatening . . .'

There's a silence.

'So . . . ?'

'So I just meant to say, I left the . . . um, the, you know, cold meat there.'

'I see. And where is this . . . meat?'

'In the drawer of the kitchen table.'

'Oh. Right. I'll go and get it.'

'Wait till your mum's not around though, maybe?'

'Of course.'

'So – see you back at college next year, then?'

'Exactly. See you next year!' And she's gone, and I just stand there in the hallway, the telephone receiver in my hand, staring into space.

I can hear the telly in the lounge.

'Which K's three laws accurately describe the motion of the planets around the sun?'

'Johannes Kepler,' I say, to no one at all.

'Correct!'

I have absolutely no idea what I'm meant to do now.

22

QUESTION: Finding its origins in the 31-syllable 'tanka', which Japanese poetic form consists of 17 syllables, arranged in lines of 5, 7 and 5?
ANSWER: The haiku.

Rebecca Epstein's response is to laugh. She lies on my futon in the student house on Richmond Hill, and laughs and laughs, kicking her Doc Martens with sadistic glee.

'It's not *that* funny, Rebecca.'

'Och, no, trust me, it is.'

I give up, and go and change the record.

'I'm sorry, Jackson, but it's just the idea of them all hiding in the woodshed until you've definitely gone . . .' This sets her off again, so I decide to go into Josh's room and get more home-brewed beer.

I'm with Mum for another eighteen hours before I decide to go back to college. Once again, I tell her it's because I need some specialist books from the library, and she shrugs, only half-believing, and by ten o'clock, I'm on the doorstep again, rejecting the same groceries.

On the train back, I start to cheer up a bit. So what if I'm spending New Year alone in a student house? I can get some work done, read, go for long walks, play music as loud as I want. And tomorrow, on New Year's Eve, I'll fight the ridiculous tradition that says we have to go out and get drunk and have fun. I'll stay in instead, and not have fun. I'll still get drunk but I'll read a book, and fall asleep at 11.58 p.m. That'll teach them, I convince myself, without really knowing who 'they' are.

But as soon as I arrive back at the student house, I realise I've made a terrible mistake. As I open the front door, a waft of warm, yeasty gas from Marcus and Joshua's home-brew Yorkshire Bitter hits me, and it's as if the whole house had just burped in my face. I go into Joshua's room, and find the plastic barrel bubbling and hissing near a fully-on radiator. I open the window to let some of the intestinal gas out.

No one's back yet, obviously, which is what I'd hoped, but I don't think I was prepared for the house to be quite *this* empty. So I decide to go to the mini-market on the corner. It's 5.45, the optimum time for buying reduced-price food.

The purchase of reduced-price food isn't something one should enter into lightly. The dented canned goods are generally safe, but with 'fresh' produce, frankly it's a minefield. As a general rule of thumb, the degree to which the price is reduced is proportional to the danger involved in actually eating it, so the trick is to go for something that's still a bargain without actually giving you stomach cramps; a measly 10p off a pound of blue-grey braising steak is hardly worth the risk, but a whole chicken for 25p is just asking for trouble. Also beef and chicken are generally safer than pork and fish. Old pork is no fun for anyone, whereas with old beef you can at least kid yourself that it's not 'off', it's just 'well-hung'. The same applies to strongly flavoured foods; it's not 'off', it's 'spicy'. It is for this reason that the curry is in many ways the classic reduced-price item.

In the mini-market, me and an old lady with a Zapata moustache eye each other warily over the chill cabinet. As it's so soon after Christmas there are a great many lethal turkeys here, as well as a leg of lamb which looks as if it's in danger of climbing out of the chill cabinet and walking back to the farm by itself. Generally it's a pretty disappointing haul, so I decide to go for the dehydrated Vesta curry, at 75 pence off and, as a special treat, a tub of banana-flavour Nesquick and a pint of milk.

But the elation is short-lived. By the time I've got back, had some Nesquick, boiled the kettle, dissolved the bright yellow curry powder in a saucepan and eaten it, I'm feeling like Robinson Crusoe. The house is empty, it's raining outside, Josh's portable telly is locked in his wardrobe, and it's rapidly becoming clear that the so-called best years of my life are never going to happen.

Snap out of this. Do something about it.

I steal some change from the copper-jar in Josh's room and pile the coins on top of the payphone in the hallway.

But who to call? I contemplate phoning some guy called Vince I met at a party, but don't want to sit in a pub with just one other man, and also don't have his number, and can't remember his surname or where he lives or pretty much anything about him. Lucy Chang's back in Minneaopolis, and also thinks I'm a racist. Colin Pagett's still got hepatitis. I *nearly* call Patrick before I remember that I don't even like him. Finally I decide to call Rebecca Epstein, because Rebecca's a Law student and, as Law's a proper subject, there's a good chance that she'll actually be doing some work.

She lives in Kenwood Manor and as her corridor's the same as Alice's, I have the number. After about twenty rings a Glaswegian voice finally answers.

'Hello, is that Rebecca?'

'. . . yeeeeess?'

'It's Brian, here.'

A pause.

'Brian Jackson?' I offer.

'I know which Brian. What are you doing back?'

'I got bored, that's all.'

'God, me too.' Another pause. 'So . . . ?'

'So I just wondered, what are you doing tonight?'

'Waiting for you to call, obviously. Is this a *date*?' she says, as if she were asking 'is this a *turd*?'

'God, no, I just wondered if you wanted to go to the pictures or something. They're showing Pasolini's *Gospel According To St Matthew* at the Arts . . .'

'Alternatively, we could go and see something *enjoyable* . . .'

'*St Elmo's Fire* at the ABC?'

'Would that be Pasolini's *St Elmo's Fire*?'

'*Back to the Future*'s on at the Odeon . . .'

'How old are you exactly? . . .'

'*Cocoon* at the ABC . . .'

'God help us . . .'

'You're very opinionated, aren't you?'

'I know. Scary, isn't it? Are you sure you're up to the job, Brian?'

'I think so. So what do you want to do?'

'Got any booze?'

'Twelve gallons of it. It's all home-brew, though.'

'Och, I'm not fussy. You're in Richmond House?'

'Yep.'

'All right, give me half an hour.'

She hangs up, and suddenly I'm scared.

Forty minutes later, she's sat on my bed drinking home-brew and laughing at me. As usual, she's wearing her uniform, which really does look like a uniform; black DMs, thick black tights under a blue-black denim mini-skirt, a v-necked black jumper under the black vinyl military-style belted coat, which I have yet to see her take off. Her short hair is glossy with Black-and-White pomade, and has been pushed up into a little, oily quiff in front of her black, peaked worker's cap. In fact everything she wears seems designed to suggest a long tradition of tough, manual labour, which is strange really, because as I recall her mum's a ceramic artist and her dad's a consultant paediatrician. In fact Rebecca's only concession to conventional notions of femininity is a thick smear of glossy ruby-red lipstick and a great deal of heavy mascara that makes her look intimidating and glamorous at the same time, like the Hollywood branch of the Baader-Meinhof gang. She even smokes like a film star, Bette Davis or someone, but a film star who rolls her own. In fact, if anything, she looks a little more attractive than usual this evening, and I find myself worrying that she may even have made an effort.

When she finally stops laughing, I say, 'Well, I'm glad you find my sex life funny, Rebecca.'

'Surely it's only a sex life if there's sex in it?'

'She could have actually been telling the truth.'

'Yes, Brian I'm *sure* she was telling the truth. I told you she was a cow, didn't I? And don't look all po-faced. You know it's funny, otherwise you wouldn't have told me about it.' She puffs on her rolly, flicks the ash down the side of the futon. 'Anyway, serves you right.'

'What for?'

'You know what for. The bourgeois wank-fest. Call yourself a Socialist, but in the end you're just like all the other social-climbers at this university, all ready to roll over and have your stomach rubbed by the so-called superior classes . . .'

'That's not true!'

''Tis true. Closet Tory! . . .'

'Stalinist! . . .'

'Class traitor! . . .'

'Snob! . . .'

'Inverted snob! . . .'

'Proto-yuppie! . . .'

'D'you want to get your Doctor Martens off my duvet?'

'Scared I'll ruin this *exquisite* fabric?' But she does move her feet, and then shuffles along to sit next to me, and taps her glass of warm beer against mine in reconciliation.

'Why's your bed-frame behind your wardrobe?' she asks.

'I thought I'd, you know, turn it into a futon.'

'A *futon*, eh? Well let me tell you, Brian, a mattress on the floor does not a futon make.'

'That was almost a haiku,' I say.

'How many syllables in a haiku?'

I know this one. 'Seventeen, arranged 5-7-5.'

She thinks for maybe one second, then says:

A mattress on the
Floor does not a futon make.
Smells surely follow.

. . . then she goes to drink, but stops to pluck off a strand of Golden Virginia that's got matted in her lipstick, a gesture that's so extravagantly cool and languid that I find myself staring sideways at her lips in case she does it again. Then she catches my eye, and I babble out, 'How was your Christmas, then?'

'We don't do Christmas, we're Jews, we *killed* Christ, remember?'

'So how about, what's it called, Passover?'

'Hanukkah. We don't do that either. For someone who's representing our glorious establishment on *University Challenge,* Brian Jackson, you're surprisingly ignorant. How many times do I have to tell you, we're Socialist Non-Orthodox Jewish Anti-Zionist Glaswegians.'

'Doesn't sound much fun.'

'Believe me, it's not. Why d'you think I'm here with you?'

I think I'll try my hand at Jewish humour.

'Still. Christmas Schmistmas!'

'*What?*'

'Nothing.'

She scrutinises me for a moment, then half-smiles . . .

'Anti-semite.'

And I smile back. I suddenly find myself feeling fantastically fond of Rebecca Epstein, and want to make a tentative gesture of friendship. I have an idea.

'Which reminds me, I got you this! Happy Hanukkah!'

It's Alice's unwanted Joni Mitchell album. I lost the receipt. Rebecca looks at me questioningly, 'For *me*?'

'Uh-huh.'

'Are you *sure*?' she asks, an East European checkpoint-guard who suspects my passport might be fake.

'Absolutely.'

She takes it between finger and thumb, and peels back a corner of the wrapping. 'Joni *Mitchell*.'

'Uh-huh. D'you know it?'

'I'm familiar with her work.'

'So you've got it?'

'No. No, I'm ashamed to say I haven't.'

'Well, let me play it to you . . .'

And I take it from her hand, go to the record player, take off Tears For Fears, and put on *Blue*, side 2, track 4, 'A Case Of You', surely one of the most exquisite love songs ever committed to vinyl. After we've listened to the whole of the first verse and chorus in silence, I ask, 'So. What d'you think?'

'I think it's brought on my period.'

'Don't you like it?'

'Well, to be completely honest, it's not really my thing, Brian.'

'It will grow on you.'

'Hmmm,' she says, doubtfully. 'So, big Joni fan are you?'

'Sort of. To be honest, I'm more of a Kate Bush man.'

'Hmmm – that figures.'

'Why?'

'Because, Brian, you *are* the Man with the Child in his Eyes,' she says, and sniggers into her beer.

'So what are you listening to at the moment, then?'

'Lots of things. Durutti Column, Marvin Gaye, the Cocteau Twins, some early blues, Muddy Waters, The Cramps, Bessie

Smith, Joy Division, the New York Dolls, Sly and the Family Stone, some dub. I'll make you a compilation tape, see if I can wean you off all this fanny-music. You know, you have to be careful with these singer-songwriters, Brian. They're fine in moderation but if you listen to too much of this stuff, you will actually grow wee vestigial breasts.'

'Well, if you don't want your present, just say . . .' I say, getting up to change the record.

'No! No, I'll keep it. I'm sure I'll grow to love it. Thank you very much, Brian. Very Christian of you.'

And then I sit back down next to her, and we sit in silence for a moment. Then she takes my hand, squeezes it pretty hard, and says, 'Seriously – thank you.'

Ten minutes later, we're lying on the bed, and somehow the same hand seems to have found its way into her bra.

They say that the personal is political and it's certainly fair to say that, like her politics, Rebecca Epstein's kissing is radical, forthright and uncompromising. I'm lying on my back and she's pushing my head down into the pillow, and her front teeth are grinding against mine, but I'm determined to give as good as I get, and I'm grinding back, so it's only a matter of time before we take off all our enamel. The combination of the booze and the fumes from the calor-gas heater have made me feel heady, a little panicky even, but it's fun too, like when you're at school and you're being bundled. The thick emulsion of the lipstick creates an airlock around our mouths, so that when she finally pulls her mouth away I almost expect there to be a popping noise, like in a cartoon when a sink-plunger's pulled off someone's face.

'Is this all right? she asks. Her lipstick's smeared round her mouth now, like she's been eating raspberries.

'Fine,' I say, and she's on me again. She tastes of brewing yeast and Golden Virginia and the scented oiliness of the lipstick. For my part, I can't help worrying about the Vesta curry I had earlier. Should I pretend to need the toilet, and go and brush my teeth? But then she'll *know* I've brushed my teeth for her sake, and I don't want to appear conventional. Is bad breath in some way *un*conventional? Probably not, but if I brush my teeth, maybe she'll think I want her to brush her teeth too, which I don't, really. In fact I quite like the tobacco taste, that feeling of smoking by proxy. Best just carry on. But where to go from here? Like a ventriloquist, I try to put my hand up her top at the back, but she's still wearing the belted coat, and when I make it past the belt I find that her jumper's tucked in pretty firmly, so I try to take an alternative route, via her neckline. I have to contort my arm to do so, and bend my hand back at right angles, like the world's most inept pickpocket, but eventually I get there. Her bra is black, lacy and slightly padded, which surprises me, and for a moment I find myself contemplating the politics of this bra. Why is it padded? Isn't this a bit out of character for Rebecca? Why does she of all people feel the need to conform to conventional male-defined notions of femininity? Why should she be obliged to acquire the conventionally 'sexy' body image that actually *no* woman is capable of attaining in real life, except maybe Alice Harbinson.

Then suddenly she breaks away from the kiss, and I expect she's going to ask me what the hell I think I'm up to, but instead; 'Brian?' she whispers.

'What?'

'There's something I need to tell you. I wasn't joking earlier. When I said I was on.'

'That's okay. I'm on too.'

She looks at me quizzically. 'I don't think you are somehow, Bri.'

'No really, I am. I might not have seemed on, but I really am . . .'

She's scowling at me now. 'You're *on your period*?'

'What? Oh, I see. No, sorry, I thought you meant you, you know . . .'

'What?'

'"On-for-it?"'

'What's "*on*-for-it"?'

I think for a second. 'Slang?' I offer, hopefully, but my hand's out of her bra now, never to return. She's sat up on the edge of the bed, straightening her tights, checking to see if I've torn her jumper, and I've blown it.

'Maybe this isn't such a good idea after all.'

'I don't mind, honestly.'

'What's *that* supposed to mean?'

'I mean I'm cool about your period.'

'Oh, well, I'm glad you're *cool* about it, Jackson. Just as well, seeing as there's fuck-all I can do about it, is there?'

'I'm sorry, but I don't know what else to say.'

'I bet Alice Harbinson doesn't even *have* a period . . .'

'What?'

'. . . she probably *pays* someone to have it for her . . .'

'Hang on, what's this got to do with Alice Harbinson?'

'Nothing!'

She turns, and seems about to snap at me again, but then breaks into a smile, or a half-smile at least; 'You'd better wipe the lipstick off your face. You look like a clown . . .' I wipe my mouth with the corner of my duvet and hear her murmur, 'You *are* a fucking clown.'

'What have I done now!'

'You know what.'

'Hey, it was you who started it!'

'Started what?'

'Talking about, you know, Alice.'

'Oh for Christ's sake, Jackson . . .'

'I only mentioned her because you mentioned her . . .'

'But you're *thinking* about her though, aren't you?'

'No, of course I'm not!' I say. But I am. Rebecca holds

my gaze just long enough to be sure of the fact, then looks away.

'This is stupid' she says quietly, pressing her eyes with the heel of her hands. 'I'm a wee bit pissed. I think I should go.' I might not have been sure before, but now I definitely don't want her to go, so I clamber round in front of her, and try to kiss her again. She turns her head away.

'Why d'you have to go?'

'I don't . . . I don't know – what just happened. Can we forget about it?'

'Oh. Right. All right. Okay. I'd rather you didn't go, but if that's what you want . . .'

'I think so. I think I want to go,' and she's on her feet, pulling her coat together and heading out the door, leaving me wondering what I've done this time. I mean, above and beyond the usual, crass ineptitude. I follow her downstairs into the hallway, where she scrambles over the tangle of bicycles blocking the hallway.

'Now look – I've snagged my bloody tights . . .'

'At least let me walk you home.'

'No thanks.'

'I don't mind . . .'

'I'm all right . . .'

'You shouldn't walk back by yourself . . .'

'I'll be fine . . .'

'Really, I insist . . .' and she wheels around suddenly, and points her finger at me, and snaps, 'And I insist you *don't*! Is that understood?' We're both thrown by the sharpness of this; it may be that I even take a step backwards. We look at each other, wondering what is going on, and eventually she says 'Besides, you should go to bed. You're "on", remember?' She opens the door. 'Let's never talk about this again, okay? And don't tell anyone, all right? Especially not Alice-bloody-Harbinson. Promise?'

'Of course not. Why would I tell Alice . . . ?'

But she's already halfway down the steps, and without looking back she runs off into the night.

Round Three

‘I’m sorry,’ said Sebastian, after a time. ‘I’m afraid I wasn’t very nice this afternoon. Brideshead often has that effect on me.’

Evelyn Waugh, *Brideshead Revisited*

23

QUESTION: Striated, cardiac and smooth are three types of which tissue?

ANSWER: Muscle.

Some New Year's Resolutions

1. *Spend more time working on my poetry. If I'm serious about poetry as a literary form, as well as a way of earning extra money, then I'm really going to have to work at it, especially if I'm to discover my own distinctive voice. Remember, T.S.Eliot held down a job in a bank* and *wrote* The Four Quartets, *so not having enough time is no excuse.*
2. *Stop picking at my face, especially when I'm talking to people. If science has taught us anything, it's that picking at your skin just spreads the infection and causes scars. Just* leave it alone, *find something else to do with your hands, learn to smoke or something. Remember – no one wants to kiss a bleeding face.*
3. *Be aloof. Play it cool with Alice – she'll respect you more for it.*
4. *Become lightly muscled.*

The above were written at about 10.45 p.m. on New Year's Eve, and I was pretty drunk by then, which means that the handwriting's a bit slurred. Twenty minutes later I was asleep, thereby flouting the conventional, clichéd notion that says we're obliged to have an amazing, fun time on New Year's Eve, by having an unconventional, unbelievably shitty time.

Festivities began at 8.35, when I found a screwdriver in the kitchen drawer, and unscrewed the doors of Josh's wardrobe so that I could get to his portable television. I then sat and watched the James Bond film on ITV, joining the massed ranks of elderly widows, mental patients and everyone else who stays in on New Year's Eve. But the more I drank, the more I thought about Dad, and Alice, and the two got strangely muddled in my head so that by the time Agent 007 had foiled Scaramanga's evil plan for world domination I was pretty much a physical and emotional wreck, thereby becoming the only person in the history of the world ever to cry watching *The Man With The Golden Gun* with the possible exception of Britt Eckland. Then I pulled myself together, and wrote the resolutions.

And now, two weeks later, the resolutions still stand. True, I haven't really grappled with my poetry yet, but will soon, when I get time. And I've barely touched my face. I've also been very aloof with Alice too, largely because I haven't seen her or heard from her and have no idea where she is. In fact, socially, things have been a bit quiet since term began again. In *Brideshead Revisited*, Charles' cousin warns him that your second term at university is generally spent avoiding all the undesirable people that you met in the first term, and I'm starting to suspect that I am, in actual fact, one of those people.

But back to the resolutions. The last one needs some elucidation. I've decided that it wouldn't do me any harm to have a muscle or two, and, no, this isn't because I'm buying into some shallow, gender-based notion of what the advertising media chooses to define as 'masculine' or attractive, and it's not because anyone's started to kick sand in my face, not literally anyway. It's just that I think I've taken the tubercular look to its natural conclusion really. Also, ever since school, I've been working on the principle that you're either clever, or you're fit, and the two are mutually exclusive, but actually there's no reason you can't have both; Patrick Watts for instance, is clever and really, really fit, even if he does have personality problems. Maybe Dustin Hoffman in *Marathon Man* is a better example; he's fit *and* clever, and has integrity too, the kind of guy who runs five miles carrying a load of library books. Or, from the real world, Alice Harbinson. Alice Harbinson is amazingly fresh-faced, healthy *and* intelligent. Or at least she was the last time I saw her. Two weeks and three days ago. Ages ago.

Not to worry. I'm going to sublimate all that energy into a fitness campaign. I'm thoroughly committed to a strict daily Canadian Royal-Air-Force-style regime that involves wedging my feet under the wardrobe, having first ensured that it won't topple over on top of me, and doing sit-ups, numbering eight, and press-ups, four. This is fine, but it doesn't really feel as if I've had a proper, thorough full-body work-out, and I think I'm going to need something extra. I think I'm going to need weights. I decide to spend my Christmas money on weight-lifting equipment.

I eat a healthy, nutritious breakfast from the newsagents, a chocolate covered muesli bar and a litre of pineapple Just Juice, and scout-march (run for thirty, walk for thirty) towards the City Centre, which suddenly seems like an incredibly long way away, especially when jogging in a donkey jacket and jeans. But I keep going, along residential streets littered with the skeletons of all the Christmas trees that the bin-men are refusing to take away, every now and then giving these little pineapple-juice burps. It's not long before I get a stitch, which suggests that perhaps I need to put some work into cardio-vascular health, but this can come later. My first priority is to increase body mass and improve muscle definition. I don't want to get all stocky, like a boxer or weight-lifter or anything, just to get more of a gymnast's physique, like one of those guys on the parallel bars. If at any point it looks like I'm going to get massively over-developed then I'll pull back.

I arrive at Sport! shortly after it opens, sweating pretty heavily. This is perhaps the second time in my life that I've entered a sports shop, because up until now Mum's bought all my sports kit for me. I'm pretty nervous about going in, as if I'm about to enter a pornographer's or something. Once inside, there's definitely a whiff of the boys' changing room about the place, emphasised by the shop's manager, who's about my age, stocky and bullish, and who approaches as if he's about to flick me with a wet towel.

'Need help, mate?'

'Just looking thanks!' I say, in an ever-so-slightly deeper-than-usual voice, and I browse around the shop, appraising badminton rackets with an expert eye, before casually heading over to the dumb-bells. There they are, two of them, made of heavy-duty iron, with adjustable weights, allowing me to gradually increase the load so that I am Adonis-like, but *no more*. There's something pretty self-explanatory about dumb-bells, so once I've established that, yes, they are very heavy and made of iron as opposed to grey-painted polystyrene and, yes, I can afford them, just about, at £12.99, then I heft them over to the shop assistant. It's only when I've handed over the cash, and he's put them in a heavy-duty plastic bag and I've left the shop, that I realise that I've made an extremely basic logistical error, and it's this: I can't carry them home.

For the first twenty-five yards I convince myself that it's possible, if I walk quickly enough, and change hands when the pain of the plastic bag cutting into flesh proves too much. But outside Woolworths the inevitable happens, the bottom falls out of the bag and the weights hit the pavement with a heavy-industrial crunch that causes shoppers, young mums with their kids in pushchairs mainly, to look at me, and at the dumb-bells, and in return I give them a 'who snuck dumb-bells in my bag!' kind of look. The paving-slab seems undamaged, but one of the dumb-bells is trundling heavily off towards Boots the Chemist like a tiny tank, and I have to lunge and stop it with my foot, which causes a certain amount of mirth amongst the young mums, who are pointing me out to their kids – 'look at the funny under-developed man!' I pick up a dumb-bell in each hand and walk briskly away.

I make it to Dorothy Perkins, twenty yards away, before I have to stop again for breath. Teenage girls see the dumb-bells and grin at me as I lean against the shop window. I decide that forward momentum is the key; the trick is to keep moving. I'll be fine if I keep moving. After all, there's only maybe a mile and a quarter still to go.

Once I'm out of the shopping centre, past the ring road and into the residential streets, it becomes a little easier to take regular rests without being stared at. I wait for my breathing to stabilise, then pick the weights up, arms hanging baboon-like, and make little stooped runs along the street as if under machine-gun fire, for as long as my heart can take it. I feel like I've just been resuscitated. I'm sweaty and red-faced, my shoulders feel bruised, wrenched and sore, my arms feel cartoonishly stretched, and the metallic diamond pattern on the bar of the dumb-bells has transferred itself indelibly to the palms of my hands, making them look reptilian and raw. I have a personal tutorial this afternoon, and I'm still nowhere near home, so I pick up the dumb-bells again, and stoop and run.

Eventually, I reach the south face of Richmond Hill, stretching vertically up before me, its summit lost in low-level cloud. I manage to yomp about twenty-five yards before I slump, doubled over, against a wall. It feels as if someone's stamped on my lungs, popped them like blown-up crisp packets. I'm coughing uncontrollably, the breath rasping over the back of my throat, which is parched, causing me to retch dryly. There's a sweetly bilious taste in my mouth where I've coughed up some pineapple Just Juice, and the sweat is pouring off my face and dripping off my nose onto the pavement, and then suddenly there's a hand on my back and a voice saying, 'Are you all right, are you okay,' and I open my eyes and look up and it's Alice . . .

'D'you want me to call you a . . . Brian?'

'Alice!' breathe, pant, 'Oh . . . hi . . . Alice,' straighten up, breathe, pant. 'How are you?' I gasp, aloofly.

'I'm fine, it's you I'm worried about. I thought you were some old man having a heart attack or something . . .'

'No, no, it's me. I'm fine, really . . .'

She sees the dumb-bells, wedged under my foot to stop them bouncing off down the hill and killing a child. 'What are *those*?'

'They're dumb-bells . . .'

'I know what they *are*, but what are *you* doing with them?'

'It's a long story.'

'Need a hand?'

'If you could . . .'

She scoops up a dumb-bell, like she's scooping up a small dog, and strides on up the hill.

24

QUESTION: What was identified by Hegel as the tendency of a concept to pass over into its own negation as the result of conflict between its inherent contradictory aspects?

ANSWER: Dialectics.

I leave Alice in my bedroom, listening to my Brandenburg Concerto LP and giving my bookshelves marks out of ten while I go and make coffee. The bedroom is not in an ideal state to be honest. I've made sure that I've not left my poetry notebook or underpants lying around, but I still don't like leaving her alone in there. The kettle is taking forever to boil, so I distract myself by rushing to the bathroom, splashing my face, and brushing my teeth very quickly to get rid of some of the biliousness. When I get back to the kitchen, Josh is there, helping himself to my newly boiled water.

'Of course you do know there's a fox loose in your bedroom?'

'My friend Alice.'

'Well hellooooo, Alice. Mind if I join you?'

'Actually, we're sort of talking about work, actually . . .'

'All right, Bri, I get the message. Just send her in to see me on the way out, will you? And you might want to do something about that?' and he gestures to the corner of my mouth, where there are two little crescents of toothpaste. '*Bonne chance, mon ami* . . .' he says, and heads for the door – 'oh, and someone called for you – Spencer, is it? – says to give him a call.' I make the coffee, pick up the mugs, steal two of Marcus' biscuits, and head back into the bedroom.

Alice is reclined on the futon, flicking idly through my copy of *The Communist Manifesto*, so I hand her the coffee, and remove the cloudy glass of water and the encrusted old mugs from the side of the bed, and take a mental photograph of her head on my pillow.

'Why's your bed-frame behind your wardrobe, Brian?'

'I thought I'd try the futon thing.'

'Right. Futon. Nice.' And she looks at the postcards and photos Blu-Tacked by the bed. 'Is this your dad?'

'Uh-huh.'

She peels the photo off the wall, looks at it. 'He's very handsome.'

I take my donkey jacket off, hang it on the wardrobe door. 'Yes, he was.'

She inspects my face, trying to work out why it should have skipped a generation, then gives me one of her frowning smiles. 'Don't you want to get changed?'

I look down at my sweater, which is living up to its name and has dark, oily damp patches under the arms, and smells of wet dog. I hesitate though, bashfully; 'No, I'm fine, really.'

'Go on, get changed. I promise I won't touch myself while you're doing it.'

And, in the racy, erotically charged atmosphere that this last remark creates, I turn my back on her and take my top off.

'So what are the weights for, big guy?'

'Oh, I just thought I'd try and get a little healthier . . .'

'Having muscles isn't the same as being healthy – my last boyfriend had the most *amazing* body, but could barely walk two hundred yards . . .'

'Was he the one with the massive penis?'

'Brian!! Who told you that?'

'You did?'

'Did I? Well, yes, that was him. Anyway, your body's fine.'

'You think?' I ask, holding the jumper in front of me, like a bashful bride.

'Sort of lean and angular – it's the Egon-Schiele-look . . .'

I turn my back and pull the new jumper over my head, and decide it's time to change the subject.

'How was the rest of your Christmas break?'

'Oh, you know. Fine. Hey, thanks for coming to stay.'

'Thank you for having me. Did you get rid of the cold meat okay?'

'Absolutely. Mingus and Coltrane say thank you very much.'

'And is your nan okay?'

'What? Oh, yes. Yes, she's fine.'

She presses Dad's photo back onto the wall and, taking care not to look at me, says, 'It got a little bit . . . weird, didn't it?'

'*I* got a bit weird you mean. It was losing my drugs-virginity, I think.'

'It wasn't just that though, was it? You were . . . strange, like you thought you had something to prove.'

'Sorry. I get a bit nervous. Especially around posh peop . . .'

'Oh, please . . .' she snaps.

'What?'

'Please, don't start with that crap, Brian. "Posh" – what a *ridiculous* word. What is "posh" anyway? That stuff's all in your head, it's completely meaningless. Christ, I hate this complete obsession with *class*, especially at this place, you can hardly say "hello" to anyone before they're getting all prolier-than-thou, and telling you about how their dad's a one-eyed chimney-sweep with rickets, and how they've still got an outside loo, and have never been on a plane or whatever, all that dubious *crap*, most of which is usually lies anyway, and I'm thinking why are you telling me all this? Am I meant to feel *guilty*? D'you think it's *my fault* or something, or are you just feeling pleased with yourself for escaping your pre-determined social role or some such self-congratulatory bullshit? I mean, what does it matter anyway? People are people, if you ask me, and they rise or fall by their own talents and merits, and their own labours, and blaming the fact that they've got a *settee* rather than a *sofa*, or eat *tea* rather than *dinner*, that's just an excuse, it's just whining self-pity and shoddy thinking . . .'

The Bach concerto's rising to a crescendo behind her as she speaks, so I say, 'And you join us live from this year's Tory Party Conference!'

'Piss off, Brian! That's not fair, that's not fair at all. *I* don't make judgements about other people because of their background, and I expect people to treat me with the same courtesy.' She's sat up on the futon now, stabbing the air with her finger. 'And anyway, it's not even *my* money, it's my parents' money, and it's not as if they got it from nicking people's dole, or running sweat-shops in Johannesburg or something, they worked fucking hard for what they've got, *fucking* hard . . .'

'They didn't work for it *all* though, did they?'

'What d'you mean?' she snaps.

'I just mean they inherited a lot, from *their* parents . . .'

'And . . . ?'

'Well, it's . . . privilege, isn't it?'

'So, what, you think people should have their money buried with them when they die, like in Ancient Egypt? Because I would have thought passing money on, using it to help your family, to buy them security and freedom, was just about the *only* truly worthwhile thing you can do with it . . .'

'Of course it is, but I'm just saying, it's a privilege.'

'Absolutely it's a privilege, and they treat it as such, and they pay a *fuck* of a lot of tax, and they do their best to give something back. But if you ask me, there's no snob like an inverted snob, and if that doesn't conform to some conventional, student-approved system of socialist thought, then I'm sorry, that's how I feel. Because I'm just so fucking bored of people trying to pass plain old *envy* off as some sort of *virtue*!' And she judders to a stop, red-faced, and picks up her mug of coffee. 'I'm not talking about *you* necessarily, of course.'

'Of course not,' and I sip my coffee too, which tastes bitterly of toothpaste, and there's a pause as we listen to the Brandenburg Concertos.

'Isn't this the theme from *Antiques Roadshow*?'

'It is. Though that's not what it says on the album cover.'

She smiles, and flops back down onto the futon. 'Sorry, just letting off steam.'

'No, that's fine. I sort of agree with you. In places,' I say, but all I can think of is Mingus and Coltrane eating bowls of pasta.

'I mean, we're friends, aren't we? Brian – look at me. We're friends, yes?'

'Yes, of course we're friends.'

'Even though I'm obviously the Queen of Sheba and you're a snotty-nosed chimney-sweep?'

'Absolutely.'

'So shall we just forget the whole thing? Just forget it and move on?'

'Forget what?'

'The thing we've just been . . . oh I see. So it is forgotten?'

'It's forgotten.'

'Good.' She says. 'Good.'

'So – d'you want to come to the pictures later this afternoon or something?'

'I can't – I've got this audition later . . .'

'Right – what for?'

'Henrik Ibsen's *Hedda Gabler*.'

'Which part?'

'The eponymous Hedda.'

'You'd be a great Hedda.'

'Thank you. I hope so. Still I doubt if I'll get it. The third years have got it all stitched up. I'll be lucky if I get cast as' – cock-er-ney accent – '*Berte the bleedin' maid* . . .'

'But you're coming to the team meeting tonight?'

'Is it *tonight*?'

'First of the new term!'

'Oh God, do I have to?'

'Patrick's being very strict. He specifically asked me to make sure you came tonight, or you're off the team, he says.' He didn't say any of that of course, but still.

'Okay, I'll see you there, and we'll have a drink afterwards.' She crosses the room, puts her arms around me so that I can smell the perfume on her neck, and whispers in my ear. 'And friends again, yes?'

'Absolutely. Friends again.'

But I'm still brooding over the conversation with Alice when Professor Morrison says;

'Tell me, Brian, why are you *here* exactly?'

The question takes me by surprise. I stop looking out of the window, and turn to Professor Morrison, who's lying back in his chair, fingers laced across his little pot belly.

'Um, personal tutorial? Two o'clock?'

'No, I mean here at university, reading English? Why are you here?'

'To . . . learn?'

'Because?'

'It's . . . valuable?'

'Financially?'

'No, you know . . .'

'Improving?'

'Yes, I suppose so. Improving. And I enjoy it, of course. I like education, learning, knowledge . . .'

'"Like it?"'

'Love it. I love books.'

'The *contents* of books, or just owning a whole load of books?'

'The contents, obviously . . .'

'So you're serious about your studies?'

'I like to think so.' He doesn't say anything, just leans right back in his chair, his arms stretched behind him with his fingers laced, and yawns. 'You don't think I am?'

'Not sure, Bri. I hope you are. But the reason I ask is because this last essay, "Notions of 'pride' and 'prejudice' in *Othello*", is, well, it's really just *awful*. Everything about it, from the title onwards, is just awful, awful, awful . . .'

'Yes, well I wrote it in a bit of a hurry actually . . .'

'Oh I know *that*, I can tell *that*. But it's such an awful, vapid, fatuous thing, that I wondered if you'd written it at all?'

'Right, so, what didn't you like?'

He sighs, slumps forward and runs his fingers through his hair, as if he's about to tell me that he wants a divorce.

'Okay, well for a start, you talk about Othello as if he's this guy you know who you're a bit worried about.'

'Well that's good, isn't it? Treating him like a real individual. Isn't that a testament to Shakespeare's vivid imagination?'

'Or your lack of insight? Othello's a *fictional character*, Brian, he's a construct, a creation. He's a particularly rich and complex creation in a remarkable work of art, but all you can say about him is it's a shame he has a hard time just because he's *black*. All I learnt from *this* is that you think bigotry is "a bad thing". Why are you telling me this? Did you think that maybe I thought bigotry was a *good* thing? What's your next essay, Brian? "Hamlet – Why the long face?" or perhaps, "Why can't you Montagues and Capulets just get along?" . . .'

'Well, no, because racism is an issue that I feel passionately about.'

'I'm sure it is, but what am I supposed to *do* about it? Phone Iago's mum, tell her to get him to back off? In fact, ironically, as a discourse on race, your portrayal of Othello as a blameless, suggestible Noble Savage might almost be viewed as racist in itself . . .'

'You think the essay's *racist*?'

'No, but I do think it's ignorant, and the two aren't unconnected.'

I start to say something, but can't work out what, so just sit there. I feel hot and red and embarrassed, as if I'm six years old, and have just wet myself. I want it to be over as soon as possible, so I half stand, reach over to the table to pick up the essay; 'Okay, well maybe I should give it another go . . .' but he's not finished yet, and he pulls the pages back towards him.

'This to me isn't the work of someone who "loves knowledge", it's the work of someone who quite likes the idea of *appearing* as if he loves knowledge. There isn't a shred of insight or original thought or mental effort here, it's shallow, pious, ill-informed, it's intellectually immature, it's stuffed full of received ideas and gossip and clichés.' He leans forward, picks up my essay with his fingertips, like a dead seagull. 'Worst of all it's disappointing. I'm disappointed that *you* wrote it, and even more disappointed that you thought it worth my time and energy to read the thing.'

He pauses, but I can't think of anything to say, so I just look out of the window, waiting for it to be over. But the silence is almost as uncomfortable, and when I finally turn back, he's giving me a look that I think I'm meant to interpret as 'fatherly'.

'Brian, this morning I had a private tutorial about W.B. Yeats with a student – a nice enough girl, sure to get on, privately educated at one of the more exclusive girls' schools – and at one point during this tutorial, I had to go out to my car and get my RAC Road Atlas so that I could actually explain to her where Northern Ireland is.' I go to speak, but he raises his hand. 'Brian. When I interviewed you in this office a year ago, you struck me as a uniquely enthusiastic and passionate young man. A little unfocused perhaps, a little *gauche* – may I say gauche? Is that a fair assessment? – but at least you weren't taking your education for granted. A lot of students, particularly at a university like this, tend to treat their education as a sort of state-subsidised three-year cheese-and-wine party, with a flat and a car and a nice job at the end, but I really thought you weren't like that . . .'

'I'm not . . .'

'So what's the problem then? Is something distracting you? Are you unhappy, depressed . . . ?'

God, I don't know. Am I? Is this what it feels like? Maybe I am. Maybe I should tell him about Alice. Is simply being in love a good enough excuse for irrational behaviour? It was for Othello, obviously, but for me?

'So. Is there something you'd like to talk to me about?'

I'm in love with a beautiful woman, more in love than I ever thought possible, so much so that that I'm incapable of thinking about anything else, but she is entirely unobtainable, and finds me amusing at best, repulsive at worst, and I consequently think that I may be going a little bit mad . . .

'I don't think so, no.'

'Well, then I don't know what the problem is, because looking at your grades so far this year – 74%, 64%, 58% and for this, 53% – it would seem that you're actually becoming *less intelligent*. Which, strangely enough, is not what an education is for . . .'

25

QUESTION: Where might you find the pons, the arcuate fasciculus, Wernicke's area and the fissure of Rolando?
ANSWER: The brain.

It's true, I am becoming more stupid. Or do I mean 'stupider'?

And it's not just barely making the team for The Challenge, it's the lectures. I go in and sit down, all bright-eyed and alert, and even when it's something I'm genuinely interested in, like metaphysical poetry, or the development of the sonnet form, or the rise of the middle classes in the English novel, I find that, after about ten minutes I'm so lost and confused that I might as well be listening to a football match on the radio. I walk into a university library that's almost audibly groaning with the huge weight and breadth of human knowledge, and the same two things always happen: a) I start to think about sex b) I need to go to the toilet. I go to a lecture and I fall asleep, or I haven't read the book because I'm always falling asleep, or I don't understand the book in the first place, or I don't get the references, or I'm looking around the room at girls, and even when I *do* understand the lecture, I don't know what to say about it, I don't even know if I agree with it, or disagree. I've been given the opportunity, entirely at the state's expense, to study beautiful, timeless, awe-inspiring works of art, and my response to them never gets any more profound than 'thumbs-up' or 'thumbs-down'. And meanwhile some intense bright, shiny-haired young thing in the front row will stick up their hand and say something like 'don't you think that, formally speaking, Ezra Pound's language is too hermetically sealed to be readable in structural terms?' and even though I understand all the words individually, 'readable' and 'formally' and 'is' and even 'hermetically', I have no idea what they mean when put together in that particular order.

And it's the same when I try to *read* the stuff, it just turns to mush in my head, so that an important, profound poem like Shelley's *Mont Blanc* goes something like 'The Everlasting Universe of Things/Flows through the mind, and rolls its rapid blah/Now dark – now bla-di-da – now da-di-bla-di-da' until it crumbles and disintegrates. Of course if Shelley had released *Mont Blanc* as a seven-inch single, then I'd be able to recite it word for word *and* tell you the highest chart positions, but because it's *literature*, and it's actually intellectually *demanding*, then I just don't have a clue. The sad fact is that I love Dickens and Donne and Keats and Eliot and Forster and Conrad and Fitzgerald and Kafka and Wilde and Orwell and Waugh and Marvell and Greene and Sterne and Shakespeare and Webster and Swift and Yeats and Joyce and Hardy, really, really love them. It's just that they don't love me back.

When did this start happening? Why is nothing working out the way it should have? The brain is, after all, a muscle, and I thought that if you exercised it enough, really put it through its paces, it would become this lean, humming, electrically charged little white fist of protein. Instead it feels as if I have a head full of warm, moist matter; grey and lardy and useless, the kind of thing you find wrapped in plastic inside a supermarket chicken. In fact, now I think of it, I'm not even sure if the brain technically *is* a muscle. Is it an organ? Or tissue? Or a gland? My brain certainly feels like a gland.

And it's at its most gland-ish tonight, at The Challenge practice meeting in Patrick's flat. It's the first of the new year, and only a month to go before our first televised appearance, so Patrick is particularly on edge, especially as he's about to introduce a whole new exciting element to the proceedings.

Patrick has spent the Christmas vacation building *buzzers* – four battery-powered contraptions made from Christmas-tree lights and doorbells screwed to LP-sized squares of plywood, which he's painted with red enamel paint – and he's clearly fiercely proud of this new innovation, because I barely have time to say hello and Happy New Year to Lucy Chang, or ask Alice how the audition went, before we're sat on the sofa, buzzers on our knees. Patrick settles on a swivel office chair with a thick pad of 4 by 6 index cards, adjusts the angle-poise over his shoulder, and begins . . .

'So, your starter question, for ten points – which eighteenth century British Prime Minister was nicknamed the Great Commoner?'

I buzz. 'Gladstone?' I say.

'Nope,' says Patrick. 'Anyone?'

'Pitt the Elder?' says Alice.

'Correct. That's minus five points, Brian. I did say *eighteenth* century, didn't I?'

'Yes, you did . . .'

'And Gladstone was ninet . . .'

'Yes, I know . . .'

'Okay then. Which of the following countries does *not* have a coastline. Niger, Mali, Chad, Sudan.' I think I know this one, so I buzz and say . . .

'Sudan!'

'Nope,' says Patrick

Lucy Chang says, 'All of them, *except* Sudan?'

'Correct. So that's minus *ten* points, Brian. Okay, the vestibular nerve, the tensor tympani, the ampulae, utricle and saccule are all parts of which organ?'

I've no idea, but find that I've buzzed anyway.

'Brian?' Patrick groans.

'Sorry, I pressed by mistake . . .'

'So that's minus *fifteen* points . . .'

'. . . I know, it was a mistake, my finger slipped . . .'

'. . . What's the answer, Lucy?'

'The ear?'

'Exactly, the ear. What are you studying, Lucy?'

'Medicine.'

'And Brian, what are you studying?'

'English Litera . . .'

'Exactly. English Literature. So, Brian, you don't think maybe Lucy would be better qualified to answer . . . ?'

'I'm sure she would, but like I said, my finger slipped. These buzzers are very touch-sensitive . . .'

'So it's *my buzzer*'s fault?'

'Well . . .'

'The real buzzers on the day, you don't think they'll be touch-sensitive too?'

'I'm sure they will, Patrick . . .'

'. . . because I've used those buzzers, guys, and I can tell you, you have to be very, very sure of the answer before you press them . . .'

'Look, could we get a move on d'you think?' says Alice, testily. 'It's just I've got to be somewhere at nine-thirty . . .'

'Where?' I ask, suddenly anxious.

'Just going to see someone – is that okay with you?' She snaps. Lucy and Patrick share a look.

'Of course, but I thought we were going for a drink, that's all . . .'

'Can't now. I've got a *Hedda Gabler* re-call if you must know' and I bridle slightly, and accidentally press the buzzer.

'Sorry!'

'Actually, I don't think my buzzer's working at all,' says Lucy Chang, and Patrick snatches it off her, likes it's poor Lucy's fault, and jabs at it with the huge Swiss Army knife he keeps on his big bunch of keys. Alice and I glance at each other warily and we seem a long way from being a winning team.

After that, I don't bother answering any more questions, even the ones I actually know the answers to. I just leave them to Lucy, mainly, and Alice, occasionally, and as soon as Patrick has given his post-match analysis – don't get trigger-happy with those buzzers, always concede to the person with greater expertise in that area, listen to the question, be wary of interruptions – Alice has got her coat on and is heading for the door. Just before she exits, though, in the spirit of appeasement, she says, 'Oh, by the way, some friends of mine are having a party tomorrow night, twelve Dorchester Street, eight o'clock? You're all invited,' and then she smiles an apology at me, I think, and goes.

I walk home with Lucy Chang, who lives up the hill from me, and she's actually incredibly nice. I realise that Lucy is the first Chinese person I've really talked to outside of a restaurant environment, but decide not to say this out loud. Instead we talk about what it's like training as a doctor and she's very interesting on the subject, but very quiet, and I have to lean in to hear what she's saying, which makes me feel a bit Prince Philip-ish.

'What made you want to be a doctor?'

'My parents, really. They always said being a doctor was the highest ambition you could have. You know, actually making a difference to the quality of life.'

'And you enjoy it?'

'Absolutely. I love it. How about you, how about lit-er-a-ture?'

'Oh, I like it. I just don't know if I'm improving the quality of anyone's life, that's all.'

'Do you write?'

'Not really. I've just sort of started writing a bit of poetry.' I'm still practising saying this aloud, but Lucy doesn't sneer, not out loud anyway. 'Sounds a bit pretentious, doesn't it?'

'Oh, not in the least. Why?'

'I don't know, it's just like Orwell said; the natural response of the Englishman to poetry was extreme embarrassment.'

'Well, I don't know why. Some might argue that poetry is actually the purest form of human expression.'

'Yeah, well, you haven't read my poems.'

She laughs quietly, and says, 'I wouldn't mind reading them. I'm sure they're very good.'

'And I wouldn't mind you operating on me either!' I say, and then there's a pause while we both try to work out why this sounds dirty.

'Well, let's hope it doesn't ever come to that!' and we walk on a bit further, trying to shake off that 'operate-on-me' comment, which is still hanging in the air between us like a fart in an art gallery.

'So – dissecting anything good at the moment?' I ask eventually.

'The cardiovascular system.'

'Right. And do you enjoy that?' asks Prince Philip.

'Yes, yes I do.'

'And is that what you'd like to specialise in when you leave?'

'Surgery I think, though I don't know in what area yet. I'm torn between heart and brain.'

'Aren't we all!' I say, which sounds pretty witty to me. In fact I say it before I can actually work out what it means, so that it just hangs there in the air, too. And then Lucy comes up with a complete non-sequitur.

'Alice is cool, isn't she?'

'Yes. Yes. She can be.' It was a non-sequitur, wasn't it?

After a while. 'Very beautiful.'

'Hmm.'

After a while. 'You seem pretty close.'

'Well, yes, I suppose we are. Sometimes.' And encouraged and surprised by this new-found easy familiarity between Lucy and I, say, 'Patrick is a very strange man, isn't he? I think perhaps he . . .' but Lucy stops suddenly, and puts her hand on my forearm and squeezes slightly . . .

'Brian – can I tell you something? Something personal . . .'

'Of course,' I say, then realise what she's going to say . . .

'This is a little embarrassing for me . . .' she says, frowning.

She's going to ask me out! 'Go on, say it . . .'

'Ok-aaaay . . .' she says, taking a deep breath . . .

What should I say? Well – no. Clearly I have to say no . . .

'Here goes . . .'

. . . but how do I let her down gently, without upsetting her . . . ?

'Well . . . it's just that when you talk to me, you have this habit of over-enunciating everything, like I'm profoundly deaf or something?'

'Oh. Do I?'

'Uh-huh, you kinda lean over and nod and use very simple words, like I've got this incredibly limited vocabulary? And I don't know if it's because I'm "of Chinese Origin" or American or something, but I've never *been* to China, I don't *speak* Chinese, I don't even particularly care for Chinese food, so I will be able to understand if you just, you know, talk good old, regular, colloquial English . . .'

'Sorry. I didn't realise I was doing it . . .'

'It's okay, it's not just you, I get it *a lot*. I mean, all the time . . .'

'I'm so embarrassed . . .'

'Don't be, it's fine, it just sounds a little patronising, that's all.'

'Actually I think you'll find it's pronounced p*a*tronising!'

'Not funny, Brian.'

'No, right, of course not.' We're outside Richmond House now. 'So, will I see you at the party tomorrow?'

'Maybe. I'm not so good at parties.'

'But maybe.'

'Maybe,' and she sets off up the hill.

'By the way – can I just ask you something?'

She pauses, a little nervously 'Go on.'

'The brain – medically speaking, is it a muscle or a gland?'

'Well, it's a concentration of various kinds of nerve tissue, all with a similar, connected purpose, so technically I suppose that would make the brain an organ. Why?'

'Just wondered. See you tomorrow.'

'Bye,' and I watch her panda disappear off up the hill.

Then I turn and am about to trot up the steps to the front door when I notice a hunched shape in the shadows, slumped against the front door, head down, barring the way. I freeze halfway up the steps, and peer at the man, who runs both hands over his closely shaved head before looking up at me. I'm just coming to terms with discovering what it's like to be mugged when the dark shape lurches to his feet and speaks: 'So – who's the Asian babe then, Bri?'

And, stepping out of the shadows, I recognise the sharp, shrewd eyes of Spencer Lewis.

26

QUESTION: Frequently used in sculpture, where it is sometimes known as Florentine marble, what is the hydrous fine-grained translucent variety of gypsum formed by bedded deposits precipitated from evaporating sea water?

ANSWER: Alabaster.

'Spencer? What are you doing here?'

'Just thought I'd come and visit, that's all,' and I run up the stairs and go to hug him, and he goes to punch the top of my arm, and we do that weird little dance that boys do when they greet each other. 'And you did invite me . . .'

'Yeah, I know I did, but . . . hey, what's happened to your hair . . . ?'

He runs his hand over his head, which has been shaved right down to the scalp. 'It's the escaped-convict look – don't you like it?' he says, and I notice the thick, slurred quality to his voice, indicating that he must have got pissed on the train.

'Yeah! Yeah, it's very . . . bold. Who did it?'

'I did.'

'For a bet, or . . . ?'

'Fuck off, Brideshead. So, can I come in or what?'

'Of course,' I unlock the door and turn the hall light on, and we squeeze past the bikes in the hallway. He looks different in other ways too, his eyes look hooded and tired, smudged purple underneath, like bruises. Despite the bitter cold he's wearing just a crumpled, old Harrington that I remember from school, and as luggage he's carrying a thin plastic bag, which as far as I can tell, only contains two cans of lager.

'I did phone this morning, spoke to some posh bloke,' he says as we climb the stairs.

'That's my housemate, Josh. It's Josh and Marcus.'

'What are they like then?'

'Oh, they're all right. Not really your type.'

'So are they your type then?'

'I don't think they're anyone's type actually.' And we're outside my bedroom. I open the door.

'So – this is where all the action takes place is it? Nice . . .'

I take my coat off, and throw it casually over the dumb-bells before Spencer sees them.

'Make yourself at home. D'you want a cup of tea, or coffee or something?'

'Got any booze?'

'I think there might be some home-brew.'

'Home-brew?'

'It's Marcus and Josh's really.'

'What's it like?'

'Bit like piss?'

'Alcoholic though?'

'Uh-huh.'

'Go on then.'

And, reluctantly, I leave him alone in my room, and hurry to the kitchen to get the booze. I need a drink, too. Spencer's arrival has thrown me completely, partly because he's clearly being a bit weird and mean, and partly, I suppose, because I never expected in my life to be unhappy to see him. Also, I'm a little anxious, because I think I may have left my poetry notebook on my desk, open on a tentative new erotic sonnet that I'm working on. The first line contains the words 'breasts of alabaster', and if Spencer reads that, then I'll never hear the end of it.

And suddenly I can hear the opening of the Brandenburg

Concertos playing very loudly from my room, so I grab the mugs of beer and hurry back to find him sitting at my desk with a fag in his mouth, the Bach album sleeve in one hand, the Communist Manifesto in the other.

'So what are you these days, communist or a socialist?'

'A socialist I suppose,' I say, turning the volume down.

'Right. So what's the difference then?' I know he knows the difference, and that I'm being teased, but I tell him anyway.

'A communist is opposed to the notion of private property and ownership of the means of production, whereas socialism is about working towards . . .'

'Why's your mattress on the floor?'

'It's a futon.'

'Right. A fu-ton. Did the Asian babe teach you that then?'

'"Asian babe" – racism *and* sexism in the same phrase!' I say, slipping the breasts-of-alabaster poem into the desk drawer. 'Actually Lucy's originally from Minneapolis. Just because she's of Chinese *origin*, doesn't mean she's *Chinese*.'

'God, you're right, this beer really is piss. Can't we go down the pub or something?'

'Bit late, isn't it?'

'We've still got half an hour.'

'I've got to do some reading before tomorrow morning.'

'What have you got to read?'

'Pope's *The Rape of the Lock*.'

'Sounds racy. Do it in the morning though, yeah?'

'Well . . .'

'Come on, just a quick one?'

I know I shouldn't go, of course. But this room suddenly feels too small and bright, and getting drunk now seems like a necessity, so I say okay, and we go to the pub.

The Flying Dutchman is still busy when we arrive, and as I wait at the bar, I look across to where Spencer's standing, glaring round the room with his red eyes narrowed, puffing sourly on another cigarette. I get a pint for me, a pint and a vodka for him.

'So, a student pub this, is it?' he asks.

'Don't know. I suppose it is. Shall we see if we can find a table?'

We squeeze through to the back, holding our pints over our heads, find an empty table and settle, and there's a moment's silence before I say, 'So – how's things at home?'

'Oh – wonderful. *Really* A-1.'

'So what brings you here then?'

'You invited me; come any time, remember?'

'Of course.'

And he's silent for a moment, seems to make a decision, and then says, a little too casually 'And like I said – I'm an escaped convict, aren't I?'

'What d'you mean?'

'Well, let's just say I'm in a spot of bother. With the legal system.'

I laugh, and then stop laughing. 'What for? Not another fight . . .'

'No, I got caught, didn't I? Fiddling the dole.'

'You're joking . . .'

'No, Bri, I'm not joking,' he says wearily.

'How come?'

'Don't know – someone must have split on me I suppose. Hey, it wasn't you, was it?'

'Yeah, Spencer, it was me. So what's going to happen?'

'Don't know, do I? Depends on the magistrate I suppose.'

'You're going to court?'

'Oh yeah. They're having a crackdown apparently, so I'm up in court next month. Good news isn't it?'

'So what are you going to say?'

'In court? Don't know yet. I thought I might say that God told me to do it.'

'And are you still working at the petrol station?'

'Well, not exactly, no.'

'Why not?'

'Because I got caught.'

'Caught doing what?'

He takes a large gulp of the vodka. 'With my hand in the till.'

'You're *joking*!'

'Brian, why d'you keep asking me if I'm joking? D'you think this is the kind of thing that I'd find funny?'

'No, I just meant . . .'

'They had a camera hidden over the till, and I got caught taking the cash out at the end of the night.'

'How much?'

'I don't know, a fiver, tenner sometimes, a little bit here and there from not ringing in sweets and crisps and stuff.'

'So are they going to prosecute you as well?'

'No, they can't, 'cause I wasn't on the books. But let's just say my manager wasn't very happy. He's kept a load of my wages back and told me if he ever saw me again he'd break my legs . . .'

'So how much does he think you took?'

'A couple of hundred?'

'And how much did you take?'

Spencer exhales smoke. 'Couple of hundred sounds about right.'

'Bloody hell, Spencer . . .'

'They were paying me one pound fucking eighty an hour, Brian, what the fuck did they expect?'

'I know, I know!'

'Anyway, you're a *Communist*, I thought you didn't agree with private ownership.'

'I don't, but Marx is talking about the means of production, not the contents of the till at a petrol station. And besides I don't *dis*approve, and anyway I'm a socialist. And I just think, well, it's a shame, that's all. What do your mum and dad say?'

'Oh, they're very, very proud of me,' and he drinks about half a pint in one go. 'Anyway. The point is I'm well and truly fucked.'

'But you'll get another job though, won't you?'

'Oh, definitely – an unqualified, unemployed petty thief with a criminal record. In terms of today's competitive job market, I'm absolute fucking gold dust. Want another pint?'

'A half, maybe.'

'Well, you'll have to get them, I find myself a little embarrassed, financially speaking.'

So I head to the bar again, and get the pints in, and accept that I'm probably not going to get round to reading *The Rape of the Lock* tonight after all.

Needless to say we're the last to leave the pub. After they've called last orders, Spencer takes it upon himself to pour the remnants of other people's discarded drinks into our glasses, something I haven't done since I was sixteen maybe, so that by the time we get back to Richmond House, we're both pretty pissed. There we finish off the mugs of milky home-brew, and open the two cans of Special Brew that make up Spencer's luggage, along with the *Daily Mirror* and a half-eaten pasty. I tell him all about New Year and Alice, and my version of the encounter with her naked mum in the kitchen, and Spencer unclenches a bit, and laughs for the first time, a proper, generous laugh, rather than a sneer or a snigger.

Then I get up to change the record, and put on *The Kick Inside*, Kate Bush's remarkable but challenging debut album, and he reverts to type, laughing all the way through 'The Man With The Child In His Eyes', and taking the piss out of my record collection and the postcards on my wall. To distract him I put on the tape he made me, 'Bri's College Compilation', and we both slump drunkenly back on the futon and watch the ceiling buckling, warping and revolving over our heads as we listen to Gil Scott-Heron singing '*The Bottle*'.

'You know you're in this, don't you?'

'In what?'

'This song – listen . . .' and he crawls on his hands and knees over to the music system, presses stop and rewind. 'Listen very carefully . . .' and the song starts, a live recording, the first sixteen bars just electric organ and percussion, and then a jazz flute solo starts, and Gil Scott-Heron says something I don't quite hear . . .

'Get it?' says Spencer, excited.

'No . . . ?'

'Listen again, cloth-ears, listen properly,' and he presses rewind, stop, play, turns the volume to full and this time I hear Gil Scott-Heron say, quite clearly, 'Brian Jackson on flute for ya!' and the crowd applauding.

'Get it?'

'Yeah!'

'That's you!'

'Brian Jackson on flute!'

'Again . . .'

And there it is again – '. . . Brian Jackson on flute for ya'.

'That's *amazing*, I've never heard that before.'

'That's because you never listen to the compilation tapes I make you, you philistine *bastard*,' and he crawls back to the futon, flops on his back, and we listen to the song for a minute or so, and I decide I quite like jazz after all, or soul or funk or whatever this is, and resolve to explore the world of black music more fully in the future.

'So's Alice the one you fancy then?' says Spencer, eventually.

'I don't *fancy* her, Spence, I *love* her . . .'

'You *love* her . . .'

'I looooove her . . .'

'You loooooove her . . .'

'I absolutely, completely, totally love her, with all my heart . . .'

'I thought you loved Janet Parks, you fickle *tart* . . .'

'Janet Parks is a *cow* compared to Alice Harbinson. "Not Janet Parks but Alice do I love/Who shalt compare a raven to a dove?"'

'Whassat then?'

'*Midsummer Night's Dream*, act two, scene three.'

'Jackson, you *pillock*. So will I meet her then, this Alice?'

'Maybe. There's a party tomorrow night if you're still around.'

'Want me to put a word in for you, mate?'

'No point, mate. Like I said, she's a goddess. What about you, though?'

'Not me, mate. You know me, I'm a robot.'

'You must love someone . . .'

'Only you, mate, only you . . .'

'Yeah, well I love you too, mate, but that's not *sexual*, *romantic* love is it?'

'Oh, yeah, definitely sexual. What d'you think I've come all this way for? It's because I *want* you. Give us a kiss, big boy,' and Spencer jumps on me and sits on my chest, making wet, smacking noises, and I try to push him off, and it turns into a scuffle . . .

'Come on Bri, give in, you know you want to . . .'

'Get off!'

'Kiss me, my love! . . .'

'Spencer! That hurts! . . .'

'Don't fight it, my darling . . .'

'Get off me! You're sat on my keys, you *bender* . . .'

And then there's a knock on the door, and Marcus stands blinking in the doorway, mole-eyed behind lop-sided aviator specs, in his ruby-red towelling dressing gown;

'Brian, it's two-fifteen, is there any chance of you turning the music *off*?'

'Sorry, Marcus!' I say, and crawl across the floor towards the stereo.

'Heeeeelloooo, *Marcus*,' says Spencer.

'Hello,' mumbles Marcus, pushing his specs up his nose.

'Marcus's a lovely name, Marcus . . .'

'This's my best mate Spencer, Marcus!' I say, slipping on all the S's.

'Just keep it down, will you?'

'Okay, Marcus, nice to meet you Marcus . . .' and, once he's closed the door '. . . bye, Marcus, you *wwwwwanker* . . .'

'Shhhhh! Spencer!'

But with the music off, it doesn't seem so much fun any more, so with some difficulty, and quite a lot of noise, we get the heavy iron bed-frame out from behind the wardrobe, and tip it over next to the futon. There's a brief debate as to who should sleep where, but Spencer gets the futon, because he's a guest after all, and I lie on the bare wire bed-frame, fully clothed, beneath a pile of coats and towels, with my head on an inch thick polyester pillow, feeling the floor buck and spin underneath me, and longing to be sober again.

'So how long you staying for, Spency?'

'Don't know. A couple of days maybe? Just till I can get my head sorted out? 'S that all right, mate?'

'Course's alright. Stay's long's you want. 'S what friends are for, isn't it?'

'Cheers, mate.'

'Cheers.'

After a while, I say, 'But you're all right, mate, aren't you?'

'Don't know, mate. Don't know. Not sure. How 'bout you?'

''M all right.'

And after a while, he says, 'Brian Jackson on flute!'

And I say, 'Brian Jackson on flute . . .'

And he says, 'And the crowd go wild . . .'

And then we fall asleep.

27

QUESTION: How is the 'calumet', a central ceremonial object in Native American culture, more commonly known?

ANSWER: The peace pipe.

At about four-thirty in the morning I throw up.

Thankfully I stumble down the corridor to the bathroom just in time, but when I look up from the sink, wet-lipped, pale and shaking, at my reflection in the mirror, I nearly throw up again because it becomes clear that I have transformed in the night into some kind of freakishly hideous man-lizard, with a diamond-shaped pattern of scales all down one side of my face. I cover my mouth to suppress my scream, and then realise that it's just the imprint of the bed-frame's wire mesh on my face, so I go back to bed.

The alarm goes off at 8.15, like an ice-pick in my ear, and I lie in bed and listen to the rain pelt against the window. God knows I've had hangovers before, most days in fact, but this is a strange new kind; almost hallucinatory. It's as if my whole nervous system has been re-calibrated, so the slightest sensation – the rain outside, the light from the anglepoise, the smell from the empty can of Special Brew that's rolled under the bed-frame – all have a grotesquely exaggerated effect. All my nerve endings seem uncomfortably alive and twitching, even the ones inside my body, so that if I lie still and concentrate, I can actually feel the shape and location of my internal organs; the lungs bellowing wetly, the exhausted, perspiring yellow-grey mass of my liver slumped against my backbone, the engorged, aching, bruised purple kidneys, the hot, spasming lower intestine. I try to move, to physically shake this last image out of my head, but the noise of my hair rustling against the pillowcase sounds massively amplified too, so I lie very still on my side and look at Spencer, lying a few feet away, his mouth pouting open slightly, a damp patch of opaque saliva soaking into my pillow. I'm lying close enough to smell his breath, which is stale, muggy and warm. God, I'd forgotten about the skinhead haircut. He looks like a fascist; a good-looking, charismatic fascist, but they're the worst kind, as history tells us. What if people see me with him at the party tonight, and think that I'm friends with a fascist? Maybe he won't be here tonight. Maybe he'll have gone home. Maybe that'll be for the best.

Getting up and sitting on the edge of the bed-frame feels Herculean, and I can actually *hear* the contents of my stomach shift and settle, like a thin plastic bin-bag full of warm, gently effervescing custard. The idea of changing out of last night's clothes seems frankly untenable, so I don't, and I'm not even sure if I can lace up my shoes without throwing up on them, but I manage somehow, then pull on my coat/blanket and manage to leave the house with Spencer still asleep, and walk up the hill towards the English department. There's a steady drizzle, and a squally wind. I had this fanciful idea that I'd be able to read *The Rape of The Lock* as I walk, but the pages are getting soaked, and besides it's all my nervous system can handle just to walk without falling over.

Outside the lecture hall, I lean against the wall and rub my hands briskly over my face to try and give it some colour other than grey, when I see Rebecca Epstein striding out through the gate. For a second I imagine that she's seen me but decided to just walk away, but that can't be right, because that would mean that she's ignoring me.

'Rebecca!' I shout, but she's stomping off down the street,

the collar of her black vinyl coat turned up, head down against the rain. 'Rebecca . . . ?' I hold on to the bag of fizzy custard, and try to run without moving my head.

'Rebecca, it's Brian!'

'So it is. Hello, Jackson,' she says blankly.

'How are you?'

'Fine.'

And we walk on a little further.

'Good lecture?' I ask.

'Uh-huh.'

'What was it on?'

'Do you really want to know or are you just making conversation?'

'I'm just making conversation.'

I think I see the ghost of a smile, but maybe I imagine it because the next thing she says is: 'Shouldn't you be heading off to a lecture yourself?'

'Well, I was meant to, but I'm not sure if I'm up to it somehow . . .'

'What's it on?'

'Do you really want to know or are you just . . . ?'

'You look like shite by the way.'

'I feel like shite.'

'Good. I'm glad.'

She seems hostile. She always seems hostile of course, but more so today. We walk on a little further, with me just behind her, and I wonder how someone with such short legs can manage to walk so much faster than me.

'Becs, are you angry with me or something?'

'"*Becs*"? Who the fuck is "*Becs*"?'

'*Rebecca*, I mean. Well, are you?'

'Not angry. Just . . . disappointed.'

'God, not you as well.' She looks me in the eye, for the first time. 'I just seem to be disappointing everyone at the moment. I don't know why. I'm trying hard not to, really I am.' She stops at this, and we stand in the street in the rain for a moment while she looks me up and down.

'You do know your face is completely *grey*, don't you?'

'I know.'

'And you've got white stuff in the corner of your mouth.'

I wipe it away with my coat sleeve and say, 'Toothpaste,' though I'm not sure if it is. 'Look, have you had breakfast?'

'What about your lecture?'

I remember my resolution, to attend every single possible lecture, but Rebecca feels more important than resolutions, so I say, 'I think I'll skip the lecture,' and she thinks for a moment, then says, 'Come on then' and we walk back down the hill.

The steam and grease from the breakfast specials fog the café window, condensing on the cold glass, and dripping down and pooling on our red Formica table. Rebecca and I have got a booth to ourselves, with a mug of tea for her, and milky coffee, a can of Coke, a crispy bacon roll with brown sauce and a Mars bar for me. Rebecca's doodling in the steam on the window with her finger, while I say, '. . . he's getting done for fiddling his dole, which I think is outrageous, personally. I mean, if you think about the huge amounts that all those fat-cat businesses get to fiddle in tax evasion, and no one bats an eyelid . . .'

'. . . hmmm . . .'

'. . . I mean, what is it, a measly twenty-three quid a week or something? No one can live on that. And what do they expect people to do anyway, if there's no proper work around . . . ?'

'Uh-huh . . .'

'. . . I'd like to see some of those bastard Tories survive on that money. Anyway, I'm worried that he's going to ask if he can borrow money from me, because I can't afford to lend him money, not with grants at this level . . .'

. . . and here I stop talking because I realise that Rebecca's written the words 'Heeeelp meeee!' backwards in the steam on the window.

'Sorry. I'm being a bit boring, aren't I?'

'Well, Jackson, you know me, usually I'd love nothing better than to discuss Tory social policy of a morning, it's just, well, it's not really the important issue here. Is it?'

'No, I suppose not.' I take a deep breath. 'Sorry about the other night.'

'And do you know exactly what you're apologising for?'

Do I? 'Not exactly, no.'

'Not really an apology then, is it?'

'No. No, I suppose not.' Looking back on that evening, I suppose it was a little like getting caught up in a drunken scuffle outside a pub on a Friday night; exciting and vivid and scary at the time, but afterwards you're not sure exactly who did what to whom, or even who started it. I contemplate communicating this analogy to Rebecca, but no one likes being told that kissing them is like being beaten up outside a pub, so instead I just say, 'I presumed it was just, you know, the usual.'

'What's the usual?'

'You know, just me being useless.'

'Och, well, you're no worse than me . . .'

'I'm *much* worse than you.'

'You're not . . .'

'I am . . .'

'No, you're not . . .'

'I am, I'm appalling . . .'

'All right, Jackson, let's not get into a dialectic about it, yeah?' and she sips her tea, and seems to chew it, then says, 'Look, I got a bit drunk and made a mistake, "misread the signals" or whatever the phrase is, and I'm not particularly *angry* with you, I'm just embarrassed really. It's not very often that I make myself . . .' and she gives a little, bitter laugh, '. . . *vulnerable*, is that the right word?' Then she licks the tip of her finger, and uses it to swab the crumbs of my bacon roll from my plate. 'Still, I'm sure I'll learn to love again.'

The conversation is clearly taking on a new and intriguing personal dimension here, so I lean forward on the table and rest my head at an angle against the wet window in a style that I believe denotes a kind of wistful sensitivity, and in a low voice say, 'So, have you had, you know, bad emotional experiences, in the past then, emotionally speaking?'

Rebecca pauses, mug halfway to her mouth, then looks over both shoulders. 'Sorry, but are you talking to *me*?'

'It's a fair question, isn't it?'

'It's also none of your fucking business. What d'you want me to say? It's because Daddy never let me have a pony? I got drunk, and I fancied a bit of, human, whatever, contact, and I made a pass, and I got rejected. It's not that big a deal. Just because everyone else at this fucking place is emotionally fucking *incontinent*, doesn't mean I have to be . . .'

'I think you swear too much.'

'Bollocks I do . . .'

'I think if you swear all the time, then you're going to devalue the effectiveness of the swear words.'

'And who are you, Mary-fucking-Poppins?' she says, but smiling ever so slightly, which is as much as I can hope for, I suppose. Then she sips her tea, looks out the window, and says casually, 'Anyway, if you must know, the last relationship I had ended up in an abortion clinic, so . . . well . . . anyway, I'm not quite as free and easy about these things as some people are. That's all.'

I don't know how to react to this. Or rather, I know how to react from a political point of view, but I'm just not sure how I'm meant to react as a human being. I don't know what to do with my face. Perhaps the thing is not to get too sombre, not to make too big a deal about it.

'Who was he?'

'Just some guy from home, some guy I made the mistake of

shagging. No one you know,' she says, picking holes in my balled-up serviette.

'And he packed you in because you . . . ?'

'No, of course not. Well, not immediately. Not at all. It was complicated . . .' then she sighs, glances at me, then back down to the serviette. 'Guy called Gordon, who I was at sixth form with. First-true-love, all that crap. We'd been going out about six months, and we were going to go inter-railing together that summer, after our Highers, then take a year out and go and live somewhere abroad, see how things worked out, see if we wanted to, you know, whatever. So we set off round Europe, seeing the sights, sleeping on beaches, all very love's-young-dream, then halfway round Spain, turned out I was pregnant. So we talked it through, decided what to do, came straight back, sorted things out. And he said that we'd get through it together and he'd stick by me, which he did. But only for a week and a half. So. There you go.'

'And did you, you know, love him?' She frowns, purses her lips, but doesn't reply, just looks out the window, then back to the balled-up serviette. I don't know what to say, but feel like I ought to say something. 'Well I'm sure you did the right thing at the time.'

Rebecca's eyes flash back at me; 'Brian, I *know* I did the right thing. I wasn't asking for your *approval* . . .'

'No, I know . . .'

'. . . and there's no need to start talking in that dopey voice either . . .'

'What voice?'

'You know what voice. It does happen you know, abortion, a lot, more than you know . . .'

'I do know . . .'

'. . . and we don't all curl up into a little ball about it either, we don't all crawl away into a corner with a copy of *The Bell Jar* you know. Most women just get on with things . . .'

'I'm sure . . .'

'. . . so let's just change the subject then, shall we?'

'Okay.'

'Is that your Mars bar?' she says, and I have a tiny little moment of anxiety, because I can't remember whether or not we're meant to be boycotting Mars bars.

'Uh-huh.'

'Give it here, then.' I dutifully hand it over to her, and she takes a bite, chews it for a moment or two. 'Why's everything you eat and drink *brown*? I've never seen so much *brown* food. It wouldn't hurt you to eat the odd piece of fruit and veg every now and then, you know . . .'

'You sound like my mum,' I say.

'Well, she's a wise lady. You should listen to her. And me.' She takes another bite. 'So, have you seen her, then?' she says with her mouth full.

'Who? My mum?'

'No, not your mum . . .'

'Who, then?'

'You know who; Farrah-Fucking-Fawcett.'

'Oh, just a couple of times.'

She takes another bite, then tosses the Mars bar back across the table at me, where it lands sticky-end down. 'And do you still . . . *like* her then?'

I recognise that there's a very real danger that I could end up with a teaspoon in my eye, so I choose my words very carefully, and just say, 'I think so.'

'And what do you think she thinks about you?'

'I think she finds me . . . interesting.'

She looks at me, and goes to say something, then looks out of the window, and starts to draw in the condensation again, a smiley face. '*Interesting*, eh? Well, it's very touching of you to hang in there, I suppose. Persistence in the face of indifference. Very . . . *plucky*,' she says, with a curl of the lip.

'Yeah, well. I don't really seem to have much choice in the matter, to be honest.'

'Oh no, there's always a choice, Brian. You've always got a choice whether or not to be a complete and utter *sap*.'

When I arrive home in the middle of the day, I see Marcus coming out of the house and locking the front door. I duck behind a wall and even contemplate running away, but don't have full control of my legs yet, and besides he's seen me, and waits at the top of the steps, tapping the palm of his hand with an invisible rolling-pin.

'Hiya, Marcus!'

'Hello, *Brian*.'

I try to get past him to the front door out of the drizzle, but he's not budging.

'Sorry about last night, Marcus,' I say, you little squirt . . .

'You do know overnight guests aren't allowed on university premises, don't you?'

'Yes, I know . . .' I say, taking his aviator spectacles off his face . . .

'I mean, Josh and I might want to have people to stay, but we don't, because we respect the university rules . . .'

'I know, Marcus . . .' I say, snapping the spectacles neatly in two across the bridge . . .

'So how long's he staying then?'

'Don't know. The next couple of days? Just till he's sort of sorted himself out . . .' and I toss the broken spectacles on the ground, grind the glass under foot . . .

'Seemed to me that might take more than a couple of days . . .'

I look up to my bedroom window, worried that Spencer's still lying in bed, listening, then offer, in a low voice, 'Tomorrow? He'll be gone by tomorrow.'

Marcus weighs this up, and finally finds it acceptable. 'Okay, tomorrow. But no later,' he says, brushing past me, and I plant my foot at the base of his spine and shove him down the flight of stone steps to his death.

'Have a good day, yeah?' I say.

In the grey mid-morning light, my bedroom is a mess of bed-frames, and album covers, coats and mattresses, duvets and moist towels. There's a sort of tangy, effervescent ammonia and alcohol smell, a feeling that if I'd walked in smoking a cigarette, my bedroom would have actually exploded in my face, so I open the window wide in spite of the rain and turn on the overhead light to see if Spencer is still lolling under a duvet somewhere. He isn't. Instead, there's a note on the desk, scrawled on a piece of lined A4.

'Gone to the pub. See you later.'

The travel alarm clock on my mantelpiece says 11.55. Next to the clock is the pile of change that I emptied out of my pockets last night. There should be approximately four pounds fifty-five there, but I count it anyway, just in case.

Four pounds fifty.

And I don't know what makes me feel sadder, the idea of Spencer in a pub before noon, or the fact that I checked to see if he'd stolen my money.

28

QUESTION: Which secret Greco-Roman festivals began as events exclusively for women, later admitting men, before finally being banned by the Roman Senate in 186 BC on the grounds of their supposedly orgiastic nature?

ANSWER: Bacchanalia.

As a general rule of thumb, you know a party's in trouble when they start playing show tunes.

When Spencer and I arrive on the doorstep of 12 Dorchester Street we can clearly hear 'Gee, Officer Krupke' from *West Side Story* blaring out loudly from the living-room hi-fi, accompanied by several ostentatiously word-perfect male voices, and whilst I love Broadway musicals as much as the next man, there's a time and a place for these things. Also, the next man in this case is Spencer, who's not really a musical theatre fan, and eyes me warily.

'You sure about this?'

'If they put *Starlight Express* on, we'll leave. All right?' and then the door's opened by Erin the Cat.

'Hiya, Erin!' I chirp.

'Hello, *Brian*,' she sighs.

No one moves. I see her eyes flick up to Spencer's shaved head.

'This is my friend, Spencer!'

'All right?' says Spencer.

'Hm,' says Erin, clearly not sure if this is all right, so I hold up the bottle of wine and four cans of lager as an incentive, and finally she opens the door.

'The kitchen's through there,' says Erin, before heading back into New York's tough West Side, where the macho, street-smart Jets are being portrayed by three larky, skinny, over-excited boys from the Drama Department. To her credit, Erin takes *West Side Story* off the stereo, and puts on Sly and the Family Stone instead. 'Oh! But it's "I Feel Pretty" next!' wails one of the Jets petulantly, and I see Spencer the Shark shaking his head and running his hand over where his hair used to be, and I have the definite sensation of having arrived at a party with a cocked and loaded shotgun.

When I get back from breakfast with Rebecca, I check to see if Spencer's stolen any money, then decide to write some notes in my poetry notebook. On a new page, opposite my 'breasts of alabaster' poem, I write;

steam and grease condense
on a café's plate-
glass windows. breakfast specials

. . . then I get tired, and decide that that's probably enough for today. I don't really have the energy, so instead I lie on the futon, start to read *The Rhyme of the Ancient Mariner*, and get as far as 'It was an Ancient . . .' before the warmth and fumes from the gas heater make me fall into an appropriately narcotic slumber.

I wake up in the afternoon gloom, fully dressed and sweaty and glue-mouthed, to find Spencer sat with his feet up on my desk, reading Coleridge.

'All right, Sleeping Beauty?'

'What time is it?'

'About four o'clock?' and there it is again, that all too common pang of regret at having entirely wasted another perfectly good day. Great chunks of my life have slipped by in this manner, the long school holidays especially; my salad days apparently, the supposedly idyllic long, hot summers, all evaporated away in a hazy torpor of hangovers and pointless ambles round Woolworths, and headache-inducing afternoon naps, and video-nasties watched for the fifteenth time with the curtains drawn, and drunken bickering and name-calling, and take-away food and fitful sleep and hangovers again and then back to Woolworths. Hadn't I made some kind of resolution about all this? Wasn't this meant to have stopped by now? I'm already *nineteen*; I can't afford to let life slip through my fingers like this. So why have I done it again? I decide it's Spencer's fault, and sit up grumpily.

'Who let you in?'

'Some long-haired prick in a *velvet waistcoat*.'

'Josh?'

'"Josh." Not very friendly.'

'Were you very friendly?'

'Probably not. Why, should I have been?'

'Well I do have to live with him, so . . .' Spencer doesn't say anything, just tosses the Coleridge back onto my desk. I get a waft of lager, cigarettes and perspiration. 'Where have you been then?'

'Went to the pub. Read the paper. Walked round the shops.'

'Buy anything?'

'What with?' The same thing you bought the lager and cigarettes with maybe? I think, but instead say:

'Nice city though, isn't it?'

'Yeah, 's alright' and he rubs his hands over his face. 'So – what now?'

'Well, there's this party tonight, which should be quite cool, but I have to do some work first really . . .'

'Nah, you don't.'

'Spence, I do . . .'

'All right, I'll just sit and read or something.'

But I have to get out of this room, as soon as possible, so instead I say . . . 'or we could just go to the pictures?'

So we go to the pictures and watch the 5.15 p.m. screening of *Amadeus*, which seems to me a beautiful and profound exploration of the nature of genius, and which Spencer sleeps through.

Things perk up, as they tend to, when we go to the pub. We argue over what to put on the jukebox, blow fifty pence on the slot-machine, then sit in a little booth and have a laugh again. Spencer tells me that Tone has joined the Territorial Army.

'You're joking . . .'

'I'm not . . .'

'But he's a *nutter* . . .'

'Doesn't matter. They prefer nutters . . .'

'So they're going to *arm* him?'

'Eventually.'

'Too-oooo w-risky,' we say, in unison, and I realise I haven't said 'too-oooo w-risky' for years. Then Spencer says, 'Initially of course, they're just training him to sit on the enemy's chest and fart in his face . . .'

'. . . or just sneak up behind him and rub his knuckles really hard on the top of their head.'

'. . . then nick their stereo equipment . . .'

'. . . fucking hell – Sergeant Tone . . .'

'. . . the ultimate deterrent . . .'

'The free world sleeps safe in its bed,' and Spence gulps his pint, then adds, 'I tell you what's *really* funny – he's trying to get me to join, too. Thinks I need some order and discipline in my life apparently.'

'Tempted?'

'Absolutely. Weekends spent in a fart-filled tent on Salisbury Plain with a bunch of Tory gun-nuts. It's just the short-sharp-shock I need.'

And I see my opportunity to slip it in undetected, so I keep smiling and say 'So have you thought about going back to college maybe . . . ?'

But Spencer spots it and says, 'Fuck off, Bri . . .' Not in an unkind way, but not kindly either, just wearily. 'Anyway, university's just National Service for the middle classes.'

'So what about me then? I'm not middle class.'

'You are middle class . . .'

'No, I'm not . . .'

'Yes, you are . . .'

'My mum earns *loads* less than your parents . . .'

'It's not about money, though, is it? It's about attitude.'

'Actually, technically it's about who owns the means of production . . .'

'Bollocks, it's about attitude. Your mum could have sent you down a coal mine, and you'd still come up middle class. It's the things you say, the books you read, that film you just made me sit through, it's the way you go on school trips and spend your money on educational books and postcards instead of fags and arcade games, it's the way you ask for black pepper in the chippy . . .'

'I've *never* done that . . .'

'You have, Bri! I was with you.'

Actually, in my defence, *my* memory of the incident is that I didn't *ask* for black pepper, I *chose* black pepper, because they had black pepper there, but I don't want to labour the point. 'So you think just because someone likes reading, or wants to learn something, or prefers black pepper, or wine to beer or whatever, that makes them middle class?'

'Yeah, more or less . . .'

'Because some people might think that's a bit of a stereotype . . .'

'Look, Bri, the fact is, you call yourself a socialist, but if you'd been around during the Russian revolution, and Lenin had given you the job of executing the Czar and his family, you wouldn't have done it. And you know why? Because you'd have been too busy trying to get off with the czar's daughter . . .'

All remnants of this morning's hangover disappear after the third pint, and I am once again taken aback by the restorative and medicinal power of lager. Obviously, this party is a big opportunity for me to move things forward with Alice, and I've thought long and hard about how to play it, and have decided that the trick is to be Devastating and Aloof. Those are tonight's watchwords. Devastating. Aloof. It's therefore important that I don't get too drunk, so for supper we eat three bags of crisps each, and some dry-roasted peanuts, for the protein, then head off to the party.

When we arrive at 12 Dorchester Street, it's clear the party's at that could-go-either-way stage. Even a cursory glance around the kitchen tells me that there's a strong theatrical bias to the guest-list – most of the chorus of *The Bacchae* are here, all talking at once, and Neil whatsisname, star of last term's acclaimed modern-dress production of *Richard III* is leaning on the fridge, talking amiably with the Duke of Buckingham, and Antigone, one of the hosts, is emptying cheesy wotsits into a big bowl. There's no sign of Alice yet, and I'm unaccountably nervous, though whether it's about what Spencer will make of Alice, or what Alice will make of Spencer, I'm not quite sure.

And all of a sudden she's there, standing in the kitchen doorway, talking to Richard III. She hasn't seen me, so I lean, Devastating and Aloof, against the kitchen sink and watch her. Her hair is gathered up on the top of her head in an artfully dishevelled fashion, and she's wearing a very tight, black long-sleeved party dress made from the same stuff as leotards, scooped very low at the front, giving her this amazing sort of bib of cleavage, and I'm reminded of the outfit Kate Bush used to wear in her early stage appearances, before she decided to concentrate exclusively on her studio recordings. In fact she's a dead ringer, right down to the dark crescents of perspiration that are starting to form under her armpits.

'That's Alice,' I whisper to Spencer.

'The one with the breasts of alabaster?' says Spencer, and before I can say anything she's rushing over to us at the sink, barking 'Salt! Salt! SALT! . . .'

'Hello, Alice,' I say, Devastating and Aloof.

'Have you seen the salt? Someone's spilt red wine on Cathy's Afghan rug . . .'

'This is my best mate from home, Spencer . . .'

'Pleased to meet you, Spencer. I need a cloth, *shift* will you, Brian! . . .' she says, moving me away from the sink, and I can't help noticing the quarter-inch doily of black lace bra peeking over the top of her leotard . . .

'Here's the salt!' shouts Antigone, and Alice runs back out of the kitchen with the wet cloth.

'That was Alice,' I say.

'Well, there's clearly a real spark between you, Bri . . .'

'You think so?'

'Absolutely, just by the way she told you to get out of her way.'

I tell him to fuck off, and we leave the kitchen.

In the hallway we meet Patrick and Lucy, arriving together and both nursing identical litres of long-life orange juice, which seems strange to me, but which I put down to coincidence. I have a little pang of anxiety because I haven't told Spencer about The Challenge, but reassure myself that it's unlikely to come up in casual conversation, so breezily I introduce them.

'So how d'you know Bri, then?' asks Spencer, on his best behaviour.

'He's on the team with us,' says Patrick.

'What team's that then?' asks Spencer, swigging from his can.

'The *University Challenge* team,' says Patrick, then steps deftly back just in time to avoid the spray of lager . . .

'You're *joking*,' says Spencer, wiping his mouth with the back of his hand.

'No,' I say wearily. 'The team's us three and Alice . . .'

'You never told me that.'

'I haven't got round to it,' I say, smiling apologetically towards Patrick and Lucy.

'Fucking hell, Brian Jackson on *University Challenge* . . .'

'Yes.'

'Though technically Brian was just the reserve . . .' adds Patrick. 'If the other team member hadn't got hepatitis . . .'

'Actually *on telly* . . .' laughs Spencer.

'Uh-huh.'

'When?'

'Three weeks' time.'

'With *Bamber Gascoigne* . . . ?'

'Yes, with Bamber Gascoigne.'

'You seem to find it amusing,' says Patrick, through a tight little smile.

'No, no, sorry, I don't, it's just, well, I think it's . . . amazing. Well done, Bri mate. And you know what a big fan I am of the show . . .' and he starts to laugh again.

Patrick sniffs and says, 'Actually, I'm just going to get a drink . . .', tucks his carton of orange juice under his arm and heads off to the kitchen, followed by Lucy, who's smiling, embarrassed, and once they've gone I say, 'Nice one, Spence . . .'

'What? What have I done now?'

'You've just laughed in their faces, that's all.'

'No, I didn't.'

'Well, yes, you did.'

'Well, I'm sorry, Bri, but I've always wondered what kind of nerdy, weird, repressed nutter would want to be on that programme, and it turns out it's you, Brian. It's *you* . . .' And he's laughing again, so I laugh again too, and tell him to fuck off, and he tells me to fuck off, and I tell him to fuck off, and I find myself wondering if it's natural for best friends to tell each other to fuck off quite so much.

We decide to explore upstairs, and find ourselves outside a bedroom with a hand-made No Entry sign sellotaped to the door. We enter, and inside there's a circle of seven or eight people all sat on the floor passing round a joint, and listening to Chris with the dirty nails continuing his epic journey 'Across The Punjab Without a Toilet Roll', all to the accompaniment of early Van Morrison. Holding on to Chris's arm is his girlfriend, a toothy lank-haired miniature Chris, who I'm pretty sure is called Ruth. 'Come on, let's go,' I whisper to Spencer. But Chris hears me, turns around: 'All right, Bri!'

'Hiya, Chris! Chris is in my tutorial group. Chris, this is my best mate from home, Spencer . . .'

'*Hiya, Spencer!*' says Chris.

'. . . and this is Ruth . . .' I say.

'Actually, my name is Mary,' says Mary, turning around and waggling the tips of Spencer's fingers. 'Hi, Spencer, *really* pleased to meet you . . .' and she shuffles to one side and pats the floor, allowing us, obliging us to join the circle.

Chris passes the joint to an extremely small, snub-nosed girl with her blonde hair held back in an Alice-band, sat against the bed with her legs tucked neatly under her. I don't know her name, but recognise her as Richard III's first wife Lady Anne, and vaguely recall a rumour that she's actually a Lady in real life too, and will one day inherit a large chunk of Shropshire. She takes the joint, inhales regally, then hands it over to us. 'Guys?'

'Cheers,' says Spence, and inhales very deeply, which is strange, because he's usually strictly booze and fags, and is generally pretty contemptuous of stoners. 'So, what were you talking about?' he asks.

'India!' says everyone in unison.

'Have you been, Spencer?' asks Chris.

'No, no, can't say I have . . .' holding his breath.

'Did you take a year out, then?' asks Mary/Ruth.

'Not . . . as . . . such,' he says, then exhales slowly.

'So where are you studying, then?' asks Chris.

'I'm not,' says Spencer.

'At the moment!' I add brightly, and Spencer gives me a look, and a crocodile smile, before taking another, deeper puff on the joint and passing it on to me. I take it, put it in my mouth, cough, take it out, pass it on, and then there's a brief pause, while people sit and listen to Van Morrison and me coughing. Then Lady Anne suddenly sits up on her knees and slurs.

'I know! Let's play "If This Person Were . . ."!'

'What's that then?' says Spence, exhaling slowly.

'Well, we pick a person, and then we go out of the room, and then that person – no, that's not right, no, *we* pick a person to go out of the room, and then the people *in* the room pick *another* person, and the person *outside* the room comes back *in* and they have to go round the circle, person-by-person, and ask questions like, um, "if this person were a type of weather what type of weather would they be?" and that person has to answer and say something like "this person . . ." – the one we've secretly picked – ". . . would be a bright sunny day!" or "heavy thunder!" or something, they have to *personify* that person depending on how they perceive *that* person to be, and then the person who went *out* the room asks the *next* person "if this person were a type of *fish*, or a type of *underwear*, say, what type of *fish* or *underwear* would they be?" and that person . . .' and slowly and laboriously, she goes on explaining the rules to 'If This Person Were . . .' for maybe another two or three days, giving me plenty of time to look at Spencer, who's sitting slack-jawed, looking dazed and confused and smiling quietly to himself. I hear a crack, look down, and realise that

I'm crushing the can of lager in my hand. I decide to get us out of there . . .

'Come on Spencer, let's go get a drink,' I say, grabbing his arm, and pulling him up.

'Ohhhh, don't you want to play?' sighs Ruth or was it Mary.

'Maybe later. Just need a drink,' I say, holding up my full can of lager, and I tug Spencer towards the door, shut it behind us and thank God, we're on our way out of the room and heading back towards the stairs.

'But I wanted to play!' giggles Spencer, behind me. I look around, and he's steadying himself against the wall, and smiling woozily, so I pretend that I need the toilet, point at the door on the landing, and hide.

In the toilet I lean against the sink, look in the mirror at my great stupid, boiled ham of a face and wonder why Spencer has to ruin everything. I love Spencer, but I hate him like this, drunk and mean. Drunk and sentimental is all right, but drunk and mean is scary. Not that he gets violent, not usually, not unless he's provoked, but I have to get him to stop drinking, and short of actually prising the booze out of his hand, I don't see how I can. We could just leave I suppose, but if I don't see Alice tonight, then it's a whole week before the next team meeting, and I really can't wait that long. The fact is, I'm finding it very hard to be Devastating and Aloof with Spencer here.

And worst of all I have to work out a way of telling him that he has to go home tomorrow. Of course, while I stay here with the door locked, I don't have to deal with any of these things, but there's an urgent knocking at the door, so I go to flush the toilet, and notice that the person who used it before me has managed to pee abundantly all over the black plastic toilet seat. I contemplate wiping it down, and even have a ball of toilet paper in my hand, but decide that wiping up other people's pee is just the kind of servile, degrading behaviour that

I've been trying hard to avoid, and really not my responsibility at all. Remember – Devastating and Aloof. I flush the toilet and leave.

Alice is next in the queue.

She's standing in the doorway, talking to Spencer, laughing very hard.

'Hello, Brian!' she says brightly.

'I didn't pee on the toilet seat' I say, Devastating and Aloof.

'Well, Brian, that's . . . *good* to know,' she says, goes in and closes the door.

29

QUESTION: In which play of 1594 do old friends Proteus and Valentine fall out over the love of the beauteous Silvia?

ANSWER: *Two Gentlemen of Verona.*

'So – you've been talking then!' I ask Spencer.

'Uh-huh.'

'Nice, isn't she?'

'Yeah, she seems all right. Very sexy . . .' he says, glancing at the toilet door.

'But interesting too?'

'Well, Bri, we only talked for five minutes, but I definitely wasn't bored. Not with her in that leotard anyway . . .'

'What did you talk about then? I mean has she said anything? About me . . . ?'

'Bri, just play it cool mate. She obviously likes you, just don't push it . . .'

'You think so?'

'I'm sure.'

'Right. I'm going to the kitchen. You coming . . . ?'

'Nah, I'm waiting,' and he nods at the toilet door, so I head on downstairs, and it's only when I'm halfway down that I start to wonder what he means by 'I'm waiting'. 'I'm waiting for the toilet'? Or 'I'm waiting for Alice'?

Out of nowhere an idea starts to form in my head, and takes on the solidity of irrefutable fact: Spencer's chatting her up. He's come all this way to *seduce her*. He's heard me talk about her and he's thought, *I like the sound of that, I'll have a crack at that*. After all, it wouldn't be the first time – it's the Janet Parks fiasco all over again. The girls I fancy always fancy Spencer Lewis, and the fact that he obviously couldn't care less just adds to the appeal. Why is that? What's he got that I haven't got? He's good-looking, I suppose, even as a heterosexual man I can make an objective assessment and say that he's good-looking, and mysterious, and cocky, and irresponsible, and not particularly clean, and all those things that women pretend not to like, but obviously do. And all right, he's not Posh, but he is Cool, and Cool beats Posh in Alice Harbinson's eyes, sure as scissors beats paper. Of course, I see it all now, clear as day; the bastard's pulling a Heathcliff on me. Even as I'm thinking this I bet his hand is snaking down the top of her leotard and . . .

'What's up with you then, smiler?'

Rebecca's standing at the bottom of the stairs.

'Oh, hi, Rebecca. What are you doing here?'

'I'm not gate-crashing. I was invited, you know.'

'Who invited you?'

'The lovely Alice as a matter of fact,' she says, and takes her own little private bottle of whisky out of the pocket of her vinyl coat.

'Really?'

'Uh-huh.' She swigs her whisky. 'Between you and me, I think she's taken a bit of a shine to me.'

'But I thought you didn't like her?'

'Och, she's all right, once you get to know her.' Giggling, she prods me in the chest with the whisky bottle, and I realise that she's very drunk; not gloomy drunk or surly drunk, but frisky drunk, playful drunk, which is a good sign, I suppose, but still a little strange and unsettling, like seeing Stalin on a skateboard. 'Why, d'you think I'm being a *hypocrite*? D'you think I should go, Brian?'

'No, not at all, it's nice to see you, I just thought it wasn't really your thing.'

'Ah, well, you know me, there's nothing I like more than two hundred pissed-up drama students all having a singalong,' and she nods her head at the lounge, where Richard III, the multi-faceted Neil whatsisname, has produced an acoustic guitar from somewhere and is starting to play 'The Boxer' by Simon and Garfunkel.

The na-na-nas are still going on some forty-five minutes later. It's actually gone beyond a fade-out, and has turned into something else, a kind of trance-like mantra, harmonies and all, that may yet go on for several days. Rebecca and I don't mind too much though, because we're squeezed on the sofa at the other end of the room, passing the bottle of whisky back and forth, and laughing.

'Och, I don't fuckin' believe it – that wanker Neil MacIntyre's found a *tambourine* . . .'

'Where did he get a tambourine from? . . .'

'From up his own fuckin' *arse*, presumably . . .' she says, and swigs whisky. 'D'you think it will *ever* end?'

'I think we'll be fine as long as they don't start on "Hey Jude".'

'If they do, I'll take a pair of pliers to the fuckin' guitar, I swear.'

The party's reaching critical mass now. All the rooms in the house are heaving, and here in the lounge, people are clinging to the furniture like it's *The Raft of The Medusa* by the French nineteenth century realist painter Gericault. I should get us more drink, but Rebecca and I are in prime positions, wedged in between the six other people on the two-seater settee, and I can tell the booze has run out anyway because people keep scampering into the lounge, looking for bottles and holding them up to the light, or checking discarded cans of lager for cigarette ash on the rim. Also I don't want to move because

Rebecca's drunk, and very funny and a little bit flirty I think, breathing her whisky breath in my ear, which is helping me take my mind off 'The Boxer' and Alice and Spencer, who at this very moment are almost certainly having breathless intercourse on a pile of coats.

'. . . you know, if I ruled the world, which I fully intend to do one day by the way, first thing I'd do 's ban acoustic guitars – all right, not *ban*, but at least limit access, introduce a licensing system, so 's like owning a shotgun or a fork-lift truck, and there'd be these really draconian rules; no playing after dusk, no playing on beaches or near camp fires, no "Scarborough Fair", no "American Pie", no harmonies, no more than two persons singing at any one time . . .'

'But won't legislation just drive it under ground?'

'Which's 'xactly where it belongs, ma friend, 'xactly where it belongs. *And* I'd ban marijuana too. I mean, as if stuuuudents weren't fatuous and self-obsessed enough already. Yeah, I'd definitely ban marijuana.'

'Isn't it banned already?' I say.

'*That*'s a very good point, my friend. Objection sustained!' and she drains the last of the whisky from the bottle. 'Now, alcohol, alcohol and nicotine, they're the only *proper* drugs. 'S there anything in that can of lager by your foot?'

'Just fag ends . . .'

'Ah'll leave it then,' and she catches me smiling at her. 'What's funny?'

'You are . . .'

''N what's funny about me, mister?'

'Your opinions. D'you think you'll mellow? You know, with age?'

'Absolutely *no way*! Ah'll tell you one thing, Brian Jackson. You know that load of *crap* they tell you about how you're meant to be left-wing till you're thirty, then you're suddenly meant to realise the error of your ways and go all right-wing? Well, big fat bollocks to *that*. If we're still friends in the year

2000 which is, what, fourteen years' time – and I hope we will be, Brian, my ol' pal – anyway, if we're still friends, and I have in *any way* altered or compromised my political, ethical or moral views about tax or immigration or apartheid or trade unions, or if I've stopped marching, or attending meetings, or have turned even *remotely* right-wing, then I give you permission to shoot me,' and she taps the centre of her forehead. 'Right. Here.'

'Okay. I will.'

'Do. Do.' Then she blinks very slowly, licks her lips, and attempts to swig from the empty bottle before saying, 'Hey, listen, I'm sorry about getting all heavy with you this morning.'

'What d'you mean?'

'You know what I mean – getting all Sylvia Plath on you.'

'Oh, that's all right . . .'

'I mean, I still think you're a complete prick and everything, but I'm sorry for giving you a hard time.'

'And why am I a complete . . . ?'

'You know why . . .'

'No, go on, tell me . . .'

She smiles at me sideways, from under heavy black eyelids. 'For not having it off with me when you had the chance.'

'Ah, well . . .' and I think about kissing her for a moment, but there are too many people looking, and Alice upstairs, so I say '. . . maybe . . . some other time?'

'Oh no, you blew it, I'm afraid. Once-only offer, pal . . .' and she bops me on the shoulder with her head. 'Once. Only. Offer . . .' and we sit there, not looking at each other, until Rebecca says 'So where's your friend then?'

'Spencer? No idea. Upstairs, I think.'

'I thought he was meant to be having some kind of mental breakdown or something . . .'

'Yeah, well, Alice is helping him get over it.'

'So do I get to meet him or what?'

Rebecca and Spencer isn't a combination I'd imagined

before, and the consequences could be disastrous, but I need to know where he is and what he's doing and how far down Alice's top his hand is, so I say, 'If you want,' and we heave ourselves up out of the depths of the sofa and start to look.

We peer into each of the rooms in turn, until we find them, in a small, packed back bedroom at the top of the house, over in the corner, about two inches apart. All around them people are dancing, or not dancing, because there's not enough room, but bobbing their heads to 'Exodus' by Bob Marley, and Alice is waggling her shoulders too, slightly out of time, biting her lower lip, and, okay, they're not kissing *as such*, just 'talking', but they might as well be, considering how close they're standing. Spencer's got that annoying lop-sided charm-boy expression on his face, like he's The Fonz or something, and Alice is mooning up at him all cow-eyed and interested with her arms crossed over her leotard, as if auditioning for the role of 'country wench', shoving her cleavage up under his chin, just in case he'd missed it.

'That's him, in the corner,' I say.

'The suede-head?' says Rebecca.

'He's not a fascist,' I say, though I don't know why I'm defending him, he probably *is* a fascist, or as good as.

'Good-looking isn't he?'

'Oh, right, well, yeah, right, thanks for that, Rebecca,' I say.

'Aw, shut ya face, ya daft sod. You've got nothing to worry about on *that* score.' Is she being sarcastic? I can't tell, and I can't concentrate anyway because now Alice is actually *running her hand over the top of Spencer's head,* and giggling, and trying to pull her hand away in a sort of pathetic, girly, oooh-doesn't-it-feel-fuzzy kind of way, and Spencer's stooping, taking her hand again, and putting it back on top of his head, and grinning his stupid lop-sided Fonzie grin, and saying no, go on, have a feel, have a feel. He'll be showing her his scars from that glass-fight next, and I think, what a scam, shaving your head to make your friends think you were having some kind of crisis or breakdown, when in fact it's just a cheap trick to get beautiful women to stroke your scalp. I wonder how long it would take me to go downstairs, fill the washing-up bowl with cold water, come back and throw it over them when, God bless him, Patrick Watts goes over and does it for me by *starting a conversation*.

'. . . Oi, are you listening to me, you nutter?' says Rebecca.

'Uh-huh.'

'So are you going to introduce me or what?'

'Absolutely, let's go. Just don't get off with him though, will you?'

'Och, what do *you* care?' she says, and we head over.

'. . . and Patrick is the captain of our team!' Alice is announcing proudly, as we arrive.

'Yeah, I heard,' says Spencer, not looking Patrick in the eye.

'Oh, hiya, Rebecca!' says Alice, and, bizarrely, throws her arms around her. Rebecca hugs her back, but pulls a face at me over her shoulder.

'Spencer, this is my good friend Rebecca,' I shout over the music, and they shake hands.

'The famous Spencer. Pleased to meet you at last,' says Rebecca. 'Brian's told me a lot about you.'

'Right!' says Spencer and there's a little pause, and the five of us just stand there, all bobbing slightly, and then from out of nowhere, I find myself shouting . . .

'Hey, you should talk to Rebecca about your LEGAL PROBLEM, Spencer!'

I'm not sure why I say it, but I do. I think, in fact I'm pretty sure, it's because I'm trying to be helpful and friendly and keep the conversation going, but I say it anyway, and after a little pause, still smiling, Spencer asks, 'Why's that?'

'Because she's a lawyer.'

'I'm *studying* law, that's not the same thing . . .'

'No, but still . . .'

'So what's your legal problem then?' says Patrick, interested now.

'Spencer's getting done for fiddling his dole . . .' I say.

'You're *joking* . . .' says Alice, coming over all righteous and left-wing all of a sudden, and squeezing Spencer's arm '. . . the *bastards*. You poor thing . . .'

'Nice one, Brian . . .' mouths Spencer, smiling but not really.

'Well, if you didn't do it, then I'm sure you'll be fine,' says Patrick, loftily.

'But he *did* do it,' I say, just to clarify things.

'So you've got a job then?' says Patrick.

'Just cash-in-hand. Petrol station,' mumbles Spence.

'Except he got caught with . . .' but Spence's eyes flick across at me, and I stop speaking.

'Well then . . .' Patrick sniggers, shrugging his shoulders, 'I have to say, best of luck, mate.'

Spencer's glaring at me steadily now as Rebecca starts on Patrick: 'So what if there's no work out there?'

'Well, there obviously *is* work out there . . .'

'No, there's not . . .'

'I think you'll find there is . . .'

'There's four million unemployed!' says Rebecca, turning nasty now.

'Three million. And he's clearly not one of them, is he? That's the whole point. If he was working cash-in-hand, he obviously could get a job, but it seems that the pay wasn't good enough for his particular lifestyle, so he decided to take money from the state instead' – is he going to keep calling him 'he' I wonder? – 'you can hardly blame the state for wanting something back when they find it's been *stolen*. It is *my* money after all . . .'

Bob Marley is singing 'No Woman, No Cry', and I watch Spencer as he necks his lager, glowering at Patrick all the time from under hooded eyes. I catch his eye for just a second, then quickly look back to Rebecca, who's gone red-faced and is belligerently jabbing her finger into Patrick's chest in an attempt to tear out his still beating heart.

'It's not *your* money, you don't pay tax!' says Rebecca.

'No, but we will, we all will, a great deal of tax in fact. And call me old-fashioned, but I think I have a right to demand that it doesn't go to "unemployed" people who aren't really unemployed . . .'

'. . . even if the job pays below the breadline?'

'Not my problem! If the employee wants a better job, then there's a great deal he can do about it; join a Youth Opportunities Scheme, get some qualifications, get on his bike and look for . . .' . . . and the next words Patrick says are 'PLEASE-GET-HIM-OFF-ME-PLEASE!' because Spencer has stepped forward suddenly, jammed his forearm hard under Patrick's chin and is holding him high, high up against the wall, and even though I've seen Spencer get into fights maybe seven or eight times now, it still takes me by surprise, like suddenly discovering that he can tap-dance. In this instance, it all happens so quickly and deftly that for a while no one else outside our circle sees what happens, they just keep bobbing away to 'No Woman, No Cry'. But then Patrick starts kicking out with his legs, denting the plasterboard walls, and Spencer's forced to brace Patrick's body with his own, and is pushing his free hand into Patrick's face, squeezing his mouth together.

'Come on mate, for Christ's sake . . .' I say.

'Okay then, question number one, who's "*he*"?' hisses Spencer, his face inches away from Patrick's.

'What d'you mean?' lisps Patrick.

'Well, you keep talking about "*he*" – who's "*he*"?'

'*You*, of course . . .'

'. . . just let him go,' I say.

'And what's my name?'

'What?'

'. . . come on, please, just pack it in . . .'

'My *name*, what's my *name*, you pompous little *prick* . . . ?' says Spencer, squeezing Patrick's cheeks for emphasis, pushing his head back hard against the wall. The record comes off with a scratch, and people start to turn to watch. Patrick's face is bright red now, his teeth clenched, his toes searching for the floor, and he's spluttering through saliva and orange juice as he says, 'I . . . can't . . . remember . . .'

'Pack it in, you two!' shouts someone from the doorway, where a crowd has started to form on the landing. 'We're calling the police' shouts someone else, but Spencer's indifferent, and I hear him say, in a whisper, his forehead touching Patrick's, 'Well, the correct answer's *Spencer*, Patrick, and if you've got any careers advice you want to give to me, you'll have some respect, and give it to my *face*, you stuck-up, little . . .'

And then there's another flurry of motion as Patrick gets an arm free, and brings it up open-handed against Spencer's ear, a noisy ineffectual glancing swipe, but enough to make Spencer release the pressure on Patrick's neck, and then suddenly Patrick is lashing out, arms and legs flailing madly, hissing and spitting like an incensed child. People are screaming, and tumbling backwards out of the tiny room, and in the chaos I see Alice holding on to Spencer's arm, trying to pull him out of the way too, like some sort of movie-poster heroine, but he shakes her off and she falls back against the window frame, cracking her head loudly. I see her scowl and put her hand to the back of her head, checking for blood, and I want to cross the room to her to make sure she's all right, but Patrick is still swinging his arms round madly, lashing out at Spencer, who's crouching low, ducking out of the way, until suddenly he sees his moment. He stands, places one hand flat on Patrick's chest, holding him out of range, pulls the other arm back and then throws his whole weight forward into his fist, making contact with the side of Patrick's head with a loud, wet smacking noise, like meat slapped down on wood, sending him spinning round once, twice, and down face-first onto the floor.

There's a moment's silence, and then a sudden rush of people over to Patrick, who has rolled over on to his back, and is tentatively dabbing at his nose and mouth with his hand, checking for blood, and finding it in abundance. 'Oh, my God,' he's mumbling, 'oh, my God,' and I think he's about to cry as Lucy Chang squeezes through to the front, supporting the back of his head with her hand, helping him up into a sitting position, and I only really see three people clearly after that.

Rebecca is standing in the middle of the room with her hands over her mouth, suspended somewhere between laughter and tears.

Alice is leaning against the window frame, staring open-mouthed at Spencer, one hand rubbing the back of her head.

Spencer has turned his back to Patrick, and is flicking his hand out into the air, examining his knuckles, breathing heavily. He looks up at me, blows air out through his gritted teeth and says, 'Let's go then, shall we?'

Downstairs they're all singing along to 'With A Little Help From My Friends'.

30

QUESTION: The conditions blepharitis, ectropion, amblyophobia and heterophoria would all result in what condition?

ANSWER: An inability to see clearly.

We stride down the terraced streets in silence, Spencer somewhere close behind me. I can hear his footsteps slap the wet pavement, but I'm too angry, too embarrassed, too drunk and confused to talk to him just now, so I keep my head down and stride on.

'Great party!' says Spencer eventually.

I ignore him, stomp on ahead.

'I liked Alice.'

'Yeah, I noticed!' I say, without looking back.

We walk a little further in silence.

'I know, Bri! How about a game of "If This Person Were . . ."?'

I start to walk a little faster.

'Look, Bri, if you've got something to say to me, just say it now, 'cause this is just fuckin' stupid . . .'

'And what if I don't? You going to hit me, too?'

'It's certainly very tempting,' he mutters under his breath. 'All right, mate,' he says, 'you've made your point, just listen will you?' but I keep walking. 'Please?' he says. The word doesn't come easily, and he sounds like a petulant child, forced to say it against his will, but I stop and turn to listen.

'All right, Brian. I'm very sorry . . . for hitting . . . the captain of your *University Challenge* quiz team . . .' but he can't get to the end of the sentence without starting to giggle, so I turn again, and keep on walking. After a while I hear him running up behind me, and I flinch maybe, but then he's standing in front of me, scowling, walking backwards quickly. 'What did you want me to do, Bri? Just stand there and take it? He was treating me like *shit* . . .'

'So you decided to hit him?'

'Yeah . . .'

'Because you *disagreed* with him?'

'No, not just that . . .'

'And you didn't think of maybe arguing with him, debating your point of view, in a calm, rational way?'

'What's my point of view got to do with it? He was trying to make me look like a tit . . .'

'. . . so you resorted to violence!'

'I didn't *resort* to it. Violence was my first choice.'

'Oh, yes, very *cool*, you're very *hard*, Spence . . .'

'Well, you weren't exactly going out of your way to help me, were you? Or were you scared he'd drop you from the team?'

'I was sticking up for you!'

'No, you weren't, you were just flapping your big fucking social conscience around in front of your girlfriends. If you hadn't raised the subject . . .'

'What did you want me to do, hold his arms behind his back for you? Those are my *friends*, Spencer . . .'

'That pillock? Your friend? Fucking hell, Brian, it's worse than I thought. He treats you like a piece of shit.'

'He does not!'

'He does, Bri, I saw him do it. He's a complete wanker and he deserves what he got . . .'

'Well . . . at least he doesn't try and get off with the girls I like . . .'

'Whoa, whoa, hang on there.' And he stops me, putting one

open hand on my chest, just as he did to Patrick, before he punched him, and I wonder if he can feel how fast my heart is beating. 'You think I was trying to get off with *Alice*? You really think that's what I was doing?'

'Well, it certainly looked that way to me, Spence – all that *head-rubbing* . . .' and I go to put my hand on his head, but his other hand snaps up, grabs my wrist and holds it tight.

'You know Bri, for someone who's meant to be *educated*, you can be pretty fucking *stupid* sometimes . . .'

'Don't talk to me like that . . .' I say, wrenching my hand away.

'Like what?'

'Like *that*, like you always talk to me! What is it, Spence, this need to . . . smash everything up? I'm sorry things aren't going well for you at the moment, I'm sorry if you're not happy, but there's stuff you can do about that, Spencer, practical stuff, and you just choose not to, because it's easier to just fuck about, and fuck things up, and sneer, and take the piss out of people who are actually trying to *do* something with their lives . . .'

'What, like *you*, you mean?' he says, sniggering.

'You're just jealous, Spencer, you always have been jealous of me, just because I work hard, just because I'm clever and got some qualifi . . .'

'Whoa, hang on. *Clever?* Is that what you call it, you cocky cunt? When I first met you, you couldn't even tie your fucking shoe-laces! I had to teach you to do it. You had "left" and "right" written on your plimsolls till you were fifteen! You couldn't even get through a game of football without bursting into tears, you soft sod. If you're so clever, then how come you don't know what people say about you behind your back, how much they *laugh* at you? I've stuck up for you for years and years since your dad died . . .'

'What's my dad got to do it with it?'

'You tell me, Brian – you tell me.'

'Just leave my dad out of it, all right!' I shout.

'Or what? What are you going to do, *cry*?'

'Fuck off, Spencer, you fucking . . . *bully*.' But there's a hot itchy feeling behind my eyes, a tight knot of panic in my stomach, and I suddenly realise that I have to get away from him, so I turn around and walk back the way we came.

'Where you going?' he shouts after me.

'Dunno!'

'You running away, Brian? Is that it?'

'Yeah, if you like.'

'So how am I meant to get back?'

'Dunno Spence. Not my problem is it?'

And then I hear him say, quite quietly, almost to himself 'Go on then. Piss off,' so I stop and turn, expecting to see him sneering or grinning, but he's not. Instead he's stood quite still some distance away, under a street light, with his head tilted back, his eyes tightly closed and the heel of one hand pressed against his forehead, fingers curled up tight.

He looks about ten years old. I have this sense that I should go up to him, or at least just stand a little bit closer, but instead I shout down the street: 'You've got to go, Spence! By tomorrow morning. You can't stay in the house any more. It's against the rules.'

He opens his eyes, which are wet and red and tired, and looks at me levelly.

'And is that why you want me to go, Brian? Because it's *against the rules*?'

'Yeah. Partly.'

'Right. Well. I'll go then.'

'Okay.'

'And I'm sorry if I've . . . embarrassed you. In front of your friends.'

'You haven't embarrassed me, I just . . . don't want you around. That's all.'

I turn, and walk quickly away without looking back, and I'm sure, I'm convinced that I should feel good, and defiant, and strong about having finally stood up to him for once, but for some reason I don't. I just feel hot and hollow and stupid and sad, and I have no idea where to go.

I'm not sure how long I walk for after that. I'm vaguely aware that I've got the only keys to the house, and that the sensible thing to do would be to go home and let Spencer in. But he can always wake Marcus or Josh up; after all, I'm not my brother's keeper. I'll just give him enough time to find his way home and get to sleep, and give myself a chance to walk off the booze and the confusion, and then sneak back home and sort things out in the morning. But after an hour or so the drizzle starts to thicken into rain, and though it's really not my intention, consciously anyway, I eventually find myself outside Alice and Rebecca's halls of residence.

The front gates are locked at one in the morning to all but key-holders, so I have to clamber over the high old cast-iron railings. I manage to do so without setting off any alarms or impaling myself, but then almost immediately slip over on the smooth soles of my brogues and toboggan down the muddy wooded embankment, finally coming to rest underneath a rhododendron bush. I wipe the thick mud off my hands on wet leaf mulch, crouch under the bushes and wait for someone to come along the gravel path to the main entrance.

Ice cold water is dripping from the leaves and dribbling down the nape of my neck, and thick muddy water is starting to soak into my suede brogues, so that it feels as if my feet are wrapped in cold, damp cardboard. I'm just about to give up and head home when I finally see someone coming down the driveway to the house. I slip out of the bushes and walk a little way behind them, and when they've opened the door I shout 'wait' and they stop and turn.

'Hold the door!' The man, who I don't recognise, regards me suspiciously. 'Forgotten my keys! Would you believe it! And on a night like this!' He's looking at my shoes and trousers, which are caked with leaf mould. 'Fell over! God, I am *soaked*!' but he's not moving, so I fiddle in my wallet with numb slimy fingers, and show him my NUS card – trust me, I'm a student – and this seems to do the trick for some reason, because he opens the door and lets me in.

I slap wetly down the dark corridors, leaving a trail of compost on the parquet, until I come to Alice's room. There's a narrow ribbon of orange light under the door, so I know she's awake. I press my ear against the door, and can hear some music – it's Joni singing 'Help Me' from *Court and Spark* – and I can almost feel the warmth and light through the heavy wooden door, and desperately want to be on the other side. I knock gently. Too gently in fact, because she doesn't hear anything, so I knock again, and whisper her name.

'Who is it?'

'It's Brian,' I whisper.

'Brian?' and she opens the door. 'Oh, my God, Brian, look at you!' and she takes my by the hand and tugs me inside.

She leads me to the centre of the room and immediately takes charge of the situation, adopting the demeanour of a strict but kindly Edwardian housekeeper – '*Don't* sit down, and *don't* touch anything, not until we've dried you off, young man!' – and she starts to root through her drawers, pulling out a baggy green hand-knitted jumper, a pair of loose tracksuit bottoms and a pair of hiking socks. 'And here, you'll need this, too,' and she undoes the cord of her white towelling dressing gown, takes it off and throws it to me. Underneath she's wearing an ancient grey T-shirt, shrunk up to above her belly-button, with a print of Snoopy lying on his kennel on the front, cracked and faded like a mediaeval fresco, a pair of big, battleship grey cotton knickers, and a pair of men's black socks rolled down to her ankles, and it occurs to me that this is without doubt the most sensual and erotic sight that I have ever seen in my whole life.

'Look at you – your hands are shaking.'

'Are they?' I say, and when I open my mouth to speak, I realise my teeth are chattering too.

'Come on, get your kit off, or you'll get pneumonia,' she says sternly, hand outstretched. I'm a bit nervous about getting undressed, partly because the dumb-bells haven't really had a chance to kick in yet, and also because I'm wearing one of my old school vests, so there's bound to be a slight war-time-orphan look about me. But I seem to remember that my boxers are in fairly good nick, and I am extremely cold, so I relent. She stands next to me as I start to get undressed, and notices that my hands are shaking too much to undo the buttons of my shirt.

'Here, let me,' she says, and starts to undo them, top to bottom. 'Why aren't you with Spencer?'

'We had a bit of a f-f-falling-out.'

'So where is he then?' Why's she still talking about Spencer?

'No idea – back at my house probably.' The buttons are undone, and she backs away, so that I can take the shirt off. 'I'm *so* sorry about all that . . .'

'What?'

'You know – Spencer, the p-punch-up . . .'

'Oh, God, don't worry about that. I quite enjoyed it actually. I mean, I'd usually never condone physical violence, but in Patrick's case I'm prepared to make an exception. Wow, your friend Spencer can really *fight*, can't he?' Her eyes twinkling at the memory of it. 'I know I shouldn't say this, but I do think there's something quite exciting about men fighting, you get a sense of the appeal, you know, like in ancient Roman gladiatorial combat.' I'm sat on the edge of her desk now, trying not to get mud on it, unravelling the slimy mud-soaked laces of my shoe. 'I once went out briefly with this guy who was an amateur boxer, and I used to love going to watch him train and fight. We always used to have the most amazing, animalistic sex afterwards; all the blood and bruises and everything, there was something really beautiful and *sensual* about it. The blood on the pillow afterwards . . .'

and she stands there for a moment, with my mouldy shoes in her hand, and gives a little involuntary erotic shudder at the memory. I start to gingerly peel my wet trousers off. 'Of course, outside the bedroom and the boxing ring, we didn't have a lot in common, so it was doomed from the start really. Not a good basis for a relationship, is it? If you're only attracted to them when they're half-naked and beating someone's brains out. Have you ever hit someone, Brian?'

I'm standing in my pants and vest, so you'd have thought the answer would have been fairly self-explanatory. 'Me? God, no.'

'Or been hit . . . ?'

'Oh, once or twice – you know, just playground bundles, scuffles in pubs. Thankfully I have a black belt in hiding under tables.' She smiles, takes my clothes off me, eyes averted, and starts shaking them out, folding them neatly.

'So he didn't hurt you then?' I say.

'When?'

'Spencer, in the fight.'

'When?'

'I saw him push you against the wall . . .'

'Oh, that was nothing, just a little bump on the head. Why, can you see a bruise?' She turns around, parting the hair on the crown of her head, with one hand, and I stand close behind her, and pull the hair to one side and don't really look, just inhale. She smells of red wine and clean cotton, warm skin and Timotei, and I have this overwhelming urge to kiss the top of her head, the small raised area where the bruise is. I could get away with it too. I could lean forward now and kiss it and then say 'there you go, kissed it better!' something along those lines, but I do have *some* pride, so instead I just place my fingers gently where the redness is.

'Do you feel anything?' she asks. Alice, you have *no idea* . . .

'There's just a tiny bruise,' I say. 'Nothing much.'

'Good,' she says, and starts hanging my clothes on the

radiator. I'm still standing in my vest and pants, and a quick glance down at my boxers reveals that it looks as if I'm smuggling executive toys, so I quickly pull on the tracksuit bottoms and the old jumper that still smells of her. 'I've got some whisky. Want some?'

'Absolutely,' I say, then sit on her bed and watch as she rinses out two teacups in the handbasin. In the light of the anglepoise I notice that the flesh at the top of her thighs is very white and dimpled slightly, like risen bread dough, and as she turns sideways-on against the light I see, or think I see, a little wisp of pale brown hair escaping at the top of her underwear against the small, soft bulge of her belly.

'So what are you going to do about it?'

I snap to. 'About what?'

'Your friend, Spencer.' There she goes again – Spencer, Spencer, Spencer . . .

'I don't know – talk in the morning, I suppose.'

'So what are you walking around in the rain for?'

'I just wanted to give him a couple of hours to go to sleep. I'll head back soon . . .' I say, and pretend to shiver.

She hands me a teacup with an inch of whisky in it. 'Well, you can't go back out tonight. You'll have to sleep here . . .'

This is my cue to feign resistance. 'Oh, really, that's all right, I should head back . . .' I'm actually quite warm now, but try to make my teeth chatter artificially, which is actually a lot harder than you'd think, so I don't push it, but just quietly say, 'I'll drink this and go.'

'Brian, you can't go back out there, just look at your shoes . . . !' My ruined suede brogues are steaming on top of the radiator like hot pasties, and I can hear the rain being blown hard against the window. 'I *refuse* to let you leave. You'll have to sleep with me tonight.' The bed is single. This is a very narrow bed. *Very* narrow. More like a ledge.

'Oh, all right then,' I say, '. . . if you insist.'

31

QUESTION: Discovered accidentally by the Dutch physicist Pieter van Musschenbroek in 1746, and also by the German inventor Ewald Georg von Kleist in 1745, a Leyden jar is a sealed glass container used for storing what?

ANSWER: Static electricity.

There are things that a nineteen-year-old man such as myself might reasonably be expected to have done by now. For instance, I think you should be able to assume that, at nineteen, I'd have travelled by plane, for instance, or ridden on a motorbike, or driven a car, or scored a goal, or successfully smoked a cigarette. By the age of nineteen Mozart had written symphonies, operas and played for the crowned heads of Europe. Keats had written *Endymion*. Even Kate Bush had recorded her first two studio albums, and I've yet to eat tinned sweetcorn.

But I have to say I don't really mind all that, because tonight I'm about to crack the big one. Tonight, for the first time in my life I am about to spend a whole night in bed with someone.

All right, I should qualify that a little. Last summer I shared a one-man tent with Spencer and Tone on Canvey Island, and that was pretty cosy. I slept in the same bed as Mum for the first couple of nights after Dad died. And the night before his funeral I shared my single bed at home with my Irish cousin, Tina, but of course this last one doesn't count because, leaving aside the sombre circumstances and the incest taboo, cousin

Tina was, and remains, a deeply violent person. To clarify then, I've never, ever, in my life shared a bed as an adult for the whole night with a member of the opposite sex to whom I'm not closely related and/or afraid of. Until now.

We stay up for an hour or so, drinking whisky, sitting on the bed next to each other and talking and listening to *Tapestry* and the new Everything But The Girl album. Because I know that I'm here for the duration, I relax a little and we start to have fun again, proper fun, reliving the party, the fight, the look on Patrick's face while he tried to remember Spencer's name. She sits right up next to me with her legs crossed in front of her, her T-shirt tugged down over her belly for propriety's sake, but when she's not looking I can still see the mottled pink and white smoothness on the inside of her thighs, the beginning of a dark hollow at the top of each leg.

'By the way,' she says, 'I've got something to tell you.'

'What?' I say. *I'm in love with Spencer* or something, I expect.

'I got some good news tonight,' she says, making a meal of it.

'Go on . . .'

'I . . . am . . . *Hedda Gabler*!'

'Congratulations! That's brilliant news!' To be honest, I'd been secretly hoping that she wouldn't get the role, partly because it means she'll be rehearsing all the time, and partly because, like a lot of actors, she can frankly be pretty monumentally *boring* on the subject. But never let it be said that I don't have a huge talent for insincerity. 'That's amazing! The eponymous Hedda! You'll be great! I'm *so* pleased!' I say, and hug her and kiss her on the cheek, because after all, I might as well get something out of it. 'Hey, you are still going to do *University Challenge*, aren't you?'

'Absolutely. I've checked. The dates don't clash, even if we do get through to the second round . . .'

'Which we will.'

'Which we will.'

And then we both talk for an hour or so about the many and varied challenges involved in tackling Hedda Gabler, which isn't easy, because to be honest I've never read it, so I drift off and just look at her for a little while, and then she's saying . . .

'. . . and the really great thing is that Eilert Lovborg is being played by Neil MacIntyre . . .'

'Who's Neil . . . ?'

'You know – he was that amazing Richard III last term?'

'Oh, *him*!' I say, meaning 'Oh, the twat with the tambourine!' Neil MacIntyre's the actorly bastard who spent most of the last term hobbling ostentatiously round the student bar on a pair of crutches to 'get into character'. Many's the time I've been tempted to kick his crutches away, but Alice is obviously pretty fired up about the experience that awaits her because she's getting incredibly animated and passionate, waving her hands in the air, biting her lip, and pressing her hand against her forehead. In fact she's pretty much running through her whole performance scene by scene, so I try to stay awake by blinking heavily when she's not looking, and sneaking occasional surreptitious glances at the faded print of Snoopy on her T-shirt, rising and falling, or the pale skin on the inside of her thighs, taking little mental photographs.

Finally, after Hedda's thrown her beloved Lovborg's manuscript into the flames, and committed suicide off-stage, Alice says, 'God, I'm bursting for a pee,' and pads off down the corridor to the communal toilet. As soon as she's gone I surreptitiously have an illicit roll of her Cool Blue under-arm deodorant, and adjust the angle of the bedside radio-alarm clock in the hope that she won't see that it's gone three in the morning and start getting sleepy. But when she comes back to the room the first thing she does is yawn and say, 'Time for bed,' then goes to the handbasin and starts to brush her teeth.

'You'll have to borrow my toothbrush, I'm afraid,' she says, through a mouthful of foam. 'Hope you don't mind.'

'I don't if you don't!'

'Here you go then,' and she passes it to me, and I rinse it under the tap, but not too much, and then we stand side by side at the sink, and I brush my teeth while she takes her make-up off with blue cleanser. There's a little bit of comic business when I accidentally spit on her hand as she reaches across the washbasin for a cottonwool pad, and we catch each other's eye in the mirror, and she laughs brightly as she swiftly rinses my minty flob off her wrist. And it occurs to me that there's something a little bit cosily domestic about the moment, as if we're getting ready for bed having just hosted a delightful and hugely successful dinner party for our closest friends, but I don't say this out loud, because I'm not, after all, a complete and utter cretin.

I take the green jumper and tracksuit bottoms off in a way that doesn't seem too sexually provocative, and contemplate leaving the hiking socks on, for comfort's sake, but it's not a good look, pants and socks, so I take them off and put them by the bed, just in case.

'Do you want to be up against the wall, or . . . ?' she says.

'Don't mind . . .'

'I'll be up against the wall then, shall I?'

'Okay!'

'Got a glass of water?'

'Yep,' and she gets under the hand-made patchwork eiderdown, and I follow.

To begin with we don't actually touch each other, not on purpose, and there's some shuffling round as we realise just exactly how small the bed is. Finally we adjust ourselves into what seems like a workable position, which involves lying curled up in parallel, like quotation marks, but with me not actually daring to touch her, as if she were a live rail. Which, in a way, she is.

'Comfy?' she says.

'Uh-huh.'

'Nifty-nift, Brian.'

What? '"Nifty-nift?"'

'Just something Daddy used to say, you know, instead of nighty-night?'

'Nifty-nift to you too, Alice.'

'Turn the light out, will you?'

'Don't you mean turn the "*lift*" out?' I say, which if you ask me is a pretty witty thing to come up with at 3.42 in the morning, but she doesn't say anything or make a noise even, so I turn off the light. For a moment I wonder if this will act as some sort of catalyst to make us lose our inhibitions and unleash our potent mutual secret longings, but it doesn't, it just makes the room dark. We lie exactly as before, in quotation marks, not touching, and it soon becomes clear that the actual muscular tension required to stay rigid and not touch her is going to be impossible to sustain, like holding a chair out at arm's length all night. So I relax slightly, and the top of my thigh comes into contact with the warm curve of her left buttock, and she doesn't seem to flinch or elbow me in the gut, so I assume it's all right.

But now I realise that I don't know what to do with my arms. The right arm, under my torso, is starting to tingle, so I wrench it out from under me, jabbing Alice in the kidneys.

'Ow!'

'Sorry!'

''S alright.'

But now they're just sort of dangling pointlessly in front of me, at weird angles, like a discarded marionette, and I'm trying to remember what I usually do with my arms when I'm not in bed with someone, i.e. my whole life. I try folding these strange new extra limbs across my chest, which doesn't seem quite right either, and now Alice has shifted slightly nearer the wall, taking the eiderdown with her, so that my backside is hanging over the edge of the bed, and a draught is blowing up the leg of my boxer shorts. So I can either yank the covers back, which will look a bit rude, or risk moving closer, which I do, so that I'm now lying curled-up tight against her back, which is wonderful, and I think is technically called spooning. I can feel the rise and fall of her breathing, and try and synchronise my own with hers in the hope that this will make me fall asleep, though this seems unlikely, because my heart is clearly beating way, way too fast, like a greyhound's.

And now her hair is in my mouth. I try to flick it away by spasming an assortment of facial muscles, but this doesn't seem to work, so instead I crane my head backwards as far as I can, but her hair's still there, creeping up my nostrils now. My arms are still folded across my chest and pressed against Alice's back, so I have to lean backward and extricate my arms and brush the hair away, but now my left arm is outside the eiderdown, and cold, and I don't know where to put it, and my right arm is starting to tingle, either from cramp or an impending heart attack, and the under-arm deodorant is smelling overwhelmingly Cool and Blue, and my boxers are out in the draught again, and my feet are cold, and I'm wondering if I should maybe reach over and get the hiking socks and . . .

'Quite a fidget, aren't you?' mumbles Alice.

'Sorry. Can't work out what to do with my arms!'

'Here . . .' and then she does the most amazing thing. She reaches over and takes my arm and pulls it tight around her ribs, *under* her T-shirt, so that my hand is resting against the warm skin of her belly, and I think I feel the curve of her breast brush against my forearm.

'Better?'

'Much better.'

'Sleepy?' she asks, which is an absurd question really, considering that her right breast is rubbing against my wrist.

'Not . . . really,' I say.

'Me neither. Talk to me.'

'What about?'

'Anything.'

'Okay.' I decide to grasp the nettle. 'What did you think of Spencer?'

'I liked him.'

'You thought he was all right?'

'Yeah! Bit bloke-y, bit full-of-it . . .' she says, putting on her Radio 4 cockney accent '. . . bit ov a jack-the-lad, but I thought he was great. And he obviously *loves* you.'

'Well, I don't know about that . . .' I say.

'No, he does. You should have heard him, singing your praises.'

'I thought he was chatting you up . . .'

'God, no! *Quite* the opposite . . .' she says. What does *that* mean?

'How come?' I ask.

She hesitates, and half turns her head and says, 'Well . . . he seemed to have this idea in his head that you had . . . a bit of a crush on me.'

'Spencer said *that*? To you, tonight?'

'Uh-huh.'

So there it is. It's out there. I don't know what to say or where to look, so I roll onto my back and sigh, 'Well, thanks Spencer, thank you very much . . .'

'I don't think he meant any harm by it.'

'Why, what else did he say?'

'Well, he was pretty pissed, but he said that you were a really good guy, and well, his exact words were that you could be a bit of a twat sometimes, but that you were really loyal, and decent, and that there weren't many blokes out there like you and if I had any sense I should . . . go out with you.'

'Spencer said all *that*?'

'Uh-huh,' and I have this fleeting image of Spencer standing under the streetlight, in the drizzle with his eyes closed, the heel of his hand pressed against his forehead, and me walking the other way.

'What are you thinking?' says Alice, facing the wall again.

'Um. Don't know, really.'

'I assume it's true though, yeah? I mean, I had an idea that it might be true.'

'Is it really so obvious?'

'Well, I suppose I have caught you looking at me every now and then. And then there was our dinner date . . .'

'Oh, God, I'm so embarrassed about that . . .'

'Don't be. It was nice. It's just . . .'

'What.'

She's silent for a moment, and then sighs deeply and squeezes my hand, the kind of gesture that lets you know your hamster's died, and I brace myself for the good old 'let's-be-friends' speech. But then she flips over to look at me, pushes her hair behind her ears, and I can just about make out her face in the pulsing orange glow of the radio-alarm clock.

'I don't know, Brian. I'm really bad news, you know.'

'No, you're not . . .'

'I am though, really. Every relationship I've ever had has ended up with someone being hurt . . .'

'I don't mind . . .'

'You would though, if it was you. I mean, you know what I'm like . . .'

'I know, you've told me. But like I said, I don't mind, because isn't it better to try? I mean, wouldn't it be better to give it a go, see how we got on? It would be up to you, obviously, because you might not like me in that way . . .'

'Well, I've thought about it, obviously. But it's not even to do with *you*. I haven't really got time for that whole boyfriend-girlfriend thing, what with playing Hedda, and the team and everything. I value my independence too much . . .'

'Well, I really value *my* independence, too!' I say, though this is of course a lie of absolutely epic proportions, because what am I supposed to do with *independence*? You know what 'independence' is? 'Independence' is staring at the ceiling in the middle of the night with your fingernails digging into the palms of your hand. 'Independence' is realising that the only person you've spoken to all day is the man in the off-licence. 'Independence' is a value meal in the basement of Burger King on a Saturday afternoon. When Alice talks about 'independence' she means something completely different. 'Independence' is the luxury of all those people who are too confident, and busy, and popular, and attractive to be just plain old 'lonely'.

And make no mistake, lonely is absolutely the worst thing to be. Tell someone that you've got a drink problem, or an eating disorder, or your dad died when you were a kid even, and you can almost see their eyes light up with the sheer fascinating drama and pathos of it all, because you've got an *issue*, something for them to get involved in, to talk about and analyse and discuss and maybe even cure. But tell someone you're lonely and of course they'll *seem* sympathetic, but look very carefully and you'll see one hand snaking behind their back, groping for the door handle, ready to make a run for it, as if loneliness itself were contagious. Because being lonely is just so banal, so shaming, so plain and dull and ugly.

Well, I've been lonely as a snake all my life and I'm sick of it. I want to be part of a team, a partnership, I want to sense that audible hum of envy and admiration and relief when we walk into a room together – 'thank *God*, we're all right now, because *they*'re here' – but also to be slightly scary, slightly intimidating, sharp as razors, Dick and Nicole Diver in *Tender is the Night*, glamorous and sexually enthralled with each other, like Burton and Taylor, or like Arthur Miller and Marilyn Monroe, except stable and sensible and constant, without the mental breakdowns and infidelity and divorce. I can't say any of this out loud, of course, because there's nothing at this moment that would scare her more, short of producing an axe, and I certainly can't use the word 'lonely' because it does tend to make people uncomfortable. So what do I say instead? I take a deep breath, and sigh, and put my hand to my head, and finally this is what I come up with.

'All I know is that I think you're absolutely amazing, Alice, and stunningly beautiful of course, not that it matters, and that I just love being with you, spending time with you, and I think that, well I really think that we should . . .' and then there's a pause, and that's when I do it. I kiss Alice Harbinson.

And then I'm kissing her, actually *kissing* her properly, on the *mouth* and everything. Her lips are warm but dry at first, and very slightly chapped, so that I can feel a little hard, sharp spur of dead skin on her bottom lip, which I contemplate biting off, but wonder if maybe that's perhaps a bit audaciously sensual, biting, within the first few seconds. Maybe I could kiss it off, might that be possible? Can you kiss off dead skin? What might that involve? I'm just about to try when Alice pulls her head away, and I think maybe I've blown it, but instead she just smiles and reaches up and pulls the little flap of dead skin off her own lip and drops it down the side of the bed. Then she blots her lip with the back of her hand, glances at it to check she's not bleeding, licks her lips and we're kissing again, and it's heaven.

When it comes to kissing, I'm obviously no connoisseur, but I'm pretty sure that this is *good* kissing. It's very different from the Rebecca Epstein experience; Rebecca's a great person and a lot of fun and everything, but kissing Rebecca Epstein was all hard edges. Alice's mouth appears to have no edges at all, just warmth and softness, and despite the ever-so-slight tang of hot, minty bad breath from one of us, me probably, it is pretty much heaven, or it would be if I wasn't suddenly aware that I don't know what to do with my tongue, which suddenly seems to have grown massive and meaty, like something you see shrink-wrapped in plastic in a butcher's. Is a tongue appropriate here, I wonder? And then in answer I feel *her* tongue just tentatively touching my teeth, and then she takes my hand and moves it on top of her T-shirt, Snoopy lying on his kennel, and then underneath her T-shirt, and then after that I have to confess that everything starts to get a little bit blurred.

32

QUESTION: What was the more familiar name of the Hungarian rabbi's son Eric Weisz, famed for his feats of escapology and disappearance?
ANSWER: Harry Houdini.

The next morning we kiss some more, but with less of the ardent erotic abandon of the previous night, now that we're in daylight and she can see what she's up against. Also Alice has got a 9.15 Mask Workshop, so just after 8.00 I'm holding on to my mud-caked shoes, and heading for the door.

'Sure you don't want me to walk in with you?'

'No, no, that's okay . . .'

'You're sure?'

'I've got to get my stuff together, have a shower and everything . . .' I'd be very happy to hang around for *that*, and feel in some indefinable way that I've earnt it, but it's a communal bathroom, which obviously makes things difficult, and besides, I've got to remember, play it cool, play it cool . . .

'Well, thank you for *having* me,' I say, trying for a kind of saucy swagger that I don't quite pull off, then I lean in and kiss her. She pulls away a little too quickly, and for a moment I wonder if I should be offended, but she immediately provides a perfectly rational explanation; 'Sorry, bad breath!'

'Not at all,' I say, even though her breath actually does smell really, really bad. I don't care though. She could be breathing fire and I wouldn't mind.

'You could be breathing fire and I wouldn't mind,' I say.

She makes a sceptical 'hmmm' noise and rolls her eyes delightedly, and says, 'Yeah, well, you'd better go, before anyone sees you. And Brian?'

'Uh-huh?'

'You're not to tell anyone. Promise?'

'Of course.'

'Our secret . . . ?'

'Absolutely.'

'Completely?'

'I promise.'

'Okay – ready?' and she opens the door and peers down the corridor to check that the coast is clear, then gives me a loving little shove out of the door, as if pushing an unwilling parachutist from a plane, and I turn around just in time to see her beautiful face disappearing behind the door, smiling, I'm pretty sure.

I sit on a radiator in the corridor, and tap my ruined shoes together, flaking mud all over the parquet floor.

I float home. I've not really eaten anything except crisps and peanuts for twenty-four hours, so I'm starving hungry, and I've managed to pull a muscle in my neck while kissing Alice, which has got to be a good thing. I also have that dizzy, hollow, drugged feeling that you get when you've stayed up all night, and am pretty much running on adrenaline, elation and someone else's saliva, so I stop in the garage and get a can of Fanta, a Mars bar and a Mint Aero for breakfast, and start to feel a little better.

It's a beautiful crisp winter morning, and there are crowds of school kids holding hands with their parents, strolling to school. Standing eating the Mint Aero at a pelican crossing I catch the eye of the little girl stood next to me, who's glancing curiously at my shoes and trousers which are still caked in mud, so that it looks as if I've been dipped in milk chocolate. This strikes me as the kind of quaint picture-book image that little kids respond to, so I smile at the little girl, bend down and say aloud, in a J.D. Salinger-ish kind of way: 'I've actually been dipped in milk chocolate!'

But something happens to the words between my brain and my mouth, and it suddenly sounds as if this is the strangest and most disturbing thing that anyone has ever said to a child. Her mum seems to agree too, because she scowls at me like I'm The Child-catcher, picks up her child and hurries across the road before the lights have even changed. I shrug if off, because I'm determined not to let anything spoil this morning, because I want to keep hold of this feeling of slightly queasy elation, but there's something else bothering me, something that I can't quite shake off.

Spencer. What do I say to Spencer? Apologise, I suppose. But not too solemnly, I won't make a big deal about it, I'll just sort of say, hey, sorry about last night, I think things got a bit out of hand, mate, and then we'll just sort of laugh it off. And I'll tell him about how Alice and I made love, except I won't call it that, I'll call it 'got off with each other', and then things will be back to normal. Of course it's probably best if he does still leave today, but I'll make an effort, I'll bunk off lectures and patch things up and escort him to the train station.

But when I get back to Richmond House, he's not there. In fact the room seems exactly the same as when we left it yesterday afternoon – the bed frame, the mess of duvets and cold, damp towels, the smell of ammonia and Special Brew and Calor gas. I wonder if he's left any possessions here, and then remember that he didn't actually have any in the first place; just a thin plastic bag with a three-day old *Daily Mirror* and a stale meat pasty in it, still beside my desk where he left it. Anxious, I pick up the plastic bag, and head out to the kitchen, where Josh and Marcus are eating poached eggs and checking their share prices in *The Times*.

'Did either of you see Spencer last night?'

'No, 'fraid not,' says Josh.

'Isn't he with you?' grumbles Marcus.

'No, we got split up at a party. I thought he'd make his own way back.'

'Why? Where have *you* been then, you dirty stop-out?' leers Josh.

'Just staying over at a friend's place. My friend Alice's actually,' I say, and then remember that I'm not meant to tell anyone.

'Whoooooooooo,' they say in unison.

'Well, you know how it is, you've either got it or you haven't!' I say, put Spencer's stuff in the bin, and leave. I haven't got 'it' of course, I've never had 'it', never will have 'it', am not even sure what 'it' is, but there's no reason why I shouldn't let people think that I do have 'it', even if it's just for a little while.

Round Four

Rosemary stood up and leaned down and said her most sincere thing to him: 'Oh, we're such *actors* – you and I.'

F. Scott Fitzgerald, *Tender is the Night*

33

QUESTION: In his article of 1926, published in the review 'Lef' by the poet Mayakovsky, Sergei Eisenstein proposes a new form of cinema that relies less on the static, logical, linear unfolding of action, and more on a stylised juxtaposition of images. What is Eisenstein's name for this new cinematic form?
ANSWER: Montage of attractions.

There's a generic convention, recognisable particularly from mainstream American film, where the hero and heroine fall in love with each other during a protracted, wordless montage sequence, inevitably underscored by some sort of lush orchestral ballad, usually with a sax solo. I'm not sure why falling-in-love should be wordless – maybe because the actual business of sharing your most intimate thoughts and secrets and desires is a bit of a chore for those not immediately involved. But anyway, this sequence illustrates all the various fun things that young lovers are meant to do – eating popcorn at the movies, giving each other piggy-backs, kissing on a park bench, trying on goofy hats, drinking glasses of wine in a foam-filled bath, falling into swimming pools, walking home arm-in-arm at night whilst pointing out the different constellations etc. etc. etc.

Well, with Alice and me, the last week has been absolutely nothing like that at all. In fact, I haven't heard from her, which is fine because my new watchwords are Cool and Aloof, and I'm taking great care not to infringe on her precious independence, especially as she's so busy with *Hedda Gabler*. And I really don't mind not hearing from her. In fact, I've only telephoned her, what, five, six times during the entire week, and I haven't left messages either, so the beauty of it is that, as far as Alice is concerned, I haven't phoned her, either! Admittedly, there was one slightly sticky moment when Rebecca Epstein picked up the phone, and I had to subtly alter my voice a little way into the call, but I think I got away with it.

Instead, I've been distracting myself by listening to a lot of mid-period Bush and pouring all my feelings into a love poem that I've been working on for Valentine's Day, in three days' time, the day before The Challenge. Of course I recognise that Valentine's Day is nothing more than a cynical, exploitative marketing construct, but there was a time when Valentine's Day was a really big thing for me, and involved this huge, *Reader's Digest*-style mail-out. I'm a lot older now, more emotionally discerning, so now it's just a card to Mum and Alice and that's my limit. The Cool and Aloof thing to do with Alice, of course, would be not to send her a card at all, but I don't want her thinking that I've gone off her or, worse, that what happened between us was only about sex.

As for the poem, it's going okay, but I can't seem to settle on the appropriate verse form, and have been experimenting with the Petrarchan sonnet, the Elizabethan sonnet, rhyming couplets, Alexandrines, haikus and blank verse, and may well end up writing a limerick.

Alice, palace, chalice, phallus, malice . . .

In the end, it turns out that Patrick's nose isn't broken at all. That's not to say it isn't red and misshapen and swollen, and it's certainly taken the edge off the Action Man good looks for the moment. There's a scar on his cheek too, appropriately enough, which I think looks pretty cool and hard, but I don't tell him this.

'Does it hurt?' I ask.

'Does it *look* like it hurts?' he scowls.

'A bit.'

'Well, it does hurt. It *bloody* hurts as a matter of fact,' and to prove his point he touches it to make it hurt, then winces theatrically. We're in his neat military-style kitchen, making tea before the rest of the team arrive for the last rehearsal before our TV appearance. 'You do realise that it's still going to be like this next week? When we're on *television*? In front of *millions* of people?'

'Not *that* many millions, Patrick. And anyway, I'm sure they'll be able to cover it up with make-up or something.'

'Well, I hope so, Brian, because more or less the whole of my family are going to be there in the studio, and I don't want to have to explain that some skinhead cockney oik did it just because he didn't happen to agree with my political views.'

'That's not the only reason he did it, is it though?'

'He did it because he's a wild animal who should never have been let off his leash. He's just very lucky that I've decided not to sue.'

'No point. He hasn't got any money.'

'No wonder, too. I'm not surprised he can't get a decent job . . .'

'Actually, he's very intelli . . .'

'. . . not if that's how he behaves himself . . .'

'Well, you were being a bit . . .'

'A bit what?'

I contemplate telling him – pompous, ignorant, obnoxious, rude, patronising – but decide against it, because at the end of the day my best friend did beat him up, so instead I just say, 'Anyway, I got you this – a peace offering, to say sorry, on Spencer's behalf . . .' and I hand over the gift, a massive slab of a Cadbury's Fruit and Nut, a left-over Christmas present from Nana Jackson. This feels a bit unprincipled, because of course Spencer would never, ever dream of apologising, and for a moment I contemplate bringing the slab of Fruit and Nut down hard on the bridge of his supercilious right-wing nose, imagine the noise it would make, that satisfying loud crack, but I hand it over politely instead, because we are meant to be a team after all. Patrick mumbles a terse 'thank you very much' and stashes the chocolate on the very top of the wall-cupboards so that he doesn't actually have to share it with anyone.

The doorbell rings. 'If that's Lucy, Brian, then you should apologise. I think she was a little shaken by the whole thing, to be honest.' I run downstairs, and open the door to Lucy and her panda.

'Hello, Brian!' she says, brightly.

'Lucy, I just wanted to say that I'm really, really sorry about the fight the other day . . .'

'Oh, that's okay. I was going to call you in the week to see if . . .'

ALICE! Alice appears over Lucy's shoulder.

'Hiya, Alice!' I say.

'Hello, Brian,' she says, and gives an imperceptible smile, because after all, we have a secret.

The rest of the meeting passes uneventfully enough. There's no news about who our competition's going to be, because they like to keep it secret until the day of recording, but Patrick tells us not to be thrown if it's Oxbridge or the Open University; 'They're *very* overrated,' he says. Then there's a lot of practical stuff about hiring the minibus from the hockey team, and putting up posters in the Student Union for anyone who wants to come along and support us. One of Patrick's big-boned, right-wing pals from the Economics department has offered to drive the minibus of supporters up to Manchester, providing we can get enough people to show an interest. 'So if there's anyone you want to come along, get them to sign the form in the Student Union.'

Alice is going to invite the cast of *Hedda Gabler*, and Lucy has some medic pals, but the only person I can think of to invite is Rebecca. I'm not entirely sure that she wouldn't boo, or cheer the other side, but I decide to at least give her the option.

'Now . . .' says Patrick, consulting his type-written notes '. . . the final item on the agenda. We need to decide on some kind of team mascot!'

I don't really own anything that could qualify as a mascot, and Patrick owns nothing even remotely soft or amusing, so in the end it's a toss-up between Alice's favourite old teddy, Eddie, or the skull of Lucy's anatomical skeleton, which very wittily Alice suggests we wrap in a college scarf and call Yorick.

We go for Eddie.

After we finish, I have to run off down the street to catch up with Alice, who's got to get straight to rehearsals.

'So what are you doing tomor . . . ?'

'Rehearsing . . .'

'But during the day?'

'Well, I've got to get an essay in, so . . .'

'Fancy the pictures?'

'The pictures?' She stops in the street, looks both ways to check no one's looking, and says, 'Okay. The pictures.' We make an arrangement, and I skip home to really get cracking on that poem.

And the following afternoon, she bunks off her essay to be with me exclusively and we go to the pictures together. The cinema's not ideal, of course, because the opportunities to talk or to just look at her, are limited. Also, she wants to go and see *Back to the Future* at the Odeon, which she insists will be 'a laugh, a bit of fun', but I have something a bit more intellectually demanding in mind. So instead we go and watch the Tuesday afternoon double-bill of ground-breaking early silent film at the Arts Cinema; Dali and Bunuel's startling surrealist 1928 masterpiece *Un Chien Andalou* and Eisenstein's masterly Soviet polemic *Battleship Potemkin* (1925).

We buy a whole load of confectionery from the newsagents beforehand, because, as I point out, the mark-up on confectionery in the cinema is absolutely outrageous, and then settle down in centre aisle seats, two of only six people in the whole auditorium. The lights go down, and the atmosphere of suppressed sexual desire, like a mild electric current running through us, is almost tangible, as is the smell of damp cigarettes and curdled Kia-ora, and the cold, and the vague feeling of infestation. It's *Un Chien Andalou* first. During the startling sequence involving the slitting of the eyeball and the decomposing donkey on top of the piano, Alice leans forward in her seat with her hands over her eyes, and I rather cornily put my arm round the back of her chair, as if shielding her from Dali and Bunuel's grotesque insight into the workings of the subconscious mind.

Then the lights come up and there's a brief intermission during which we eat a big bag of chocolate-covered peanuts, drink cans of Lilt, and debate surrealism and its relationship to the unconscious mind. Alice isn't a fan. 'It just leaves me cold. It's very ugly and alienating. It just doesn't move me or involve me emotionally, that's all . . .'

'It's not *meant* to engage or involve you emotionally, not in a conventionally sympathetic way. Surrealism is *meant* to be strange, unnerving. I find it *very* emotional, it's just that the emotions that we feel are often ones of anxiety and disgust . . .' and of course the ironic thing is that, unlike the surrealists, all I want is for Alice to be engaged and involved in a conventionally sympathetic way, and *not* to feel emotions of anxiety and disgust.

Then the lights go down, and things perk up again as *Battleship Potemkin* comes on. I keep sneaking looks at her during the famous Odessa Steps sequence until she smiles back at me, and I lean across and kiss her. And thank God, she kisses me back, for quite a while actually, and it's great. There's a slight citrus/dairy clash of flavours, because she's moved on to wine gums while I'm still on chocolate peanuts, and I can't really let rip because there's a peanut kernel wedged back in my wisdom teeth, and I don't want the kissing to get too fiery or wide-ranging in case she dislodges it. In the end I needn't have worried, because Alice soon breaks away and whispers, 'I think I'd better watch the film. I want to know what happens to the sailors!' and we go back to *Battleship Potemkin.*

It's dark when we leave the cinema, and I'm feeling a little nauseous from all the sweets and kissing, but she takes my arm as we walk back through the town centre, and we talk about Eisenstein with revolutionary zeal. 'He really is the father of modern film narrative technique,' I say and, when I finally run out of that kind of dreary crap, 'Coffee and a flapjack? Or the pub? Or back to mine? Or yours?'

'Better not. I've got lines to learn.'

'I could test you?' I suggest, though something tells me I'm testing her quite enough as it is.

'Actually, I'm better off on my own,' she says, and I realise with dismay that we're heading back towards her halls of residence, and that this is the end of our falling-in-love montage for today.

Then on the ring road, just past the National Express coach station, I see something and have an idea.

'Come with me a second . . .'

'What for?'

'I've had an idea. It's going to be fun, I promise.' I ever so subtly tighten my grip on her arm so that she can't run away, and we head into the grey diesel haze of the coach station, and the Photo-Me Booth.

'What are we doing?'

'I just thought we'd get our pictures done,' I say, searching in my pockets for change.

'Of the *two of us*?'

'Uh-huh.'

'What on earth for?' she says, pulling away slightly. I tighten my grip.

'Just a souvenir,' I say, but that word isn't right. 'Souvenir', noun, from the French verb *souvenir*, to remember. 'You know – for fun!'

'No way,' she says firmly, and I wonder how I'm going to get her in there, without the aid of a chloroformed handkerchief.

'Oh, go on . . .'

'No!'

'Why not?'

'Because I look *terrible*!' she says, when of course what she really means is 'Because *you* look terrible . . .'

'Rubbish, you look fine – come on, it'll be fun,' I say, again tugging her across the station forecourt by her hand; it will be fun, it will be fun, it will be fun . . . I pull back the diesel-and-nicotine infused orange nylon curtain and we squeeze into the booth, and there's some light-hearted fidgeting about as we adjust the height of the stool and work out how we're going to sit. Eventually Alice perches on my knee, then has to get off again so that I can remove a bunch of keys and get the change out of my pocket, then nestles once more on my lap, both legs swung over mine this time, and wraps her arms around my neck. She's playing along now, and it seems as if this might even be fun after all, so I lean forward and put the 50p in the slot.

The first camera flash happens just as I'm pushing the great loose flap of hair out of my eyes.

For the second flash I take off my spectacles, suck in my cheeks and pout, pulling a sort of tongue-in-cheek male-model face, because it will be fun.

For the third photo I try relaxed, light-hearted laughter, head tipped back, mouth open.

And for number four, I kiss Alice on the cheek.

It seems that several hours pass as we wait for the photos

to come out of the machine. We stand around in the coach station in silence, inhaling diesel fumes and listening to the tannoy. The 5.45 coach for Durham is about to leave.

'Ever been to Durham?' I ask.

'No,' she says. 'You?'

'No,' I say. 'I'd like to, though. Lovely cathedral apparently.' The coach rumbles past us, belching exhaust. I contemplate throwing myself under it. Then finally, with a whirr and a click, the machine spits out the strip of photographs, which are sticky with developing fluid and smell of ammonia.

Some primitive tribes believe that having your photograph taken steals a little bit of your soul, and looking at this strip of photos it's hard not to think that maybe they've got a point. In the first, my hand and my hair are obscuring most of my face, and the only thing you can see clearly is the acne round the corners of my mouth, and the great fat mottled tongue lolling out obscenely, as if I've just been punched. Number two, the 'comedy male-model shot', is possibly the most grotesquely mirthless thing you've ever seen in your life, an effect that's reinforced by one, just one, of Alice's eyes rolling back into her head. Number three, entitled 'laughter!', is horribly bright and over-illuminated, so that you can see up my nose, past matted nostril hair into the black centre of my skull, and down into the pink-ribbed roof of my mouth, past the stubby silver-grey fillings on my molars all the way down to my epiglottis. Finally, in number four, I'm kissing Alice with a chapped, puckered haddock mouth while she winces, eyes squeezed tightly shut.

One for the wallet then.

'Oh dear,' I say.

'Lovely,' says Alice, flatly.

'Which two do you want?'

'Oh, I'm all right, I think. You keep them, as a souvenir.' And there's that word again, souvenir, noun, from the French verb *souvenir*, to remember. 'Sorry, Bri, I've got to run.' And she does. She runs.

Sat at home that evening, putting the finishing touches to the poem, and looking at the strip of photographs Blu-Tacked to the wall by my desk – me kissing Alice, her wincing – it strikes me that our fun-day-out has only been a partial success. I should forget about it of course, but I'm worried that I won't be able to sleep unless I speak to her again, so I pull on my coat and head off to the student bar, in the hope that I'll accidentally bump into her after rehearsals.

She's not there, of course. When I arrive the only other person I know is Rebecca Epstein, surrounded by her little coterie of fuckingangryactuallys. She seems pretty pleased to see me, and gets her comrades to redistribute some of the space on the bench so that I can squeeze in next to her, but the table's covered in empties; she's been alternating lager and whisky all night, and seems pretty drunk.

'Have you seen Eisenstein's *Battleship Potemkin*?' I say, keeping an eye out for Alice.

'Can't say I have. Why, should I?'

'Absolutely. It's amazing. They're showing it at the Arts Cinema all this week.'

'Okay then, let's go, shall we? I'll bunk off lectures tomorrow afternoon . . .'

'Well, actually I went to see it this afternoon.'

'On your own?'

'No. With Alice actually,' I say, as casually as I can. But Rebecca can spot that kind of thing a mile off, and pounces, 'Well, you two are awfully friendly at the moment, aren't you? 'S there something I should know?'

'We've just been spending a bit of time together, that's all.'

'Is that right?' says Rebecca, sceptically. She starts to roll another cigarette, even though she still has one glued to her lip, and it's like watching someone load a revolver. 'Is . . . that . . .'

(licks the Rizla) '. . . right? Well, Jackson, you certainly know how to show a gal a good time, don't you? A masterpiece of Soviet propaganda in the afternoon, then maybe on to Luigi's for prawn cocktail, half a barbecue chicken and two pints of Lambrusco bianco. It really is the high-life. I only hope, after a magical day out like that, she at least let you have a wee feel of her tits . . .'

The clever thing to do, of course, would be not to rise to the bait.

'Actually, we're sort of going out with each other,' I say.

Rebecca raises her eyebrows and smiles to herself. She lights her new cigarette before speaking again.

'Are you now?' she says, quietly, and picking tobacco off her lip. 'So how come I haven't seen you together round at our halls of residence?'

'We're being discreet. Taking it slow,' I say, unconvincingly.

'Right, right. So was that you who phoned up in the week to talk to her?'

'No!'

'Are you sure?'

'Yes!'

'Because it sounded awfully like you . . .'

'. . . well . . .'

'. . . putting on a funny voice . . .'

'. . . well it wasn't . . .'

'So have you *shagged* her yet?' she snarls, rollie dangling from her curled lip.

'*What?*'

'Have you had *sexual intercourse*? You know – congress, coitus, the beast-with-two-backs. Come on, you must have at least *heard* about it. After all, you're going on *University Challenge* – what are you going to do if it comes up as a question? "Jackson, from Southend-on-Sea, reading Eng. Lit, what actually *is* sexual intercourse?" "Ummmmmmm . . . Can I confer with the rest of the team, Bamber? Alice, what's sexual inter . . . ?"'

'I know what it *is*, Rebecca . . .'

'So, have you done it then, or are you saving yourself for your wedding day? Or maybe she's worried about your sexual history; after all, you can't be too careful these days. Except as I recall you don't actually *have* a sexual history . . .'

And before I even know what I'm saying, I say, 'Yeah, well, it's not like *yours* is anything to write home about, Rebecca.'

She takes the cigarette out of her mouth, rests her hand against the edge of the table, and is silent for a moment.

'Good point, Jackson. Good point.' She downs the last inch of her pint, winces. 'Touché, Jackson!' And then we sit in silence.

'I didn't mean . . .'

'. . . no, that's all right . . .'

'. . . I wasn't referring to . . .'

'No, I know you weren't.'

I decide to leave.

'So are you coming to the filming?' I say, pulling on my coat.

'What filming?'

'The *University Cha* . . .'

'When is it?'

'Day after tomorrow?'

'Can't. I've got tutorials, so . . .'

'. . . there's a list on the second-floor notice-board if . . .'

'. . . I know . . .'

'. . . just sign your name if . . .'

'. . . I'll see . . .'

'. . . I'd really, really like you to come . . .'

'Why?'

'. . . I just would. See you there maybe?'

'Aye. Well. Maybe.'

I swing by Alice's halls of residence, just in case, and drop my Valentine's card in; hand hovering by her mailbox, then taking a deep breath and letting go. Then I hang around, pretending to read the notice-boards, in case she comes back. But I don't want to run into Rebecca again tonight, so I soon head back home and arrive just as Josh is pinning a note to my door.

'Ah, there you are, lover boy. Message for you. From someone called . . .' *Alice maybe*? '. . . from someone called . . . Tone. He says you're to call him urgently.'

'Really?' I say. What on earth does Tone want? Maybe he's coming to stay too. I can't have Tone coming to stay, not with Valentine's Day tomorrow, and The Challenge and everything. I check my watch. Half eleven. I go to the payphone in the hall.

'Hiya, Tone!' I say, brightly.

'All right, Bri . . .'

'Didn't wake you up, did I? It's just I had a message to call.'

'Yeah, that's right . . .'

'Are you coming up to stay, Tone? Because if you are, it's not the best time at the mo . . .'

'I'm not coming to stay, Bri. Actually I was just wondering when you were going to come down here?'

'Well . . . not until Easter, I don't think.'

'No, I mean to see Spencer.'

'Why, what about Spencer?'

'You haven't heard then?'

I press the receiver tighter against my ear, lean against the wall.

'Heard what?'

Tone exhales into the mouthpiece, and says, 'There's been a bit of an accident.'

34

QUESTION: At whose wedding do 'funeral bak'd meats . . . coldly furnish forth the wedding tables'?
ANSWER: The marriage of Gertrude and Claudius, in *Hamlet*.

I head back to Southend first thing on Valentine's Day, before the post arrives, and get back to the maisonette on Archer Road round about noon. I've been desperate for a pee since the change at Fenchurch Street, but the toilets on the train were spectacularly blocked, so I've waited and now have this throbbing ache in my kidneys. I take the stairs at a run, head into the bathroom, and scream . . .

'OH MY GOD!'

There's a man in the bath, shampooing his hair. He starts to scream too . . .

'WHAT THE BLOODY HELL . . . !'

And then Mum's coming out of her bedroom, doing up her dressing gown, and over her shoulder I see the unmade bed in disarray, the red and white Y-fronts hanging from the headboard, the men's trousers gaping on the floor, the bottle of sparkling wine . . .

'BRIAN, WHAT THE HELL ARE YOU DOING BACK!' shouts Mum. I turn away, because she's not quite done up her dressing gown properly, and see that the man in the bath is standing up now, wiping at the shampoo in his eyes with one hand, clasping a face flannel to his groin with the other.

'What the hell's going on!' I say.

'I'm trying to have a bloody bath!' blusters Uncle Des.

'Wait downstairs!' snaps Mum.

'I need to use the toilet!' I say, which I do, urgently.

'BRIAN – WAIT DOWNSTAIRS!' She's shouting now, holding her dressing gown closed, pointing at the stairs. I haven't heard her shout like this since I was a kid, and suddenly I feel like a kid, so I go downstairs, unlock the back door, and pee in the corner of the garden.

I'm in the kitchen waiting for the kettle to boil when I hear Uncle Des and Mum sneaking down the stairs, then whispering furtively in the hallway, like a pair of teenagers. I think I hear 'I'll call you later', then the sound of a kiss, the sound of my mother *kissing* Uncle Des, then the front door closes, and I hear the fizz of a match being struck, the sound of Mum inhaling, breathing out slowly, and then she's stood behind me in the doorway, wearing a powder blue tracksuit, sucking hard on the fag in one hand, holding a greasy glass of sparkling wine in the other.

The kettle's still not boiling.

Finally Mum says, 'I thought you were going straight to the hospital?'

'I missed lunch-time visiting. I'm going later.'

'I wasn't expecting you.'

'No, well, obviously not. So – something wrong with Uncle Des's bath is there?'

'Don't take that tone, Brian . . .'

'What tone?'

'You know what tone,' and she drains the remains of the wine. The kettle finally clicks off. 'You making coffee?'

'Looks like it.'

'Make me one. Then come into the lounge. We need to have a little talk.'

Oh, God. My heart sinks. We're going to have a little talk, a frank discussion, a heart-to-heart, a one-to-one. We're going to talk to each other like adults. I've managed to avoid this kind of thing so far. Dad died before he could do the 'when-a-man-and-a-lady-really-like-each-other' number, and I think Mum must have assumed that either it was never going to be relevant, or that I'd find out about the strange mystery of physical love by myself one way or another, which I did I suppose, after a fashion, up against a wheelie bin at the back of Littlewoods. But there's no getting away from this one. I pluck two mugs off the tree, spoon in the coffee powder and try to work out what to think. I try to imagine that there's some kind of innocent explanation to Uncle Des being in our bath at one in the afternoon on Valentine's Day, but can't. All that comes to mind is the obvious explanation, and the obvious explanation is . . . unthinkable. Uncle Des and Mum. Uncle Des from three doors down and my mum in bed together in broad daylight, Uncle Des and Mum having . . .

Kettle's boiled.

Mum's in the lounge, drawing deeply on a Rothmans and peering through the net curtains. I hand her the mug of coffee and sit glumly on the sofa, in silence, and I find myself wondering if this is what it feels like to be told by your wife that she wants a divorce.

I notice my Valentine's card on the mantelpiece, a Chagall postcard. 'I see you got a card, then!'

'What? Oh yes. Thank you very much, sweetheart. Very nice.'

'How d'you know it was from me?' I ask, a feeble attempt at light-heartedness.

'Well you wrote "To Mum" on it, so . . .' and she tries a smile, then turns back to the window and blows smoke at the window pane, exhaling so hard that the net curtains move. Finally, she says, 'Brian, your Uncle Des and I are having an . . .' and she's about to say 'affair', but plumps for 'having an . . . relationship.'

'For how long?'

'A little while now. Since last October.'

'Since I went away you mean?'

'More or less. He came round for a curry one night, to keep me company, and one thing led to another and well, I was going to tell you Brian, at Christmas, but you weren't around much, and I didn't want to do it over the phone . . .'

'No. No, I can imagine,' I mumble. 'So is it . . . serious?'

'I think so. Well . . .' and she sucks on her fag again, purses her lips, exhales and says '. . . as a matter of fact we've been talking about getting married.'

'*What?*'

'He's asked me to marry him.'

'Uncle Des?'

'Yes.'

'*Marry* him?'

'Brian . . .'

'And you've said *yes*?'

'. . . I know you don't get on, I know you don't like him, but I do, I like Des a lot. He's a good man, and he likes me, and he makes me laugh. And I'm forty-one years old Brian, I know that must seem ancient to you – God knows it feels ancient sometimes – but you'll be forty-one one day, sooner than you think. Anyway, I'm still, I still, well, I still get *lonely*, Brian, I still like a bit of company every now and then, a bit of . . .' she draws on her cigarette, looks at the floor, '. . . well, I'm sorry, but your dad's been gone a long time now Brian, and Des and I aren't doing anything wrong. I won't be made to feel like we're doing anything wrong . . .'

But I'm still trying to take things in. 'So you *are* going to marry him?'

'I think so . . .'

'You don't know?'

'Yes! Yes, I am going to marry him!'

'When?'

'Later in the year sometime. We're not in any rush.'

'And then what happens?'

'He's going to move in here, with me. We're thinking . . .'

and she pauses, nervous again, and I can't imagine what else she could possibly have to tell me '. . . we're thinking of turning it into a B and B.'

I think I laugh at this, not because I find it funny, or any of this funny in fact, just because I don't have another appropriate response.

'You're joking.'

'No, I'm not.'

'A Bed and Breakfast?'

'Uh-huh.'

'But there's no room!'

'Not for families – for singles, or young couples, businessmen. Des is going to convert the loft' – she glances at me nervously, then back at the net curtains – 'and your room. We thought we'd maybe clear out your room.'

'And what happens to my stuff?'

'We thought you could . . . take it with you.'

'You're throwing me out of my room!'

'Not throwing you out, just . . . asking you to move your stuff.'

'To university?'

'Yes! Either that or throw it away. It's just a lot of books and comics and model planes, Bri, it's not anything you're going to need. You are a grown-up after all . . .'

'So I am getting thrown out!'

'Don't be daft, of course you're not. You can still stay in the holidays if you really want to, and over the summer . . .'

'But isn't that your peak season . . . ?'

'Brian . . .'

'Well, that's very good of you and Uncle Des, Mum, but how much do you charge per night?' I can hear my own voice now, high-pitched and wheedling.

'Don't be like this please, Brian . . .' Mum says.

'Well, what d'you expect me to do? I mean, I'm only getting thrown out of my own house . . .'

And then she spins, and turns to me, and jabs at me with the remains of her fag and shouts, 'It's not your house any more, Brian!'

'Oh really!'

'No, I'm sorry, but it's not! You were here, what, one week at Christmas? One week, and even then you couldn't wait to get back to college. You don't come back at weekends, you don't phone for weeks, you certainly don't write to me, so, no, actually, no, this is not your house. It's *mine*. It's the house I live in *by myself*, just me, every bloody day, day after day, since your dad died, this is where I've slept every night on my own, and that, that there, that bloody settee, that's where I've sat nearly every night on my own, watching the telly or just staring at the wall, while you're away at college, or if you do deign to stay here you're out with your mates, or hiding in your room because you're so bloody obviously bored of talking to me, your own mother. D'you have any idea what that's like, Brian, being here all by myself, year after year after bloody, bloody year . . . ?' but then her voice starts to crack, and she clasps her face with her hands and starts sobbing, great heavy, wet sobs and once again I realise that I have absolutely no idea what I'm supposed to do.

'Hey, come on, Mum . . .' I say, but she just waves her hand at me, gesturing for me to keep away.

'Leave me alone, please Brian,' she says, and I'm tempted to do as she says, because it would be easier after all.

'. . . Mum, there's no need to get . . .'

'Leave me *alone. Just go away* . . .'

What if I pretend I haven't heard any of this? The lounge door's still open after all. I could just go out, come back in an hour or so, let her calm down, just go. After all, that's what she's told me to do, that's what she wants, isn't it?

'Please Mum, please, don't cry. I hate it when you . . .' and I can't finish the sentence because I find that I'm crying myself, and I cross over to her and fold my arms round her and hold onto her as tightly as I can.

35

QUESTION: Circles of standing stones at Lindholm Hoje near Alborg in Denmark indicate that it was a site for which ancient ritual?

ANSWER: Viking burial.

I meet Tone at two-fifteen in The Black Prince on the sea front. There's no one in apart from a couple of tubercular old geezers nursing the last warm inch of their pints and reading dog-eared copies of the *Sun*, but it still takes me a moment to notice him because I'm instinctively looking for light-blue denim, not the charcoal single-button suit, white socks and light-grey slip-ons that he's wearing today.

'Bloody hell, Tone, what's happened to your hair?' The Viking look has gone, and instead he's got a neat short-back-and-sides with a parting slightly too far to the left. Tone, in a suit, with a parting.

'Had it cut, that's all.' I go to ruffle it, but he karates my hand away, not quite playfully. I want to keep things light-hearted so I say, 'Here, are you wearing gel?'

'A little bit. So what?' he says, then takes a sip from the half-pint of lager in front of him. I don't think I've ever seen Tone holding a half-pint glass, and it's playing tricks with scale, like he's some sort of giant.

'D'you want another drink?' I ask.

'I'm all right . . .'

'Another half then? . . .'

'I can't . . .'

'Go on, you wuss . . .' I cajole, light-heartedly.

'Can't. I've got to get back to work,' he says.

'Surely you've got time for a . . .'

'I don't want another half, all right?' he snaps. I go and get myself a pint and sit back down.

'So – how's work?'

''S alright. I'm out front on the shop floor now, so that's why . . .' and half apologetically, he tugs on the long thin lapel of his suit.

'Which department?'

'Hi-fi and audio.'

'Great!'

'Yeah, well. It'll do. And there's commission, so . . .'

'Spencer told me about you and the Territorials.'

'Did he? Have a good laugh about it, did you?'

'No, course not . . .'

'I don't suppose you *approve*.'

'I didn't say that, did I? I mean I am a unilateralist, and I think we should definitely reduce defence spending and plough some of that money into social services, but I still understand the need for some form of . . .' but Tone's looking at his watch, not really interested. 'So have you seen Spencer?' I say.

'Of course I've seen Spencer,' he snaps, and I accept that, for today at least, it's going to be impossible for me to say *any*thing that doesn't piss *some*one off.

'And how is he?' I ask.

'Well, considering he's been through the windscreen of a Ford Escort, he's pretty good actually.'

'So what happened, Tone?'

'Don't know, exactly. We were down the pub Friday as usual, and after closing he wanted to go on into London, to a club or something so we could keep drinking, and I said no, 'cause I was working the next day, and he was pretty pissed, but he went anyway, took his dad's car. The next thing I knew was two days later when his mum called and said he was in hospital.'

'Was anyone else hurt?'

'No . . .'

'Well thank God for that . . .'

'. . . just our mate Spencer,' he adds, with a sneer.

'I didn't mean . . . I just meant . . . And is he in trouble? I mean, legally?'

'Well, he was over the limit, he's only got a provisional licence, it wasn't his car and he wasn't insured, so, yeah, from a legal standpoint, things aren't looking too rosy.'

'And how's he . . . feeling?'

'I don't know, Brian, ask him yourself, will you? I've got to get back to work,' and irritably, he drains the rest of his half, takes a packet of mints out of his pocket and pops one in his mouth, without offering me one.

We step outside the pub and walk along the street back towards the pier. The wind's blowing rain in off the estuary, and Tone folds the two thin lapels of his jacket over to protect his shirt and tie as we march on up towards the High Street.

'So you staying over tonight?' he asks, clearly not caring much either way.

'No, can't I'm afraid.' I wonder if I should tell him that I'm on *University Challenge* tomorrow, but decide against it. 'Got a tutorial tomorrow, first thing, so I'm going back later. But I'll be back at Easter I think, so . . . see you then?'

'Yeah, well, whatever.'

'Tone – have I done something to, you know, piss you off?'

He snorts. 'Whatever gave you that impression?'

'Was it something Spence said?' No reply. 'What did he say, Tone?'

Without looking at me, Tone says, 'Spencer told me about coming to see you. It didn't sound as if you were much of a mate to him, Bri. In fact it sounded to me as if you behaved like a bit of a cunt. That's all.'

'Why, what did he say?'

'. . . doesn't matter . . .'

'I couldn't let him stay any longer, Tone, it was against the rules . . .'

'Oh, well, if it was against *the rules*, Bri . . .'

'He was the one who started the fight, Tone . . .'

'Look, I'm not interested, Bri, that's between you and Spence.'

'So I suppose it's my fault he decided to get pissed-up and drive into a tree as well?'

'I didn't say that, did I? Just sort it out Brian, all right?' and Tone hurries on up the street, head down against the rain, then pauses for a second, half turns. 'And try not to be too much of a twat about it. Yeah?' Then he turns and hurries off back to work, and I find myself wondering if I'll ever see him again.

36

QUESTION: First isolated by F.W.A. Serturner in 1806, what is the common name of the narcotic analgesic derived from the unripe seeds of *papaver somniferum*?
ANSWER: Morphine.

A morning in May 1979, three days after Dad's funeral. I'm lying on the sofa with the curtains still drawn, watching Saturday morning television in my school uniform. Technically of course, I don't need to be in school uniform, but I tend to wear it all year round anyway, because it's easier, and I don't really know what else to wear; my concession to the weekend is that I don't put my tie on.

The relatives have all gone home and it's just Mum and me now. Mum's not at her best, and has taken to sleeping in late, then padding round the house in her dressing gown, leaving a trail of dirty mugs and cigarette ends, or dozing curled up on the sofa all afternoon and on into the evening. The whole house has a hot, grey, sickly aspect, but neither of us can quite find the energy or motivation to draw the curtains and open a window, empty an ashtray, turn the television off, wash up the dishes, cook something other than spaghetti hoops. The fridge is still crammed with left-over cake, cling-wrapped sausage rolls and flat bottles of cola from the wake. I'm eating cheese-and-onion crisps for breakfast. This is pretty much the worst time.

When the doorbell rings, I assume it's one of the neighbours popping round to check up on Mum. She answers, and I hear a voice in the hall that I don't recognise, then Mum's opening the lounge door, dressing gown held closed for propriety's sake, and putting on the funny 'well-spoken' voice she uses for important visitors.

'There's someone here to see you, Brian!'

She steps to one side, and Spencer Lewis walks in.

'Alright, Bri?'

I sit up straight on the sofa. 'Alright, Spence?'

'What are you doing?'

'Nothing.'

'Glass of Coke, Spencer?' asks Mum.

'Yes, please, Mrs Jackson.'

Mum backs discreetly out of the room, and Spencer comes and sits next to me on the sofa.

It's hard to over-emphasise the significance of a visit from Spencer Lewis. It's not like we're even mates or anything; we've barely spoken before – maybe just a bit of name-calling on the football pitch, a nod of recognition in the queue for the ice-cream van. There seems to be no possible explanation as to why someone as cool, popular and hard as Spencer Lewis should come and visit me, the kind of nutter who wears his school uniform on a Saturday. But here he is, sat on the settee.

'What you watching?'

'Swap Shop.'

'I bloody hate Swap Shop,*' he says.*

'Yeah, me too.' I sniff sardonically, though secretly I like it. We sit in silence for a moment or two, then he says, 'I accidentally called your mum Mrs *Jackson. D'you think she minds?'*

'Nah. She's alright,' I say.

And apart from that, he doesn't mention Dad dying at all, or ask about the funeral or 'how I'm feeling', thank God, because that would just be embarrassing – we are twelve-year-old boys after all. Instead, he sits and drinks flat cola and watches telly with me. He tells me what bands are crap and what bands are good, and I believe him, and agree with everything he says. It feels like a film star's come to visit, or someone better than a film star, someone like Han Solo. And it feels like an act of absolute kindness.

Spencer's left leg is broken in three places, his right in two. His collar bone has snapped, which is particularly painful because it's impossible to set a collar bone in plaster, so he can't really move the top half of his body. His arms seem to be okay, though there are some cuts on the palms of his hand and his forearm from broken glass. Thankfully there's no damage to the spine or skull, but six of his ribs are fractured where they impacted against the steering wheel. This makes breathing painful and unaided sleep almost impossible, so he's on quite a lot of medication. His nose is broken, red and swollen, and the brow over his right eye is badly split, and contains six thick black stitches. The eye itself is deep black and purple and swollen, and remains half-closed. The top of his head meanwhile is peppered with dark red scabs from the shattered windscreen, clearly visible beneath the still-short hair, and there's more stitches in his left ear where the lobe was partially torn off by the broken glass.

'But apart from that?'

'Apart from that I'm actually feeling really good,' says Spencer, and we both laugh for a while, before sinking back into silence.

'You think *I* look rough! You should see the tree!' he says, not for the first time I suspect, and we laugh again, Spencer sniggering and wincing at the same time, because of the pain from his ribs and collar bone. He's on pills, of course. He's not sure what they are exactly, but it's definitely something a bit stronger than aspirin, some kind of opiate he thinks. And it seems to be doing the trick, because there's an uncharacteristic mirthless smile lurking around the corner of his mouth. Nothing disturbing, not like Jack Nicholson at the end of *One Flew Over The Cuckoo's Nest*, just a strange sort of vaguely inappropriate amusement. His speech, usually so sharp and direct, is groggy and distant, as if a hand were pressed over his mouth.

'Still, the good news is they've postponed my court case about the dole-fiddling thing . . .'

'That's good.'

'Yeah, almost makes this all worthwhile. Haven't got any fags have you?'

'Spencer – I don't smoke.'

'I'm gasping for a fag. And a pint.'

'It's a *hospital*, Spencer . . .'

'I know, but still . . .'

'What's the food like?' I ask.

'Not particularly tasty.'

'And the nurses?'

'Not particularly tasty.'

I smile, and make a noise to show that I'm smiling, because I'm out of his eye-line, and he doesn't seem to be able to move his head too well. 'And what about all this . . . ?' I indicate the plaster-cast on his legs, his bandaged hands . . . 'are there going to be any, you know, legal . . . repercussions?'

'Don't know yet. Probably.'

'Bloody hell, Spencer . . .'

'All right Bri, don't start . . .'

'. . . well, you must have known that something . . .'

'You haven't come all this way to tell me off, have you Bri?'

'No, of course not, but you have to admit . . .'

'. . . yeah, I know – don't smoke, don't fight, don't fiddle your dole, don't drink and drive, wear a seat-belt, work hard, go to night-school, get your qualifications, go on a scheme – you're like a fucking walking-public-information-film sometimes, Brian . . .'

'. . . sorry, I . . .'

'. . . we don't *all* do the sensible thing all the time, Brian . . .'

'. . . no, I know . . .'

'. . . we can't *all* be like you . . .'

'. . . hey, I don't always do the sensible . . . !'

'. . . you know what I mean, though, don't you?'

—and he doesn't shout any of the above, because he can't shout, he just sort of hisses it between his teeth, before lapsing into silence again. There's something I know I have to say, and haven't quite found the words yet, but I'm about to open my mouth to try when he says, 'Pour us some water, will you?' I pour him a plastic cupful, hand it over, and as he strains to sit up straight, I can smell his breath which is hot and metallic.

'Anyway . . .' he sighs, letting his head fall back on the pillow '. . . how's Alice?'

'Oh, alright. I stayed over the other night, so . . .'

'You're joking – really?' he says, smiling sincerely, turning his head on the pillow to look at me. 'So you're actually going out with her, then?'

'Well, we're taking it slowly,' I say, a little bashfully. 'Really, *really* slowly actually, but yeah, it's good.'

'Brian Jackson, you dark horse . . .'

'Yeah, well, we'll see.' I sense that this is the time to do the proper, adult thing, so I take a deep breath. 'Alice said you put a word in for me. At that party.'

'Did she?' he says, without looking at me.

'I was a bit of a wanker to you, wasn't I?'

'No, you weren't . . .'

'I was, Spence, I was a complete wanker . . .'

'Bri, you're fine . . .'

'I don't set out to be a wanker, you know, it just sort of happens . . .'

'. . . let's just forget it, yeah?'

'No, but still . . .'

'All right, if it makes you happier, Bri, then yes, you were a complete wanker. Now can we forget about it?'

'But how are you feeling, though . . . ?'

'What about . . . ?'

'. . . about, you know, *things*?'

'In general, you mean? Don't know. To be honest, I'm just really tired. Tired and a little bit scared, Bri.' He says this very quietly, and I have to lean forward in my chair to hear him, and notice that his eyes are red and wet. He senses me looking at him, and puts both hands vertically over his face, pressing his eyes hard with his fingertips, exhaling slowly and deeply, and I feel twelve years old again, sad, embarrassed, with no idea what to do now – some sort of act of kindness I suppose, but what? Maybe put my arm around him? But I feel awkward about getting up out of my chair, anxious about the other people in the ward seeing, so I stay where I am.

'It's meant to be scary though, isn't it?' I say. 'You know, life, this bit of it. That's what people say . . .'

'Yeah. S'pose so . . .'

'It gets better . . .'

'Does it?' he says, his eyes still covered. ''Cause it seems like I've just fucked *everything* up, Bri . . .'

'Rubbish! You're fine, mate, you're going to be absolutely fine,' and I reach across, and put my hand on his shoulder, and squeeze it. The gesture feels clumsy and self-conscious, leaning forward in my chair with my arm outstretched, but I stay like that for as long as I can, until his shoulders stop shaking. Eventually he takes the hands away from his eyes.

'Sorry – it's these painkillers,' he says, wiping his eyes with his cuffs.

Shortly afterwards, we run out of things to say, and even though I've got plenty of time, I stand up and grab my coat.

'Hey, I better run, or I'll miss my last connection.'

'Thanks for coming, mate . . .'

'Pleasure, mate . . .'

'Well, not a *pleasure* . . .'

'Well, no, but, you know . . .'

'Hey, aren't you going to sign my plaster-cast first?'

'Yeah, yeah, of course,' and I go to the end of the bed, grab a biro from one of the clipboards and find a blank space to write. There are a lot of 'best wishes' and names I don't recognise, and a 'serves you right, you twat' and 'The Zep Rule!' from Tone. I think for a moment, and write, 'Dear Spence. Apologies and Thanks. Break a leg! Ha-Ha! Loads of love, your mate Bri.'

'What have you written then?'

'Oh – Break a leg . . .'

'*"Break a leg"! . . .*'

'You know – good luck. It's a theatrical term . . .'

And Spencer looks at the ceiling, laughs through his teeth and says slowly, 'You know Brian, you really can be the most unbelievable prick sometimes.'

'Yeah, Spence, I know mate. I know.'

37

QUESTION: Which third century Christian martyr, either identified as a Roman priest and physician who died during the persecution of Christians by the emperor Claudius II Gothicus, or as the Bishop of Terni, also martyred in Rome, has, since the fourteenth century, had a feast day in his name allocated specifically as a festival for lovers?

ANSWER: St Valentine.

Whenever I hear Edith Piaf sing '*Non, je ne regrette rien*' – which is more often than I'd like, now that I'm at university – I can't help thinking 'what the *hell* is she talking about?' I regret pretty much *everything*. I'm aware that the transition into adulthood is a difficult and sometimes painful one. I'm familiar with the conventions of the rites of passage, I know what the literary term *bildungsroman* means, I realise that it's inevitable that I'll look back at things that happened in my youth and give a wry, knowing smile. But surely there's no reason why I should be embarrassed and ashamed about things that happened thirty seconds ago? No reason why life just should be this endless rolling panorama of bodged friendships, fumbled opportunities, fatuous conversations, wasted days, idiotic remarks and ill-judged, unfunny jokes that just lie on the floor in front of me, flipping about like dying fish?

Well, not any more. I've decided that enough is enough. On the train home, contemplating the latest round of incredible fuck-ups, I resolve that I'm going to have to change my life.

Generally speaking, I resolve to change my life on average maybe thirty to forty times a week, usually at about two a.m., drunk, or early the next morning, hungover, but this one is a big one, I'm going to live life *well* from now on. Being Cool and Aloof clearly isn't working for me, and probably never will, so instead I'm going to concentrate on living a life based on the central tenets of Wisdom, Kindness and Courage.

When the train finally pulls into the station, I make a start on my wiser, kinder, braver life. I find a call-box on the platform, check that I have enough change, and dial the number. Des answers; now it's out in the open, I suppose there's no reason why he shouldn't.

'Hello?' he says.

'Hi! Des, it's Brian here!' I say, bright as a button, then realise that I've unconsciously called him Des, not Uncle Des, though whether this is a symptom of my more mature attitude to life, or a Freudian response to the fact that he's having sex with my mother, I'm not entirely sure.

'Oh. Hello there,' he says, bizarrely sounding scared of me, though God knows why, since Des weighs about fourteen stone, and besides it's not as if I can punch him down the phone line. There's a pause as he re-adjusts the receiver. 'Sorry about, you know, flashing my fella at you this morning. Obviously we were going to tell you, about me and your mum . . .'

'Des, really, it's fine, completely fine,' I assure him, and catch sight of my reflection in the call-box glass, grinning like a circus clown. 'Is Mum there?' I ask, which is a pretty stupid question really, considering it's her house.

''Course. I'll pass you over,' and I hear a rustle as he puts his hand over the receiver, mumbles something, and then Mum picks up.

'Hello?' she says warily, the receiver not quite near her mouth.

'Hi, Mum.'

'Hello, Brian. Did you get back home alright?' she asks, over-enunciating slightly, which means she's drunk.

'Uh-huh,' I say, and there's a silence, and I have a fleeting desire to hang up. But then I remember my new watch-words, Wisdom, Kindness, Courage, so I swallow hard and start speaking.

'Look, hi, I just wanted to say . . .' what do I want to say? . . . 'I just wanted to say I've thought about it and I'm really, really pleased about you and Des, and I think it's fine that you're getting married, really I do. In fact I think it's a great idea, and he's a really nice bloke, and I'm sorry if . . . well, it was a shock that's all . . .'

'Oh, Brian . . .'

'And I'm okay about the B and B too. I'll come down in the Easter break and clear out my stuff and then it's all yours. Like you said, it's only a load of model planes, after all. So what I'm saying, what I mean to say, is that I think it's a good thing. I'm . . . pleased you're happy.' There's no reply from the other end of the line, just the sound of Mum's breathing, shifting the receiver from one hand to another. 'As long as you don't expect me to call him "Dad", that's all!' I say, as light-heartedly as I can manage.

'Of course not, Brian . . .' and she's about to say something, then decides not to, stops.

'Well, that's it really. You're still coming tomorrow?'

''Course I am – wouldn't miss it for the world.'

'And you're sure you can afford it, the train fare and everything?'

'Brian, don't worry about that . . .'

'The ticket will be on the door, in your name . . .'

'Oh, and Brian? There's one other thing . . .' The pips are going and even though I can feel the weight of the loose change in my pocket, it feels as if I've said all I need to say. 'Got to go now Mum, out of money . . .'

'Brian, I need to ask you something else . . .'

'Go on then, quick . . .'

'Can Des come, too?' and then the line goes dead.

I stand in the phone-box with the receiver in my hand. The fact is I'd always expected Dad to be there. Not *literally*, obviously, not with him being dead and everything, but in my head, it had been Dad sat in the audience, next to Mum, smiling, clapping, putting two thumbs up, and Mum must have known this too, otherwise she wouldn't have been so nervous about asking. And now it's not Dad, but *Des*, some bloke called Des, who I don't really know and I don't really like, and . . .

I take change from my pocket, pick up the phone, dial the number, and Mum picks up almost immediately.

'Mum?'

'Oh, yes, Brian, I was just going to ask . . .'

'I heard you Mum. Of course you can bring Des.'

'Oh. Okay.'

'I'll sort out the ticket tomorrow.'

'Oh. Okay then, Brian. If you're sure . . .'

'I'm sure.'

'Bye then.'

'Bye then.'

And I hang up.

I stay in the phone-box for a while after that, standing, thinking, well, it's early days but the Wisdom, Kindness, Courage policy seems to be working out pretty well, so far. I think I might even have done something *good* for once. And even though I should go home to work out what to wear for the filming tomorrow and get a good night's sleep and everything, I decide to go and see Alice, because it is Valentine's Day after all, and she'll have read my poem by now.

38

QUESTION: Adam Heyer, Frank Gusenberg, Pete Gusenberg, John May, Al Weinshank and James Clark were amongst the victims of which bloody event on North Clark Street, Chicago in February 1929?

ANSWER: The St Valentine's Day Massacre.

'Listen Alice, I've been doing some thinking, about us, and, well, there's this great poem by the Metaphysical poet John Donne, *The Triple Foole*, which goes "*I am two fools I know/For loving, and for saying so/In whining poetry*" and I think, well, *I*'ve been a bit like that. What I mean to say is I've been coming on a bit strong, what with dragging you kicking-and-screaming into the photo-booth and that crazy, bad poetry in the Valentine's card and everything, and I know how important your independence is, and that's fine by me, it really, really is. I'm in love with you of course, massively so, but that's not important, that needn't get in the way, because at the end of the day I think we get along really well, that we're good friends, soul-mates even. I'd certainly rather spend time with you than anyone in the world, really I would, even though I know I can be a complete prick sometimes. Most of the time in fact, and, alright, look, I'm not completely stupid, I know you don't love me *now*, but you might do, mightn't you, one day? I mean you might grow to? It is possible, it does happen, and I've got patience, loads and loads of patience, and I don't mind waiting. So what I'm trying to say is – let's wait and see. Just wait and see what happens. Let's not push things, let's just keep spending time together and have some fun. And wait. And see. Okay?'

That's what I'm going to say to Alice when I see her, more or less. I'm not sure if I can get away with the John Donne quote, because I'm worried it might come across as a tiny bit pretentious, but I'm going to see how it plays in the moment. I'm going to say all of the above, nothing more, and see how she takes it, but not get into a big, heavy discussion, and then I'm going to pull on my coat, go home and get a good eight hours' sleep. And I'm definitely not going to try and kiss her. Even if she asks me to stay and make love to her or whatever, I'm going to say no, because it's The Challenge in the morning. We've both got to be fresh for The Challenge. Like boxers – no sex before a fight.

I'm standing outside her door. I knock.

There's no reply.

I knock again. Wisdom, Kindness, Courage, Wisdom, Kindness, Courage . . .

'Who is it?'

'It's Brian.'

'Brian! It's nearly midnight!'

'I know, sorry, I just wanted to say hi!'

I hear her get out of bed, the rustle of her pulling on some clothes, and then she peers round the edge of the door, in the Snoopy T-shirt and a black pair of knickers.

'I'm actually asleep, Bri . . .' she says, rubbing her eyes.

'Are you? God, sorry. It's just I've had a bit of an eventful day, and I wanted to talk to someone about it.'

'Can't it wait 'til . . . ?'

'Not someone. You.'

She bites her lip, and tugs the front of her T-shirt down with her spare hand.

'Oh, come on then.' And she opens up the door. I go and sit on the edge of the unmade bed, which is warm to the touch from where she was sleeping.

'So – how was Valentine's Day?'

'Oh fine, fine . . .'

'Get anything special?' I ask meaningfully. 'In the post this morning? Get anything nice? . . .' I wish she'd come and sit next to me.

'Ye-eees, I did, thank you Brian, and it was a lovely, lovely poem.'

Why won't she come and sit next to me?

'You really think so? Phew! Because I was a bit embarrassed about it. It's the first time anyone's actually read anything I've written so . . .'

'No, I thought it was lovely, really. Very . . . frank. And . . . raw. Emotionally. Quite derivative of e.e.cummings I thought, well not *derivative*, inspired by, it reminded me of him, I mean. In fact I think there were some lines that I actually recognised . . .' Hang on, is she accusing me of *plagiarism*? '. . . but anyway, it was lovely, really. Thank you. I was very . . . touched . . .'

'That is assuming it was from me!' I say light-heartedly. 'What poem! I didn't send any poetry!' I'm jabbering, I know I am, but she smiles, and scratches her elbow and makes a tent of her T-shirt by stretching it down and hooking it over her bare knees. And I'm struggling to keep things light-hearted now, because I can't help noticing that on the desk behind her, looming over her shoulder, is a massive bouquet of perfect red roses slumping sideways in a huge, battered aluminium saucepan of water that she's nicked from the communal kitchen. Of course there's no reason why she shouldn't receive Valentine's gifts from other men, I'd be a fool not to realise that she would, I'm not naïve, she's bound to, what with being beautiful and popular and conventionally sexually attractive and everything, but this bouquet is just . . . vulgar. So vulgar that I'm trying not to draw attention to it, and to focus instead on my small, sincere, little heartfelt hand-crafted home-made poem. But there they are, looming over her shoulder, stinking up the place like cheap air-freshener, that big fuck-off bunch of perfect fucking red fucking roses . . .

'Lovely roses!' I say.

'Oh, those!' she says, doing a little double-take over her shoulder, as if they'd somehow crept up behind her, like Birnam bloody Wood . . .

'Any idea . . . who might have sent them?' I say, lightly.

'No idea at all!' she says. It's some posh bastard obviously. That's a whole term's grant there, slumped in that saucepan of water. And of course she knows who they're from; because what's the point of being that generous if you're going to remain anonymous?

'Well – was there a card attached or . . . ?'

'Is this *any* of your business, Brian?' she snaps.

'No. No, I suppose not.'

'Sorry! Sorry, sorry, sorry, sorry, sorry . . .' she says, and gets out of her chair, and puts her arms round me, and gives me a stooped hug. I look down along the length of her back, where the T-shirt has ridden up, and put one hand on the warm bare skin just above her underwear, which incidentally seems to be made of some sort of translucent black mesh or lace or something, and we stay like that for a time, while I stare at the roses lolling in the saucepan.

'Sorry . . .' she whispers in my ear. 'I'm *such* a bitch for snapping at you, it's just we had a really long, difficult rehearsal tonight, and I think I might still be in character . . .' then she sits next to me and laughing, says, 'God, did I really just say that? That is without a doubt *the* most pretentious thing I've ever said in my life . . .' and we're both smiling again, and I wonder if I might try for a kiss, but then remember my new mantra. Wisdom, Kindness, Courage.

'Look, I really ought to be getting back to bed now, Brian. Big day tomorrow and all that . . .'

'Of course, I'll go . . .' and I half-stand, then sit down again. 'But can I just say something first . . . ?'

'O-kay,' she says warily, sitting down beside me.

'Don't worry – it's nothing scary. I just wanted to say . . .' and I take her hand, take a deep breath and say, 'Alice . . . Okay, listen, Alice I've been doing some thinking, about us, and, well, there's this great poem by the Metaphysical poet John Donne, *The Triple Foole*, which goes "*I am two fools I know/For loving, and for saying so/In whining poetry*" and I think, well, I've been a bit like that. What I mean to say is I've been coming on a bit strong, what with dragging you kicking and screaming into the photo-booth and that crazy, bad poetry in the Valentine's card and everything, and I know how much you value your independence, and that's fine by me, it really, really is. I'm in love with you of course, massively so . . .'

'Brian . . .' she says.

'. . . but that's not important, that needn't get in the way, because at the end of the day . . .'

'Brian . . .' she says.

'. . . hang on, Alice, just let me finish . . .'

'. . . no, Brian, you *have* to stop . . .' she says, standing up and crossing to the far side of the room. 'This isn't right . . .'

'But, it's not what you think it is, Alice . . .'

'No, I'm sorry, Brian, I can't take it any more. Let's get this over with . . .'

And the strange thing is, she doesn't say this to me, she says it to her wardrobe.

'Come on, Neil, this isn't funny any more . . .'

'That's strange,' I think, 'why is she calling her wardrobe *Neil*? What does she call her chest of drawers!' I wonder, as she knocks on Neil the Wardrobe's door with the flat of her hand, and the door opens slowly by itself, as if in a conjuring trick.

There's a man in the wardrobe.

He's holding his trousers in his hand.

I don't understand.

'Brian, this is Neil,' says Alice.

Neil unfolds out of the wardrobe, gets to his feet.
'Neil is playing Eilert Lovborg. In *Hedda Gabler*.'
'Hello, Neil,' I say.
'Hello, Brian,' says Neil.
'We were . . . *rehearsing*,' says Alice.
'Oh,' I say, as if this explained everything.
And then, I think, I shake his hand.

The Final Round

'What do you think of her?'

'I don't like to say,' I stammered.

'Tell me in my ear,' said Miss Havisham, bending down.

'I think she is very proud,' I replied, in a whisper.

'Anything else?'

'I think she is very pretty . . .'

'. . . Anything else?'

'I think I should like to go home now . . .'

'. . . You shall go soon,' said Miss Havisham, aloud. 'Play the game out . . .'

Charles Dickens, *Great Expectations*

39

QUESTION: 'Once there were four children named Peter, Susan, Edmund and Lucy.' So begins the most famous work of a scholar, novelist and Christian apologist. But what is the name of the book?

ANSWER: *The Lion, the Witch and the Wardrobe.*

The cliché about meeting famous people in the flesh, of course, is that they're often disappointingly a lot smaller than they appear on the screen. But in real life Bamber Gascoigne is actually a lot bigger than I'd imagined; very slim, and smiley, and surprisingly good-looking, like a benevolent character from C.S. Lewis who's about to take you on an amazing adventure, but with sex appeal. The four of us are stood in a line in the TV studios, waiting nervously, and he's working his way down the line, a little like a Royal Variety Performance.

Alice is avoiding me, and is first in the line, so I can't hear what she's saying to him but presume that she's attempting to seduce him. Then Patrick, who's practically doubled over with humility, and is making a big show of having met him before, this time last year, and is acting as if they're big, big pals, like they've been on holiday together or whatever. Bamber's very charming, smiling a lot, and saying, 'Yes, yes *of course* I remember you!' when he's probably thinking 'who the hell is *this* idiot?'

Then Lucy, who is incredibly quiet and nice as usual, and then it's my turn. The question is do I call him Bamber, or

Mr Gascoigne? He approaches, shakes my hand, and I say: 'Pleased to meet you, Mr Gascoigne.'

'Oh, please, call me Bamber,' he says, grinning broadly, taking my hand in his two hands. 'And your name is?'

'Brian, Brian Jackson,' I mumble.

'. . . reading?'

'Eng. Lit.' I say.

'Beg your pardon?' he says, and leans in.

'Eng-lish Lit-erature,' I say loudly, over-enunciating this time, and I notice Bamber recoiling, almost imperceptibly, and guess that it's because he can smell the alcohol on my breath, and has realised that I'm pretty much pissed out of my head.

Despite the best efforts of the licensing authorities, the fact remains that no matter how late it is, you can always get a drink if you need it badly enough.

After I run from Alice's room at Kenwood Manor, I walk the streets for a while, trying to calm down, trying to stop shaking, until I find myself outside The Taste of The Raj, a curry house that doubles as a sort of Indian speak-easy; you can drink pretty much all night, as long as you're always within ten feet of an onion bhaji.

Tonight, at just gone midnight, the place is empty. 'Table for one?' asks the solitary waiter.

'Yes, please,' and he shows me to a booth at the very back of the restaurant, near the kitchen. I open the menu, and notice that The Taste of The Raj is offering an extra-special, bitterly-ironic Valentine's Day Menu for couples out on a romantic date, but decide that even though the menu represents good value for money, I doubt if I'd be able to swallow anything. Besides, I'm not here for the food. I order a pint of lager, two poppadoms, an onion bhaji, and a gin and tonic.

'No main course, sir?'

'Maybe later,' I say. And the waiter nods mournfully, as if

he understands the sometimes brutal workings of the human heart, and goes to get my booze. I've finished both the pint of lager and the gin and tonic before I even hear the ping of the microwave from the kitchen behind me. The waiter slides the warmed-through onion bhaji in between my elbows on the table, and I offer up the empty glasses.

'Another pint of lager, and a gin please. No tonic this time,' and the sad-eyed waiter nods wisely, and sighs, and heads off to get my order.

'And, excuse me?' – I shout after him – 'could you make the gin a double?' Half-heartedly, I pick the crust off the onion bhaji and dip it into the sweet, watery mint yoghurt, and when the waiter returns with my drinks, I sip the top inch off the pint and pour in the gin, stir it with the handle of my fork, and think about all the things that I know.

I know the difference between a pterosaur, a pteranadon, a pterodactyl and a ramphorhynchus. I know the Latin name for most of the common domestic British birds. I know the capital cities of nearly every country in the world, and most of the flags too. I know that Magdalen College is pronounced *Maudlin* College. I know the complete plays of Shakespeare except *Timon of Athens*, and the complete novels of Charles Dickens except *Barnaby Rudge*, and all the Narnia books, and the order in which they were all written, approximate in the case of Shakespeare. I know every lyric of every song Kate Bush has ever recorded, including B-sides, as well as the highest chart position of every single she's released. I know all the French irregular verbs, and where the phrase 'toe the line' comes from, and what the gall bladder's for, and how oxbow lakes are formed, and all the British monarchs in order, and the wives of Henry VIII and their fate, the difference between igneous, sedimentary and metamorphic rocks, and the dates of the major battles of the War of the Roses, the meanings of the words 'albedo', 'peripatetic' and 'litotes', and the average number of hairs on a human head, and how to crochet, and the difference between nuclear fission and fusion and how to spell deoxyribonucleic and the constellations of the stars and the population of the earth and the mass of the moon and the workings of the human heart. And yet the important and most basic things, like friendship, or getting over Dad dying, or loving someone, or just simply being happy, just being good and decent and dignified and happy, seem to be utterly and completely beyond my comprehension. And it occurs to me that I'm not clever at all, that in fact I am without a doubt the most ignorant, the most profoundly and hopelessly stupid person in the whole world.

I start to feel a bit blue, so to cheer myself up I order another pint of lager and another double gin, pour the gin into the lager, stir it with my fork, dip a shard of poppadom into the mango chutney, and the next thing I remember is waking up in my clothes at 6.30 in the morning.

'Brian! Brian, wake up . . .'

'Leave me alone . . .' I say, and pull the duvet up over my head.

'Brian, come on, we're late . . .' Someone's shaking me by the shoulder. I push their hand away.

'It's still night-time – go away.'

'It's 6.30 in the morning, Brian, we're due at the studio at 9.30, and we're not going to make it. Come on, get up . . .' and Patrick yanks the duvet back. 'You've been *sleeping in your clothes*?'

'No . . . !' I say indignantly, but pretty unconvincingly, since I clearly am asleep, and wearing clothes. 'I got cold in the night, that's all . . .'

Patrick yanks the duvet off completely.

'You've still got your shoes on!'

'My feet got cold!'

'Brian – have you been *drinking*?'

'No . . . !'

'Brian, I thought we had an agreement – an early night and no drinking before the match . . .'

'I have *not* been drinking!' I slur, hauling myself upright, hearing the gin and lager and the onion bhaji settling in my stomach.

'Brian, I can smell it on your breath! What's your mattress doing on the floor, anyway?'

'He says it's a *futon*,' says Josh from the doorway, shivering in his underpants. Marcus peers, blinking over his shoulder.

'I had to wake your flatmates up to get in,' explains Patrick.

'Ooooops. Sorry Josh, sorry Marcush . . .'

'I don't believe it – you're still drunk!'

'I'm not drunk! Five minutes – just give me five more minutes!'

'You've got *three* minutes. I'll be waiting downstairs in the car,' snarls Patrick, and flounces out, followed by Josh and Marcus. I sigh, rub my face with my hands, sit on the edge of the futon.

I remember Alice.

I go to my wardrobe, and take out Dad's brown corduroy jacket.

The journey to Manchester is pretty grim. We're travelling in Alice's 2CV, and she gives me a patronising little no-hard-feelings smile, which I pretend not to see as I clamber in the back, the crisp packets and shattered cassette cases crunching underfoot. I tug the door shut by means of the length of washing-line that passes for a door-handle, and the exertion causes me to belch a little, the air hissing through clenched teeth. Dr Lucy Chang detects this, makes her diagnosis, and gives me the hospital smile that they teach her to use as part of her training. I pull my coat up under my chin like a blanket as we set off, and try to ignore the lurching of the 2CV, which apparently seems to have no suspension at all, and feels like the Waltzers at a fun fair.

Needless to say good old Patrick has prepared several hundred questions for the journey as a fun, fun warm-up, all meticulously typed on 6 by 4 index cards, and he insists on bellowing them out *very loudly* over the noise of the 2CV's lawnmower engine as we judder along the motorway at a steady 55 miles per hour. I resolve not to answer any of them, just to teach them all a lesson. The trick about getting through today is to remain dignified. Pride and Dignity, that's the key. That, and not throwing up on myself.

'Three bonus questions on battles. What year was the Battle of Blenheim fought? Anyone? No one? Lucy?'

'Seventeen . . . twelve?' suggests Lucy.

'Nope. Seventeen-oh-four.'

'Where is the Bulge, as in the Battle of the *Bulge*? Anyone? The *Bulge*? Anyone have any idea at all? The *Bulge*. Come on, think about it, the *Bulge*, the Battle of the *Bulge* . . .'

'Holland!' I mutter from under my coat, partly just to stop him saying 'Bulge'.

'The Ardennes in *Belgium*,' says Patrick, clicking his tongue and shaking his head. 'Question number 3. Also known as the Battle of the Three Emperors, the Battle of Austerlitz was fought between which . . .'

'Patrick, can I just ask, what is the actual *point* of all this?' I say, leaning forward in my seat. 'I mean, do you honestly think that, by some miracle, *any* of these questions is going to come up in the actual quiz? Because if not, it's a bit of a pointless waste of everyone's time, isn't it?'

'Brian . . .' says Lucy, a hand on my arm.

'It's a *warm-up*, Brian!' screeches Patrick, leaning round in his seat so we're face to face. 'A *warm-up* for those of us who aren't quite as *fresh* this morning as we maybe ought to be?'

'I don't know why you're getting at me!' I say, shouting now. 'What time did *you* get to sleep last night, Alice?' and she glares at me in the rear-view mirror, her cool, contemptuous head-girl glare.

'Brian, we'll talk about it later, alright . . . ?'

'Talk about *what* later?' asks Patrick.

'Nothing,' says Alice, 'nothing at all . . .'

'So is it just the four of us today then, Alice, or have you got someone hiding in the boot?'

'*What?*' says Patrick.

'Brian, not *here*, alright . . . ?' hisses Alice.

'Will someone *please* tell me what's going on . . . ?' barks Patrick.

'Okay, everyone! Okay! Let's all . . . just listen to some music shall we?' says Lucy, the peace-maker. One hand is holding on to my arm, kindly but firmly, and I almost expect to see a hypodermic syringe in the other hand, so I slump back into my seat, pull my coat up high over my head again to try to get some sleep, and we listen to a warped, warbling cassette of 'The Look of Love' by ABC over and over and over again, all the way to Manchester, until I think I'm going to start screaming.

Shortly after I accidentally breathe booze in Bamber Gascoigne's face, he disappears off to his office to look through the questions and it's left to our old friend Julian, the nice young researcher, to unveil the opposition for the first time. It's just as we feared. One word. Oxbridge. Patrick forces a great big smile, and the sound of his teeth grinding together echoes round the studio.

The four of them amble casually across the studio floor towards us in a long line, like gunslingers. They've all gone for the matching blazer-and-tie look, and are all wearing college scarves and spectacles in a further attempt to intimidate us. Theirs is an all-white, all-male team, so I suppose we can at least congratulate ourselves on striking a blow for sexual equality by having two women on our team, even if one of them is a vicious, deceitful, scheming, two-faced witch.

Of course, our rivals have yet to discover Alice's true

nature, so they all make straight for her, and cluster round as if they're asking for her autograph, while Patrick bobs uselessly at the edge of the circle, desperately trying to shake someone's hand, anyone's hand. Their captain, Norton reading Classics – a complacently handsome broad-shouldered, floppy-haired type, the kind of good-looking bastard who looks as if he rows everywhere – is shaking Alice by the hand and refusing to let go. 'So – you must be the mascot!' he drawls lecherously, which strikes me as a pretty obnoxious and chauvinistic thing to say, and I have a moment of feminist indignation on Alice's behalf, but then I remember last night, the wardrobe. Besides, Alice doesn't seem to mind, because she's laughing too, and biting her lip, all doe-eyed, and tossing her freshly washed hair, and Norton tosses his lovely, glossy hair back, and she tosses her hair in return, and he tosses his, and she tosses hers, and it's like some mating ritual on a wildlife programme. I'm ashamed to say that the words 'prick-tease' enter my head, but because the phrase is both gender-specific and misogynist, I suppress it, and instead stand just outside the group, with no one to shake hands with, and watch. Lucy Chang spots me, comes over, takes me by the elbow and introduces me to Partridge, a peachy-skinned, balding nineteen-year-old from Saffron Walden, reading Modern History, and I smile, and smile, and chat, and smile and wonder if there's somewhere I can go and have a little lie-down.

But there's no time, because Julian is jollying us over to our seats for a quick rehearsal, just for fun, with him standing in for Bamber. Needless to say, Patrick has fixed the seating plan, so that I'm at the very, very end, as far away from him and Lucy as possible, more or less in the next studio, in fact. Alice sits between us, which would have been fun twenty-four hours ago, but now is just pure misery, and we sit there, staring blankly and silently ahead, as Julian reminds us that it's only a bit of fun, only a game, the important thing is to enjoy ourselves. The desk and buzzers all feel surprisingly shoddy and make-shift, as if someone's knocked them up in a woodwork class, and I can actually see the bare light bulbs that are illuminating my name on the front of the panel. I could unscrew one if I wanted to, maybe steal it after the show and keep it as a souvenir, as a kind of studenty, undergraduate lark. I think about pointing this out to Alice, then remember that we're not meant to be talking to each other, and feel sad again. Julian, meanwhile, is inviting us to try out our buzzers, just to get the feel of them. We all do so, and I lean forward over the front of the plywood desk, to see my name flashing on and off. Jackson. Jackson. Jackson . . .

'At last! My name's in lights!' says Alice. I don't look at her of course, but can tell by her voice that she's smiling desperately. 'You know, I always thought the only way I'd get my name in lights is if I changed it to Fire Exit!' she says, but I don't smile, I just tap out some Morse code on the buzzer; dot dot dot, dash dash dash . . .

'Strange, isn't it? Finding ourselves here! After all this time . . . !'

But I still don't reply, so she reaches across and takes my hand, pulls it off the buzzer.

'Brian, talk to me, please,' says Alice, unsmiling this time, then in a whisper, 'Look, I'm sorry about last night, and I'm sorry if you feel I've led you on, but I never made any promises, Brian. I was always honest with you, always very, very clear about how I felt. Speak to me, Brian, please? I can't bear you not speaking to me . . .'

I turn to her, and she looks sad and beautiful and tired around the eyes. 'I'm sorry, Alice, but I don't think I can.' She nods, as if she understands, and then before we can say anything else Julian is clearing his throat and the rehearsal is beginning.

'The final separation between the Eastern and Western

Christian churches, sometimes known as the East–West Schism, happened in which year?'

I think I know this one, so I buzz.

'Fifteen-seventeen?'

'No, I'm sorry, I think you may be thinking of The Reformation. I'm afraid that's a five-point penalty.'

'Ten fifty-four?' says Norton, with the floppy hair, reading Classics.

'Correct,' says Julian, and Norton smiles and gives his lovely hair a victory toss. 'So Norton, that's ten points, and your team now get the chance to answer three bonus questions on the Roman Gods . . .'

And ironically, of course, I actually know all the answers.

At the end of the fifteen-minute rehearsal, which is just for fun, just to get us all relaxed, remember it's only a game, we've lost by 115 points to 15. Standing in the scenery dock behind the set, Patrick is so angry that he can barely speak. He just walks in tight little circles, clenching and unclenching his fists, and squeaking. Actually squeaking.

'Good, aren't they?' says Alice.

'They're okay,' says Lucy, 'they got lucky, that's all. Partridge is the one to watch . . .'

'. . . three years I've been waiting for this, three years . . .' mutters Patrick, walking in his tight little circle.

'. . . we're just a little on edge, that's all,' says Lucy, 'we just need to lighten up a little! Start to have fun, relax!'

I suddenly need a drink. Is there a bar in the building, I wonder? 'Maybe we should all just go to the bar, have a pint or two, just get loosened up a bit?' I suggest.

Patrick stops walking. '*What?*' he hisses.

'You don't think it's a good idea, then?'

'Brian, you answered *eight* starter questions during that rehearsal and got *six* of them wrong. That's *minus thirty points . . .*'

'That's not true . . .' I insist. 'Is it?' and I look to Lucy for some support, but she's just staring at her shoes. Patrick turns on her.

'*Lucia, dimmi, parli Italiano?*' and, embarrassed, Lucy says, '*Si, un pochino.*'

Then to Alice, '*E tu Alice, dimmi, parli anche tu l'italiano?*'

'*Si, parlo l'italiano, ma solo come una turista* . . .' sighs Alice.

'He's asking us if we speak Ital . . .' whispers Lucy.

'I know what he's asking, Lucy!' I snap.

'So, do you speak Italian?' asks Patrick.

'No! No, not as such . . .'

'And yet *Lucy* does, and *Alice* does, and *I* do, and yet it was *you*, Brian Jackson, *you*, the *sole non-Italian speaker* on the team, who felt qualified to attempt to answer a starter question on Italian musical terms . . .'

'No one else was buzzing, so I thought I'd have a stab . . .'

'And that's the problem with you, isn't it Brian? It's just stab, stab, stab with you, *stabbing* away in the dark, getting it *wrong* every time, but just *stabbing* away, over and over again, just getting everything wrong, wrong, wrong, wrong, wrong, wrong, wrong, and losing the game, and dragging us all down with you.' His face is bright burgundy now, the same colour as his university sweatshirt, and inches away from mine . . .

'Hey, come on guys, it was just a rehearsal,' says Lucy, trying to squeeze in between us while Alice stands a little further off, her hands over her face, peeking through her fingers.

'. . . I don't even know why I let you on this team in the first place! You turn up pissed and reeking of booze, you act like you know it all when in fact you know *nothing*. As far as this team is concerned you're a complete dead-weight . . .' his hands on my chest, fingers splayed and I can feel a fine spray of his saliva on my cheek . . . 'we'd probably be better off with some bloke off the street, even that stupid bloody mate of yours, Spencer, you're both as pig-ignorant as each other.

It's like they say, you can take the boy out of Essex, but you can't take . . .'

And I suppose he must carry on talking after that, because his mouth continues to move, but I don't really hear what he's saying because all I'm aware of is his hands tugging on the lapels of Dad's brown corduroy jacket, pulling me up on to my toes. That's when I make my decision, that's where something snaps – except it doesn't really *snap*, just stretches – and maybe it's the mention of Spencer, or the remnants of last night's booze, but that's the point at which I decide to head-butt Patrick Watts. I take a little leap up into the air, not a basketball player's leap by any means, just a little spring on the balls of my feet, and I bring my head down as hard as I possibly can into the very centre of his screaming burgundy face. And I'm ashamed to say that I have a fleeting but intense sense of pleasure and satisfaction and righteous vengeance before the pain finds its way to my brain and everything goes black.

40

QUESTION: In T.S. Eliot's *Love Song Of J. Alfred Prufrock*, the evening is 'spread out against the sky . . . ?'

ANSWER: '. . . Like a patient etherised upon a table.'

'As a Glaswegian, born and bred, I think it's safe to say that what we're looking at here is an absolutely *classic* misunderstanding of the basic principle of the head-butt,' says Rebecca Epstein. 'The whole point of a head-butt is to bring the *hard* part of your forehead down with as much force as possible on to the *soft* part of your opponent's nose. What you've done here, Brian, is bring the *soft* part of your nose down against the *hard* part of his forehead. Hence the blood and the loss of consciousness.'

I open my eyes and find myself lying on my back on two office desks pushed together. Lucy Chang is standing over me, brushing my fringe back out of my eyes, holding up three fingers and asking, 'How many fingers am I holding up?'

'If I get the answer wrong, do we lose five points?'

She smiles. 'Not this time, no.'

'Then the answer is three.'

'And the capital of Venezuela is . . . ?'

'Caracas?'

'Attaboy, Mr Jackson,' says Lucy. 'I think you're going to be just fine.'

We seem to be a couple of floors up; looking out over the back of the TV studios in the *University Challenge* production office; reference books scattered everywhere, photos of past winners on the walls. I turn my head to the side and see Rebecca, sat on the edge of a desk opposite me, looking pretty – not pretty, because the word 'pretty' is reactionary and gender-specific, but *attractive* – in a long, plain, clingy black dress under a black denim jacket, swinging her Doc Martens backwards and forwards.

'You came, then?'

'Oh, aye. Wouldn't have missed *this* for the world. There I was on the minibus with a bunch of pissed-up Young Conservatives all with their college scarves and their ironic teddy-bears, and paying *three quid* towards the petrol I might add, which is an absolute *rip-off* if you do the maths, and I thought, Christ, what am I doing here? This is *hell*! And then we arrive and we're all getting a wee pre-show tour of the studio, and we turn a corner just in time to see you lying on the floor unconscious in a pool of your own blood, and I thought, well, there you go, if that's not worth three quid, then I don't know what is.'

I look down, and see that I'm wearing just trousers and a vest, the same vest I've been wearing for the last thirty-six hours, which is dappled in blood down the front, and has a tang of gin to it. In fact, it's more than just a tang. It's fumes. I'm giving off fumes.

'What happened to my clothes?'

'We ravished you, Lucy and me, while you were unconscious. Don't mind, do you?'

Lucy blushes. 'Alice is washing your shirt in the ladies' washroom, trying to get it dry under the hand dryer . . .'

'Is the jacket all right?'

'The jacket's fine . . .'

'. . . it's just it was my Dad's jacket . . .'

'It's fine, really . . .'

Gingerly I sit up sideways, on the edge of the desk, and imagine that I can feel my brain shifting too, buffeting against the sides of my skull. Lucy holds up the mirror from her make-up kit, and I take a deep breath and look. It could be worse I suppose; my nose seems no more lumpy and misshapen than usual, though there's a dark waxy rim of what looks like red crayon around each nostril.

'How's Patrick?' I ask Lucy.

'Not a scratch on him,' she says.

'Pity,' I say.

'Hey, that's enough now,' she says, but smiling conspiratorially. Then with a straight face, 'There is a problem, though.'

'What?'

'Well . . . I don't think they're going to let you do the show.'

'*What?* You're kidding!'

'I'm afraid not.'

'But why not?'

'Well, you did assault our team captain.'

'I didn't *assault* him! I hit him *once*! And he provoked me, you saw that, he was lifting me up by my jacket! And anyway, I'm the one who got hurt! How can I have assaulted him if I'm the one who got hurt? . . .'

'And that, m'lord, is the case for the defence,' says Rebecca.

'I know, Brian, but still, Patrick's not happy. He's got a friend, from the Economics Department, who's prepared to take your place at the last minute . . .'

'You're kidding . . .'

'You can't really blame him, Brian. You turn up stinking of booze, get a whole load of questions wrong, then try and break his nose . . .'

'But my mum's here and everything!'

'It's only a stupid quiz, Brian,' says Rebecca, still swinging her feet.

'But she's come all the way from Southend! . . .' and I can hear my voice crack slightly, which is pathetic in a man of nineteen, I know, but I wanted so much to be on the show. I have a sudden vision of me trying to explain to Mum why

I'm not out there after all. It's going to feel like being sent home early from school, it's so embarrassing, so shaming that I can't bear to think about it.

'What does Julian say?'

'Julian says it's up to Patrick. He's with him at the moment, talking it through . . .'

'And what do you think?'

Lucy frowns for a moment, then says, 'I think that if you both promise to play nice, and stop behaving like children, and agree to work together as *a team*, and go a little easy on the buzzer, then I think that, yes, you should do the show . . .'

'Well, can you say that to him for me, Lucy? Please?'

And she sighs, checks her watch, looks at the door, and says, 'I'll see what I can do,' then she heads out, leaving me and Rebecca in the production office, sat on the edge of opposite desks, about fifteen feet apart from each other, both swinging our legs and trying to ignore what I think is called 'an atmosphere between us'. When the silence becomes too uncomfortable, Rebecca nods towards the door.

'She's nice.'

'Who?'

'Lucy.'

'Yes. Yes, she is. Really, really nice.'

'So why don't you go out with *her* then?' says Rebecca.

'. . . What?'

'. . . I just think she seems nice, that's all . . .'

'. . . because I don't want to! . . .'

'. . . but you just said she was nice . . .'

'. . . lots of people are *nice* . . .'

'. . . not *beautiful* enough for you, is that it? . . .'

'. . . I didn't say that, did I? . . .'

'. . . not *sexy* enough? . . .'

'. . . Rebecc . . .'

'. . . because, let me tell you, you're no oil-painting yourself, pal . . .'

'. . . no, I know . . .'

'. . . sat there in your blood-stained vest . . .'

'. . . all right . . .'

'. . . which is none too fresh I might add, even from here . . .'

'. . . thank you, Rebecca . . .'

'. . . so why not, then? . . .'

'. . . because she probably doesn't like me! . . .'

'. . . how d'you know? If you haven't asked? You didn't see the way she was looking at you while you were in your coma . . .'

'. . . rubbish . . .'

'. . . brushing your hair out your eyes and everything, it was a very touching scene . . .'

'. . . rubbish! . . .'

'. . . lovingly sticking toilet-roll up your nostril, it was actually quite erotic . . .'

'. . . Rebecca! . . .'

'. . . it's true! If I hadn't been here she'd've probably had your kecks off too, and you none the wiser . . .'

'. . . rubbish! . . .'

'. . . so why are you blushing then? . . .'

'. . . I'm not! . . .'

'. . . so why don't you ask her? . . .'

'. . . ask her what? . . .'

'. . . ask her *out* . . .'

'. . . because I don't . . .'

'. . . what? . . .'

'. . . I'm not . . .'

'. . . go on . . .'

'. . . in . . . love with her . . .'

'. . . same as you're not with me?'

'. . . *what?*'

'. . . you heard . . .'

'. . . Rebecca, can we? . . .'

'. . . what?'

'. . . talk about this later?'

'. . . why not now?'

'Because!' and I take a deep breath, the first for some time. 'Because I've got other things on my mind. Okay?'

'Okay,' she says. 'Okay, point taken,' and she slips down off the high desk, tugging her long dress, as if she's not quite got the hang of it, crosses the office and sits next to me on the edge of the table.

'Is that a frock you're wearing?' I say.

'Fuck-off it's a frock. It's a *dress*. How's your head?'

'Oh, you know. A bit sore.'

She reaches into the inside pocket of her coat and pulls out a quarter-bottle of whisky.

'Care for some medicine?'

'Better not.'

'Go on, hair of the dog?'

'It was a different dog. Gin.'

'Och, that's just plain *nasty*. You do know gin's a depressant, don't you?'

'I think that's why I was drinking it.'

'Hmmmmmmm, self-pity *and* self-loathing – a winning combination. No wonder women find you irresistible. You're quite the Travis Bickle.' And she takes a swig from the bottle, offers it to me again. 'Trust me, scotch is definitely the way to go.'

'They'll smell it on my breath,' I say, but she reaches deep into her other pocket, and pulls out a packet of extra-strong mints. 'Go on, then,' I say. She passes me the bottle and I take a long swig, then pop a mint in my mouth, letting the tastes combine, and we look at each other and smile, and sit there, like school kids, feet dangling off the edge of the desk.

'Of course, you know Alice has been seeing someone else?' I say.

'Uh-huh.'

'That guy Neil, the one who played Richard III last term, always hobbling around in the student bar . . .'

'The cunt on crutches . . .'

'That's the one. I suppose you knew.'

'Well, I saw him scuttling out of her room a couple of times so let's just say I had an inkling . . .'

'Or a *hunch*?' She looks at me quizzically, 'You know, like a *hump*, like Richard III . . . ? So why didn't you tell me then?'

'Not really any of my business, is it? Your love life.'

'No. Maybe not,' and I have to confess that, even with all that's happened, and Alice and the knock on the head and everything, that I think about kissing her, tucking the mint to a back corner of my mouth with my tongue, and leaning over and kissing her right now, just to see what would happen.

But the moment passes and instead I look at my watch.

'They're taking their time.'

'Who?'

'The jury.'

'Want me to go and check?'

'Yeah, that would be great,' and she pushes herself off the edge of the desk, and heads for the door. 'Put a good word in for me,' I say.

'I'll see if I can think of one,' she says, adjusts her dress, and goes, and I'm left alone.

I always get a bit fidgety by myself with nothing to read, especially sat in a vest, but thankfully this office is crammed with books – mostly reference books, but still books – so I pick up the *Oxford Dictionary of Quotations*, which they'd been using as a pillow, and that's when I see it.

On the desk.

A blue clipboard.

On the clipboard are some photocopied A4 sheets. It has Julian the researcher's name handwritten at the top, so I assume it's just his production notes. He must have brought it with him when they carried me up here, and just left it on the desk. The A4 sheets aren't particularly interesting – just the names of the team members, a seating plan, list of crew names, all that kind of stuff. But in front of this is an envelope, a thick manila envelope that feels as if it contains two packs of playing cards. I unclip the envelope the clipboard.

The envelope isn't sealed. Or it is, but barely, just a half-inch of glue holding it closed. All I'd need to do is slide my thumb along the . . .

I throw the envelope down on the desk, as if it had just become blisteringly hot.

Then I nudge it, pushing it away across the desk with the tip of a fingernail.

Then I nudge it again, the way you nudge something to check that it's dead.

Then I grab one corner, pull it back towards me.

Then I pick it up in two hands, hold it on my lap, look at it.

Then I slide it back down the desk again, as far out of my reach as possible.

And then I think 'oh bollocks to this' and I reach over and open it.

41

QUESTION: James Hogg, Saint Augustine, Jean-Jacques Rousseau and Thomas de Quincey all have what literary genre in common?
ANSWER: They all wrote 'Confessions'.

When I was doing my O-levels, just before the Chemistry multiple-choice paper, I had a mild case of gastric flu. That was what I was calling it anyway, and because it's contagious and I had a fever – well, not a *fever*, just a very slight temperature – I was allowed to take the exam un-invigilated in a tiny little office next to the staff room, because that's the kind of school-kid I was; absolutely and entirely trustworthy.

And I cheated.

Not in any major way, you understand. I just checked that no one was coming, got my revision guide out and very quickly looked up the periodic table to check the valency of potassium or magnesium or something, then put it back again, and that was it.

Also, incidentally, when I played Scrabble by candle-light with Alice in Suffolk just after Christmas, I pulled out an 'E' and an 'S' and swapped them both surreptitiously for 'Z' and 'X', hence 'Amazed' and 'Foxed' on triple word scores.

And that's about it, cheating-wise. I'm not proud of myself in either instance, but apart from the shame and what I believe Sartre would call the 'bad faith' involved, the worst thing is the nagging sense that the cheating was unnecessary. I'd have won anyway, and all the cheating did was taint that sense of victory. As Mum, and Sartre, would probably say, 'you're only cheating yourself.'

But this isn't Scrabble or O-level Chemistry, this is much more important. This is *The Challenge*, and there are at least eight good reasons why it seems a perfectly reasonable idea for me to cheat. 1) It's on telly for a start. Everyone I know will see it, Spence, and Tone and Janet Parks, all my old teachers, and Professor Morrison, and that bastard Neil MacIntyre, and then of course there's 2) the studio audience; Mum's out there, and Des, my stepdad-to-be, and Rebecca, and Chris the Hippie, and that cow Erin. And then there's 3) my team-mates Patrick and Lucy, especially Lucy, who I've been letting down, and who deserves so much to win, and 4) Alice of course, who thinks I'm an idiot and a drunk and a liability and a fool, and who I think I might still be in love with, and besides 5) I might not even *be* on the team, so all this ethical wrestling could be academic anyway, and 6) in a way, this situation isn't even my fault, it's Julian's fault, for putting temptation in my way, and 7) *everyone* would do the same in the circumstances, *everyone*, and besides 8) I'm only human.

And that's why I decide to do what I do, which is *technically* cheating, but into which I introduce a strong element of chance; I will allow myself to look at *one* card, and one card only, that's all, I swear. But I'll have to be quick. I run over to the door, open it a crack, look both ways, don't see anyone, run back to the desk, take the cards out of the envelope.

They're divided with elastic bands into two piles, one of starter questions, another of bonus questions. I cut the pile of starter questions, about two-thirds of the way through, place the two cut piles carefully on the desk face down, so that I can put everything back precisely in the right place, close my eyes tightly and pick a card from the top of the exposed pile, holding it about three feet away from my closed eyes.

I can feel the blood beating in my eye-lids.

I open my eyes and see, neatly typed . . .

QUESTION: How is the Dickensian character Philip Pirrip better known?

. . . and I feel a little flush of irritation because I *know* this one, it's easy, it's Pip in *Great Expectations*. What's the point in wrestling with this kind of ethical dilemma if I know the answer already? And even though I'd made a strict deal between myself and God, or whoever, that I would only look at *one* card and one card only, I grab another, the next in the pile, and turn it over.

Now *that's* better . . .

QUESTION: The state of California is bordered by three states of the USA and one Mexican state; what are they?

ANSWER: Oregon, Nevada, Arizona and the Mexican state of Baja ('Lower') California.

Oregon, Nevada, Arizona, Baja California. Perfect – just hard enough to look impressive, but not so hard as to make me appear freakish. *Oregon, Nevada, Arizona, Baja California*. But is that pronounced Baja, or *Baya*? Doesn't matter, I'll make that part of my answer; I practise saying it aloud, acting naturalistically; 'Oregon, eh, Nevada, um, Arizona? And Baja . . .' (little smile, because my Spanish is a little rusty) . . . 'or is that perhaps *Baya* California?'

But what if Lucy knows the answer, too? I bet she does. Doesn't matter, as long as one of us gets there before the other team. In fact, it would actually be better for Lucy to answer, because then my conscience will be clear. *Oregon, Nevada, Arizona and Baja California*. Quickly now, put them back in the right place in the pile, tap the edges together against the desk, wrap the elastic band round, once, twice, put both piles in the envelope and lick it, but not too much, just either side of where I broke the seal, reattach it to the clipboard, put the clipboard back exactly where I found it, practise again, aloud. 'Oregon, eh, Nevada, um, Arizona and is it Baja California? . . .'

I go to the window, look out over the rooftops and chimneys of Manchester, and think about what I've got to do now. An apology to Patrick first, sincere, humble but not grovelling, acknowledging that we both got a little carried away, but still maintaining Pride and Dignity. Then make some kind of temporary peace with Alice, show that, yes I'm upset with her, but that she's making a terrible mistake with this Neil guy, it's her loss. And then I just have to prove to her what she's been missing; with style and grace and modesty and with Alice by my side, I'm going to win this game. *Oregon, Nevada, Arizona and Baja California . . .*

There's a knock at the door, and Patrick enters looking sombre, but flanked by Alice and Lucy, both of whom are trying to conceal their smiles.

'Patrick.'

'Brian.'

'Apologies for earlier.'

'Apology accepted.' Then he clears his throat, and Lucy gives him a little encouraging poke in the ribs. 'Well, um, look, I've been talking with Lucy and Alice here, and we've decided that maybe we've all been getting a little carried away, a little over-excited, what with the studio lights and everything, and – anyway, we've all decided that we'd very much like you to stay on the team.'

'Thanks, Patrick,' I say, giving a solemn little nodding bow.

'Thank you, Brian,' bowing back.

And Lucy is winking at me and laughing, and giving me the thumbs-up discreetly at waist level, and Alice is holding out my clean, newly ironed shirt and Dad's brown corduroy jacket.

'Okay, then,' I say. 'Let's go and kick some ass!'

42

QUESTION: In E.M. Forster's novel *Howards End*, how does Leonard Bast meet his unfortunate end?
ANSWER: A bookcase falls on top of him, and his heart gives way.

But before we go and kick some ass, we have a cup of tea and some plain biscuits, then I go to the gents' and wash my armpits with liquid soap and start to feel a little better. Then we go to separate dressing rooms to have a little bit of make-up applied. When your skin is as bad as mine, this is potentially a pretty embarrassing experience, but a nice girl called Janet does me, and it's really just a case of damage limitation; a little spot of cover-up and just enough powder to stop the oily droplets from my sebaceous glands glistening under the studio lights. Three of us don't take long; Patrick's had his university sweatshirt ironed, and his hair sealed safely beneath a solid transparent carapace of hairspray, and Lucy's changed into a very clean, neat, buttoned-up shirt, and has put on a little lipstick and pinned her hair back with a butterfly hair-grip. We stand around in the corridor, chatting amiably, and it strikes me how nice she looks, and I'm trying to work out a way of telling her this without sounding creepy, when Alice steps out of her dressing room.

She's wearing a long, tight black sheath of a dress, high at the neck, and tapered towards her ankles, some form of fish-net hosiery, and strappy black high-heeled shoes, despite the fact that her legs will never appear in front of the desk. She looks like a film star, glowing, luminescent, and I suddenly feel sick again.

'You think it's too much?' she says.

'Not at all. Alice, you look wonderful,' says Lucy. Julian comes to fetch us, clutching the infamous clipboard, and gives a little double-take when he sees Alice. 'Okay then, ladies and gentlemen, when you're ready?' and we follow him down the corridors to the studio. I stand behind Alice so that I can watch her walk.

The other team are taking their seats when we arrive at the studio, and we can hear the applause and shouts of their supporters as we stand in the wings. Then Julian gives us a nod, and it's time to make our entrance into the gladiatorial arena. I follow Alice as we cross to take our places, and hear a collective intake of breath from the audience, stage-crew and cameramen stopping and staring, whispering into their mouthpieces, and an audible hum of admiration beneath the applause and whoops and cheers. She hitches up her dress slightly as she slides behind our desk, as if sliding into a limousine, and someone in the audience actually wolf-whistles, which from a sexual–political point-of-view I don't really approve of, but which causes a roll of laughter through the studio. Alice laughs and holds our mascot, Eddie the Teddy, in front of her face, and it's just like Mum always says – 'beautiful *and knows it . . .*'

We settle in our seats, and smile at each other as the excitement dies down.

'Peace?' she says.

'Peace,' I say, and then we peer out into the audience. Rose and Michael Harbinson are there, and Rose gives a proud little wave.

'Nice to see them with their clothes on!' I say, and Alice gives me a reprimanding slap on the wrist. Mum, who's in the second row just behind Rebecca, gives me a little fingers-only wave, and two thumbs up, and I wave back.

'Is that your mum?' asks Alice.

'Uh-huh.'

'She looks nice. I'd like to meet her.'

'I'm sure you will. One day.'

'Who's the man with the Tom Selleck moustache?'

'Uncle Des. Not a real uncle, we just call him that. As a matter of fact, he's marrying Mum.'

'Your mum's getting married again?'

'Uh-huh.'

'That's brilliant news! You didn't tell me that!'

'Well, I was going to, yesterday night, but . . .'

'Yes. Oh. Yes, of course. Listen, Brian, that thing with Neil, it isn't really going anywhere . . .'

'Alice . . .'

'It was just a fling, it doesn't mean that you and me . . .' but she doesn't get to finish, because Bamber's making his entrance now. The crowd's applauding and cheering, and Alice takes my hand, and squeezes it tight, and my heart starts to beat faster, and it's time to finish this thing, once and for all.

And of course eighteen minutes later we've lost.

Or as good as, anyway. It's 45 points to 90, but Partridge, the peach-fluff-faced balding child, is clearly some incredible genetically enhanced mutant freak who's been created in a secret laboratory somewhere, because he just keeps firing out correct answers, on every conceivable subject, one after another '. . . *Pope Pius XIII, The San Andreas Fault, Herodotus, 2n-1(2n-1) where both n and 2n-1 are prime numbers, potassium nitrate, potassium chromate, potassium sulphate* . . .' and all this from someone who's meant to be doing Modern History and who looks about six years old. It isn't even fair to call it *general* knowledge, it's just *knowledge*, pure concentrated knowledge, and I decide that, at the back of Partridge's head somewhere, there's a small concealed button, and if you press it his face pops open revealing banks of diodes and microchips and flashing l.e.d.s. Meanwhile their captain, Norton, from Canterbury reading Classics, barely needs to do a thing, just pass on the correct answers to Bamber in his lovely, low, well-modulated voice, then lean back and stretch and play with his lovely, lustrous hair and shoot meaningful, see-you-afterwards looks at Alice.

Patrick is starting to panic. There's a damp rim of sweat forming round the neck of his burgundy sweatshirt, and he's starting to get trigger-happy and make mistakes, terrible mistakes, his trembling finger jabbing at the buzzer in a desperate attempt to pull something back.

Buzz.

'George Stephenson?' says Patrick.

'No, I'm sorry, that's minus five points.'

'Brunel?' says Partridge.

'Correct! That's ten points . . .'

Buzz.

'Thomas Paine's *The Rights of Man*?' pleads Patrick.

'No, sorry, that's minus five points . . .'

'Paine's *The Age of Reason*,' says Partridge.

'Correct! That's another ten points . . .'

And so it goes on. Alice and I meanwhile are worse than useless. She gets one question wrong, saying Dame Margot Fonteyn when it should be Dame Alicia Markova, and I'm barely opening my mouth at all, just nodding madly at whatever Lucy says during team consultations. In fact, if it wasn't for the amazing Doctor Lucy Chang we'd actually be in minus figures by now, because for everything Patrick gets wrong, she gets one right, just quietly, modestly. 'The study of bees?' – Correct – 'I think therefore I am?' – Correct – '*Zadok The Priest* by Handel?' – Correct – and at one point, I find myself leaning past Alice and watching Lucy, pushing her glossy black hair behind her ear, modestly looking at the floor as the crowd applauds her, and I think about what Rebecca said; maybe I should have asked her out? Why didn't I think of that? Maybe that's the answer. Maybe, if this thing with Alice doesn't work out . . .

But what am I thinking about? We're losing 65 points to 100 now, and the freaky boy Partridge is answering three in a row about the mathematical theories of Evariste Galois or something *completely* incomprehensible, and I'm just sat here dumbly staring at the back of our mascot's head, and we're losing, losing, *losing*, and I realise that even with Oregon, Nevada, Arizona and Baja California up my sleeve, the only way we can possibly win is if someone in the audience, Rebecca Epstein say, takes Partridge out with a high-powered sniper's rifle.

And then something amazing happens; a question that I know the answer to.

'*Porphyria's Lover*, in which the protagonist strangles his beloved with a braid of her hair, is a narrative poem by which Victorian poet?'

And *no one buzzes*. No one except me. I buzz, then try to open my mouth, which seems to be stuck together with flour-and-water paste, and manage to get the words out.

'Robert Browning?'

'Correct!'

And there's applause, actual *applause*, led by my Mum I have to say, but it's applause none the less, and we've got a crack at the bonus questions . . .

'. . . which are on plant-cell structure!'

Alice and I groan audibly and slump back in our chairs, redundant. But it doesn't matter, because Doctor Lucy Chang's there, and what Doctor Lucy Chang doesn't know about plant-cell structure isn't worth knowing. She polishes them off without breaking a sweat.

'. . . parenchyma . . . *collen*chyma . . . is it sclerenchyma?'

Oh yes, it *is* sclerenchyma, and the crowd are cheering again, because we're back in the game, 90 plays 115 now, and I'm awake again, because I now know that I – no, not *I*, but *we*, the team – can win this after all.

'Another starter question, the Dickensian character Philip Pirrip is . . . ?'

Know it.

Buzz.

'Pip in *Great Expectations*,' I say, clearly and confidently.

'Very well anticipated,' says Bamber, and there's a round of applause from the audience, and a wolf-whistle even, I think from Rebecca, who I can see in the front row beaming away, and I imagine that this is what it might feel like to score a goal. I try not to smile though. I just look serious and confident and my mind is racing because I know what's coming up soon. '*Oregon, um, Arizona, eh, Nevada and Baja – or is it Baya? – California?*' But keep calm, keep calm, bonus questions first, a potential fifteen points, plus the ten I've just won for us, enough to put us in neck and neck, 115 all, but it all depends on what the bonus questions are about . . .

'And your bonus questions are all about opening and closing lines from the plays of William Shakespeare.'

'*Yesss!*' I think, but don't say, or show in my face, 'I can do these, I *bet* I know these.' The opposition harrumph of course, slump down in their chairs because they know they'd have been able to get them right too, and Norton, reading Classics, tosses his hair despondently, but tough luck boys, because they're *ours* now. Alice must be feeling confident too, because she glances at me, nods and smiles, as if to say 'Come on then, Bamber, do your worst, it won't matter, because me and Brian are soul-mates and together we can handle *anything* you throw at us' and here it comes, the first bonus question . . .

'Which play begins with the lines, "Hence! home you idle creatures, get you home/Is this a holiday?"'

Know it.

'*Julius Caesar*,' I whisper to Patrick.

'Sure?' says Patrick.

'Absolutely. Did it for O-level.'

'*Julius Caesar*,' says Patrick, decisively.

'Correct!' says Bamber, and there's a smattering of applause, not much, just enough, before the next question is on its way.

'Which play ends with the words, "Myself will straight abroad; and to the state/This heavy act with heavy heart relate."'

Know it. *Othello*.

'Is it *Hamlet*?' Alice whispers to Patrick.

'No, I think it's *Othello*,' I say, kind but firm.

'Lucy?' says Patrick.

'Sorry. No idea.'

'I really am ninety-nine per cent sure it's *Hamlet*,' says Alice again.

'Brian?'

'I think *Hamlet* ends with something about bodies being taken out and shots being fired. The "heavy act" here is the death of Desdemona and Othello, so I'm fairly sure it is *Othello*, but if you want to say *Hamlet*, Patrick, then by all means go with *Hamlet*.'

And Patrick looks between us, Alice and I, makes his choice, turns back to his microphone, and says 'Is it . . . *Othello*?'

'It is *Othello*!' and the crowd goes wild. Patrick reaches down the length of the desk and rubs my forearm matily, and Lucy winks, and Alice looks at me, this glowing look of gratitude and humility and genuine *fondness*, a look that I've never seen from her before. Her hand reaches underneath the desk between us, rubs my thigh and then finds my hand and squeezes it, rubbing my hot damp palm with her thumb, and now she's squeezing her strappy black shoe in between my two great, flapping fat feet, and rubbing my ankle, and we look at each other for what must only be a second but seems like forever, and the applause goes on and on and I smile, despite myself, but Bamber's speaking again, saying . . .

'Your final bonus question; Which play ends with the sung lines, "But that's all one, our play is done/And we'll strive to please you every day"?'

Know it.

And still holding hands under the table, as one, in perfect unison, Alice and I whisper, *'Twelfth Night!'*

'Twelfth Night?' says Patrick

'Twelfth Night is correct!' says Bamber, and the crowd applauds, and still secretly holding Alice's hand under the desk, I peer out at Rebecca in the audience, and she's sat up in her seat, whooping and whistling with her fingers in her mouth, and clapping with her hands up above her head. Mum's sat in the row behind, putting two thumbs up, and Des is clapping too, leaning across, saying in her ear, 'How the hell does your son know all this stuff? You must be so proud!' or something like that I imagine, and under the sound of the applause I think I hear Alice say something like 'you're absolutely *amazing*', and then Bamber's saying:

'Very well done! That brings you neck and neck, with four minutes left on the clock, so still plenty of time for both teams. Here we go then, fingers on the buzzers and your next starter question, for ten points. The state of . . .'

Know it.

And still holding on tightly to Alice's hand under the desk, with my right hand I reach for the buzzer, and buzz, and say, with absolute clarity: 'Oregon, Nevada, Arizona and Baja – or is it pronounced Baya? – California?'

And then I sit back in my chair and wait for the applause.

And it doesn't come.

Nothing.

No applause, just this terrible silence.

I.

I don't.

I don't understand.

I look to Alice for some explanation, but she's just staring straight at me with this strange, confused half-smile on her face, which initially I take to be awe, frank awe at my brilliance, but which changes in front of my eyes and settles into something much, much worse. I look down the desk, and there it is again, the same look, from Lucy and Patrick, a kind of horrified . . . contempt. I look out into the audience, and see that it's a serried rank of silent black holes, mouths hanging open under mystified frowns, except for Rebecca, who is leant forward in her chair with her head in her hands. There's a growing rumble from the studio audience, and then someone starts to laugh, loud and hysterical, and with a sudden spasm of pain and regret that feels like pitching backwards into space, I realise what I've done.

I've answered the question correctly before it has been asked.

Bamber Gascoigne is the first to break the silence.

'Well, rather remarkably, that *is* in fact the correct answer, so . . .' his finger's in one ear, consulting with the control room, and then he's saying '. . . so I think perhaps we'd better . . . stop . . . recording . . . for a moment or two?'

And underneath the desk, Alice lets go of my hand.

Epilogue

A little Learning is a dang'rous Thing;
Drink deep, or taste not the Pierian Spring:
There shallow draughts intoxicate the Brain,
And drinking largely sobers us again.
Alexander Pope, *An Essay on Criticism*

I know that something good is going to happen.
And I don't know when,
But just saying it could even make it happen.
Kate Bush, 'Cloudbusting', *The Hounds of Love*

43

THE FINAL QUESTION: At 160 miles long on its East-West axis, the largest of the Greek Islands, with its administrative centre at Heraklion, which Mediterranean island was the home of the first true European civilisation, the Minoans?

ANSWER: Crete.

12th August 1986

How-di stranger! ('Howdy?' Sp.!?)*

How ya doing? Bet this is a surprise, after all this time! Yes, the postmark on the front is correct – I'm actually abroad for the first time. Somewhere hot too! I even have a tan, of sorts, or will have when the peeling stops. Rather predictably I 'over-did it on the first day' and was in quite a lot of pain for a while, and had to eat standing up, but am better now. (My skin's cleared up too, but you don't need to know that!!!) I've also learnt to snorkel, subject to panic-attacks. Food is great – lots of burnt meat, absolutely no vegetables. Today I ate my first piece of Feta cheese. Hmmm – little bit like salty packing material. Do you remember that time we went to Luigi's, and you wore that ball gown?

Anyway.

Your postcard arrived just before we left, and was a nice surprise, and a relief too. After our little, um, adventure, I thought perhaps that you might still be a bit angry with me. Do you ever see Patrick? Is he recovered yet, or is my name still mud? Send him my regards, stand back and watch his face change colour.

I think that's really great news about you playing the role of Helen Keller next term. I imagine that it's going to be a real challenge. Still, at least there's no lines to learn! What was it Noel Coward said about acting being all about not bumping into the furniture? Ha-ha! Sorry!!! Not funny. Seriously, really, really well done. You'll be a great Helen. Maybe I'll come down and see you in it, especially as I missed your Hedda (as the remorseful goalkeeper once said! Geddit? A football joke! Ha-ha!) It would be good to see you again, after all this time. There's loads to tell you . . .

. . . and I have to stop writing at this point, because I can hear her coming up the stairs from her early evening swim, so I quickly tuck the airmail letter inside the book, throw myself on the bed, and pretend to be reading *One Hundred Years of Solitude.*

In the end, it was Julian the nice young researcher that I felt most sorry for. For my story to make any sense, I had to drop him in it a bit.

Basically it went like this; while I was lying on the desk I'd accidentally knocked the clipboard, his clipboard, the one he'd left behind when they carried me up there, onto the floor, and the envelope had burst open, scattering the question cards all over the floor. Naturally, as soon as I realised what the cards were I'd put them back in the envelope straight away, but obviously I must have noticed what was written on one of the cards before I could get it out of sight. You know, sort of *subliminally*.

And they were pretty nice about it, considering that they had to scrap the recording and send everyone home. I mean, they weren't like the Gestapo or anything, they didn't shine an anglepoise in my eyes or rough me up, because I suppose *technically* I hadn't done anything wrong. Nothing that I could be prosecuted for, anyway.

Of course they had to disqualify the whole team, because even though I insisted that it was only me involved, and completely my fault and everything, they couldn't risk it. So that was it. That was the end of The Challenge. For everyone.

And I have to admit, the whole affair was pretty embarrassing. So much so that I didn't feel I could really travel back with the rest of the team, because I wasn't sure that they'd let me in the car with them, and I was pretty certain that I wouldn't be welcome on the supporters' minibus. So I went back to Southend with Mum in Des's van instead, squeezed in the front seat. You know that footage that you see on the news, of criminals being rushed out of police stations hidden under a grey blanket? Well, it was a bit like that. As we drove out of the car park, I could see the others standing around Alice's yellow 2CV and Patrick looked as if he was shouting and kicking the tyres of the car, and Lucy was trying to calm him down, and Alice was leaning up against the car, still in that wonderful black dress with Eddie the Teddy dangling from one hand, just looking so sad and beautiful. I caught her eye as we drove past in the van, and she must have said 'Look, there he is!' or something, because they all turned, and, well, there isn't really any obvious way to behave in a situation like that, there isn't really a facial expression to adopt, so I just mouthed the word 'sorry' through the glass.

I'm not sure if they saw it.

Patrick started shouting something that I couldn't make out, and looking around for something to throw, and Alice just shook her head very slowly.

But I noticed that Lucy waved, which I thought was really nice of her.

When she's safely asleep, having her early evening doze, I go out onto the veranda that overlooks the sea, sit at the wooden table, and carry on writing.

Sorry about that. Got interrupted. Where was I? Yes, maybe

I could come down and see you do your Helen Keller thing, though it's quite a long way to travel. I'm moving to Dundee you see. I've got a place, starting next October. Eng Lit again, though up there they just call it 'Literature', as I think it's a bit of an issue. It feels quite good, having a fresh start and all that. I am hopeful for the future, and hope to concentrate a bit more on my studies this time . . .

I told Mum the same story that I'd told the authorities, and I think she believed me, though she didn't say much at the time. But in the early hours of the next morning, when we finally arrived back in Southend and I walked up the stairs to my old bedroom, she said that it didn't matter, and that she was proud of me anyway, and it was nice to hear her say it, even if I wasn't sure it was actually true.

Then the next afternoon I phoned the English Department, and said that I wouldn't be back for a week or so on account of a sudden illness. But word must have got around already, because Professor Morrison didn't even ask what was wrong with me. He just said that he quite understood, that it sounded like a good idea, and to take as long as I wanted. So I spent most of that week in bed, sleeping mainly, reading, not drinking, waiting for the smoke to clear.

But some smoke you know is just *never* going to clear. After two weeks had passed and I still hadn't really left my bedroom, I decided that maybe it was best not to go back after all. So Des and me drove up one afternoon in his van, picked up all my stuff while Marcus and Josh were out, and drove home the same afternoon. Then I went back to bed, and pretty much stayed there, until Mum insisted that I go and see the doctor, and after that things started to seem a little bit better.

The rest of the year I spent back in my old job at Ashworth Electricals, the toaster factory. I think they were pleased to have me back. Mum and Des had to put the grand opening of their B-and-B empire on hold for six months, but they were pretty good about it, and Des is all right I suppose. Spencer was up and about by April, and got a suspended sentence and a pretty hefty fine. But I managed to get him a job in Ashworth Electricals with me, and so I got to spend a bit more time with him, which was good. I didn't tell him the whole story about what happened, and he didn't ask, which was maybe best. I saw Tone a bit too, but not so much, because he always seems to be away on 'secret manoeuvres' on Salisbury Plain.

What else? I read a lot. I wrote some poetry, most of it pretty rotten, some short stories, and a radio play; a first-person, stream-of-consciousness interior monologue based on *Robinson Crusoe*, but updated, and from Man Friday's point of view. I listened to *The Hounds of Love* over and over again, and decided that it is almost certainly Kate's best album.

And then in June, completely out of the blue, I got a phone call.

Anyway, must close soon. I can smell burning meat, which means it's nearly time for dinner!!!

Looking back, it was a funny time, wasn't it, Alice? Strange, I mean. The metaphor (or do I mean 'simile'???!) that keeps coming back to me is that it's a bit like when I was a kid and Dad would buy me an Airfix kit. I'd sit down at the kitchen table and before I even opened the box, I'd make sure that I had all the right tools, the right kind of glue and all the right paints, matt and gloss, and a really, really sharp craft knife, and I'd promise myself that I was going to follow the instructions absolutely to the letter, and really take my time, not leap ahead, not rush things, proceed with care, concentrate, really, really concentrate, so that at the end I'd have this perfect model plane, the Platonic ideal of what a model plane should be. But somewhere along the line things would always start to go wrong – I'd lose a piece under the table, or smudge the paint, or a propeller that was meant to revolve would get glue on it and stick tight, or I'd get paint on the see-through cockpit, or the transfers would tear as I slid them on – so that when I showed it to Dad there was something about the finished product that was somehow just . . . not quite as good as I'd hoped for.

I've been attempting to use this extended metaphor as the basis of a poem, but haven't quite cracked it yet.

Anyway, all the best for the new academic year. I'll drop you a line as soon as I'm settled and then maybe we can . . .

'Who are you writing to?' she says, her eyes blinking sleepily in the evening sun.

'Just Mum,' I say. 'How was your swim?'

'Very refreshing. Except I've got something in my hair.'

'Want me to pick it out?'

'Yes, please,' and without putting on her top she strolls out on to the veranda, and sits down on the floor between my knees.

'D'you want to put some clothes on first, maybe?' I say.

'D'you want a smack in the teeth, maybe? . . .'

'People can see! . . .'

'So what! God, Jackson, I swear, it's like going on holiday with Mary-fucking-Poppins . . .'

'You know, you really do swear much too much.'

'Just shut your face and look, will you? See anything?'

'Uh-huh. Looks like oil or tar or something.'

'Is it coming out?'

'Not really.'

'Think it might be easier to do in the shower?'

'Yeah, maybe.'

'So – you coming then?'

'Yeah. Alright.'

So here we are. It's early days of course. The original idea when we talked on the phone was that as we travelled around we'd definitely get separate bedrooms, or at least a room with two single beds in, but that plan proved too expensive, and sort of fell to bits on the third night, after a very long, frank conversation and a whole bottle of Metaxa brandy.

But, anyway, like I say, here we are. I'm not really where I expected to be, or even necessarily where I *wanted* to be, but then, who is? And I didn't expect her to be here with me either, to be honest. She still swears too much of course, but she makes me laugh a lot too. Which doesn't sound like much, but actually didn't even seem possible just a few months ago. So it's all right.

It's actually pretty much all right.

All young people worry about things, it's a natural and inevitable part of growing up, and at the age of sixteen my greatest anxiety in life was that I'd never again achieve anything as good, or pure, or noble, or true, as my O-level results. And I suppose I still might not. But that was all a long, long time ago. I'm nineteen now, and I like to think I'm a *lot* wiser and cooler about these things.

Author's Note

Thank you to the following for their permission to reproduce copyright material:

Howards End by E. M. Forster, extract reproduced by permission of the Provost and Scholars of King's College, Cambridge, and the Society of Authors as the literary representatives of the E. M. Forster Estate.

Love Cats, Words and Music by Robert Smith and Lawrence Tolhurst © Fiction Songs Ltd. All rights reserved. Used by permission.

Get Up (I Feel Like Being A Sex Machine), Words and Music by James Brown, Bobby Byrd and Ronald Lenhoff © 1971 Dynatone Publishing Co., USA, Warner/Chappell Music Ltd., London W6 8BS. Reproduced by permission of International Music Publications Ltd. All rights reserved.

Cloudbusting, Words and Music by Kate Bush © 1985. Reproduced by permission of Kate Bush trading as Noble & Brite, London WC2H 0QY.

Perfect Skin, Words and Music by Lloyd Cole © 1984. Reproduced by permission of EMI Songs Ltd., London WC2H 0QY

Life on Mars, Words and Music by David Bowie © 1971. Reproduced by permission of EMI Music Publishing Ltd./Moth Music/Tintoretto Music, London WC2H 0QY.

Words by Joni Mitchell taken from the songs *The Last Time I Saw Richard* and *Big Yellow Taxi*. By kind permission of Sony/ATV Music Publishing.

A New England by Billy Bragg, lyrics reproduced by kind permission of BMG Publishing UK.

The Love Song of J. Alfred Prufrock © T. S. Eliot, *Collected Poems 1909-1962*, reproduced by kind permission of Faber & Faber Ltd.

Tender is the Night by F. Scott Fitzgerald, first published by The Bodley Head, extract reproduced by permission of David Higham Associates.

Brideshead Revisited by Evelyn Waugh, copyright © Evelyn Waugh 1945, extract reproduced by permission of PFD on behalf of the Evelyn Waugh Trust.

The Lion, the Witch and the Wardrobe by C. S. Lewis, copyright © C. S. Lewis Pte. Ltd. 1950. Extract reprinted by permission.

Every reasonable effort has been made to contact all copyright holders, but if there are any errors or omissions, Hodder & Stoughton will be pleased to insert the appropriate acknowledgement in any subsequent printing of this publication.

If you have enjoyed *Starter For Ten*
don't miss David Nicholls' new novel

One Day

Available in paperback from 4 February 2010.

www.oneday-twopeople.com

Praise for *One Day*

'A totally brilliant book about the heartbreaking gap between the way we were and the way we are ... the best weird love story since *The Time Traveler's Wife*. Every reader will fall in love with it. And every writer will wish they had written it.'
Tony Parsons

'The ultimate zeitgeist love story for anyone who ever wanted someone they couldn't have'
Adele Parks

'The funniest, loveliest book I've read in ages. Most of all it is horribly, cringingly, absolutely 100% honest and true to life: I lived every page.'
Jenny Colgan